Chauncey Crafts Hotchkiss

A colonial free-lance

Chauncey Crafts Hotchkiss

A colonial free-lance

ISBN/EAN: 9783337056858

Printed in Europe, USA, Canada, Australia, Japan

Cover: Foto ©Andreas Hilbeck / pixelio.de

More available books at **www.hansebooks.com**

A COLONIAL FREE-LANCE

BY

CHAUNCEY C. HOTCHKISS

AUTHOR OF IN DEFIANCE OF THE KING

NEW YORK
D. APPLETON AND COMPANY
1897

CONTENTS.

vii

CONTENTS.

A COLONIAL FREE-LANCE.

CHAPTER I.

" 'TWIXT THE DEVIL AND THE DEEP SEA."

I THANK God I am no coward, else that which I am
about to write would be unwritten for loss of subject
matter. Nor do I make a boast of my bravery, seeing it
is a thing born in a man and not of his own making.
For, as it ill becomes a woman to take to herself the
credit of her beauty (for the reason that it is fashioned
by a power not her own), so would it appear vainglori-
ous in me to laud myself for not playing the part of a
child when necessity demanded the action of a man.
And, furthermore, if in the following I seem to make
much of my quickness of brain and power of arm, let me
here disclaim all unjust pride in the matter, for my
size and strength are things I owe to a cause higher
than myself, and as for my wits, why, they are but
those God gave me, and they worked as he saw fit to have
them.

As for bravery, I take it to be as much a part of a
man as the fashion of his nose or set of his chin—by
no means a thing for which he can claim self-merit
(though I know the world holds a different opinion),
and is but little more than sound nerves soundly strung,
having nothing to do with rectitude of purpose. For

1

the world has witnessed the righteous trembling in fear of the consequence of a righteous act, while the hardened villain ascends the scaffold with a smile of set determination to die without a tremor.

These things I say in self-justification for what follows. I have known fear, but, thank God! not the fear that paralyzes action. In a measure I felt it when I first openly lifted my voice against the King, and, later, the very day on which my story opens.

We were then somewhere northward of the Delaware capes, with as fair a sea under and about us and as fair though hot a sky above us as ever fell to my lot to see. I say we, meaning the schooner Phantom, short-handed with two blacks and a mate, and myself, Donald Thorndyke, master, bound from Norfolk to New London with a cargo of scrap lead to be turned into bullets, and five hundred pounds in good British gold secretly built into the bulkhead of the cabin. This latter, with the schooner, being the sole property I possessed, were further protected by a double set of clearance papers, the false especially forged by my own hands to deceive such of the ships of his gracious Majesty George III as by chance might be encountered betwixt the two ports.

And there was no small chance of such an encounter, as one may well know by glancing at the history of the United Colonies in the year of grace 1778.

I had been held long in Norfolk for the lack of a mate with a knowledge of navigation, being myself by no means a blue-water sailor, only dodging about the coast in years past on the laudable mission of besting the King's customs—a practice which had been winked at by the authorities up to the time of the breaking out of hostilities. And this profession injured neither credit nor character, for such were the unjust commercial laws with which Parliament had compassed us that the term

of "smuggler" bore no opprobrium in those days.
More was it a title of virtue in the mind of each good
colonist, and to this trade was I bred by my father,
who stood to be as stanch and God-fearing a man and
one above a mean act as ever listened to a parson or
issued orders from a quarter-deck. Until two years
agone he had been my compass, rudder, mainstay, and
entire trust, but the coast fever of the tropics had cut
him down, and no more would I meet his brig fresh
from Jamaica somewhere off shore, and fill up with con-
traband goods to be distributed as my judgment saw
fit. No more would he greet my mother and sister in
the long, low kitchen hard by the heights of Gay Head
and talk of our getting to be forehanded. No more
would I hear him in the "captain's room" of the "Anchor Watch" Tavern, damn his glorious Majesty for
being a pig-headed Dutchman with a ring in his nose,
or deliver a tirade in good set terms against Bute,
North, Germain, and the rest, who were leading him to
the loss of his American colonies. That was all in the
past. Now I was ripe for my voyage and home.

But it was by no means an easy matter to come by
a navigator of any sort at that time. The war had
absorbed such talent long since, and traders were at a
discount, owing to the risk with no chance for prize
money. So it was with great satisfaction that at last I
met with one, John Lounsbury, a man I had slightly
known in Westchester before the war was well on. He
being set to get East, was willing to act as mate on my
own terms; and, though I knew him to be of shady
character, and with morals to be spoken about behind
one's hand, I was glad enough to get him, especially
as he seemed so loud against the King, and, when he
knew what was under my hatches, so well pleased to be
able to pilot a load of metal on its first trip toward the
vitals of his Majesty's hirelings.

And thus it was that on the 18th of June, 1778, we were, as I said, a little northward of the Delaware capes, with a small wind due east and on the starboard bow, and the land a low, blue cloud over the schooner's taffrail.

It was smothering hot in the cabin, where I had but just finished fisting up the log. The clock had barely gone three when Lounsbury hailed me from the deck in a fashion not to be borne, being neither respectful nor seamanlike, and at variance with his usual custom.

"Below there! Thorndyke! Lay up here!"

Now, I make no profession of being a patient man, especially in the face of injustice or bold disobedience; and, as disrespect on my own quarter-deck has a savor of each, I was not far behind his words when I stepped out of the companionway.

A negro was at the wheel, and the mate was striding the weather side of the deck with a spyglass under his arm, a pipe in his teeth, and a very easy, self-satisfied set to his countenance.

He was a short, burly man, bearing a heavy, bronzed face, and having a smile the meaning of which might be anything. His light blue eyes were always half closed, in a manner to be called a squint in another man, but his actions had been bluff, good-natured, and open, and the fellow had hitherto always shown a sense of respectful humor in our intercourse.

As I strode up to him, I marked him slew his little eyes around to take me in from their corners, but he made no move to face or give me particular notice. I guessed then that something untoward was in the wind, and took the shortest way to arrive at the bottom of it.

"Mr. Lounsbury, I'd have you find it convenient to address me as captain on my own vessel, and bear yourself with decent respect in so doing."

For an answer he turned his back to me, and spat

over the rail, then facing about again, burst into a loud laugh. I looked at him as though he had suddenly been bereft of wit, at which he sobered down, and then broke out with a scowl:

" Faith, 'tis a fine farce finely played."

" What the devil has come to you? " I vociferated.

" Well, we'll belay all an' drop the curtain," he continued, setting his back against the rail and jerking his thumb over his shoulder. " Ye may be captain, but 'twill soon be captain o' nothing—d'ye see?—savin', of course, ye come to tarms with Jack Lounsbury. Do ye mark that, an' that, an' that? " he went on easily, turning and pointing to three sails that were well up on the horizon.

Then something of the matter came to me at once. That they were British ships I well knew, for the French were not yet due to arrive, and American privateers moved not in flocks. In wonder at my mate's actions and words, I had not marked this rising danger, but at a glance saw that escape by flight was useless, as the oncoming vessels were spread out from east to south and rapidly sailing down on a fresh wind, which they were evidently bringing with them. To pass through them unnoticed was unhoped for; to be chased was to proclaim my character.

Lounsbury was no coward, I knew; but that he was a traitor to me, or mad, I had small doubt. His manner and words heated my temper, but now that I must have recourse to deception, I let him bide the while, and turned attention toward getting out of the danger bearing down from windward. Putting a curb on my temper, I said:

" You will get up the British ensign and ·hold the course. We will clear them yet." And with this I turned toward the companion.

Now, whether he feared I was about to arm myself,

and preferred to take me as I stood (which was more
than most men dare attempt), or whether his plans
were ripe for action, I know not; but he interposed his
square figure betwixt me and the door, and with a
mighty patronizing air spake thus:

"Faith, captain, I had no call to harrow ye, seeing
the game is in my own two hands; but list' a bit, an'
we may yet be comrades again. No matter how I know,
but I *do* know ye look to cozen yonder ships by false
papers, seeing 'tis impossible to dodge them, as they
have the weather gauge of ye an' ye are in the bight
of the land. Now what use might be yer papers should
I see fit to damn ye as a rebel with a cargo of rebel lead
consigned to rebels? About as much sarvice as a rabbit's
tail to a cow in flytime. Ye be a man o' sense an' have
little liking, I take it, for a taste o' either Cunningham *
or one o' the prison hulks, an' ye can escape them both
if my standing by ye will help, by just handing over
the bit o' gold ye have snugged away below."

The shock of this demand with the knowledge of
what might lay in store for me caused me to lose thought
of all else save how the fellow had gotten so familiar
with my private affairs, and to this day I have never
entirely fathomed it. And it was here I was clutched
by fear of the danger bearing down on me, for my best-
laid plans were rendered valueless by the scoundrel I
had too easily taken on trust. I can not account for
his insight, save that he had probed my locker when I
was absent (this fact being plain enough), and had in
some mysterious way come at the fact that I possessed
treasure which, by search, he had discovered hidden
somewhere beyond his reach. Be this as it may, I saw
that my secret was no longer mine alone.

It is very possible my emotion showed in my face,

---

* The British provost marshal at New York.

and he, mightily astray in guessing my temper, doubtless thought I was completely in his power. And, in
fact, for the moment I might have confessed as much
had I given thought to it. Before I could gather words
to frame an answer, he continued, though with a lowered
voice:

"'Tis five hundred pounds to the penny, I fancy;
if more, ye can keep the rest. Did ye play Jack Lounsbury for a suckling? I started this voyage on your
tarms, but we'll finish on mine. Have ye slept since
the war began that ye knew not the color o' Lounsbury
o' Rye? Come, now, speak out!"

"Then ye looked to fall in with yonder ships, did
ye, ye scoundrel?" said I, while I gathered myself together.

"Ay, two o' them. The one to cast is a flight o'
luck."

"What are they?"

"The tail o' Howe's fleet from Philadelphia. Ye
may swear that Clinton has evacuated the place an' is
marching across Jersey for New York. So it was to
be. Am I plain enough? They be bound for the same
place, an', d—n it, man, shall we go with them or no?
Speak out!"

"Does any one know of my private matters save
yourself?" I asked, as I knitted my strength to fulfill
the purpose I had arrived at.

"None o' that, now! I see yer game! What I know,
I know! An' ye think if I am made 'way with, all's safe."
With this he backed a pace, and, drawing a pistol from
his pocket, presented it full at me. "Now," he continued, with a devilish look in his half-closed eyes, "ye
are my prisoner an' I captain; an' as for the matter o'
that, I have been all along."

I had guessed the man was armed. Knowing me,
he would hardly have had the daring to thus speak to

my face without means of defense. Of his possible
backing by the crew, I had given no thought (which
came near making an end of me), but my wrath was
boundless, and, as his firearm came nearly within reach,
I quickly stretched out my left hand and struck up the
weapon, then with an oath I made a step forward and
planted my right fist in his face. The blow fell far
too short to bring him down, only knocking his pipe
from his mouth; but, as if surprised, his little eyes
opened wide as he turned under its force, and again
with all my power I struck him fairly beneath his left
ear.

Though it may be unbecoming in me to chronicle
my own strength, the blow was a fearful one. It lifted
his clean off his feet; the pistol and spyglass went
spinning into the larboard scupper, where he followed
them, falling with a crash, the blood spurting from his
ears, nose, and mouth. I had little doubt that I had
killed him, and as little care, but with a natural instinct
I followed and bent over him.

At that instant the fresh wind from the south struck
us. Possibly we had lain in a calm for a space while
the breeze veered from the east, but of that I have no
knowledge, only, as we presented a full beam to the
blast, it lurched us to larboard, and caused me to
straighten myself to get a balance.

It was well I did, and I have since looked upon that
gust as an interposition of the Almighty to save me
from the knife of an assassin, for as I shifted myself I
caught a glimpse of the bare feet of a negro making
toward me. He was on me in a breath. I saw the glitter of his knife, and wheeled in time to catch the descending blade in my left arm just above the elbow.
With a mighty wrench I twisted about, breaking the
steel in my flesh, and, catching the fellow by the throat,
held him for one instant, then, lifting him, flung him

clean over the rail into the sea. From first to last he uttered no sound, and if ever he came to the surface I saw him not.

In the maddened fury possessing me my wound felt no more than the prick of a needle, though I found the steel was through and through the flesh. Plucking it out, I ran forward with the determination of taking the status of the remaining hand, but I could not find him at first, for both galley and forecastle were bare of everything human. As I came up from the latter, I saw him astride the starboard spreader of the foremast with a pistol in his hand. I doubt not that he would have shot at me as I passed under him on my way forward, only that the helm being relieved of pressure, the vessel had gone into the wind, and the violent motion of the headsails and tremor of the mast under the thunderous thrashing of the foresail, made an aim impossible. His attitude and the pistol told the story of the part he was expected to play in the mutiny which had probably been hatched before leaving Norfolk. But the cowardly cur had either skulked at the last moment or I had been too rapid for him, and he had swarmed up the shrouds to be out of reach, and there sat looking down at me. I passed no words with him, but, running back on the larboard side, fetched my rifle from the cabin, and, standing by the break of the poop, drew a bead on him and commanded him to drop his pistol and come down. At first he demurred, then whimpered, and, finally dropping the pistol, swung himself to the halyards, down which he slid to the deck, where, falling to his knees, he began begging for his life, his black face turned to a sickly green through abject terror.

The blood I was losing from my arm (and it was a sight) took it from my head, and my temper was a trifle less murderous by the time the fellow had come within

2

my power. I had traded on his ignorance, as, had he
but known my gun was uncharged, matters might have
taken a different complexion. Sternly ordering him
below, I drew the slide over the hatch, and then, feeling
my life was safe from him, fetched a deep breath and
took a look about me.

The ships were in fair sight by this, the one eastward doubtless a troop ship bound for New York with
re-enforcements for Sir Henry Clinton, who had already
begun his call for help, and kept it up through his administration. The ship to the west looked to be a man-
of-war, judging by her size and rig, but 'twas the third
that caused me the most uneasiness—a fine, large
schooner coming down before the wind, and now about
four miles away.

That the Phantom was her object I nowise doubted.
To pass myself as a royalist bound from Savannah to
New York with lead for his Majesty (that being the
gist of my forged papers) would hardly do in the face
of one dead man lying in the scuppers and a single
black hand driven below. But I saw nothing else to
be done, for to have my true colors known would be
to lose liberty and property at once. To fight was impossible; to run, as far out of the question.

Be the upshot what it might, my arm demanded
my first attention, and I passed into the cabin, where
I made a shift to stop the flow of blood, bind it up, and
get it into a sling. Owing to the twist of the knife,
'twas an ugly gash, though, fortunately, no artery was
severed, and in the end it served me a good turn instead of being a source of great trouble.

My next step was to get my papers into proper shape
by destroying the regular clearance, and 'twas here I
discovered the cause of the tone of my mate, for, though
there had been taken nothing of value besides, the
locker showed itself to have been rifled of the false

documents. To be without credentials showing my business on the high seas were as damning as to openly sail under the flag of the colonies, and the discovery of the theft left me for the moment high and dry. Bethinking me, then, of the bare possibility of Lounsbury having carried the matter with him, I jumped to the deck for the purpose of overhauling his body.

A glance seaward showed the schooner now about two miles away, but bearing straight for me. I could easily imagine the perplexity that possessed them at sight of the actions of the Phantom, for, as the helm was still free and all plain sail made on her, she hove into the wind for a space, and there hung in irons with a thunder of canvas overhead; then filling on the opposite tack, she staggered off, until, rounding up again, the entire performance was repeated. For all the world she was like a man well slewed with liquor, using the width of the road in his journeying.

That which lay before me to do must be done quickly. Lounsbury sprawled on his back, so that access to his pockets was an easy matter. There was nothing in his pea-jacket save the junk carried by a seaman, though I soon discovered that around his body was a belt stuffed full of papers. But the stolen ones were not among them, and I felt a sense of hopelessness come over me as the certainty of their loss was forced on my mind.

But it was not for long. A hasty glance at the belt's contents at once opened my eyes to the character of the man before me, and caused me to come to a sudden determination regarding my future action. 'Twas a desperate resolve, but, saving some untoward circumstance, it insured liberty, or, at least, immunity from present imprisonment, although it would put my fortune in jeopardy. It was no time to look far beyond the present; freedom was worth more than fortune, and even that might not, in the end, be lost; so, throwing the belt overboard, I placed the papers carefully in my pocket and went forward.

The pistol dropped from aloft I found on the deck, and with it in my hand I slid back the hatch cover of the forecastle and called to the black to come up. This he did, blinking mightily as he struck the strong light, when, clapping the weapon to his ear, I swore I would blow his brains out, and, if necessary, follow him to the ends of the world to do it, if he breathed a word of my ever having been master of the Phantom.

The fellow was bound to be a source of anxiety to me as long as he had the power to speak, but I could not well murder him outright. Fortunately, his patois was well-nigh unintelligible to ears untrained to the dialect of the Southern negro, and, if my plan worked, he would ere long meet his deserts in one of the British prison hulks, the horrible reputation of which was now widespread. I have small doubt that he thought he was coming to his death when I ordered him up, for, like the slave he had once been, he cringed and writhed at my feet, begging for his life in a manner both disgusting and pitiful. Yet, for all his gratitude at my promise to spare him on the condition of his silence, I felt that, were it in his power, he would have knifed me as I stood. I had no fear that he knew of my hidden gold, Lounsbury having been far too shrewd to take for partners men of the character of the crew, he probably having seduced them with promises of some ready cash, backed with visions of prize money and the high favor of British officers. I had a warrant for thus believing, for my mate had suddenly lowered his voice as he referred to the treasure below, in all likelihood for the purpose of concealing from the man at the wheel its presence on board the schooner.

To the fellow at my feet, whose name, I now mind

me, was "Stofe" (probably a corruption of Christopher), I made no promises for the future, only saying I would hold my hand for the present, and then ordered him to take in the jib and staysail, that the Phantom might lay in the wind and meet her fate as soon as possible.

Indeed, I had expected ere this to have had a shot across my bows and another one into me for not obeying the hint of the first, an action which had so far been impossible. I fancied (and afterward found I was right) they were nonplused at the queer seamanship displayed by the drunken progress of the Phantom. It had been thought, mayhap, that, as but two men showed on our deck, we had a host below, and that, in the disguise of a simple trader, we were intending to delude them and lay them aboard with little ceremony; or, failing in this, were adopting some uncouth mode of warfare on the sea, as strange to them as is the Indian land method to the European regular.

It was with a feeling akin to shame that when the forward halyards were let go I had the negro bend the Stars and Stripes to the ensign halyard, placing the flag union down and under the flaming bunting of the enemy. These were hoisted to the mainpeak, and thus I had set a sign of surrender before surrender was called for, but as part of my plan it became a hard necessity.

CHAPTER II.

Now the headsails being let go with a run and hanging loose over the bow, the foresail and its traveling blocks giving out a deafening protest against its slack sheet, the mainsail joining in the thundering chorus, and the wheel jerking violently hither and thither with the kick of the rudder, we were sufficiently beyond the usual order of things to suit my purpose, and my trump card, in the shape of a dead man lying in the scupper, lay clear to the eye of any who might board us. The sight was uncanny enough, and my instinct was to have the negro heave the body overboard; but, as it was to be a silent witness to the story I was about to tell, I let it bide, though, as the sequel showed, 'twould have saved me a sight of trouble to have followed my first impulse.

I confess that my heart beats took on additional force and frequency as I stood and watched the schooner's nearer approach. She came on to within easy gunshot, and swung into the wind, all of a flutter from stem to stern, and then " lay to " with her headsails full aback. From the scarlet flag at her peak to her clean cutwater she was an object of beauty, though in a light air I doubt she would have slid her keel through the brine with greater speed than would the Phantom, which had been built for fleetness and rapidity in stays.

With my wits by this time well about me, and my

wound bleeding but little (as was shown by the few drops that now dripped from my fingers' ends), I stood by the helm and took in every detail of the enemy, from the crowd at her davits to the long brass piece forward of the foremast, the gun being trained point blank at me.

The stranger worked with the alacrity of a man-of-war, for the schooner had barely lost her way when I saw a boat drop from her larboard quarter and pull toward us, while another came around her bow and followed. They were both filled with well-armed men, as could be seen by the glitter of musketry, and the way they came over the whitecaps showed their temper. It showed temper, too, in the smart manner they boarded me, the first boat hooking on to the main channels, the men clambering out with scarcely a shout and no questions, and in a twinkling I beheld half a score of them on my deck, they, I fancy, being mightily surprised at having met with no resistance.

The crisis was now at hand, and I played my first card with something of the desperation of a ruined gambler. Striding up to an officer whom I saw coming aft with bare sword in hand, I said:

"Ye show scant courtesy in boarding me, sir. Had you turned up an hour agone, 'twould have been to some purpose."

"Who in h—l are you? Where's the captain of this ship?" was the excited rejoinder.

Now there was something about the tone of his voice, the way of calling a schooner a ship, as well as the getup of the man himself, that, angered as I was at his reply, made me back a pace and look at him. A quick glance showed me I was not dealing with a man bred to the sea, much less to the regular service, for, though I then had small knowledge of the uniforms of the British, I knew that which graced the back of the officer before me was not of his Majesty's navy. I knew it by

its cut and garniture, and the land flavor of the man
lay also in the fact that he wore a forage cap and carried a cavalry sabre instead of a cutlass. His face, too,
lacked the true sea tan, its fair complexion showing the
effects of unusual exposure to sun and wind. What his
rank might be I had no idea, and speculation was lost
in the quick retort that naturally rose to my lips.

" Who are you, sir, to tumble aboard a prize of his
Majesty's in this fashion? Ye stand in need of a lesson
in marine manners as well as marine matters. Do ye
hope to judge of a craft's cargo by a squint at her hatch
cover, or of a man by the cut of his jib? Think not to
deceive yourself or me! I know my rights, and also
know the difference betwixt the cry of a sea bird and a
henhawk! "

If I had any doubt as to the official position of
the officer, it was set at rest by the subdued laugh that
came from the group about us. Piqued by the sound
of mirth from those he had no power to punish, his face
turned to an ugly red, and, lifting his sabre as though
to cut me down, he shouted:

" You insolent dog! I will make you sweat for this!
Lay hold of him, some of you! Tie the villain up!
Damnation! are you all cowards? " he continued, as
there was a shuffle of feet, though no one approached me.

There is no telling what might have been the upshot
of this dispute had there been no interruption, for the
fellow seemed determined to use his sabre on me. But,
fortunately for one of us, we were joined by another
officer, whom I afterward found had come from the
second boat.

" Hold hard, Scammell! You are not handling one
of your own dragoons! What is this all about?—You
fly the signal of a prize, sir," he continued, turning to
me; " how comes it you are alone? Who and what are
you? "

"I am Captain Jack Lounsbury, bearing instructions from Sir Henry Clinton, as that cockatrice might have found ere this had he used a smooth tongue. This is my prize—a Yankee schooner laden with lead for New London, and taken by me single-handed. There lies her skipper, and all but one of her crew are overboard." And with this I pointed to the body of my mate.

I had hardly spoken when two marines came aft with the negro Stofe betwixt them. He was trembling like a sail in the wind, and hung his head as though he had lost all strength to lift it. I was looking for an exposure on the instant, but the officer waved them back with a motion. There was an unspoken but plainly shown respect for me in the demeanor of the crowd as it spread away. The two officers stood for a moment in undisguised wonder at the recital of my prowess, giving alternate glances at the body and myself, and then the last comer, who was plainly the one in authority, spoke.

"You alone did this?—By Saint George, Scammell, you came near getting into a mess! I promised to show you a sea scrimmage, but not the kind you were hatching.—Let us have further warrant of these facts," he continued to me. "Who was he?" pointing toward the scupper, "and when did this happen? Let us come by the papers."

"Yonder fellow is Donald Thorndyke, the master till I overcame him," I answered. "I shipped as mate. If you will go below, we can come by the whole matter," I replied, not caring to extend my yarn with the negro within hearing. "Or, better, we can take what we there find and go aboard before your captain, where the whole matter may be boiled down at one sitting."

"'Twould be a saving of time, certainly," he answered, "but we'll hear the yarn while the schooner is

being searched; of course, you understand the importance of the form." And he turned to a sea corporal
and gave him the necessary orders. "Now, sir, I am
at your service," he said, crossing the deck toward the
cabin companion. Hesitating there, he seemed to hang
in the wind for an instant, and then strode over to the
body.

"Did you shoot him?" he asked, as he bent over the
prostrate form.

"Nay, I struck him," I answered.

"Faith, then," he returned, sizing me up with a side
glance, "I'd sooner take the chance of a bullet than a
blow from that fist if you struck in earnest! Did he
wing you at the onset?"

"Nay, nay; 'twas a nigger striving to knife me in
the back. Let's below. Mayhap ye have a doctor aboard
who will fix up a bad cut."

Through all this I was conscious of the eye of Scammell fixed on me. Whether or not he was suspicious of
me, or whether he was still boiling under the dressing
I had given him, there were no means of telling. I saw
plainly the resentment he made little effort to conceal,
and felt that I had made an enemy who would be mighty
glad to cross swords with me on the slightest provoca-
tion. He was twenty-eight or thirty in years, or about
my own age, and was under me not two inches in stature,
which is speaking well for him, as I stood three inches
above six feet, unshod. By weight and brawn I well
overmatched him (as I did most men), especially in the
latter quality of physique; but he made a typical dragoon officer, and would be a formidable antagonist in
any field.

I might hope for little mercy if ever I fell into the
power of this man, for mercy was a quality which,
strained or unstrained, he and his fellows had naught
to do with. This I made sure of on getting into the

cabin, where in course of conversation it turned out that he was a captain in De Lancy's Loyal Legion, a body of Tory cavalry half freebooters and half in the regular service. I had heard of them, as who has not? Betwixt New York and Philadelphia and the country surrounding both places they were a terror, their malignancy equaling if not surpassing the rapacity of Tryon himself.

I itched to get my fingers on him then and there, that there might be one less bloodsucker aboveground, but policy held me from committing an act which probably would have at once wrought ruin to my plans and left my poor mother without a son. I was, therefore, bound to treat him with civility, which I did when a word to him was necessary, but I fancy we each knew the other was but skipping over the thin ice of politeness.

Being, as it were, in the enemy's lines, I followed the bent of the lieutenant, and laughed loudly and long over the puzzlement (as he called it) into which the Phantom had led them. I drank to the King and damned the rebels; told a story of being a free lance under elastic instructions from Sir Henry Clinton, and how I had taken the vessel by killing Captain Thorndyke and besting the crew. In short, I put myself into my mate's former place as nearly as was possible, following his coarse manner and uncouth language, exhibiting the rough-and-ready character befitting a fellow of his breeding.

But, beyond Sir Henry's signature, never a line did I show them or tell the nature of my orders; and that for the best of reasons, for I knew little of the business myself, not having had the opportunity to more than scan the papers I had taken from the body.

The regular clearance discovered the schooner to be a Yankee trader. There was a Yankee sailor captured

and a Yankee captain dead, and why should there be
suspicions?—and there were none in the mind of the
lieutenant; but of his friend, the dragoon, who had
come aboard for a bit of dangerous play (and had nigh
achieved his wish), I was not so sure.

In my turn at questioning, I found that the enemy
was the Sprite, an American capture, refitted and re-
named, one of the last of Howe's fleet (as Lounsbury
had surmised), bearing two passengers beside her usual
complement of men, and bound for New York to meet
General Clinton, then on his overland trip from Philadelphia to that city.

Now we had been sitting below for upward of an
hour, drinking my rum and making game of the rebels
on land and sea (though once, when I spoke of John
Paul Jones, I saw I was on dangerous ground, and belayed my tongue, cursing the liquor for having loosed
it), when the companion way was darkened by a marine, who, jerking a salute, said, with a scarcely controlled grin:

" We have another prisoner, sir."

" Another! " exclaimed the lieutenant, starting up
and giving me a stern look.—" What's the meaning of
this, Lounsbury? Are you dealing fairly? "

I was as surprised as he, and had no answer to make,
but before my confusion became manifest the marine
again spoke.

" 'Tis the dead man come to life, sir. We were
flushing him an' the deck, an' 'twas the water as fetched
him, sir."

" Glad I am 'tis no worse," said the officer with a
light laugh. " I feared I smelled a trick. You American born are the devil and all at playing deep games,
and, faith! for a second I thought you might have coz-
ened me. Let us to the deck."

I had sudden reason to turn my curse from the

liquor, for had it not been in me I doubt not I would have fallen backward. Like a drowning man, I had visions passing through my mind with a rapidity that makes description impossible. My very strength gave out for the moment, but there was enough left to get me to my feet and follow the others to the deck.

I have faced death since, and well-nigh shaken hands with it, but never did the knowledge of its nearness affect me as did the words of the marine; and 'twould take more than money to make me go through a like thirty seconds, or the time it took me to get from the cabin.

Lounsbury had been moved, and lay on his back on the deck with his head resting on the edge of the helm grating. He was soaking from the sousing that had brought him to life, but I sent up a mental thanksgiving on the discovery that it had not also brought him to reason. The sole sign of vitality lay in the fact that he breathed. There was a hoarse and hollow tone at each heave of his broad chest, which I knew to be due to his broken head; and though I felt him to be a deadly enemy and a charnel house for morals, there was a pity in it to see the abject helplessness of the once powerful figure as it sprawled on the hot, white planking.

Scammell stooped for the man's pulse, peering closely into his face the while, and then for a moment the whole load of anxiety came back on me as he straightened up and said:

"I have seen this fellow before, though I fail to place him as Thorndyke. He looks like the chap who escaped from the rebels after spiking the guns near White Plains. But that was before we took New York. Why the d—l can't I remember names?"

Here again was mighty dangerous ground, for Scammell was right, though I knew nothing of it then nor

until after the war was over. The spiking of the guns
was an old story, but it had been long agone, and I was
only aware of the bald fact. However, I felt that he had
struck a scent, which if followed up (and I fancied him
the man for it) might, nay, would, be likely to drive
me to bay.

It was well, then, that at that moment a recall gun
sounded from the off-lying schooner. It seemed to wake
the lieutenant to the fact that time had gone, and that
the sun was well toward its setting. Without more ado
a guard was left on the vessel until a report could be
made to the captain of the Sprite, and with the others
I went along, that I might again tell my tale and get
my knife-thrust into proper dressing.

CHAPTER III.

A VOLUNTARY PRISONER.

DARKNESS was well settled on the sea, though there still hung a faint, hot glow in the west when I had finished my business on the Sprite.

Barring the baleful eye of Scammell, there had been nothing to mar the proceedings in making a report in harmony with my story. The dragoon's silence and steady gaze were a trifle disconcerting, and the knowledge of the captured black (who had been conveyed to the Sprite), coupled with the feeling that Lounsbury might return to his senses and spring a mine beneath me, served to keep my nerves at a tension which became well-nigh unbearable.

There had been a number in the elegant cabin, but of them I wot not, save that most of them got hot with liquor. For a sight of it had been taken, even the captain having his judgment crossed and his jollity increased by constant recourse to the bottle.

And here let me say that, in my poor opinion, both the length and cruelty of the war were helped more than a little by this never-ending taking aboard of " Dutch courage." Had it made men battle in proportion to their boasting, 'twould have served some proper end, but I never found that I could fight better with eyes and wits tangled with liquor, and, in fact, though I preach not, never touched it when in trouble save as on this occasion—to keep up appearances.

23

And even on this occasion I had still the upper-hand of what I drank, and noticed that Scammell was nursing himself as well; but, aside from we two, 'twas a noisy crowd that tumbled to the deck to see me back to the Phantom.

I had made myself mighty popular during my short stay aboard. A change of berths had been offered me, but I had small notion of leaving my own craft with its hidden cargo, though I put it on the ground of for-feiting prize money if I deserted her. A crew of five men were given me (which would make a small claim for salvage in favor of the Sprite), and now, with the doctor, who was to give a hand to Lounsbury, I stood by the side while laying a small wager on the race to New York.

I had little heart in the laugh and last hand shake to the rest, and was about putting foot on the side steps to pass to the boat that was swinging high and low on the running seas, when my attention was caught by the face of a girl who rose through the companion and stood startlingly clear against the black background of the night. The bright lamplight from the cabin flooded and brought out every detail of her features. It was but the face and bust I saw, the open door cutting off the lower part of her figure, but 'twas the face of an angel, and for an instant I forgot to move, looking at her as I would at a beautiful picture.

And a picture she made as she stood there turned toward us. High breeding showed in the delicate con-tour of chin and cheek, dark eyes and clearly cut straight nose, but 'twas the small mouth with its fine red lips half open as though in inquiry that held me by its sweetness, while the mass of auburn hair, dressed high, as was the fashion of the times, gave a touch of per-fection to her countenance.

The vision—for 'twas more akin to a vision than

reality—lasted but a breath, for Scammell thrust his form betwixt us, and made rapid steps toward the companion way, while I, with a hand wave to the others, joined the doctor in the boat.

The surgeon, a tall, raw-boned Irishman, afflicted with a strong after-dinner hiccough and a desire to talk, settled back in the stern sheets, and voluntarily fell into an explanation of a lady being on board the Sprite.

" An' ye know not Mrs. Badely, Sir Henry's light-o'-love? 'Tis a shame that King's officers be made to dance attendance to that ilk. Her ward seems to be o' different clay, though. A bonny lass she is, an' a lonely one, having no great love for her guardian, as 'tis plain to see, an' few to turn a word with, saving Scammell. Did ye mark the way he slid to her when she lifted o'er the hatch? 'Tis in my mind he's jealous o' the deck her foot lights on, an' he hangs about her like a brooding hen. 'Twas a sorry move Sir Henry made when he lit on him for a guard o' honor to Mrs. Badely and Gertrude King. Bad for him, I mean, since 'tis plain he's struck between wind and water by the lass, though, in my mind, she'll have little to do with the likes o' him after setting foot ashore."

From this and other rambling talk I gathered that the Sprite was taking two ladies from Philadelphia to New York—ladies high in favor with General Clinton —and that one of them, Mrs. Badely, was the famous beauty to whom the doughty knight had given his heart without the honorable accompaniment of his hand and name. Her notoriety had even spread beyond the British lines, and much of the opportune inactivity of the enemy was explained as due to the fascination of his mistress and the inability of the commander to withdraw from her influence and take the field.

Of the younger lady I had never heard, nor, after

3

my fleeting glimpse of her, could I make myself believe
that her nature was tainted. Scammell was the official
guard of the two for the trip, which accounted for the
dragoon being at sea, and, according to the doctor, he
had become deeply enamored of his younger charge,
the fair Gertrude King. Doubtless it was a desire to
cover himself with glory and dazzle the eyes of his love
which had led him to take a hand in boarding the
Phantom, but I gave over interest in the whole matter
by the time the boat reached its destination.

The half-slewed Irishman made but hasty work with
Lounsbury. The unconscious man had been removed to
the cabin, and lay in my berth with eyes fast closed, still
breathing like a pump. The doctor looked at him
frowningly, felt of his head and pulse with a careless
air, and then gave his diagnosis.

"Flip a sovereign, cap'n, and bet on its fall, and ye
will have as good a notion of how the case will turn out
as myself. There's no knowing at all what the man
will come to. He has had the devil's own shock. 'Tis
concussion and mayhap fracture, mayhap structural
lesion of the brain. Who knows? He may die, he may
live, but he'll be a bit fashed in his wits if he pulls
through, and ne'er be the lad he was. What's one dead
rebel more or less? Let him lie and take chances.
Have you a drap o' potheen to say good-night on? I'm
off."

I felt like kicking the man for his heartlessness, but
gave him a drink and saw him started for his own craft;
then getting the crew together, I set them to work,
and in short order we were under way.

The surgeon's words had not tended to depress me.
The passion possessing me when I struck my mate had
passed away, and if he would live and remain " fashed "
until I had cleared from the muddle into which I had
been forced, I would pray for his final recovery.

It was an easy matter to sail for New York. As the schooner now bore, wing on wing, that port lay fair off the end of the jib boom. The Sprite sailed something less than half a mile on our larboard beam, and thus we went for hours, each holding her own. In the early light of the following morn the wind suddenly lightened, then shifted to the north, and by the time I had made Sandy Hook, where the bulk of Howe's fleet lay waiting the arrival of the British army, the Sprite was some miles to windward.

I had forgotten the race. The sick man had most of my time and attention, for he had taken to raving, and was finally lashed to his bunk. His speech was but an uncouth mouthing of words that meant nothing, and when at last, in the lower bay, the schooner was formally taken possession of, I passed the care of him to others, and began to look sharply to my own affairs.

It was two days after the mess on the Phantom before we dropped anchor off the city, coming to a final rest near the upper limb of the bight of the small bay below Corlears Hook, on the Sound River.*

There had been more than a little fuss and many questions put by the authorities before I stepped ashore. Answers, too, were given, which might have been picked full of holes had suspicions arisen in the minds of the reigning powers; but owing to the disorder due to the retreat of Clinton from Philadelphia, and the arrival of his army, which had now boarded the fleet at Sandy Hook, confusion ran riot in all branches of government, and saved me from much fine lying.

There had never been a moment when I could have gotten at the gold in the cabin without exciting suspicion. In fact, I had but little time to study the

---

* East River.

papers I had appropriated and still had on my person; and now, well-nigh destitute from want of cash, I had the misery of seeing the King's broad arrow painted on the bows of the Phantom and of finding myself turned ashore.

I was not greatly troubled by my lack of ready money. I held indorsed documents for a claim on my own ship for prize money for capturing her, and could easily turn it into gold by allowing a liberal discount; but it went to my heart to see the broad arrow (which marks the King's property), and know the craft was, by hook or by crook, a prize in possession of the enemy.

But if my comparative poverty caused me no great uneasiness, I was worried over the fact that I had two living witnesses against me, one of whom, the negro, was capable of damning me with his evidence could he but obtain the ear of an official. It struck me forcibly, too, that I was fairly within the enemy's lines and under a false name and character. It were one thing had I been caught at acting a part on the high seas and on my own schooner, but quite another to be discovered under the existing circumstances. The first could have made me a prisoner of war at most; the second would damn me as a spy, and give me short shift to the next world by means of a rope.

At that time it might have been possible for me to have left New York and gotten on my way homeward. But it did not happen to lie in my blood to turn up with the report of having forfeited everything save liberty and life. With a weakling it would have passed; with me 'twould look as though I had thrown away all for the sake of lightening my heels, and would likely injure my reputation.

Aside from this, there lay hidden close at hand five hundred pounds, and none, save Lounsbury, had fathomed the secret. It was my all, barring the schooner, though that was not a total loss, as the admiralty papers in my pocket bore witness. No man willingly foregoes two thousand, four hundred and odd dollars in gold rightfully his own, unless he be a coward; and that, I maintain, I am not. And so by my fortune I determined to stand until it should be sunk, blown up, or otherwise lost.

There was more than this pecuniary interest which sealed my determination to stay where I was for a space and risk the future. And that—the war.

Lest my reader think I had been a laggard in the conflict which had now been on better than two and a half years, let it be known that I had been active against the enemy, both afield and afloat; noticeably in the whaleboat warfare on the coast.

I had made more than one lobster-back wish he had stayed in Merry England (unless he was at once set past wishing), and helped dig a mighty hole in the King's exchequer by destroying his property. But that was in the past, and runs not with this tale.

I could illy abide the discipline of the army, though with the patriots discipline was but a trifle more than a name. It suited me best to be my own master and fight in my own way (not that I quarrel with the mode of another man, and armies are necessary), and never would I have more than earned rations had I stood in the ranks and moved forward or backward on the word of command.

Determined then not to run, it took me but a short time to conceive that in my present position I could well serve the great cause which to no man was dearer than to me. Washington, I knew, had few agents within the lines of the city, and these I might never hope to know, they, like myself, being hooded under the mask of Toryism.

This last fact was a hitch. I might become a storehouse—a very mine of information on the strength, weakness, and contemplated movements of the enemy, but be without the means of unloading my knowledge. To force a way through the lines was to take one's life in one's hand with small chance of keeping it, and this would become necessary in my case, for on a close examination of Lounsbury's papers I found nothing in the shape of a pass save an old one signed by General Howe, which had opened a way out of Philadelphia.

The rest of the documents proved to be of no value to me, as they related to matters concerning the kidnaping of some unnamed party in Norfolk and an investigation with a view of British occupation of that unimportant town.

From the moment I had found these papers until my landing I had given no thought to the future, my first business having been to provide for my own safety. This now being accomplished (for the present, at least), I fixed matters to my taste in this wise: I would become a spy (a fair name in a good cause), and as a rampant Tory, half freebooter, and half swashbuckler (as became the character of the man into whose shoes I had stepped), I would peer and pry, and, when finally loaded sufficiently to warrant it, go to Clinton and, on the plea of past services and in the name of Lounsbury, demand a pass through the lines.

I would not turn my back on this fair prospect and become a common soldier. Nay, like Lounsbury himself (who was now lying somewhere in the city), I had been a free-lance, and a free-lance I would continue to be.

Difficulties and obstacles were forever obtruding themselves in my mind. The danger I put aside, for war being no pastime, I must incur danger in any active hostility or sit at home and play the boy. Both duty

and self-interest demanded my standing where the force
of circumstances had placed me, and I hailed my determination with grim joy.   Three years agone I was
a colonist—which had been a small matter—but since
the Declaration I had been an American, a title to be
proud of, and now, though not in the field, I would
prove worthy of the name.

CHAPTER IV.

NEW YORK at this period was a scene of confusion.

The fear of the French, which had occasioned the evacuation of Philadelphia, had brought a horde of twelve thousand soldiers to be set down among five thousand others, where but scant preparations had been made to receive them. What with the smart of the lashing administered by Washington at Monmouth on their march across New Jersey, the weakness of Howe's fleet, the fear of a sudden movement on the city by the Americans, and the intense heat of the weather, the army was in a state bordering on panic.

It was an army, too, that through rank and file had been demoralized by inactivity and debauch, and nothing could have been more apt or prophetic than the remark made by Franklin when it became known to him that the Delaware had been opened by Howe: "Philadelphia has succumbed to the British, but they in turn will succumb to Philadelphia."

It had been even so, but the effect had become apparent in New York. The civil law had long been prostrate; the military authority lax. Now the British were waking in the condition of a man after a night's dissipation, battling with a muddled brain, and feeling the internal economy fairly out of gear. Fraud, fear, and incompetence reigned in every branch of the service, and betwixt fire, vandalism, and the necessities of war, New York, which had never known and was never to know the dignity of battle, suffered as no besieged city could suffer more.

All this suited my purpose, as well as directly favored my interest. The influx of a host of newcomers saved me from being prominent as a stranger, and the extra preparations for the defense of the town, together with the knowledge that the French were at last upon the sea, diverted attention from small naval ventures.

I had feared the Phantom would be immediately refitted and armed for sound or river cruising, and was mightily pleased to have the days go by and see her, as the saying goes, "taking root to the bottom."

Never did the sun set without my having a look at her swinging at her anchor. She lay off the half-deserted shipyard, which became a favorite haunt of mine when I tired of the mask I wore and wished to ease into my true self.

And there I would walk up and down, and each day watch the growth of the muck that had fouled her cable on the ebb and flow of the tide. She had not even been dismantled, and, for aught I could see, was without a guard save at night; but to have gone out to her and worked upon the cabin bulkhead would have been impossible. The boat from her larboard davits had been taken away, but the dingey still hung over the stern, as tantalizing as a cup of water just beyond the reach of a thirsting man.

A sweet sight (but a melancholy one) the schooner made to me as she swung on the broad river well from land, the fair light of an evening over her, mellowing her lines and diminishing the rustiness of her sides. Beyond her was the bald work of Fort Sterling (built and deserted unharmed by the patriots two years be-

fore), standing clear and yellow above the height of
Brookland.*

Off Wall Street lay many of Howe's fleet, though
the largest number was posted south of Nuttens Island,†
in readiness to oppose the French, who were daily expected.

But in the fair harmony of sky and land and water
there was one discordant note. The horrible hulk of
the Jersey, within easy scope of the eye, was directly
opposite, and more than once did I see her unload her
dead, and could almost hear the cry of "Down, ye
rebels, down!" as the patriot prisoners were driven
below at sunset.

Excepting in the shipyard and through the sparsely
built district lying betwixt the line of fortifications and
the city proper on the westward side of the island, there
was scarcely a rood of land to which I could flee and
not come in contact with the evidence of war. The
quiet desolation or barrenness of the former and the
broad, green meadows, the song of birds, the harmoni-
ous hush of Nature and calmness of the evening skies
at the latter point, were in marked contrast with the
hell lying close at hand. Had the devil come on earth
in his proper person, as some poet has made him out
to have done, and landed in New York, he would have
rubbed his hands and switched his barbed tail in glee
at the work of his emissaries who were serving him as
but few so-called Christians serve the Almighty.

Barefaced inhumanity stalked before society and
caused a laugh. Cruelty had become a pastime. Domesticity was dead. Robbery seemed set to the music
of a popular song, so universal it became, nor was it
confined to the confiscation of property belonging to
patriots. An uninitiated stranger would have found

---

* Now Brooklyn.   † Governors Island.

some difficulty in determining whether this brilliant assemblage was exerting itself as much toward suppressing
a rebellious people as it was in making war on the King's
treasury.

There may have been honest men in New York during the summer of 1778, but as yet I had failed to
strike them. Every one with whom I had to do was
a gambler, a thief, or a drunkard—frequently all three—
and I dare swear that, were the truth known, one term
or the other applied to the whole army, from Sir Henry
Clinton to the last subaltern, and from the bowelless
villain of a provost marshal, Cunningham, to the lowest besotted turnkey under his thumb.

New York had ceased to be a town. It was nothing
more than a fortified camp, in which neither justice
nor mercy might be found. Morally, it had become a
vast, open sore, spreading its corruption beyond itself.
Virtue was a weight on man and woman (I speak but
of the rule), and power the only recognized right.

I was mightily depressed at this time. Seasoned
though I was, I shrank from life as I saw it, and sickened of those into whose company my policy forced
me. In fact, I might have made a shift to get myself
from this sink of heartless depravity, only my gold still
swung at the end of a cable within pistol shot of the
shore, and none knew it.

Many a night had I lain awake hatching schemes
to get aboard and recover it, but they were worse than
foolhardy, as I knew after a second thinking, so I took
it out in watching and biding my time.

As the days sped, I had little or no fear for myself. Lounsbury was probably well under ground by
this, for I had heard nothing of him, and, if the negro
was a prisoner in a hulk, he might as well have been
in a tomb.

Of what was taking place in the world outside I

knew nothing save from rumor, and rumor oft contradicted itself. The only report seemingly sure was that Washington had sat himself down on the Hudson just north of the Harlem (the very spot from which he had been driven two years before), and was there awaiting the arrival of the French fleet in order to strike a blow. And there he remained inactive, for the French did arrive early in July, and, finding Howe's fleet drawn up to receive them, but peered into the bay, and then turned tail and sped away to Newport on the fruitless mission of blockading that port.

In the seemingly open yet wholly secret life I led I made many friends—mostly pothouse companions—to whom I listened but spoke little, fearing to be recognized as an impostor. I kept both ears and eyes on the alert the while, fighting shy of broils, yet holding the respect of the roughest of the camp offscouring, owing to my size and apparent strength. I even dared make a map of the lower defenses of the city; but it was so disguised, so crossed, and recrossed in a manner clear only to myself that I would have trusted it to the eye of any of them without fear of their coming by its true nature.

This I did not to be idle, for nothing happened in the way of military movement, or even threatened to, for some weeks after my arrival. By then I was practically a prisoner, for without a pass and a clear statement of business I could not have gotten beyond the lines, which now extended across the island from the heights of Corlears Hook to the Hudson.*

My wound healed in the space of two or three weeks, but still I kept the arm in a sling, using it in privacy that the muscles might not weaken or stiffen from lack of exercise. The sling saved me from many awkward

---

* On about the general line of the present Grand Street.

questions, for when asked why I did not join the army or apply for a berth in the fleet, I had but to point to it, gently moving the limb, and say, "All in good time," adding for weight that I had no call to further serve his Majesty until he paid me the money I had already earned.

But for the arm, backed perhaps by the way my muscle filled out my coat sleeve, I would have been pressed into the service whether or not, and the sling being a safeguard, I let it bide.

I had taken quarters in the tavern of the "King's Arms," on King Street,* near the Broadway, making terms on credit, an easy matter with my prize-money claim in my pocket. 'Twas the gathering place for Tories of the better sort, and but little affected by the military, the dashing element of which favored Fraunce's, on Broad Street.

But my time was not spent here. 'Twas the "Bull's Head," on the Bowery Lane,† and near the inner line of defenses, that saw the most of me.

The spot was but a step from hades, but a great place for much coming and going and hearing the news; and then 'twas near the shipyard off which lay the Phantom. Never a day passed without one broil, and often two or three, most of them ending in more or less bloodshed, and one of them put a stop to the life I was then leading.

I mind me it was on a cloudy Saturday forenoon early in August, though through the wet in the air and the veiled heat every pore oozed as if one had raced. There had been but few about. I was half dozing under a locust in the tavern yard when I became conscious that two men had but just settled themselves at a small table

---

* Now Pine Street.
† On the site of the old Bowery Theater.

near me, and was thoroughly wakened by hearing the
name of " Scammell " in connection with some matter
they had been discussing.

One was a boyish-looking naval officer, seated with
his face toward me, the other being in dress a cross
betwixt a soldier and a civilian. Like the officer, he
wore a sword, but I could see no more of him than the
broad of his back.

Using but the tail of my eye, I marked them begin
a game of cards for stakes, for I could hear the clash
of coin, and after a hand or two he of the back
spoke.

" Does Clinton know the man? "

" Nay, but he knows of him and what he has done,"
was the answer. " I was told last night that he has
been about. There's something afoot outside, and he'll
be needed. 'Tis a wonder he has not turned up for another job; Clinton is liberal with the King's cash! I'll
give you a pound to find him."

There was silence for a moment or two as the officer
drew in a stake and dealt the cards.

" I wish I could get fingers on this same King's
cash! " the unknown remarked. " Card-playing for
shillings is small truck for a man, and ye have had all
the luck. Could I pass myself off, d'ye think, an' do
the work instead o' the chap yer after? "

" Nay; you're no sailor, and have but a shady record
for pluck."

" Then 'tis a sailor you want! As for shades an'
records, 'tis but a case o' the pot an' kettle! It's the
way ye naval chaps have of robbing a man of an honest
living! Now I've lost time with ye because I fancied
I scented cash. All last night I won nothing save a
sore head for this morning. Come! ye but stave me
off from the job. Play, then, for something save shillings and crowns an' thin wine. I'm sick of it. I'll

lay ye the pound ye offered on the better o' three hands,
an' then quit, win or lose."

" God knows I'm willing to quit! " was the return.
" I've played all night and am fagged. I'll play you
the pound for the last." And the officer yawned as he
tossed the cards to his opponent.

Now I knew this to be nothing less than the trick
of a blackleg. To lose on shillings and win on pounds
was a common practice with them, as it is to this day.
The officer must have been green not to have seen
through it, but I had little sympathy for any one wearing the scarlet, and, in truth, was interested in seeing
how the game would be played and possibly hearing
more of Scammell.

Doubtless I had been taken for a drunken drover as
I sat with my chin on my chest and my chair tilted
against the tree; anyway, they gave me no notice.

One hand was played to the advantage of the officer.
That was to be expected. Then another went smoothly
enough in behalf of the fox, after which, though without moving, I looked sharply for the end.

The method was slightly unusual, though conceived
and executed with skill. They had each been in the
habit of tilting back on the rear legs of their chairs
as they picked up their hands and conned them. As
the last card was dealt and the balance of the pack
laid aside, the officer settled himself backward, while
the fellow nearest me did the same thing but a second
later. It was then the fine play came in. Seeming to
lose his balance, to save himself from a fall he threw
out a foot which caught beneath the officer's chair,
sending that party over on to the broad of his back
and bringing himself down on the four legs of his seat.
With the rapidity of a skilled villain, I saw him draw
cards from his pocket, throwing those dealt him on to
the surplus pack, then slamming his false hand face

down on the table, he jumped to the assistance of his companion.

The officer accepted the rough apologies offered him, and, after dusting himself with his handkerchief, played out the hand. It fell to his lot to lose, and he paid with a good grace.

As was usual, the winner proposed a parting dram and set up a loud clamor for the waiter to fetch a bottle of rum, swearing he would have no more of the like of the wine he had been drinking, the empty bottle of which stood betwixt them on the table.

Now had the waiter been forthcoming, I would probably have less of a tale to tell. But 'twixt the heat, long hours and the present lack of custom, he had doubtless fallen asleep and was deaf to the calls given him. Anyway, after fruitless bawling by the winner, the officer took a hand in the matter by turning his attention to me, for he shouted:

"Here, ye lazy son of a bullock pricker! step out and find the waiter, and be damned to you!" at the same time hurling the empty bottle at me.

The glass missile struck me fairly on the wounded arm, about an inch above where the negro's knife had entered. For an instant it gave me exquisite pain, but the sling did much to deaden the force of the blow, though it had naught to do with lessening the towering anger to which both words and bottle had brought me. In six strides I was on them, and upsetting the card-sharper, chair and all, with my open palm I dealt the naval man a blow in the face, laying him backward in the dust where he had been but a short time before.

With this my anger slipped away from me like breath from polished steel, and I saw but the comic side of the two sprawling in the dirt.

Never could I hold heat longer than a wire (though I take it as readily), and had they been quick to acknowledge the mistake that had been made, I would have cried them quits, and even joined them in a dram.

But it was not so to be. After a few seconds' bewilderment, the officer scrambled to his feet, and, pulling his sword from its scabbard, paused as though to take his bearings for an onset. He was no more than twenty years of age, carrying plenty of the marks of dissipation on him, and what with his dust-whitened clothes, his boyish proportions, and his dirty face, he looked, with his drawn sword, like a ruffled bantam.

I should have been obliged to hurl the table at him in self-defense (which would have been ill for him) had not at that moment a cavalryman on a black charger driven full tilt into the tavern yard, reining up close to us.

CHAPTER V.

A TRIANGULAR QUARREL.

I KNEW of no reason to fear him, but it gave me a start to recognize Scammell, in the full uniform of a captain in De Lancy's marauding Tories. He threw a quick glance about him, taking in the angry belligerent and his friend, who had picked himself up and was standing at a safe distance with his blade in his hand, as though waiting a favorable opportunity to rush in and take a part in the muss. Though I fell under the Tory's eye, he did not at once recognize me, for I had my beard at about a ten days' growth, and was something more than picturesque in the shabbiness of my dress. He immediately claimed the attention of my opponent by calling him by name.

"Hello, Belden! Something put out again, eh? What the devil's the matter now? Have you not had lessons enough in your own set that you must fall afoul of pothouse loungers? What's amiss?"

"That villain has dared lay his hand on me, and, by God! he's bound to pay the penalty!" burst out Belden, for the first time finding his voice.

"Which villain?" asked Scammell, as he threw his leg over the saddle and came to the ground with the bridle in the crook of his elbow. "Faith, you look as though odds were against you. I see two of them. 'Tis your good luck I had a thirst that needed slaking. On my soul, whom have we here?" he exclaimed, scowl-

ing, as with a second look he identified me. "Is it a
fair quarrel, Belden? I'll weight your pockets with
five pounds if you'll hand your rights to me, unless 'tis
a matter of cheating at cards.—What, sirrah!" he demanded, walking toward me with a malignant look
to his rather fine features, "you were quick to offer
me a lesson awhile since. Are you as ready to take
one yourself at this meeting? How is it you have outraged my friend and your better?"

"Let them alone, yer Honor!" interposed the card-
sharper, approaching. "'Tis a tie cause for the both.
One was hit by a bottle, the other grounded by a fist.
Can't we have a trifle o' fun with a hawbuck without
interferences? Faith, the bullock man shall have my
sword, an' we'll see which is the better carver! I'll
back him, too, an' ye may back yer friend the popinjay,
who's one merit lies in not knowing when he's well
beaten. Come, now! we'll to the Kalchook Hill * an'
have it out. I'll——"

"What! you villain you! you low thief! Get hence,
or I'll scalp you!" interrupted Scammell, turning on
him. "Kalchook Hill, you dog! You would never
go so near the gallows on your own free will."

"Gallows, is it?" returned the fellow, still holding
his ground. "I tell ye, Scammell, capting though ye
be, ye are riper for the gallows than am I, an' this I'll
back in any way ye name."

Scammell, instead of falling on the fellow in a fury,
an act I looked for, snapped his fingers in his face, and
with a look measuring him from head to foot, replied
contemptuously:

---

* Kalchook Hill was a small elevation near the Collect, a fresh-
water pond, which was on the site of the present Tombs. The
gallows used for military execution stood between it and the
Fields, or present City Hall Park.

"You dirty dog! Mighty brave you are in the knowledge that a King's officer would ne'er cross swords with such scum. I'll give you one minute to be gone, and, failing, I'll see you tied up and lashed. If you know me so well, you know 'twill be done." And with this he turned his back on the sharper, who, far from obeying the hint to leave, stepped away but a few paces.

"And now, my wild sea bird," said the Tory, re-directing his attention to me, "are you willing to clear yourself with my friend here? Give a fair explanation of this affair if you can, or perhaps you would like to make a fine point of the matter with me in some quiet spot. I might doubt my rights to honorably cross swords with such as you in a matter as private as this, but I will forego all objections and ask no terms. Ah! but you have an excuse; you will doubtless plead a wound."

The deep insolence of his last remark turned my dislike of the man to a sudden hatred. 'Twas not the words, but his more than unbearable manner of utter-ing them that roused my ire and brought me to the pitch of action. Had he been nearer, I would have served him with my fist as I had served Lounsbury, and would have regretted it at once for its lack of dignity. Forgetting for the moment my assumed rôle, I stood where he had found me, and answered:

"Captain Scammell, my calling is the sea. You are but a marauding bushwhacker, nor can the curse be rubbed off you by a title or hidden by fine trappings, and did you but know it you would be honored by cross-ing swords with me. As for an explanation, I will sat-isfy you so far as to say that I punished your friend for insulting me, and, by the God above me, if you wish to carry this further, I will punish you worse than I did him! I could but defend myself from him, a boy whose back I could break across my knee, so he goes harmless. As for you, I will fight you within the hour and ask for no second."

"Good!" he broke in. "You gave the name to the weapon. Let it be swords, and at once. Remember," he went on with an oath, and working himself into a rage, "ask no quarter of me. Up or down I give no mercy; let à l'outrance be the word."

"Nay," said I, fanned to an equal heat by his blood-thirsty manner and the fury in his eye—"nay, then, I will not kill you, villain as you are, but, should I disarm you, or you slip, I will beat you with the flat of my sword until you roar for quarter, or I break every bone in your foul hide! 'Twill be scant mercy, as you were better killed outright. Now look to it, for this I will do, or my name is not Thorn—Lounsbury!"

I caught myself just in time, and started violently as I discovered the trip of my tongue. Both the others likewise gave a jump, but it immediately transpired that each had a different cause.

It was Scammell who first showed his reason for thus starting, and that was through the insult I had offered him in degrading him by a threatened beating. White with rage, he threw aside the bridle, and drawing his heavy sabre, advanced on me with a torrent of oaths.

Before I could do more than whip my left arm out of its sling and lift the bulky table in defense (for I was unarmed), the young officer sprang between us.

"Hold hard, Scammell!—Lounsbury! Are you Captain Lounsbury? Lounsbury, of Rye? By my faith! but I came near making a bull of it!—This thing can go no further now, Scammell. I've been looking for the man high and low for a week. Clinton wants him at once—at once! The order comes from headquarters. What, man! Hold hard!"

"Hold hard yourself!" shouted the Tory, as he

tried to dodge the young officer. "No further now! Do you think I'll brook such words to my face and wait for formalities? Ay, Lounsbury it is; and of Rye and the Phantom and the devil, for aught I care! What can Clinton want with such a man? Stand aside, you salt fish, and let me meet him!"

"Call me no fish, you butcher-bird!" snapped Belden. "What ails your humor to-day? Has the heat gotten your head? You first pick my own quarrel away from me, and then flout me for looking to my own interests. Has the fair Gertrude hipped you, that you spleen so quickly? I tell you my orders are imperative."

"'Fore God, you sprat! An' you dare twit me in public on my private affairs!" shouted the Tory, turning his wrath on the naval officer. "Use but her name again, and I'll spit you as you stand, you half a man! How! Will you, too, fight?"

Stung by his words, and more than stung by the reference to his short stature, Belden had whipped out the sword he had sheathed and thrown himself into the fencer's attitude.

"Fight? Ay, I'll fight! Put aside that meat axe and use a gentleman's tool. I'll show you that half a man is better than a whole brute. My wrist is as fine as yours, for all your brawn."

That Scammell's blood had o'ercome his brain was plainly apparent by the way he threw his heavy sabre to the ground and ran toward the card-sharper. But that fellow, anticipating his wants, brought up the point of the weapon which he still held, and presenting it at the breast of the oncomer, retreated a few steps and cried out:

"Nay, nay! Ye shall not have it. Settle yer brawl as best ye may, but my sword is mine, an' with me it shall bide. By the look of it, ye must settle with the three of us. Pull out o' the pickle, an' ye can; ye shall ha' no help or steel o' me."

Now while this was going on I had not been idle with either brain or body. I saw at once that Lounsbury had become a personage of importance, and that he was unknown to Clinton by sight. That something of moment was on hand was also discovered, and it evidently lay in my power to thwart the matter and confound the British. At the same time, it would probably spread open a path for me to leave the city, and possibly in some manner show me a way to lay hands on my gold. It was a fair chance to act upon, and I could in no wise let harm come to the young sailor until I knew more or had been piloted on my way.

This was with my head. With my body I simply moved to where lay Scammell's sabre, and picked it up.

As I did so, the baffled officer turned and saw the action. Foiled at every point, and now unarmed and compassed by three armed men, he swore and fumed like a baited animal.

I saw the folly of his total loss of temper, for had he not parted with it he never would have been placed in his present position. He had quarreled and wellnigh fought with three men in as many minutes, while his blind fury had brought him to where he was worsted and degraded at once.

As he stood there, too proud to retreat and unable to advance, he glanced hastily in every direction. In his desperation he was doubtless looking for his horse and his pistols in the holsters, and had he found them there would have been bloodshed. But his high-spirited animal, frightened at my act of swinging aloft the table and the shouts that followed, had tossed up head and tail at once and gone galloping from the yard, now being nowhere in sight.

And thus we stood for perhaps the space of half a

minute (though it seemed longer), while at a distance
gathered a number who had been drawn hither by
the noise of the brawl. 'Twas a mighty awkward predicament for Scammell, but Belden finally put a period
to the matter, and opened a way for the Tory to retreat. Slipping the point of his sword into its scabbard,
he thrust it down with a ring, and cried:

"Avast, all hands! We're nothing short of a pack
of fools. Each of us has had a thrust at his neighbor,
and each in turn has stood between two others. 'Tis
the prettiest muss I ever saw, so d—n me! 'Twas all
beginnings and devil of an ending. Let's make it up.
—Come, Scammell, you might well go halfway to meet
half a man. By my faith, that's not bad.—Lounsbury,
I was a bullock myself, and ask pardon for the bottle.
So there's my sop.—Who's next?"

Now my heart warms to a man who is quick to take
fire, whose wrath is like the touch of a match to gun-
powder, the force of which is gone when its work is
done; just as I hate the sullen spirit of one who nurses
the last spark and sulks until its heat dies for lack of
fanning.

The generosity of the boy—for he was little else—
struck home to me, and I was about offering my hand,
when Scammell, quick to take advantage of the turn
of affairs, spoke up:

"So let it be if you say so, Belden! I am overhot
from the ride from the outer lines at Kingsbridge. I'll
willingly pass you and yon fellow"—indicating the
trickster with a jerk of his head—"but I'll not be quits
with your new *protégé* save but for the time you need
him. If Clinton wants him, I'll spare him the while to
do his dirty work, for on honorable matters he would
ne'er employ such a man while his betters go begging.—
How now, sirrah?" he continued, turning and advancing toward me. "You are glad enough to accept the

respite, I doubt not. Will you name time and place to receive your deserts?"

"'Tis against my nature to duel in cold blood; but, as my word is passed, I'll carry through my promise. Where do you put up?"

"At the King's Arms, truckler!"

"Then, sir, you lie close to the rod, for there I stay also. For the time to meet you, that must rest with Sir Henry. For the place, that your howls be not heard by your fellows, I make it the clump of trees in Lepner's Meadows.* You doubtless know the spot. As to the hour, I will enlighten you at your quarters as soon as may be.—Now, Mr. Belden, I am at your disposal. Shall we get to headquarters?"

Saying this, I threw to the ground the Tory's sabre and turned from him. Instead of stooping for his side arm, Scammell stepped around so as to again be before me, and, though there was no abatement to the malicious hatred in his eye, his voice fell to a hoarse whisper as he said:

"By my faith, sir, it were better you had stood and been run through than to have put into my head the matter you have just given me! More than that. It were better that you had the devil and his horde against you than Walter Scammell!"

And bending, he picked up his sabre, sheathed it, threw a careless salute to Belden, and walked off, the card-sharper joining the throng about the tavern door.

---

* Lispenard's Meadows, an extensive tract of drained swamp-land beyond the then city limits, through about the center of which now runs the present Canal Street.

CHAPTER VI

A FAIR PROSPECT.

LEFT alone with Belden, that worthy looked me over slowly, and then holding out his hand, said:

"On my soul, Lounsbury, you had best shrive yourself! To tell the truth, I'm mightily afraid of that fellow, who is no less the brute I called him because I offered to cry quits. He would be invincible with a rapier, only he holds the light weapon with too light a hand. He is all points and tricks, and, unless you disarm him, it looks to go hard with you. You will never get by his guard."

"Thanks," said I, laughing, and taking his hand. "I've a trick or two myself. What does the general want with me now?"

"I have but a fraction of the matter, and know my place too well to talk of it. Let us step out; but, man, you'll never appear at headquarters in such a rig! You would be barred at the door!"

"'Tis but the service of a razor and a shift of clothes I need, and will soon have. Will you bear me company to my lodgings?"

He agreed to this, and we set out down the Bowery Lane to the Fields, past the provost prison * and poorhouse, and so along the Broadway, chatting like two old friends as we walked.

---

* Now the Hall of Records, City Hall Park.

'Twas a strange coincidence, I thought, when I found my companion was attached to the Sprite, having been on board even at the time I was telling a false tale of myself in her cabin, he having been laid up below through a wound received in a duel while in Philadelphia. A jolly, light-hearted, dissipated boy he was, but as rampant a worshiper of royalty as has fallen to my lot to meet.

He could tell me nothing of Mrs. Badely and her ward, Gertrude King (the latter toward whom I had an instinctive leaning), save that they had long ago left the schooner and were in sumptuous quarters on Queen Street. Scammell's passion for the young lady was no secret to him, and he made a coarse joke at the expense of both, for which I could have wrung his neck.

But all were alike in those days, it seemed to me, and not once did I hear a woman respectfully spoken of, though the maligners of the sex professed a readiness to lie down and be trodden on when in the presence of the least of the ladies of fashion. Such a fulsome aping of fine manners on the streets and off; such back-bending and courtesying, froth, and hypocrisy; such affectation in speech and attitude; such utter prostration before the god of mode and folly as was practiced by these puppets of the King in this small copy of the court, never before or since has it been the fortune of man to see. Insincerity, heartlessness, and an absurd sensitiveness regarding so-called points of honor ruled the day. And these were the spirits who were expected to subdue the hardy yeomanry of America!

But this is neither here nor there.

Well shorn, with a decent ribbon for my queue, a suit but a shade or two the worse for wear, and a sword at my thigh for effect, we set off for our destination, Belden having washed his dirty face and generally groomed himself.

At this time Clinton's headquarters was on the Broadway, at No. 1, and opposite the Bowling Green, being the same dwelling wherein Washington had established himself while the patriot troops occupied the city.

'Twas strange to me that the British commander should have hit upon this house, not only because of its association, but from the fact that it was, with some few mansions to the north, cut off from the rest of the city by the broad swath of ruin caused by the great fire of September, 1776.

This conflagration had started (God knows how!) near the Whitehall, and, under the fanning of a strong wind, had burned northwest, crossing the Broadway below Trinity Church, and from there laying low everything clear to the Hudson and northward to nigh the city limits. Trinity went with the rest, but by some mercy St. Paul's was spared, as well as King's College,* the fire stopping just short of Robinson Street,† on which stood the latter.

No attempt had been made to rebuild or even clear the ruins, and now 'twas a dangerous neighborhood, as the offscourings of the camp had taken possession of the whole area, and utilizing old walls, beams, and sails, had established a colony of violence and filth, which went by the name of Canvastown.

It might have been pleasant for Sir Henry to look from his south windows over the grand Battery, the bay, and the fleet beyond, but I take it he little cared for the view east, with its black desert of devastation, or to see in the Bowling Green, right beneath his knightly nose, the hacked pedestal that had but lately borne the desecrated statue of his Majesty of England.

But notwithstanding its isolation 'twas a fine man-

---

* Columbia College.   † Now Park Place.

sion, this Kennedy House, as it was called, and well
fitted in its interior for the uses to which it was put.
Broad halls and large rooms furnished ample space
for the brilliancy usually gathered there, but to-day it
was comparatively deserted.

Had I been alone I should have had infinite trouble
in getting in at all, but Belden soon opened a way past
the guards at the door, only to meet disappointment in
the end, for Sir Henry was at dinner, and, as was his
wont, would let nothing short of a rebel invasion prevent its slow completion.

He sent word that he would see Captain Lounsbury
in private at three o'clock on the morrow, and also sent
a sealed paper bearing my assumed name, which I was
requested to read against my return.

As I was primed and cocked for action, his char-
acteristic delay chafed me, and, unknown to him, came
nigh to putting a mighty spoke in my wheel.

However, there was nothing for me to do but wait,
though with the possibilities of a duel on my hands and
my coming interview with Clinton, I had e'en enough
to occupy my mind and save time from dragging. My
instructions, too, were to be read, and giving good-day
to Belden, I set off up the Broadway, determined to
both walk off a growing nervousness and seek a quiet
spot in which to con my paper.

No house should hold me in such sweltering weather,
so on past the Fields with its outlying barracks I went,
to where the Broadway dwindled to a mere cart track,
and finally ended in a cow pasture closed by a pair of
bars.

'Twas the edge of Lepner's Meadows, and, with the
view of planning the details of my intended battle, I
made my way to the clump of trees near its center,
where, throwing myself on the close turf, I broke the
seal of the papers.

The contents made me start as even a shot near my ear would fail to have done. The matter was short, and ran thus:

" In the name of his Majesty George III, of England, etc. You are by me instructed and ordered. Take five men of your own selection and man the schooner Phantom, captured by you while sailing against the interests of his Majesty. With this vessel you will repair to General Pigot, at Newport, R. I., with dispatches and instructions to be given you. Newport now being invested by the French and the rebellious subjects of his Majesty, you will enter the harbor of Newport under the guise and flag of the rebellious colonies, bearing out the deception to the extent of casting away the vessel on the coast of Rhode Island, or in any other way reaching or putting yourself into communication with General Pigot. You are to make requisition on the Commissary Department for such stores and supplies as you may deem necessary, and report to me for further and secret instructions on the completion of arrangements, which shall not be later than ten days from date."

This paper was undated, unsigned, and showed hurried construction. I saw at once that it was given me to test my willingness to undertake the adventure. It was to be but a dispatch-bearing mission, with spying as a side issue, unless modified in some manner by the secret instructions referred to. But should these prove a demand to kidnap or even assassinate Washington himself, I would be found ready to undertake the task on any terms, so great had become my desire to leave the city.

Five men I could easily get, though not a soul I knew who could help me carry out the scheme that leaped to my brain on the first perusal of the paper. Yet even alone I would undertake to bring the Phantom with five prisoners into a patriot port could I once get the vessel clear of the bay.

I felt the strength of ten men within me as I hatched the plot, and only prayed for the morrow and the meeting with Clinton; for Scammell, the duel, and all else faded before the glowing light of the future. I worked myself into an ecstasy the like of which I had not experienced since, when a boy and beset with home-sickness, I hailed the date of my return to the arms of my mother. My property and my liberty were to be set within reach at once, and beside them I would place honor, the last by carrying back a batch of prisoners.

It was small wonder that I acted the boy again, and you who have never known the sudden loosening of tightened heartstrings and the childlike joy resulting, know little of the upper scale of human happiness.

But I did not hold myself long at this height. The practical fact that I must name date and hour when on this very spot I should stand and fight for my life, forced itself upon me.

The ground was well hit upon, being screened from all sides by the trees, which would also keep the sun from the eyes of either combatant. It was fairly open, level, and free from underbrush.

The morrow would be the Sabbath, and, though war is no respecter of days, I would not desecrate it by fight-ing out a private quarrel. Therefore I set my mind for the meeting at sunrise of Monday, that I might have the business off my hands and prepare for what I con-sidered the greater adventure.

Now I had little doubt of the result of this conflict. Unless Scammell was different in sword play from those I had met either in sport or earnest, he would be dis-armed ere he had well begun. It was through a trick which depended more on sheer strength than great skill, for of the latter I had little more than a fair ability to

defend myself without seeking to pass the guard of a
practiced swordsman.

It was simply that I would use a rapier of greater
weight than my opponent (which would be but natural), and at the proper time throw my guard wide open
by lowering my hand. On the instant of the onset
which would be sure to follow, I had but to step back
a pace and bring up my weapon with all strength and
speed, the fairly sure result being that the sword of
my adversary would be driven from his hand or the
blade fly to pieces by the force of the blow. Whether
this trick is allowable save under the rule that "all's
fair in war," I scarcely know, but in sport I had tried
it often, and with never a failure, even though my opponent knew my intention.

With the hint of Scammell's light hand which had
been given me by Belden, I was sufficiently without
worry to take with full zest the apparent good luck
which had come to me, and, with no thought of an
untoward slip in my fair prospects, I returned to the
King's Arms, and there wrote a note in set terms in-
viting Scammell and his second to meet me the day and
hour on which I had determined.

This being dispatched to his room to await his coming, I ate my evening meal, and then sallied to the shipyard for my usual look at the Phantom.

She still swung in the old spot, with an easy grace
and an apparent unlifting of her forefoot, an effect
caused by the sheer of her deck lines. My soul went
out to her, for she seemed to know me and strain at
the cable like a high-mettled steed that only needed
the word to take the bit and be off. Rusty she was,
and foul besides, but, rusty and foul, she could outpoint
half his Majesty's heavy-going cruisers, and I waved
my hand at her as I would have done to my lady had
I one, swearing to give the word ere that day fortnight.

How little I knew we would both be well tried by then!

I waved my hand to her and turned to go, when my eye caught a huge coil of black smoke rising from near the river's edge far down the city. That it was a fire on shore I made out at a glance, nor did I give it more than passing notice until, on entering the streets again, I became aware of the concourse pouring in that direction. Soldiers by companies, disarmed and bearing buckets, were hurrying toward the conflagration, but not until reaching the King's Arms and ascending to the fine cupola that surmounted it did I know that the fire was of vast extent. And even as I looked it spread from house to house, threatening to assume the proportions of the great scourge of two years before.

Now with interest well sharpened I made haste to get to the scene of the burning and be of use—a thing not so easy to do, owing to the press of a mass of people who stood about useless and curious, watching the play of the great sheets of flame, and giving exercise to their voices when their hands might have been of better service.

I soon saw, however, that there was no organized effort to suppress the flames, and without order my arm was no better than the weakest. But of this second mighty fire in New York, in which upward of three hundred buildings were destroyed, I have little to do. Looking back from these later days (for I am an old man now), it seems as though the smoke had beckoned me to its source that I might take my next step in the quickening drama of my life, the plot of which was to lead me through travail and bloodshed, that in the end I might be fitted to enjoy the great happiness it has been the will of God to vouchsafe me.

5

CHAPTER VII.

A SINGED PATRIOT.

AFTER being driven from one street to another by
the scorching of the advancing flames, I finally turned
into an alley and stood partly protected against the
baking radiation by the corner of a building.

Betwixt the heat of the day, the fire, the smoke, and
my fruitless exertions, I was as wet as though fresh from
the river, as black as a coal-burner, and not in the fair-
est of humors. My coat and hat (my best ones, too)
were burned by falling embers, and the sword I had forgotten to put off was hot to the touch and bothered my
legs exceedingly. My eyes burned as though peppered,
and the roar of the mad element, the falling of walls,
and crashing of breaking timbers were at times well-nigh
deafening. Blasting hot draughts drove down the way,
and a suffocating pall of smoke swept through the street
as though pushed from behind by a whirlwind. Nothing was visible ten paces off, and why I remained where
I was useless, and where my situation was becoming
as dangerous as it was unbearable, I can nowise account
for, save that I was ruled by Fate, against which no
man need combat.

I was about stepping from the mouth of the blind
alley in which I had been standing, when the figure of
a man sped out of the smoke and dashed against and
then passed me, reeling from the blow and staggering
into the recess behind.

Slight as he was, the speed at which he had been

going nearly took me off my legs, and I had barely recovered my balance when a dozen armed soldiers ran
by, shouting and swearing, as though in chase. With
the last of my stock of patience exhausted, I turned on
the fellow who had run into me, and found him at the
end of the *cul-de-sac*, with his back to the wall, and two
blackened fists held up as if to defend himself to the
last.

Conceiving that I had caught a thief, a ransacker of
deserted houses, if not an incendiary, I clinched him by
the collar fo drag him forth for delivery to his pursuers,
but the fellow dealt me so smart a blow in the face that
for a second it caused me to see lights.

I was in the mood to cuff him into insensibility, and
might have done so had he not spoken, or rather gasped:

"'Fore God, I thought you a redcoat, and tried to
vex you into killing me! If you have the heart of a
man, do not deliver me to them again!"

"Who are you?" I demanded, loosening my hold
and trying to get at his features through the black that
covered them, though I made out no more than that
part of his face was overgrown by a young beard well
singed, the rest being so grimed that he might have
worn a mask and been no safer from recognition.

"On your mercy, then," he answered; "an escaped
prisoner."

"From where?"

"The den lies in the heart of the fire by this."
And rolling up his eyes, the whites of which showed
pitifully against his burned skin, he hesitated, and then
broke out again:

"What is it to you who or what I am? If you love
justice or hope for it yourself, let me go!"

"Come, then," said I, softened more by his manner
than his words, "we will roast here in three minutes.
Let us get into better air." So, taking him by the arm,

I led him into the street, where the smoke was so dense
that it became necessary to grope one's way. Once we
were in danger of suffocation, but the wind whirled
aloft the thick muck for an instant, and gradually we
worked to a fairer spot, though still hard by the fire.

And here it was I noticed that the hair of his head
was burned off on one side, his coat scorched to tinder,
and his breeches hanging in shreds.

But I had no sooner brought him to where we could
take a whole breath and see a few rods in advance than
he held back, darting his glances in every direction
as though in fear of detection. Had I not kept a close
grip on him, he would have broken away and fled, being
more like a frightened animal than a man.

"Now, once for all," said I, with a great pity stirred
by his miserable condition as well as admiration by his
gameness, "what are you—a criminal or a prisoner of
war?"

"Nay, no criminal," he answered, looking me fairly
in the eye and drawing a long breath.

"What then? A prisoner of war—an escaped patriot?"

"You can be no Tory to have used the word 'patriot,'" he answered hastily, with a sudden lifting of his
head.

"You are right," I returned quickly. "If you are
hunted as a rebel, you have found a friend and I the
same. We were each in need."

"Then, for the love of God, let me go! There will
be a price on my head! It is death to hold me here!
I was to be hanged as a spy, but the fire set me free."

"A spy! By the Lord, from your looks you might
be a second Shadrach! What name are you under?
Come, let us work into safer quarters," said I, full of a
sudden fever, for it never occurred to me to be doubtful
of his statement.

"Nay, then, I am best alone. Let me go, man; your grip is crushing my arm! I have a friend, and, once with him, I am safe. I believe you to be true. Know me as Rex."

"One second more, then!" said I, loosening my grip. "Where can we meet?"

He had drawn from me apace and was prepared to run, but halted long enough to throw back: "The Dove—Kingsbridge Road—if God be willing I get so far. See Nick Stryker." And with this he disappeared into the smoke.

This incident happened so quickly that I had met him, taken his status, and he had gone before I realized that I had not gotten from him a tithe of the knowledge I wished.

The "Dove" was no puzzle, but of Nick Stryker I had never heard. The former was a tavern somewhat back from the Kingsbridge Road, about seven miles from the city, and near McGowan's Pass,* the latter probably the host of that house of call.

I knew the place from having stopped there before the war, and, in fact, the upper island was as familiar to me as to the majority of its inhabitants, but at that time there was no Nick Stryker holding forth at the Dove. Years and the vicissitudes of war had doubtless changed many features of the country above the town, and might well have changed the proprietors of a tavern. So to it I determined to go as soon as I could come by a pass from Clinton.

How the spy could run the barriers was a peg further than I could see, but he seemed full of resource, and evidently knew his business. Doubtless, thought I, his friend is powerful, and will put him on his way. I berated myself for having let him go. I would have

* McGowan's Pass is now included in Central Park.

stood by him in the face of a platoon, so hungered was
I for one in whom I could confide and who could assist
me in the plan which still boiled in my brain.

Find him again I must. The name of " Rex," being
but Latin for " the king," I guessed to be only a pass-
word through which his allies might come by him, and
this conjecture was all I had to assist me in my intended
search. But it was something to go on, connected with
the rest, and with no further attention to the vast conflagration, I made my way out of its vicinity.

Within two hours of the time I left it a deluge of
rain, which had been threatening all day, came down
and quenched the flames. For my own interests I
looked upon the flood as providential, and it was as
well for the interests of the thousands of patriots shut
up in the city, as, had it not been for this interposition
of Heaven, the entire town would have been swept by
fire, and the imprisoned inmates of the packed sugar
houses might have shared the fate of the buildings
themselves.

It did not surprise me that on reparing to the King's
Arms I found Scammell had not returned to receive my
note, nor did I greatly wonder when told the next
morning that he had not been in overnight. The confusion attending the fire might easily account for many
irregularities, and what cared I, after all? I had done
what I promised him, and he might take up or leave
the matter as he saw fit. As for myself, I busied me
with my damaged clothing, that I might be presentable
at headquarters in the afternoon, and when these were
in as fair a shape as a clumsy bachelor could make
them, I had nothing to do but pass the time.

Of all the days of the overheated summer of 1778
that of Sunday, the 8th of August, was the most terrific in point of temperature. By high noon no man
might stand the sun's rays unprotected, and the heat

radiated from the streets as from a furnace. Indoors was but little better than without, yet for that little I remained in my rooms and well-nigh stripped myself for comfort.

Being now in the best of humors, I ordered a measure of rum and a jug of water, and with these before me sat me down to build air castles for the morrow. Great waves of heat surged through the open windows, and the drowsy stillness made me nod. Not wishing to sleep, I brought out the paper received from headquarters, and opened it as I had done for the tenth time at least.

I had reread but a few lines when I was attracted by the sound of distant thunder, and going to the window, beheld a mighty bank of blue-black clouds towering above the western horizon, the topmost ridge mingling with the thin column of smoke still rising from the burned district. Not a breath of air stirred the hanging leaves of the trees before the door, nor was a soul in sight save a small squad of redcoats that just then swung round the corner from the Broadway and entered the tavern bar.

The coming of a tempest has always been a delight to me, and I watched with suppressed emotion the advance of this, which presaged unusual violence. As I looked, the first great gust of wind came tearing up the Broadway, bending low the trees and bearing with it a mighty van of dust and rubbish. Hurriedly slamming down the windows, I turned to don some clothing and get below, when, through the din of clashing branches, swinging blinds, and rushing wind I heard a thunderous knocking at my chamber door, which was opened ere I moved to answer, and in the gathering gloom I beheld Captain Scammell hastily enter and close the heavy portal behind him.

CHAPTER VIII.

THE HINT OF THE EARTHQUAKE.

THE advent of this man, whom all the laws of dueling prohibited seeking me at the present stage of affairs, occasioned something of a shock. The manner of his entry, the tragic aspect of Nature, and the sickly-green light enveloping everything within and without; the clamorous advance of the storm, and perhaps as much as anything, the sudden revulsion of temper caused by seeing him, threw me for the moment off my mental balance, and I stood without moving, gazing at him as I might have gazed at an apparition.

As we thus faced each other, I noticed that he was hatless, coatless, and without side arms, the latter fact causing me further surprise, as I was aware of the extreme pride a British officer has in his sword and his reluctance to lay it beyond his reach.

Hard upon these details came three others of different nature. I saw at once that the man was intoxicated, though not beyond his own control; that in his left hand he had an open paper, while his right, which still hung by his side, held a cocked pistol, though this I would not have seen but for the sudden gleam of a flash of lightning. It gave me a quick realization of the fact that I was in great danger and without the means of combating it, for my sword was in the closet, while both pistols and rifle lay unloaded in a corner.

The crash of thunder following the flash for a time

made words impossible; and action was equally out of the question, for in the midst of the bellowing, and while I was casting searching glances about the room for some means of defense, he raised the weapon and leveled it at me.

I could fathom no motive for his thus attacking me, save the heat in his rum-maddened brain, and, was he impelled by drink, my position was doubly critical. Had there been a ghost of a chance to act in the aggressive, in this desperate moment I should have availed myself of it; but not even that really formidable weapon and guard, a chair, was nearer than the table, and to have made a move toward it I felt meant certain destruction. A sudden attack on him was out of my power, for betwixt us intervened the broad table itself, which made it impossible to avail myself of the tactics I had used with Lounsbury. There was naught for me to do but stand as I was and await the terrible issue.

However, as he remained silent, I managed to find my voice, and, as the thunder rolled in the distance, I shouted:

"Captain Scammell, are you so demented or so cowardly and so lost to honor that you will murder the man you challenged to fight in the field?"

Without a swerve of the arm, he answered sternly:

"Sit down!"

Even thus beset, it irked me to obey him like a schoolboy, but I realized that, armed, under the existing circumstances he was far stronger than I with all my sinews. Wisely, then, I swallowed my ire, and, approaching the table, seated myself with the hope that he would come within reach.

He was not slow in following, for he stepped forward and carefully slid into the chair opposite, though not for a second uncovering me with the muzzle of his pistol, or, for that matter, taking his eye from mine.

And here we sat while flash and crash followed each other in quick succession. My brain worked rapidly enough, but as the seconds sped no way could I find to rid me of the shining ring of steel confronting me or turn for a moment the equally brilliant glint of his eye, each of which acquired clearness with the fitful lighting of the room.

The table was too broad for an onslaught, and now that we were closer, I could see the nerves of the man were at full tension, and that on the slightest hostile move on my part he would pull the trigger.

I hoped lightning would strike the house and put an end to the situation, which at last began to have its effect on me; and I take it that no man can long stand the scowl of a loaded barrel backed by a determined yet silent enemy without undergoing more or less strain.

I was even wishing that the heavens would let loose a bolt and finish the matter, or that the man opposite would open his lips and speak, despite the roar, when I felt the floor beneath me tremble, as though the house was shaken by a mighty power. It passed in the instant, and as it did so the thunder faded away for the moment, and Scammell, lowering his hand, let it rest on the edge of the table, whence the pistol held me full in the chest. Then he spoke, and perhaps because the excitement indoors and out had partly sobered him, his words came clearly:

"I have here your d——d message in my hand, but, as you may well guess, it is forestalled. There will be no fight between us to-morrow morning."

"Because you deem it safer to murder me now?" I returned calmly. "Give me but——"

"Shut your mouth!" he interrupted, letting go his temper. "Do you think I am here to bandy words with a rebel? Captain Donald Thorndyke, *alias* Lounsbury, you are close on to the end of your rope, and you'll find that end has a noose in it, you cursed spy! What!" he continued, rising in his increasing rage, and immediately reseating himself, while his voice grew louder, " do you think I am a fool, or so blind that I may not see through a riddle? I have found you out, hide and hair—Thorndyke, of Martha's Vineyard—smuggler—rebel—spy! Had you escaped me this day, and been off on Clinton's business, which doubtless lies there" (pointing to my papers, which lay on the table), " I would have hunted you down had it cost me my commission. Escape me? No, by the gods! From the beginning I fancied you the fraud you are, and at the Bull's Head, by your words and fine airs, you made me sure of it. You slipped your rôle. You'll find your hen-hawk has sharp eyes, and, giant though you be, you will see that a seamew is nothing in his grip. Nay, I have not come to shoot you down as you deserve, but I know your infernal tricks, and mean to hold you where you belong. I take it 'twill afford me more pleasure to see you dance at a rope's end than dirty my hands with your blood, save you make it urgent. Let me clinch the matter now, and then make you ready to march. *Below stairs at this moment is Lounsbury in the flesh,* and with him a file of men to take you off. This bit of play was for my own pleasure, and, having had it, I'll be your valet and stay by your heels until you are safely delivered to Cunningham. Now God rest your miserable soul! Have you aught to say before I give the word to the rest?"

To state that I was unaffected by these words, which were poured forth in a torrent as though my tormentor feared interruption, would be false. I saw my plans for the future, my very hope for life itself, swept away together, and nothing but a blank, broken only by a vision of the gallows, danced before my eyes.

To say that he had the satisfaction of seeing me visibly quail would be equally false, for, though my heart beat thickly enough, I sat unmoved and looked at him as though in a dream. I even essayed to speak, but words would not come, for my throat was clinched by invisible bands.

"Are you crushed at last?" he exclaimed, with a grim smile, though without shifting his eye or aim. "Oh, you shorn Samson! I am well paid for your cursed insults."

He was still speaking when again the heavy shake came to the flooring. But now it did not pass into a gentle tremor and fade away; instead, it grew stronger and stronger until every rafter took up the motion and the whole house trembled as though with an ague. Greater grew the shaking until the building rocked, the bed slid away from the wall, the table shifted, the glass and bottle on it rang together, and the pitcher danced so violently that the water within it splashed from its top. A square of plaster from the ceiling fell to the floor with a crash, filling the room with dust; but through all Scammell never winced, showed wonderment, nor bore a less threatening attitude.

In the course of the seconds through which this endured he held me as he probably would have done had the roof fallen about our ears, so determined was he to take me. I knew the nature of the turmoil at once, for when in the Indies with my father I had experienced it. It was not caused by the earth shaking from the rolling of heavy thunder, for just then the voice of the storm was confined to the roar of a terrific downpour of rain. It was an earthquake—a rare phenomenon in this latitude, and its rarity, its severity, and its results before my eyes, trifling as were these, woke me from my trance and again gave full play to my wits.

Fascinated and partly stunned as I had been by the fiendish face of my enemy and the full significance of the evil fortune into which I had suddenly fallen, like him, I sat through the commotion. Every unimportant detail about him, from the broken pearl button on his shirt front down to the grains of powder in the pistol pan and the fine edge of the flint in the lock, found a force of attraction to the eye only known to those who fall into sudden hopelessness or deep depression.

But with the dancing of the tableware a quick idea shot through my brain, and showed me a last desperate chance to extricate myself from the coil about me. Natural phenomenon in the shape of a breeze had saved me from the knife of the negro, and now 'twas an earthquake that might open a way for my deliverance by splashing water from a pitcher.

Straining my nerves to conceal the new hope that had sprung to life, I began to act. Never had I felt my muscles knit firmer or been less in need of stimulant than when, sinking back as if at last overcome by the combined shock of his words and the convulsion of Nature which had now passed, I said slowly and as though dazed:

"I am but a prisoner of war, sir. I was forced for my own safety to come to New York. I am no—spy— I will go—but—you—let me drink. I feel lax and— dizzy."

"You have none of the Indian in you, you pale-livered sneak!" he answered. "Drink, then, and gather your spunk and legs for action. Beat me with the flat of your sword! 'Fore God! But wait till I can shift my eye from you! Drink, and then move before we have another quake, and the walls about us—'twill be your last dram."

With apparent effort I raised myself, reached for

the bottle, and poured out a stiff measure of liquor, which I drank off; then taking the pitcher, I made as though to fill the glass, but as I tipped it, with a sudden movement I whirled full half a gallon of water over the pistol, drenching the priming and making the weapon useless. With this action I sprang to my feet.

Scammell was quick, but not quick enough. The water had but reached the powder when I heard the snap of the descending hammer, and saw his first motion to gain his legs; but, following up the drowning of the fire-pan, I lifted the heavy table and overturned it on him, pushing him backward, where to the floor went man, furniture, and crockery with a terrific crash.

At that moment there came a vivid flash of lightning, and hard upon it an appalling peal of thunder. Though almost blinded and deafened by the bolt, I sprang round the overturned table, and seizing the first thing coming to hand, which proved to be the water jug still unbroken, I grasped the struggling Tory by the throat and with all my force brought down the heavy earthenware on his uncovered head.

The pitcher flew to fragments, leaving but the handle in my grasp, while Scammell became limp and collapsed.

This action took place during the interval at which the thunder was the loudest, and was probably the reason that caused the noise of the fall of the table to be unnoticed by those below. But, as though it had been insufficient, another violent convulsion followed, which came and went with the suddenness of the explosion of a park of artillery.

I had but gotten to a standing position when a concussion rocked the house to its foundation. It sprang not from the earth below this time, but from the air above, the vibrations of which dashed the hanging glass from the wall and caused the window panes to

fly in pieces into the room. It was not of the nature of
an earthquake, still less like thunder near or afar; much
it resembled the blowing up of a magazine, though not
until afterward did I come to know this as the solution
of the matter. The flash that had lighted my attack
on Scammell had struck a powder ship just from England as she lay at anchor off Wall Street, and no vestige
of it or those aboard was ever discovered.*

The vicious nature of the shock was unlike the grad-
ual coming and going of the earthquake, and that it
had occasioned more alarm I soon knew by the shouts
that came from beneath my window. Rushing to it,
through the shattered panes I beheld men running from
the opposite houses, while in the yard below was the
squad of soldiers, which had pressed from the tavern
in a panic when it seemed that the building would fall.

My safety still demanded immediate action, for
should curiosity or distrust impel the guard to come upstairs, I would be undone. That move would drive me
to bay, and either oblige me to finally surrender or die
like a rat in a hole.

But I had determined a course of procedure by the
time I had finished getting into my clothing. Hastily
setting the table upright, I stooped over the body of
Scammell. I expected to find him dead, and was surprised to discover that he was still of this world, the
thickness of his curly hair and a possible crack in the
jug having saved him from a crushed skull. He was
completely stunned, however, and with little ado I
dragged him into the closet and shut the door.

My sole chance of escape now lay in getting to Clinton and procuring a pass, which might be used ere a hue

---

* This combination of intense heat, violent storm, earthquake,
and explosion actually occurred in New York city, Sunday, August
8, 1778.

and cry was raised after me, and I fancied the hour was not far from that appointed for the meeting. It was possible that Clinton had been informed of the falsity of my name, though I argued if that had been the case Scammell would never have approached me in the manner he had done. At all events, the risk must be taken.

At first sight there seemed no means of leaving the house save by the stairs or a drop of twenty feet or more from my side window; but, upon investigation, I discovered a pent roof beneath the windows of a room near the end of the hall, and upon going into the chamber I saw the apartment was probably the quarters occupied by my late assailant. Upon the bed lay a military hat, coat, and a sabre, while from a hook hung a long cloak used by cavalry officers.

Appropriating the latter, I stepped from the window to the roof, creeping to the eaves which came to within ten feet of the ground, and from there dropped.

So far I had been unobserved, and it took me not many moments to get into the street and below the tavern, working from there a roundabout course through the east side of the town or until I dared come out on the Broadway.

I had little fear of immediate pursuit, as none save Belden had an inkling of my mission to Clinton; and this, with the prevailing excitement due to the explosion and everywhere manifest, placed me out of danger for the time.

With the cloak about me, both as a disguise and a protection from the rain which was still falling though rapidly diminishing, I strode down to headquarters, and there boldly sent in the name of " Captain Lounsbury " to the general in chief. It relieved me greatly to note no signs of an unusual stir about the place, nor did the guard at the door show more than a passing interest in me as he turned me over to the flunky within the hall.

Being ushered into the same great saloon I had known the day before, I waited with natural impatience for recognition. I was not far from my appointed time, for the clock on the mantel showed it was but quarter of three, nor had I cooled my heels for long before a lady entered. I caught but a glimpse of her, seeing little more than that she was richly dressed, but marked her apparent familiarity with the place in the way she immediately swept from the room without giving an opportunity for the announcement of her name.

However, I was struck by the deference of the uniformed attendant as he backed away from her, and her ladyship had not been gone above five minutes when he returned. With a glance askant at my costume, he requested me to follow him. We traversed the length of the hall to an apartment at its end, where, throwing wide the door, he loudly announced " Captain Lounsbury!" and retired, while I entered to find myself in the presence of the lady who had left the saloon but a few minutes before.

CHAPTER IX.

GENERAL SIR HENRY CLINTON.

CONCEIVING that a blunder had been committed, and that I was unwittingly an intruder in a private room, I was about to make an apology for my presence when the lady half rose from the partly reclining position she had assumed, and with a gentle wave of her hand said:

"You are Captain Lounsbury? Come nearer, please. Sit here against the light, that I may have a look at you!" at the same time indicating a chair near the great window, which was swung open and led to a small balcony without.

Her voice was sweet, but even in these few words I noticed the affectation of inflection so common with ladies of fashion, and her original position, which she immediately regained after thus addressing me, was a pose pure and simple, doubtless taken for the purpose of exposing her fine arm and the graceful curves of her small though equally fine figure.

"Madam," I replied, advancing a pace or two, "I have not the honor of knowing you as well as you seem to know me. By what name——"

"Mrs. Florence Badely," she interrupted, with a smile which discovered her small, white teeth, and accentuated the rather infantile prettiness of her face. "I have taken the liberty of asking to see you ere you met Sir Henry. A woman is a better judge of a man than one of his own sex."

"And in the present case to what end, madam?" I asked, bowing and taking the chair to which she had motioned me.

For an answer she slowly raised a pair of double-bowed gold eyeglasses, deliberately and silently scanning me from head to foot.

"Well!" she broke forth irrelevantly. "I protest, Captain Lounsbury! You are almost a gentleman! Were your face but less red and your figure less gigantic, in a proper costume you would not be amiss. Your leg is none too delicate, but you have fine eyes and teeth, and your hair also is excellent. I am quite provoked! Sir Henry has deceived me, though it is now perhaps just as well that you are not ill-favored. Are you so hard-hearted, Captain Lounsbury? You scarce look a kidnaper!"

Her reference to kidnaping brought me sharply back to the rôle of Lounsbury, whose papers had shown kidnaping to have been one of his accomplishments. Under the sharp eye of this lady, whom I now knew to be Clinton's reported light-o'-love, it would not do for me to make a slip. That in some manner she had to do with my coming secret instructions I instantly surmised, but no conjecture on my part could clear the mystery of the nature of this interest. Deeming it policy to refrain from discussing the matter, I simply said:

"Madam, my leg is not exactly that of a dancing-master, nor has my figure the grace of a courtier, but they are the gifts of God, and have seen service in this broil against the King. As for the small compliments, I am your debtor."

"Now really, Captain Lounsbury, you have quite a neat gift at retort also." But she got no further, as at that instant a door concealed by heavy hangings was suddenly thrown open, letting in a burst of noisy laughter from what might have been a dozen men, the sound of jollity being mingled with the clinking of glasses and clattering of coin. The door then shut, and was evidently securely fastened, as I heard the turn of a key and the shooting of a bolt; the curtains were pushed aside, and there entered a man, whom by his uniform alone I knew to be the commander in chief of the British forces in America.

Sir Henry gave me but a passing glance as I rose to my feet. He stepped forward, and taking the hand of the lady, who barely shifted her position to greet him, bowed low over it, repeatedly kissing the finger tips.

The broad light from the window fell full upon him, showing him to be a man of but medium height, though stout and pale of face. His eyes were dark, his nose long and slightly dished at the bridge. The mouth was sensual, and bespoke his character at a glance, though his face was by no means coarse or weak. His brow was not broad, but it was smooth and open, and his brown hair, greatly puffed about his ears, was tied into a queue behind and profusely powdered.

But he was not a striking figure despite the gorgeous uniform of scarlet and gold adorned with the waistcoat ribbon and brilliant star of his knightly order. Something there was about him which impressed me with the littleness of his nature, and there was a lurk in his side glances wholly incompatible with an honest, fearless spirit. Undoubtedly he was a man proud of his rank and power—a man much given to self-communion and silence. His official standing was indicated by the single heavy epaulet adorning his right shoulder. His sword, with its belt wrapped about it, he carried in his hand.

"I declare, madam," he said, as he straightened himself and walked to a handsomely appointed table, on which he deposited his sword, "you have braved the storm and stolen a march on me, as you promised. Have you other charms to pit against the terrors of tempest and earthquake? You are the queen of graciousness to thus honor me. Do you find Lounsbury to your liking?" And as he pronounced the name he recognized my presence by a look and an almost imperceptible bending of the head.

"Now I protest, Sir Henry!" said Mrs. Badely, rising and affecting petulance as she adjusted her costume. "You interrupted me before I had come to conclusions. The affair is none of my making, and I am broken-hearted at its necessity. Oh, necessity is such a dreadful word!—Is it not, Captain Lounsbury? —Really, Sir Henry, I supposed you would not come for an hour yet, but, now that you are here, I will leave you to settle with the captain while I look after my recreant ward. Sir Henry, I feared I would have found her with you.—Ah! Captain Lounsbury, one's children, be they ours by law or nature, are such a trial—such a trial!—When shall I know of your decision, Sir Henry?" Then with an upward look and clearly affected archness, "You will honor me to-night, will you not, Sir Henry?"

What answer Clinton made I never knew. He held out his hand to her, the fall of lace from his cuff almost covering it, and with a step as unnatural as that in the minuet escorted her into the hall, closing the door behind him.

He was not absent long. I had but time to take in the details of the elegantly furnished apartment, from its carved fireplace behind the table to the carved casing of the window overlooking the Hudson, when he entered rather hastily, his face no longer bearing its genial

expression, and with something of a businesslike air
seated himself at the table, motioning me to take the
chair opposite.

Before speaking he cast quick glances at me, instantly removing his eye from mine as he met my gaze,
but immediately returning to the charge. Finally, he
began quite sharply:

"Are you Captain Lounsbury?"

My heart leaped at the question, and I pulled myself
together with the firm intention of laying violent hands
on him if he had discovered the fraud, but I answered
quietly and with an unswerving look:

"Yes, your Excellency."

"General Knyphausen has always vouched for you,
but you hardly appear the desperado I had been led
to expect. Your physique and carriage make you an
excellent agent—if—you have subtlety behind."

His manner was unsuspicious, and this relieved me.
Bowing, I answered:

"I have seen service, your Excellency, and have always rendered a good account of myself."

"So I am told," he replied. "You are a remarkable
man. You look and speak like a gentleman, yet your
record is shady, sir; still," he put in hurriedly, "I am
not criticising. War has its necessities. You read the
order given you yesterday?"

"Yes, your Excellency."

"Are you prepared to act on its suggestion?"

"Yes, your Excellency."

He stopped as if perplexed, and passed his hand
across his brow.

"You were not successful in your mission to Norfolk! Why did you not report?"

"The party was out of reach," I ventured, hazard-
ing the guess that he referred to the kidnaping business.
"But I made amends later. I have been ill from

a wound," I continued, pointing to my sling, which through all the excitement in leaving the King's Arms I had not forgotten.

"Will you undertake a similar errand—here in the city, and in connection with the trip to Newport?" he asked, looking at me and then away.

"Yes, your Excellency, if it be feasible."

"It is feasible; it is easy, and you shall be well rewarded. Have you money?"

"No, your Excellency; I have nothing but my promise of prize money. I am living on the credit of that."

"Indeed! Have you the paper with you, properly indorsed?"

For an answer I took it from my pocket and laid it before him, at the same time realizing with a start that the communication given to me the day before had been left in my room in the hurry of escaping from the tavern. He picked up the document I laid before him, glanced at it, and then, rising, went to a bookcase, which on being opened disclosed a small strong-box. This he unlocked, and taking from it several rouleaux of coin laid them on the table.

"You must have money; you can not get ready without it. You will have many expenses. Listen! I shall not intrust you with a packet to General Pigot. The venture is too hazardous. Tell him to hold Newport to the last extremity, and I will start to his relief within two weeks. I shall also communicate with him by land."

He arose again, and clasping his hands behind him walked up and down the floor. I saw that the man was wishing to come to a point against which just then he was shying, and, as time was an object to me, I hoped to help him over the difficulty by remarking:

"The matter of the cruise is plain enough, but your Excellency hinted at secret instructions."

"Yes, yes," he answered. "It was that I referred
to a moment since." He hesitated, and then pointing
to my arm, continued, "Perhaps your wound would
cripple you for active service?"

"No, your Excellency," I answered hurriedly; "it
is about healed."

"Will you, then—undertake to—to—in short—to
abduct a—a person and—and *perhaps* deliver her to
Pigot?"

"It is a woman, then?"

"It is a woman. In fact, my position is delicate—
I must not be known in the matter. She is troublesome
to—— Well, her brother is about to be executed. I
wish to save her from this knowledge. Do you follow
me? She is to be the victim of an unauthorized out-
rage; the motive to be your own. No ill treatment,
no *unnecessary* violence, of course. You shall be paid—
you shall be well paid. Get the boat ready—be ready
within five days. Can I rely on you? Then report for
final details. Is there anything more?"

"Yes, your Excellency, there is more. I shall need
a pass. Some of my men are without the lines."

"Very good!" he returned, sitting down and pulling
paper toward him, on which he wrote rapidly; then
pushing the writing away, he began talking with the
feather of the quill betwixt his teeth.

"Here is your pass," said he, laying his hand over
the paper and looking hard at me, "and there is your
gold. There is more to come. No violence—no *brute*
violence. What would you do if necessity demanded
your sinking the ship? If—if—if——"

The pen in his mouth gave his voice the character
of a snarl; his eyes flashed, and he bent forward eagerly.
I caught a glimpse of the villainy of this man, and
without winking promptly replied:

"Save myself, your Honor!"

As though smitten by a revulsion of feeling, he started back and exclaimed:

"No! no! Not that! Great God! not quite so quick! What a tool you are! Is there no other way? Let me think; let it rest as it is until you report.—Ah! what is the meaning of this?"

The last remark was drawn from him by a noise of controversy in the hall without, the sudden opening of the door, and the entry of a female unannounced. She was veiled, but before the door had fairly closed behind her, with a graceful move of her arm she uncovered her face, and I involuntarily came to my feet as I recognized the young girl whose beauty had struck me as I was about leaving the Sprite.

Her eyes were red from weeping, and, indeed, the tears on her cheeks were as apparent as the few raindrops on her silken hood, as well as on her plain though elegant costume. Over her white brow and from under the back of her head covering there strayed a few locks of hair, which some might have called red, but red they were not, being the richest of auburn, and of such a nature that the damp of the air had curled them into a mass of crisp waves.

If tears were on her cheeks, there were none in her voice as she advanced before the Englishman. As she came to within a pace of him she halted, and demanded in a low, firm tone, which for all its firmness was sweet:

"Sir Henry Clinton, where is my brother?"

Clinton dropped his eyes, while a heavy frown contracted his smooth forehead. For an instant he appeared about to give way to temper, but finally unpuckered his brows and replied easily, as though patronizing a petulant child:

"My dear Miss Gertrude, you must ask your aunt."

"Call your Mrs. Badely no aunt of mine, Sir Henry. She may be my guardian, but none of her blood flows in my veins. Be that as it may, sir, she has but this moment referred me to you. My brother has been gone a week. You have promised each day that I should see him the next. Sir Henry, where is my brother?"

The decidedly defiant tone of the last demand made me wonder at the audacity of the speaker, but instead of arousing the temper of the man to whom it was addressed, it made him rather draw into himself, though not without an effort at self-control. Again he rose and paced the floor behind his desk, but finally stopping in his walk, took a long breath as if he had arrived at a determination, and suddenly turning to me, said:

" Captain Lounsbury, the plan I mentioned will remain in abeyance.—My dear Gertrude," he continued, addressing the girl, " I have been trying to save you from pain, but, as you will have the truth, I will give it to you. Your brother has been discovered acting in the interests of the enemy. His offense was clear, and he has acknowledged it. He was arrested one week ago this day. He was tried fairly, convicted, and sentenced to be hanged as a spy. Yesterday he perished in the fire at Cruger's Wharf before the sentence could be executed."

Now at these words I guessed this was the girl whom I had been expected to kidnap and make way with, and my first impulse, quickly controlled, was to blurt out the fact of her own danger. It had become plain, however, that Clinton could not screw his courage to going the length of even indirectly taking her life, much as he wished for some reason to be rid of her. It was strongly forced on me that he was being used as a cat's-paw by the woman who was known to powerfully influence his actions, even to the extent of altering the plans of a campaign. As he finished his statement, I knew he had told the girl an untruth, or he had been lying to me, as he had informed me that the brother was about to be hanged, no mention having been made of his death by fire. Instantly there came to mind my encounter with the scorched patriot, and I instinctively strung the two together.

I expected to witness the collapse of the girl as the British general completed his sentence, but there came nothing of the sort. Instead, she stood tall and graceful, with lips apart and eyes widely strained. Her color faded a trifle, but after a breath or two she answered stoutly:

"General Clinton, that is false! My brother held no communication with any one beyond the lines at Kingsbridge. You have overshot your mark. It was I, sir, who informed General Washington of your intended movement into the Jerseys, but my poor brother has been doomed because he is in possession of facts which would compromise Sir Henry Clinton were they known abroad. I, too, know them. Work your will on me, a girl—I care not; but if you injure a hair of the head of Beverly, all England shall know how Mr. Henry Clinton obtained his knighthood, together with other matters which would make interesting reading.* By his appearance, here is doubtless one of your familiars," she went on, indicating me by a fine look of intense scorn. "Order him to apprehend and make way with Gertrude King, who, by the help of God, has been, is now, and always will be, devoted to her own land and its liberties!"

---

* Two years before, General Clinton had challenged Lord George Germain, of the British ministry. In fear of his life, Germain promised Clinton a title and the command of the army in America if he would withdraw the challenge. Clinton did so, obtained leave of absence from America, went to London and was knighted by the King. Returning, he succeeded General Howe, who resigned shortly before the evacuation of Philadelphia. The affair caused great scandal at the time.

As she uttered these words she was sublime. Her figure swayed slightly, her eyes sparkled, and her voice rang like a bell. There was no effect of bravado, but it was apparent that with her there had come a crisis, and she had thrown off her mask, either because it was no longer of use or for the purpose of sacrificing herself for her brother. Her great beauty, her youth, her fearlessness—ay, even the grace of her pose, set off by her faultless costume—gave weight to the words which on her listeners produced profound though widely differing emotions.

My own first feeling was that of utter insignificance as I marked her great courage and heard the inspiring eloquence of her last sentence; my next that, if necessary, I would risk my life to assist her if my way to do so was made plain. My admiration, my respect was beyond measure. I was almost moved to defy Clinton to his face there and then when that party exposed the spirit in which he had listened.

He had halted and whirled about as she threw at him the falsity of his statement, and as she progressed, his face turned from white to red and from red to purple. On her finishing, he hung a moment as though to gather the full import of her words, and then banged his fist on the table as he exclaimed:

"You doubly damned rebel wench! You spy! How dare you use such language here and to me? So you have taken advantage of your housing with—— My God! what a fool your aunt has been! Madam," he suddenly thundered, "you are under arrest——"

"Sir," she said, cutting him short, "if I am, I will be released. You have now an opportunity to confiscate my property as you have my brother's. Doubtless this sum will also go to enrich your paramour. You have taken me for a child, but I am not the helpless girl you think me. I know your motives. They are money, and fear, and Mrs. Badely. And now I have but one demand, General Sir Henry Clinton, and one more statement. Your personal secrets are safe with me conditionally, and my property you are welcome to, as you will but hold it until the right prevails; but this I will have now—a pass beyond your lines at Kingsbridge. The statement will simply show the extent of your falsity and the ease with which it is overcome. My brother——"

At that moment the hall door for a second time was thrown open violently by a female, and now it was Mrs. Badely who re-entered. There was no affectation about her as she hurried in and closed it behind her. With her hand on the knob, her face blanched to an ash color, and her whole figure trembling, she pointed to the defiant girl and burst out:

"She is a traitor! she is a traitor! Let her not go hence! O Sir Henry! Sir Henry! he has escaped! He has been back and—taken—all—those——"

She got no further, but, tottering slightly, gradually sank to the floor in a real or pretended faint.

CHAPTER X.

THE HEROISM OF GERTRUDE KING.

GENERAL CLINTON stood as if stricken with catalepsy, while I sprang to Mrs. Badely. Discarding the useless disguise, I threw my sling from me and, lifting the lady, bore her to the couch. As her aunt sank to the floor the girl had given a violent start, and, as though taking for granted that the escaped party referred to was her brother, she raised her hands and exclaimed fervently, "Thank God! thank God!" Then the emotion she had bravely suppressed when her misfortune seemed at its height overcame her on the relaxation of the strain, and she broke into a torrent of tears.

Giving no further attention to Mrs. Badely, I turned and looked at Clinton. He had sunk into his chair, and was undergoing a strong inward struggle, but the expression of his face boded little good to the girl who still stood before him. In a moment he straightened himself, and pointing to the weeping maiden, sternly said:

"Captain Lounsbury, call my orderly, and see that this woman is placed in confinement. Report to me when it is done."

It appeared that the moment had arrived when I must declare myself, for to allow this heroic girl to suffer the indignity of arrest while I could prevent it, was not in my books. I was about to turn on him with my answer when she lifted her head, and, directing her

wet eyes toward Clinton, said as firmly as she had before spoken:

"General Clinton, I care little for what you may
do to me. The only load I had has been lifted. My
brother is free! Listen to me! He was never arrested
as a spy, never tried in any court, never condemned to
be hanged! I knew he was to be secretly removed from
his prison; of that I was informed by one of your own
officers, and I came here to demand his whereabouts.
Is not my so-called beauty as powerful for my interests
as your commands for yours? Look to yourself, Sir
Knight! What I know of you will find a ready ear, but,
Sir Henry Clinton, you will scarce have the courage
to demand an earldom from the one who hears it."

The utterly fearless way in which she spoke, coupled
with sarcasm and a taunt the nature of which I then
knew nothing, drove the British general into a fury.
Springing to his feet and again slamming the table, he
shouted:

"Arrest her, sir! Arrest her instantly! Stop her
vile mouth! Good God! am I to be thus bearded by a
self-confessed traitress?"

By this I had gotten to a pitch of spirits that ripened
me for any deed insuring the safety of the gallant girl,
and yet my head was left clear enough to see the possible consequences of my act.

"Nay, Sir Henry," I replied clearly, but without
moving, "I shall never arrest her nor see her arrested
here; rather would I see her canonized. Do your own
dirty work."

"Hell and furies!" he thundered, fairly bounding
from the floor. "What means this treason? You are
under arrest yourself, sir! What, sir! you defy me?"

As he spoke he moved from behind the table and
took a couple of strides toward the hall; but seeing his
intention was to call the sentry, and that for me it was

now the whole pace or the scaffold, in an instant I was ahead of him, and, quickly locking the door, threw the key through the open window.

I was none too soon. Through the heavy mahogany I heard the approach of hurried footsteps, and the knob twisted while yet my hand was on it.

With an oath Clinton turned toward the table and grasped his sword; but again I anticipated his action and was before him. Laying my left hand on the weapon, I pressed it down, while with my right I pushed him into his chair and held him there. He paled as though fearing immediate assassination, and gasped, then after a fruitless effort at freeing himself, he shouted:

"What! Captain Lounsbury, would you murder your commander?"

I rapidly shifted my grip, and to prevent his further clamoring placed my hand over his mouth, pinning his head fast to the back of the chair.

"Call me not Lounsbury!" I exclaimed in my excitement. "I have been damned by that name weeks enough! Know me as Donald Thorndyke, an enemy to the King.—Quick, now!" said I, turning to the girl. "Here is a pass ready written. Get away—out of the window! I will cover your going." And with that I snatched the writing from the table and held it toward her.

By this there was a violent knocking at the door and some shouting in the hall, but, taking no notice of the shortness of time allowed for her escape, the girl stepped close to me, and, peering into my face with undisguised surprise upon her own countenance, said:

"Are you from Washington?"

"Nay, miss," I answered, "I am but a free-lance; not from him, but for him to the end. Hurry your leaving; and God bless you for a brave lass!"

" But you—but you! Must I take the sacrifice? "

" I am already known and outlawed. Hurry! Heaven help the first man who enters this room now! If you would prevent bloodshed, leave at once. I will follow betimes. Live for your brother's sake! Get gone—get gone! "

Taking the paper I had pushed into her hand, she gave me a smile that was a benediction, the memory of which comes to me as I write. Turning, she hastened to the balcony. I saw her gather her skirts, climb over the light iron rail and drop—a matter easily accomplished, as the window sill was a scarce six feet from the soil of the garden below.

And then I turned attention to myself and my own desperate situation.

There was nothing to do but follow her immediately if I hoped to escape, but, knowing that every second's delay helped the maiden, I still held the general so that he could neither cry out nor prove aggressive, and so continued holding him for perhaps the space of a minute.

In the meantime the attacks on the door were becoming more violent, and even the one through which Clinton had entered was now being tried. Mrs. Badely, who had been unattended through the episode, suddenly recovered her senses and lifted herself upright on the couch, when, seeing me apparently strangling her lover, she set up a shrieking that must have driven to desperation those without.

It was my final moment. Casting a quick look over the table for anything in the matter of writing that might be used as a pass, my eye spied the rolls of money which had been given me, but nothing else of service was in sight and there was not an instant to lose in investigation. Releasing Clinton, I jumped for the gold, swept it into my pocket, and seizing Scammell's

7

cloak as I went, ran to the window, barely evading
the grasp of Mrs. Badely, who made a bob at me and
would have hung like a leech had she fastened to my
clothing.

In less than a second I was over the rail, and, landing on the turf, took to my heels, pointing myself to
the earthworks of the deserted " Oyster Battery," which
had been erected by the Americans exactly in the rear
of headquarters and on the edge of the Hudson.

This battery, grass-grown, dismantled, and neglected as useless by the British, I knew would be no
permanent cover, but its embankments made a temporary shield betwixt me and a possible shot from the
house had my line of flight been discovered. It was a
fair post for a minute's observation and reflection, and,
bounding through an empty embrasure, I dodged down,
and then raising my head above the edge of the works,
looked back.

To my astonishment I was not at once pursued,
though two or three figures appeared at the window I
had gone through, all others being seemingly deserted.
I had to thank the day for my good fortune, as the
Sabbath was a time for general relaxation, and were it
not for that my chances would have been next to
naught. Few soldiers were about, a corporal's guard
only being before the house when I entered it, but that
there would soon be wild confusion and a general turning out I had small doubts.

The banks of the Hudson at this point terminated
in a steep bluff, at the bottom of which was a narrow
strip of beach. Once on the sands, I might run along
screened from those at a distance, but could easily be
headed and captured like a fish in a purse net. I took
the risk, however, and sliding down the steep, sped
northward for some ways, coming to the top undiscov-
ered and at the edge of the burned district.

Into this wilderness of destruction I plunged, but soon slackened my pace to a walk to avoid marked observation from those who inhabited the shanties abounding throughout the ruins. I was fairly safe for the present, and decided there to halt and take stock in myself and circumstances, especially as I had no definite plans before me.

It came to me that I was now doubly damned—first, as a spy; second, for doing violence to the person of the highest functionary in America. I was without means of escape from the city, and entirely unarmed. I would be hunted like a wolf, and with less mercy from one quarter at least. In short, though I was then breathing free air, I was in desperate straits, and, being so, it took little reflection to see the necessity for acting like a desperate man.

I came, then, to this decision: I would attempt a return to the tavern, recover my arms and the paper of instructions, the last which might at least add weight to my assumed character and help me in forcing my way through the lines—a move that had become imperative, and might be successful if I acted with dispatch. Then to the Dove I would go, and throw myself under the protection of Stryker, whom, I had reason to believe, was one of the true men secretly helping the patriot cause.

Of the brave girl to whom I had sacrificed the pass (an act I did not for a moment regret) I thought much. Like me, she was marked for destruction; like me, she had now two virulent enemies, for I could not help believing that Mrs. Badely was at the bottom of Clinton's desire to remove her from a field which threatened the social supremacy and interests of that lady. I wondered how she had fared and in what direction she had fled.

But I was in no position for long wonderment.

Rising from my seat, I walked on until I had reached
a point opposite King Street, then coming out into the
Broadway, crossed it and got myself to the rear of the
tavern. The man who interfered with me now would
be past praying for, but to my surprise I met with no
opposition on passing through the kitchen and bounding up the back stairs, marking only the frightened
looks of the two women who were cooking.

In a moment I gained my room. It was in a terrible
state of confusion. Bloody bedclothes strewed the
floor, the mattress was ripped open, blood was upon
the table (doubtless Scammell had been laid thereon),
and the dust of plaster covered everything. Scammell
himself was gone, and likewise was gone the paper I
had counted on. My arms, however, were unmolested.
The ammunition had been swept from the shelf to the
floor in probable search for treasonable documents
(which search also accounted for the general disorder),
but no part of it was missing, nor, barring the paper,
had any of my personal property been taken from the
room. I felt new strength as I fastened on my sword
and stuffed the pistols in my belt, then, taking my
rifle, I went out the way I had gone in, and still without opposition.

And still without opposition or interruption I regained the burned district. It had been a miracle, but
I was now no better off than before, save that I was
armed and commanded the lives of at least three men
when the attempt should be made to take me.

I was aware that the wilderness of blackened walls
and charred timber, which seemed such a haven at
present, would be about the first region over which an
organized search would be prosecuted. The very un-
likelihood of my returning to the tavern had made it
possible for me to enter, regain my arms and leave unmolested, while the darkest holes of the city would be

thoroughly scoured, and that at once. To burrow into a crevice in this field of desolation might be possible, but it would end in starvation and final discovery. To disguise myself was not possible, nor, had I the means, would it have availed me much, as my unusual size would have made disguise of little more than temporary benefit. My line of flight, which might easily be traced along the sands of the strip of beach, pointed plainly toward the region which I was now traversing, and to remain in its vicinity was tantamount to placing myself within easy reach of my pursuers. I had but one expedient, and that to elude capture until nightfall by placing myself where there was the least liability of search, and, under cover of darkness, boldly attempting to force the lines at a spot remote from the regular roads of travel.

To this end I bethought me of taking to water, and by swimming outflank the defenses; but I soon realized that the banks of either river would be doubly guarded by sentinels and patrol boats, though, aside from the risk, I gave over the idea, as the attempt would necessitate my complete disarming.

Turning northward, therefore, I kept within the limits of the black desolation until I reached its upper termination. Leaving it behind, I cut through the grounds of King's College, walking with apparent carelessness, then on to the hospital, through its confines, and still onward over a garden or two and a field until I had arrived at the edge of Lispenard's Meadows.

I dared not trust myself to its broad open; I could have been too easily marked from a distance, so I turned me toward the Hudson, keeping the while close to the shrubbery which defined the meadows' limits, and finally took refuge under a chestnut tree, though ere long I was up it and as far toward its top as I durst venture.

Years after I looked in vain for this tree, but it had fallen under the axe, as fell all the heavy timber on the island during the terrible winter of 1780.

I was now wet through. The cloak I had continued to wear to prevent easy identification, together with the recking weather and the showers of water which had poured from the wet leaves, had saturated me, and I was anything save comfortable as I sat astride a bough and waited for the day to end.

It was something after five o'clock, but as yet I had discovered no signs of pursuit in my direction. To beguile the time, I reloaded my rifle and pistols, though I laid more reliance on my strength of arm and hardness of fist to overcome a single guard than I did on firearms. The great wet meadow stretched before me like a green sea, broken only by the clump of trees which was to have been my dueling ground on the morrow, and the sluggish brook taking its rise from the Collect, cutting in twain lengthwise and draining the plain which had once been a dangerous and pestilence-breeding quagmire. The thunderstorm had passed, but the sky was yet heavily overcast, promising a dark, wet night (which suited my purpose), and by the time the sun set and I swung myself from my lofty perch the rain was coming down, not in torrents, but with a steady drip-drip that told of a decided change of weather.

I had no preparations to make, nor from the point at which I had been hiding had I a long distance to go before coming to the line of defenses. This line was not a continuous embankment, but consisted of short breastworks and redoubts at no great distance apart, every foot of the intervening spaces being patrolled by sentinels. I had resolved to strike the line near its center, or about midway betwixt the Kingsbridge and Greenwich roads, and so walked straight over the meadows, crossing the brook and feeling my way up the rising ground of the northern boundary of the great field.

It was not yet dark, but through the gloom I soon made out that I was exactly in the rear of a redoubt. Retracing my steps, I worked eastward, then again headed north, and this time found myself at the end of a slight dip of the ground, with fortifications on the heights at either hand. The way between appeared un-obstructed by military works, though what guard was there posted I could not guess, and as yet it was too light to attempt the passage.

Still protecting my primings, I threw myself on the sodden ground, and in this fashion lay waiting, while the minutes dragged and the half hour seemed length-ened to an age. I say half hour, but it might have been more or less. There was no sound save the patter of the rain, the dismal chirrup of a forlorn tree toad, and an occasional hail of a guard. Finally, the gloom grew to dusk, the dusk to darkness, and that to pitchiness in the tree-shadowed passage which lay before me. And now I girded myself for the attempt, fully conscious that my life and death hung finely balanced.

I had first thought of crawling through the line like a snake, belly down, but the distance and nature of the ground made such a course impossible unless I was to take the whole night to it, and if discovered I would be taken at a disadvantage. Rising, therefore, I stepped behind a tree, slung my rifle across my back, and drew my cloak well about my sword, throwing back the gar-ment in a manner that left my right arm free. From this cover I slipped to another and another, and so on-ward until I found myself at what I thought to be the edge of a small clearing beyond, but I could neither see nor hear aught ahead, a fact causing me some per-plexity. I was debating the feasibility of advancing boldly and risking an encounter, or staying until I could locate the sentinel I knew must be near, when to my right I caught the shadow of a man walking across my line of progress. As he came close I heard him humming a tune below his breath, and hoped he would pass on that I might step over his beat unnoticed. There was nothing white about me but my face, and I bent it low that it might not betray me. On he came until he reached the tree under which I was standing, and there halting, leaned his gun against the bole and put his hand into his pocket, presumably for tobacco, for I heard him spit forth a quid.

He was within a pace of me, and why he did not feel my presence I can not guess. But I was in a predicament, for should he turn I was lost. If I moved forward or backward I was lost, but if I took matters into my own hand, I might clear the barrier with one blow, and with a sudden shifting of my position I threw the weight of my nerves into my right arm and struck out.

My fist took the man fair in the temple. I doubt if he ever knew what struck him, for he went down with no other sound than that occasioned by the fall of his body.

CHAPTER XI.

I HAD never before and have never since in cold blood struck violently an unarmed man. God knows I recoiled as I felt the plates of this fellow's skull give beneath my fist, and, though I knew my act to be a righteous one, and that had I been discovered I would have had a foot of cold steel in my vitals, I could not at once overcome the feeling of having committed murder.

Whether or not the man was a sentinel I could not tell. The shiftless way of leaning his gun against a tree and humming made me doubt it, but it mattered little—he was an obstacle whose removal was necessary. I was fairly sure there was more to overcome beyond, but resolved to try strategy in passing unless driven to open violence, and even then my fist should not be my mainstay. With my temper inflamed, it boded ill for the man who crossed me; but with pulses slow and even, it went against my grain to spill human blood, especially that of one doing his duty, and this fact alone would have made me a poor soldier for the ranks.

Now I unshipped my sword, drew my cloak about me, and walked on as openly as though I was an officer of "grand rounds." It was miserable going. In the darkness I seemed to find and stub every stone and shoot into as many brambles as might be discovered in a ten-acre wood lot. I passed unchallenged through

97

the shallow ravine, and was wondering if by chance I had already cleared the lines, when the works of an advanced redoubt rose against the dim sky, and at the same instant there came the ring of a musket and a voice called: "Halt! Who's there?"

It was not my plan to halt, or answer either, for that matter. I had located the voice to the right, but could see no one, and was fairly sure that only the noise of my progress had been marked, and not myself. Therefore I swung toward the left and hurried along as rapidly and silently as I could, soon having the pleasure of hearing the sentinel stumble across my trail some distance in the rear.

I had now the redoubt to flank, and, as the woods had been cut down at its front as well as on either side, there was an open space for me to traverse. Here I lowered my dignity by getting on to all-fours, and, holding my blade betwixt my teeth, I crept slowly onward, taking advantage of every stump and fallen tree as a post to halt and listen. But these latter were none too frequent, and I used at least an hour in getting the few hundred feet which lay between the works and the abatis protecting them. Having gained the abatis, I rose and felt my way through the tangled branches of the felled timber, making a deal of noise I thought, but finally got past and into the woods beyond. These woods proved to be but a strip, and a narrow one at that, for I soon came to a road which served me only in showing my location, as I knew of one crossing from the Kingsbridge road to another leading to the village of Greenwich.

I was well satisfied with myself and my progress, considering that the worst was passed, but my pride underwent a sudden fall when, as I was putting my leg over the snake fence, a voice came out of the darkness:

"Halt! Who goes there?"

"A friend, but without countersign. Where are you?" I returned easily, though I made a mighty start. "Then stay where you be, or I fire!"

"Very good! Come to me," I answered, swinging myself back and retreating to a tree near by, and from that to another.

It gave me infinite relief to hear the tramp of a horse, and know the man was a mounted vidette, and in the course of a few seconds he went by me to where I had answered him, though by then I had retreated along the line of the road and was forty feet away. Halting his horse, he again challenged, but, on receiving no answer, fired his pistol into the woods and began cursing like a pirate.

I knew there would be trouble now, and, indeed, the echo of the shot had scarce died away when I heard galloping coming from either direction as his fellows hastened to join him. It would not do for me to linger in the vicinity, so I leaped the fence and crossed the highway above him, gaining the opposite timber just before another horseman swept by toward the point of alarm.

At this juncture I thanked my stars for three things: First, for the wet and blackness of the night; second, that the lines I had run were the third or inner lines, comparatively illy guarded and but half manned, established to be used only in case of the fall of the outer defenses; and, third, that my present destination lay not beyond the next obstruction. I never would have dared attempt the passage of the "barrier gates," as they were called, a strong and continuous work across the neck of land below Fort Washington; and even had this been possible, the outpost of the British army at Kingsbridge would have floored anything without a pass or wings. There, in the face of the army of Washington, now but a few miles distant, it would have become almost a matter of creeping betwixt the legs of the sentinels.

I was not possessed with a great curiosity regarding the outcome of the trouble I had raised on the road, and got myself away from its locality as rapidly as was consistent with rough ground, thickly growing trees and underbrush, and pitchy darkness. I felt I was safe at last, safe from immediate disaster, and then awoke to the fact that, save from being warm instead of cold, I was in about as miserable a position as any man unhurt and shaking a free foot could well be. I had eaten but little during the day, and a man of my size and activity soon hungers, though as yet my hunger had not become a serious matter. I was drenching, without shelter and without prospect of shelter, and miles from any possibility of a helping hand. To stumble onward might land me in some difficulty from which I could not easily recover. I was now at a distance from the cross road, and knew not if I was bearing out of my line northward or toward one of the two great highways, to approach either of which was fraught with the greatest danger.

Therefore I determined to settle where I was until a glimmer of dawn should show me my way onward. I had no choice of spots, and so sat me down on the stump I had but just fallen over, and, drawing my cloak about my head, emulated the extremest patience of Job, who, for all his troubles, had never been beset as was I.

Not for an instant did I nod or cease my watchfulness through all the long hours. The rain, noted for its impartiality, seemed to belie the adage and focus on me as though I sat beneath a gargoyle. Toward daylight, which came none too early, the heat had gone from my blood, and something like a chill took its place, and with the first sign of lividness in the clouds above I set out, more from an instinct toward flight than from any definite plan. The Dove was my destination, but it was only to be approached by night, and it was scarce an hour's walk from where I sat. Nothing could be gained by wandering aimlessly, yet such was the spirit of flight within me that even movement partook of the nature of safety, and the loadstone attracting me lay still to the northward. Toward the north, then, I turned.

The birds had begun to stir in their nests and twitter sleepily as I came to the edge of the woods and beheld the checker of farm fields and woodland from the elevation on which I was standing, a fine-drawn mist so blurring the distance that it seemed infinite. I went on, and by sunrise crossed the Minetta water, striking westward that I might get into the wilderness above Greenwich, reaching that almost primeval forest toward noon.

But it is useless to follow my old trail here. I did it years after with great satisfaction to myself, calling up a cloud of memories that brought back my lost youth, albeit it brought (as it does now) a mist before my eyes as well. Through that afternoon I wandered well toward Bloomingdale, and as the shadows fell, cut eastward near the old Apthorp mansion and across the wild land which lies a beautiful waste about the center of the island.*

I was now close to the Kingsbridge road again, and not half a mile from the Dove. The storm had cleared with the going down of the sun, leaving the air cool and pleasant, but, though I am a lover of Nature and prone to mark the effect of storm and sunshine, I remember little of this evening save that it was a gorgeous one, with a moon, something less than half grown, swimming in the sky like a cleft coin.

---

* Now Central Park.

Not a morsel of food had passed my lips for more than four-and-twenty hours. I was tired, not from the miles of walking or manifold exertion, but from lack of nutriment, and, more than all, from the moral effect of knowing I was being hunted like a wild animal. My clothing had well-nigh dried on my body, but I was still damp. I had not even the comfort of tobacco, for, though I possessed it in plenty, I could get no fire, my tinder box having been wetted in the soaking I had endured. I had fled from the sight of man as Satan flies before the sign of the cross, but by the time I had gotten on my journey thus far I cared little for Nick Stryker, Rex, the British army, or the devil himself. My sole yearning was for food, and the sun had not sunken fairly behind the Jersey hills when, against all reason, I rose from my last hiding place near the road-side and strode into it, making my way toward the tavern as fast as I could walk.

My arms were like lead. The gold in my pockets and the bullets in my pouch had fifty times their weight as I splashed through the mud, but I was protected by a divine Providence, for no soul saw I going or coming while I was on the great thoroughfare. When I turned into the lane leading to the tavern some of my reason returned to me, and I slipped over the fence that I might not approach too directly the front door. There were no horses under the shed as I passed it, a fact that gave me assurance, and on peering through the bar window, I marked that the room was unoccupied.

The bar of the Dove was, like many of the taverns of the day, as much a refectory as a bar, and the general assembly room of the house. As I have said, it was deserted, and barren of light as well, the far corners being so immersed in gloom that I could barely make out the tables under the curtained windows. My advent within brought an answering sound of steps, and there entered a black man, half waiter and half hostler, as I made out by his apron, the table knives in his hand, and a general smell of the stable he brought with him.

Without ado I asked for food—food of any sort, hot or cold, with a bottle of wine, or, failing in that, stimulant of any description. I thought the fellow was frightened at my fierceness, and showed him I meant to pay for all I demanded by pulling from my pocket a few pieces of gold and exposing them. He slipped behind the bar and brought out a bottle of rum, setting it on a table in the darkest corner of the room, and then hurriedly went out, saying I should be served without delay.

Left to myself, I took a stiff dram and looked about me. The room was decidedly barren in appearance, the only attempt at ornamentation being in the boughs of green stuff that had been piled into the vast fireplace. The rafters overhead, somber with age, were black in the increasing darkness, and the walls, unwhitened for months and perhaps years, were deeply scored with names and coarse mottoes graven by sword points or bayonets, and smutted by candles held against the rough plaster. The bar took up a space near the entrance, the floor was clean and sanded, and the only furniture in the room consisted of an immense settle in the corner by the chimney, one long table with a bench betwixt it and the wall, and four or five smaller tables with accompanying chairs. In strong contrast with the prevailing dinginess of the apartment were the two windows in the rear of the room, their curtains of plain stuff as white and stiff as crusted snow, and the panes as sparkling and brilliant as newly minted coin.

With an eye to future action in case of mischance, I went to the windows and found them unfastened. The view looked east and showed an infield with a stream on one side, which I knew must drain the ponds

and swamps of the lower Harlem flats in the vicinity
of McGowan's Pass, and empty itself into the Sound
River.*

The sight of its brush-grown banks and the oncoming night suggested a way of escape, but a boat would
have been necessary, and even with this there were the
jaws of Hell Gate and the river patrols to overcome.

I think I had plumbed the depths of every possible
chance to get off the island and on to the main, but
saw no way out. The Hudson was too wide to swim;
the Sound River too boisterous in either run of the tide,
and even better guarded than was the land. To pass
the Harlem was not possible, both banks being sen-
tried by the enemy, and thus I was held betwixt the
" barrier gates," the lower lines, and the two rivers. In
time every foot of this ground would be scoured, and the
end looked to be that I would succumb.

But the end was not yet. I was well armed and
stronger by a dram than when I came in. I left open
the windows, changing my seat to the long table, partly
stretching myself along the bench to render me less
conspicuous. From here I commanded a view of the
front door and all within the room, being myself quite
in the darkness.

Thus I waited for a full quarter of an hour with
dead silence all about until the black brought in my
food and a candle, setting the light at the end of the
table farthest from me, pulling down the windows,
and drawing the curtains, though it was far from being
chilly. I was about to resent this disposition of the
candle as a piece of impertinence, as it barely cast a
shadow at that distance, when I suddenly considered
the advantage of being in gloom, and so let it bide. I

---

* This stream, now culverted, still runs under the city in the
neighborhood of East One Hundred and Tenth Street.

finished everything before me in short order, and, as
though the man had anticipated my wants, my plate
was immediately recharged with a liberal supply of
ham and eggs, while a bowl of bonnyclabber was placed
beside it.

Now, instead of withdrawing as he had done before, the black sat himself opposite me, with every wink
the whites of his eyes snapping in the light of the distant candle. After watching my jaws gradually slow
down as I drew near the end of the supply, and while
I gave a long sigh of relief and comparative comfort,
he leaned slowly forward and, speaking softly, said:

" Yous hungry, sah! "

" Slightly," I remarked; " I have e'en had a hard
day of it."

" Who be you lookin' fo'? " he asked abruptly.

" What's that to you, you black rascal? " I answered
with a forced fierceness that made him grin. " Who is
the host here? "

" Nat Burns, sah; he's away, sah. I looks to de
house den. I t'au't you might be 'spec'in' some one,
sah."

" Not I," I replied, having no desire to confide in
a negro hostler. " Has any one been here to-day? "

" Yes, sah," he answered, rolling his eyes. " Heap
o' soldiers, sah. Deys makin' de house upset all froo
lookin' for somebody."

" Looking for whom? " I asked, now mightily interested.

" Two or free pussons an' a young gal, sah. But dey
nebber finds dem here, no, sah! When am you goin'
on, sah? "

I had hard work to restrain my curiosity about those
who were being looked for. If the girl was Gertrude
King, and I felt fairly sure of it, then she, too, had
escaped arrest so far, though it gave me a strange feel-

8

ing about the ribs to think that she might be suffering even as I had been. To his question I carelessly answered:

"Not to-night, at all odds." For I at once considered that if the house had been searched, it was the safest place I could find in which to abide.

"Ah! by the way," I inquired easily, "know you of a party named King?"

"King?" said he, rising and taking up the candle. "No, sah; no King, 'ceptin' the good King Gawge."

He held the candle so that for the first time I had a good look at him. I saw then that he was not a full-blooded negro, his hair being silky and waved, his nose straight, with fine nostrils, and his mouth lacking the thick lips as his skull lacked the prognathous development of the true African. His hide was abnormally black, however, and his tongue that of the Southern darkey improved by contact with the purer speech of the North. With all its fine points his face bore no signs of great intelligence, and as he looked at me, it was almost expressionless.

I feared that if it ever had been, the tavern was now no longer a refuge for those of my party, for it seemed clear that Nick Stryker had lost the proprietorship, his place having been taken by one Burns (of whom I had never heard), whose very hostler was of rank Tory breed. I was glad I had not put myself into the darkey's hands, now even being afraid to ask for Stryker for dread of arousing suspicions against me.

"If yous boun' to stay all night, sah, I soon hab nice room, sah," he continued, while I was watching him, and taking the light with him, he went out with no apology for leaving me in the dark.

Being alone again, I filled my pipe and awaited his return with the means to light it. The difference betwixt the man I had been an hour since and was at that moment was amazing, so great is the power of nutriment to lift both body and spirits. I was ready for another night's wandering if needs be, though I thanked my stars for lack of the necessity. Stretching myself along the bench, I was almost dozing from sheer comfort when I heard the tramp of horses in the yard, and the next minute the door opened and two boisterous voices rang through the room demanding lights and service.

The violent rattling of a chair on the floor, which one of the newcomers had used as a means of gaining attention, had hardly ceased when the negro returned with the candle. I could not see the faces of either of the parties from my position (which I deemed advisable to retain), naught but their legs showing, but for two they made a vast noise. The negro, without seeming to notice my apparent absence, placed bottles and glasses on the table farthest removed from mine, and the two, after ordering a meal, sat down and began drinking.

And without stint they drank, if one could judge by the sound of pouring. The single candle but broke the gloom of the apartment, though it was helped out by the moonlight, which streamed through the south windows and over the sanded boards. By it I made out that one of the party was a cavalryman, his muddy boots and short clothes proclaiming the fact, as well as the sabretasche that trailed on the floor by the side of his heavy sword. The other, also booted and armed, was not of the ranks, for his breeches were not embellished or of striking color (his coat I could not see), while the hat he flung under the table was but a nondescript slouch without a cockade.

That they had accidentally met was at once made plain by the first words that passed between them after the negro left the room.

" An' ye are from the north! " said the soldier. " It
were a fine chance that brought us together, for I am
nigh spent an' must ha' traveled back on an empty
belly had we not crossed."

" Have ye no news o' either o' them? " asked the
civilian earnestly, ignoring the former's remark.

" Nay, man. 'Tis the coldest scent I e'er put nose
to. Scammell's an ass to think they fled together, an'
twice an ass, too, to look for a flying man an' woman
along the main highway! Have any of your gang lit
on news? This failure puts me twenty poun's out o'
pocket, for I was to ha' that if I could but locate the
woman; the man he feels sure of."

" Why of him? "

" That he's not tellin' the likes o' me, though I
think he means to lure him."

" Lure him! the fool! " said the civilian. " The
man who can overcome Scammell with an ewer, throttle
Clinton an' run the lines on his fist is no bird that can
be touched with salt. Faith! 'tis nothing but cold lead
an' steel that can take him, an' I wish I might cross
swords with him, for all his bigness."

" Well, by the piper! " broke in the soldier, banging his fist on the table, " I'm fain to meet him myself.
I'd show him sword play——"

" Shut up, ye brag! He'd make but a pinch o' ye!
Better stick to the woman, who'd come easy when ye
sighted her! What's the outcome along o' Belden? "

" Belden! " said the soldier, with a laugh and an
oath; " Clinton will ne'er forgive him for bringing forward such a mountain o' fraud. He's e'en a prisoner
on board his own ship, an' Scammell is in the old man's
bad books for havin' blabbed something to the girl—I
wot not what. There's the devil's own muss below,
made worse by the fact that both man an' woman ha'
gone up to heaven or downward, for no sign o' them

is on the island, an' they ha' not had time to get off it
by plain means."

"The girl had a pass, I was told."

"All passes were stopped, though not in time at
the lower lines, to my thinking. I fancy the man is in
the woods to the west, an' the lass hiding in the city."

"Well! well!" said the civilian, stretching his legs
under the table and refilling his glass. "Here must I
bide till the rest come up. To the devil with rebel spies,
man an' woman! I wish I had known that Thorndyke
was not Lounsbury when I had him unarmed. 'Twould
ha' been worth a pile; but a bigger pile this day could
I get him."

Now all this was mighty interesting, and I lay as
still as the bench beneath me until the civilian's last
remark. Something there was in his voice that struck
me as familiar, while his reference to having met me
made me more than curious. Carefully lifting my eye
above the table's level, I beheld the card-sharper of the
Bull's Head, his companion being a non-commissioned
officer and a total stranger to me.

CHAPTER XII.

A FIGHTING QUAKER.

HERE was I at last pinned down to close quarters. I had hoped they would eat, then drink themselves drunk and leave, but the sharper's intention of remaining all night, if necessary, together with the known hardness of head of the average trooper, made the hope a forlorn one. It seemed that I was to be confined to the bench for hours unless some chance should free me, and I had resigned myself to this when the black came in with food for the two, and at the same time the door reopened, there entering a man whom even in the dim light I knew to be of a different stripe than the others.

He was a Quaker, and so infirm that he walked slowly and heavily with the aid of a staff. Giving the two at the table a wide berth, he wended his way to the rear of the room and, seating himself on the settle, ordered a plain meal of milk and bread and butter.

There was nothing remarkable in the advent of a tired Quaker, but his appearance caused the sharper and his companion to draw their chairs together and whisper, though after a moment's close talking the former shouted across the room:

"Hello, snuffy! Where be thee from?"

There came no immediate answer to this, whereat the trooper swore roundly and repeated his fellow's question in a louder voice.

"I travel from the Kingsbridge and beyond, friend," was the final answer returned in a feeble treble.

"To where, then, thee son o' drab?" mimicked the gambler, as he put in his turn at insulting the old man.

"To a friend in the city—a Captain Scammell, of De Lancy's regiment. Mayhap thee knows him?" was the innocent response.

But, innocent as it was, it had its effect on the two, who were at once more respectful in both tone and words.

"Ye'll not find him, then," volunteered the trooper. "He has a sore head an' a broken heart—the one from a scrimmage an' the other through loss o' his lady. Ha' ye seen aught o' a runaway beauty on yer travels— a tall young lass with a painted head?"

"Does thee mean a young girl with hair inclined to red?" asked the traveler, with something of interest in his voice.

"Ay, that same," returned the trooper, bringing his feet under him and half rising.

"Yea, friend. I met with a female, though scarce a beauty, and with hair as thee describes. She was tired and wan as she came from the woods near Day's Tavern, by the Hollow Way, and asked me for victuals. But, friend, I was unprovided, and, indeed, in these times fear stragglers, be they male or female."

"Was the same tall an' fine o' skin, an' with dark eyes?"

"Ay, I think she was of proper height, and her eye was dark, if I do not err."

"'Fore God, an' I believe it the lass, Lowney!" said the trooper, starting up and for the first time giving the card-sharper a name. "I'm off on the scent.— Where away did she go, old man?"

"Back to the woods, as I saw her," was the answer.

"What woods? In what direction?" hurriedly asked the redcoat.

" Thee knowest the woods and orchard where Washington worsted Howe on the heights of Harlem? That
is the spot, friend. It strikes me she might be fair
enough after food and rest. I would not have her
harmed through me. Thee had——"

" Damn your thees an' thous an' Washington an'
being worsted!" shouted the trooper excitedly.—" I'm
off, Lowney. Tell the rest when they come. 'Tis a
fair day that bid ye stop me for a sup in this place. I
will requite ye yet. Give me a Quaker for truth an'
good luck. Alloh, lad!" And with a rattle of metal
he was out of the door, while in a moment I heard his
horse putting from the yard full tilt.

As I listened to the Quaker's description of the girl,
of whose identity I doubted as little as did the trooper,
my heart sank within me. I considered the suffering
she had undergone to make necessary her asking food
of a stranger on the high road, and was fast getting
to the point of leaving my place of concealment, dis-
patching the man Lowney, stealing his horse, overtak-
ing the trooper, and rescuing the girl myself, and all
without a thought of my own risk, when an accident
put an end to this sudden dream of heroism and caused
me to face stern facts.

'Twas but natural that I had taken a quick dislike
to the Quaker, who had innocently been the means of
setting a pursuer on the track of the patriotic girl, and
'twas also natural that I wished to see more of him than
his legs and the butt of his staff. To the end of satis-
fying my curiosity, I lifted my head as before, but was
seemingly less cautious with my foot, for, moving it
unthinkingly, I tilted my sword, which must have but
just balanced on the edge of the bench, and sent it
crashing to the floor with (to me) a racket that might
have been made by a falling house.

Both the Quaker and Lowney gave a start as the

sharp sound echoed through the room, the former dropping the spoon he was carrying to his mouth, while the
latter sprang to his feet and looked toward the darkened
corner in which I had been hiding. The two candles
in the large apartment gave but scant light, but, scant
as it was, it proved enough for the sharp eyes of the
gambler who evidently caught sight of a face, for with
an oath he cried, " What have we here—a drunkard
or a deserter? " and advanced toward the table.

And now it appeared that I would be suddenly
forced to do the very thing that but a moment before
had been buzzing in my brain as only a dream. Concealment being no longer possible, I would face matters
as they fell out, and trusted to put all into execution
before help in the shape of the negro or others without
might arrive. Ere Lowney had covered half the space
betwixt us, I stooped for my sword, and, jumping to the
bench and from that to the table, drew the blade.

As the advancing man beheld my figure loom suddenly on high, for the beams of the ceiling barely
cleared my head, he stopped short and stepped a pace
or two backward, drawing his sword the while, then
with a voice which might have been heard a furlong,
he shouted:

" By the great Jehovah! 'tis Donald Thorndyke, or
his spook from hell! Are ye run to ground at last? If
ye be no ghost, surrender in the name of the King!
—Ho, old man! here is the devil himself; get to my
holsters and fetch the firearms!—Hither, ye black
rascal! help me hold him here! Help here, I say!
Damn the closed door!—Boy! boy! Oh, what a pass
is this! "

Waiting for no action on the part of the old Quaker,
and hoping to forestall the negro, I leaped to the floor,
and in an instant the swords of Lowney and myself were
crossed in combat.

The onset was so sudden that it drove the man backward against his table, which, with the candle and earthenware, was upset, though the crash did not mar the fellow's guard. Taking advantage of the opening thus made, I sprang between him and the door, and then the battle began in grim earnest.

The light was far too uncertain to permit my putting into practice my well-worn stroke, and Lowney was much too wary and too skillful in fencing to allow me to at once come at him by any other method. I was fairly sure of tiring him and in the end beating down his guard, but at present I had enough to do in looking for his tricks and avoiding his furious lunges. In the half light of the room the fire flew bright from the steel in the energy of the parry, and my opponent hurried his fatigue by wasting breath in a constant string of oaths.

I will not go so far as to say how this certainly would have ended had there been no interference, but the end came in a manner totally unlooked for. I had worked the fellow backward through the room, hoping to get him where he could retreat no farther, and had forced him well toward the heavy settle whereon still sat the Quaker, when that white-haired patriarch rose with an exclamation, and seizing his staff, stepped behind Lowney and brought the stick down on his bared head, felling him to the floor a senseless carcass.

Though the blow was serviceable to me, such an act of war on the part of a Quaker made me turn on my ally and regard him with astonishment.

" 'Twas a foul thing to take a man from behind when engaged in front, my friend," I broke out, " and, though I give thanks for good intentions, 'twas an unseemly act, and you belie your cloth!"

" Thee has small time to pick fine holes in my service, friend," he answered hurriedly. " Turn thee to the window and see my motive. I wish to make friends with thee, but we must hurry! Look yonder!"

I looked as directed, and to my amazement saw a squad of British cavalry about turning into the lane leading to the tavern. There was scant time for me to run for my arms and get to the window, but, as I was about to throw open the casement, the Quaker laid his hand on my arm.

"Not that way!" he cried. "It is swamp land, and thee would be mired in the night. Upstairs—'tis safer for now—leave the rest to me."

With mighty nimbleness for so old a man, he drew me toward the kitchen, and, throwing open the door, pointed to a set of boxed-in steps leading above, and then quickly drew back, closing the door behind him.

I had but gotten up the short flight when I heard him go to the barroom entrance and shout for help with all the might of his cracked voice. In a moment I heard the clatter of arms as the men entered the lower room, and at the same time the negro came bounding up the stairs behind me.

The moonlight through the hall window just showed me his black face as he ran toward me, and with a will to sell myself at high cost I lifted my sword to cut him down when he cried in a hoarse whisper, and without the slightest trace of dialect:

"Hold up, man! I'm yer friend! This way!"

As he spoke he indicated a door the latch of which he lifted, and, throwing it wide, placed his finger on his lips as he pointed to a passage with a window at its far end. With the words, "I have no time to explain; lie quiet till I get back!" he turned and left me, running downstairs as quickly as he had come up.

Now from the moment I had crossed swords with Lowney till the present the time had been so short that it was as nothing. I was not confused as regards los-

ing my head, but mighty strange it seemed that two
friends had so suddenly arisen, and this fact was a trifle
bewildering. In some blind way the Dove was still a
Whig station (unless treachery lay hidden about),
though what had become of young King and how I
could come by Nick Stryker, were still puzzles. In the
face of the action and words of the Quaker, whose blow
had saved me from immediate capture, I could but think
he was not what he had seemed to be, even if he was a
Quaker at all. That he was a friend to the cause was
plain enough now, though at first, with the feeling
that every man's hand was against me, I even thought
his sending me above might be but a trap to take me
alive. But this could not be, for on going to the
window I saw the casement opened on a roof that
sloped easily to near the ground—a common arrange-
ment in architecture in those days, and one that still
holds.

I had been alone a bare five minutes when through
the still night air I heard the sound of voices and the
clattering of hoofs from the yard, and guessed that
some of the troopers below had gone in haste to the
north, for, my window being on the south side of the
house, I saw nothing of them as they passed. All below
became silent as the confusion melted in the distance.
My nerves were like harp strings as I stood and listened,
but, as the time went on and nothing occurred, I
breathed a trifle easier, and finally gathered enough
confidence to reprime my firearms. Had it not been
for the damp I knew was in them, I should have used
a pistol on the gambler at the start.

For all of an hour I waited in the passage, which
turned out to be little more than a narrow lumber room,
but at last I heard the door below open, and even as I was
hoping for some one to guide me to my next move, the
negro was before me. Like a spirit he entered the pas-

sage, for no sound of steps had heralded his coming, and the only words he spoke were:

" Pull off yer boots and follow me! "

His own were in his hand, and obeying, I trailed after him in and about two or three rooms and a hall, coming at last to a flight of steps that led us down and out by a back way.

It was something like waking from a nightmare to breathe the outer air again and not feel the cramping of close quarters. Motioning me still to follow, he bent himself like an Indian seeking footprints, and thus we passed beneath the rear bar windows, soon being at a distance from the house and toward the stream I had noticed. Under some low bushes we stopped long enough to pull on boots, and then onward we went, now bearing toward the east and through a swamp, which would have been fatal to me had I attempted to traverse it alone.

Save to caution my going, not a word my guide spoke, nor did I ask a question, only stepping close behind him as he made his way through a blind path he evidently well knew. Presently we came to something like a rod of firm ground slightly overgrown with coarse weeds and low shrubbery. Here my guide halted, and, turning about with a chuckle, said:

" Considering they know nothing of yer going, ye be safe enough here."

" What the devil——" I began, but he interrupted me.

" 'Tis plain enough, my friend. I know ye now, an' thought I did at first. Did ye mark me draw the light from ye at the table and shut the windows? "

" How did you know me? "

" Are ye not the man who bearded Clinton? Who would not know ye after the day's rumpus with searchin's an' descriptions? Are there two o' yer shadow on

the island? Is not yer name Thorndyke? 'Tis lucky
ye fell afoul o' Nick Stryker instead o' others."

"By the 'Mighty! Are you Nick Stryker?" I
asked, a light bursting on me.

"Nick Stryker is my name," he answered.

"I thought you said Nat Burns was——"

"Who ever saw Nat Burns?" he broke in. "No
one. He's always away. Come, now, I've little to tell.
What brought ye to the Dove?"

"To find one calling himself Rex——" I began, but
he stopped me by an exclamation.

"Rex! an' ye asked for a man o' the name o' King?
I know none such, but Rex—why, he it was that laid out
the Tory and saved yer neck. An' ye knew him not!
Well, on my soul, 'tis scarce a wonder!"

"Is it possible? No more than a brother unborn
would I have known him. Is Lowney dead?" I asked.

"Ay, he's dead, an' ye ha' the credit o' it. Did ye
not hear a party putting after ye to the north? We
have no time to palaver. Stay here until I guide the
Quaker hither; he's makin' blind fools o' an officer an'
three men over the body o' the Tory, but his risk is
great. I tell ye that Rex is sore beset himself, an' I
would hang higher than Haman were my position
known. Ye each need the other, for 'tis beyond me now
to more than help ye out of the muss ye have just gotten in."

"What is the man's real name?" I asked as he
turned to leave me.

"Ames," was the short answer as he made off, and in
the small light of the moon that was now close to its
setting I marked his figure grow less and less until the
shadows swallowed it.

Now I saw where I had made a mistake in not
closely following directions and asking for "Rex" in
the first place. And equally stupid had I been in de-

termining that Nick Stryker was openly known by his name. When I inquired for "King," it had never entered my head that Rex could be aught but the brother of Gertrude, and it now came to me that mayhap Clinton was inside the truth when he said that youth had perished in the flames. How, then, could the poor girl have fared since she left me? Yet her brother had escaped, according to Mrs. Badely, and 'twas possible the girl had known where to join him. Either Clinton had lied or his mistress had been deceived, and 'twas a fair muddle to clear. Stryker had known me through reputation and description, and if my act had become celebrated so might have hers, and I determined to ask him if he knew aught of the girl for whom I had now more than a passing interest.

However, the matter was not to be cleared by thinking, and as just now I had need of my brains in my own behalf, I put it aside and came home, as charity should.

Where was I to pass the coming night? Where was I to procure bread for the morrow? I would not fast again, though it came to entering a house and demanding food at a pistol's point. What was the end of it all to be? Even now I was held prisoner by a quaking bog, and had put myself into the power of a man who, in my mind, was no more a negro than was Rex or Ames an aged Quaker.

'Twas foolishly weak in me, but as one hour went far into another and nothing chanced, I took a blue turn, thinking of home and my old mother and my sister, and their worry and wonderment at my long absence, finally getting myself into a mood that was made up of universal doubts, and, were it not that I had a sense of shame left, I fairly think I might have whimpered like a sick child.

Indeed, there was nothing in my surroundings to

prick my pluck. When the moon set, a darkness almost like that of the night before came down on me. The dew was like rain on all about, and not so much as a stone, wet or dry, was there to rest upon. The unusual fast, the lack of sleep, the unceasing danger and present inactivity made me look at matters with a jaundiced eye. The night voices of the swamp were well-nigh deafening, and I was like to lose my head betwixt the vociferous bellowings of the frogs and the strain under which my nerves had so long been strung, when, as though they had come from below, the figures of Ames and Stryker were before me.

CHAPTER XIII.

A HOUSE OF REFUGE.

LIKE smoke in a gale my vapors vanished with the sound of a human voice. It was Stryker who spoke:

"Come, now, put yer hands on my shoulders an' let me have ye out o' this. There be no time to lose."

"Where do we go?" I asked.

"Thee will be guided by me, friend," said the Quaker. "Let us get beyond this quagmire, and I will pilot thee. I will now make the rear."

So saying, he took me by the flap of my coat, and I, placing my hands on Stryker's shoulders behind, we three moved off into the bog in an opposite direction from that we had come.

The negro must have had the eye of a bat and the nose of a hound to make his way over such a ground in such a darkness. There were many turnings in the path, and more than once did I see the reflection of the stars in the black water that was almost under foot. More than once was there a loud splash as we disturbed some ancient croaker of the swamp, and now and again a tall clump of bushes or a mass of rank August growth came out of the gloom ahead like human figures. I think we must have walked in this close Indian file for something over half a mile before the ground began to rise and the sod felt firm beneath me; but when it did, Stryker stopped and turned about.

"Now I leave ye," he said. "Ye know yer way on-

9   121

ward, Ames, an' ye can be safe till sunrise at least. I
charge ye both to keep away from the Dove. I can
do no more for ye, though much I regret it. I must
not be suspected, and, were a spy caught in my house,
I would be undone and my days of usefulness to the
cause be over. Tell No. 5 that all is right thus far. I
will hear of ye fast enough if ye be taken. God bless
ye both for true men! An' now good-night. I must
hurry back."

Without a word being spoken in return, he started
on a dogtrot in the direction of the morass from which
we had just escaped. As he disappeared, I turned on
the Quaker with the determination of settling a few
small matters, and abruptly asked:

"Is that man what he seems—a negro?"

"Yea, and thee has seen as devoted a patriot as the
colonies know," he answered. "As for his race, 'tis
anomalous. His parents' blood was almost white, but
he bred backward, as men sometimes do, and is blacker
than the average negro. And he has talent for a go-
between. He can mimic so that the evil one might
take him for a double. Did he not fool thee?—Ah!
Nick," he continued, apostrophizing the absent man,
"an' were it not for thy color thy name would be great
in the field, though not so great as is thy big heart!"

"Would I had known it!" I answered. "I would
have atoned for the black thoughts I had of him. And
now, friend Ames," I continued, "I have fancied you
other than you are. Had I known what I now know,
'twould have saved a deal of trouble. But, first, I owe
you my life for what you did for me, as, had you not
sighted the redcoats and acted, I would——"

"We're quits, friend, we're quits, did thee but know
it," he interrupted. "Let us not stand here; we have
Turtle Bay ahead and no bed nearer. The way is long
and rough, seeing we are debarred the highway. Thee

be well armed; give me a pistol, for as a Quaker I have not so much as a bodkin."

"Being no Quaker, then spare me your thees and thous," said I, thrusting a pistol into his hands.

"But I am a Quaker, in truth, friend," he answered.

"A Quaker, and fight!"

"I am a follower of one Elias Hicks, who takes a wider path than the orthodox. But the blood is not thick in me, though I am of the Quaker stock. I fall into the style when in need of concealment, and carry it out fairly well—eh, friend?"

"Faith," said I, "I take it you're on a broader path than Hicks e'er trod. That blow would have read you out of meeting were you a true broad-brim. And how did you cozen the party at the tavern?" I asked as we stepped out.

"By sending most of them to the north after thee," he answered. "To the rest I outlied the father of lies, and ended by getting them into a fair state of drunkenness, and after, as an old man, I pleaded fatigue and went to bed. I am in bed now, friend, to them."

Though he still clung to the Quaker style of speaking, he had laid aside the voice and actions of the old man he had represented, making a strange combination with his long, white hair, broad-brimmed hat, youthful tones, and sprightly behavior. Through all his words there was an undercurrent of dry humor, which seemed to take no account of the deep danger we were in, or the, to me, absolute blankness of the future.

Nor was this due to bravado or wonderful courage (though he lacked none of the latter), but, as he afterward told me, to the fact that with the failure to get help from Stryker—a help he had accounted as certain—he had given over hoping, and took a desperately calm view of the next day or two, surely believing that

by then all would be over. Yet withal he in no wise
abated his vigilance, though he considered the hand of
death was near him, and when, finally, there opened
up a bare chance for our escape from the island, he said
it was as though he had come back from the grave.
Ay, and so did I. It was as though a suffocating hand
placed over my mouth had been suddenly withdrawn.

On the start he told me little of himself (though
I had thought to find him communicative), and I had
to drag from him that he had left a brother at Turtle
Bay, whom he was now journeying to rejoin. The
youth was but a year or two younger than himself, and
fairly helpless, having been stricken by the Almighty
with dumbness from birth, though not with its usual
accompanying curse—deafness. From helping the great
cause in some way both brothers were under a ban, and
my companion's life was forfeit if he was taken.

Now as black as seemed my chances, I felt the weight
of the old adage of life and hope being akin, and I was
by no means overjoyed in knowing that we might be
handicapped by a helpless youth should some chance
open a way out from the surrounding danger. And this
I frankly told my companion, though to me he made
no reply.

For the most part he walked a pace or so ahead of
me, and thus we went along, going easily enough while
crossing open fields, but fairing sorely when we struck
woodland or plowed ground. Perilously near, too, we
went to dwellings, even stopping at a well hard by one
to drink, though first making sure there were no dogs
about. I never would have dared this had I been alone,
but my companion laughed at the risk, and I followed
his lead, though it then struck me as strange that I
should let this stripling take the upper hand in our
expedition. The truth is, I was fagged and not myself,
and though if driven to a corner would have fought like

a shrew, I had no head for fine points on that night, and was growing timid.

Anon we took to the high road for a space to flank a swamp, and once a dog went wild at the smell of us, but we were unmolested. Not a house showed a light (though that was small wonder, it being past midnight), and now we felt the breath of the damp that rose in the cooling air, and could even mark the pondlike appearance of the mist as it lay in some black hollow of the land. Through brooks, small swamps, and pools we went, I with heavy boots going dry-shod, though Ames, with but pumps and stockings, was wet to the knees, and I could hear the scrunching of water in his shoes as he walked. But there was little to choose about him after I had pulled him out of a ditch into which he stumbled, though he made a joke of it even while his teeth were chattering from the chill of his sousing.

It was fearful going in the dark. The Dove lay five miles from Turtle Bay by road, but, with our circling and retracing, we must have gone three or four more. For the most part we spoke little, and, though much remained to talk about, I was in no spirits to ask questions—or answer them either, for that matter. With me there was now no thought of what lay behind or before, all that remained of my wits being a stupid, stubborn determination to get on and reach our destination, be it what it might.

I take it 'twas past one o'clock, and I had been following my leader in an aimless fashion for half an hour without a word between us when he halted and laid his hand upon me, pointing toward a house with the bulk of a barn looming through the gloom behind it. I seemed to wake then, and notice the glimmer of water stretching beyond, and knew we were on the bank of the Sound River.

"Is this the place, then?" I asked, as I tried to

make head or tail of the bleak building that stood against the faint sky like a black block.

He grunted an assent and climbed a fence, I following tamely behind, but instead of proceeding to the house, we cut around it, and finally entered what might have been a disused cow shed built against the rear of the barn. Going to the end, he laid his ear against the rough boards of the barn and began scratching gently. Nothing coming of this, he fumbled about, and presently, to my great astonishment, a broad board came away in his hand, leaving in the barn's side a long, black hole that looked to lead into the bowels of darkness.

Ames pushed me toward the opening, and I squeezed through, feeling solid boards under my feet, and being greeted by such a strong smell of old hay that I might have been in the heart of an ancient rick. And this proved to be the case, for I soon heard the story of this hole of refuge. It had been made inside the barn and beneath the mow, and was now scantily covered with the little hay the British had a habit of leaving farmers to take the curse from their wholesale robbery. There was no entrance to this concealed den save the loosened board, and all cracks and openings being stuffed with wisps, from the outside this part of the building seemed bursting from fullness.

'Twas the finest masking of a retreat that could be imagined, and here one might lie and escape hanging (if he ventured not abroad), though there would be starvation to grapple with, and no small danger of smothering, for the heat was vile, the air heavy, and there was no means of ventilation.

My companion followed me into this inclosure, quickly readjusting the board, and, as though familiar with the place, struck his steel and got a light in a pierced tin lantern, which he set on the end of an up-

turned log serving as a table, on the top of which lay
a scrap of paper.

This he seized, and, bending low to the glimmer,
read the contents while I took in the details of the
queer apartment. The rough boards of the room were
barren of everything save a rifle hanging on a nail, and
the wisps of hay that penetrated each crevice from the
mow without. A heap of small arms lay in one corner;
in another was a sleeping bunk filled with straw, at the
foot of which was a closely strapped bundle filled, as
I afterward found, with provisions to be used in the extremity of being driven to this retreat for a protracted
stay. It was a hiding place pure and simple, and not
one to be defended save by secrecy, for a brand touched
to any part of the structure would reduce it to ashes in
less than an hour.

"'Tis all right!" said Ames, raising his head as I
finished my brief survey. "We are not bound to this
hole yet. We may go to the house and sleep like mod-
ern Christians for once more at least. Come!"

Extinguishing the light, he loosened the board, and
we passed out, the night air coming to the lungs like a
cooling balm after the heat and closeness of the contracted den.

"There is little danger for the next few hours," he
whispered as we made a straight line for the house.
"The redcoats were here this noon and searched the
place, but my—the boy was then in the barn. They
will hardly try here again until they have beaten up
other quarters. 'Tis a sorry outlook, Thorndyke! Have
you not in your head a way off this island? Think hard,
man! We must both think hard, and then take chances
however desperate. You are willing that we pull together?" he concluded interrogatively.

In his earnestness he dropped his assumed manner
of speech, and there was an appeal in his voice that

made me think it was not for himself he was most anxious. However, I could give him no comfort, only saying that I had small head for thought until I could clear
my brains with sleep, but that if taken, though it were
barren of gain, I would send some of the enemy ahead
of us to announce our coming. Then I laid my hand
in his and swore I would stand by him, and his brother,
too, if need be (though such swearing seemed useless
in the face of matters), telling him I would be but an
ungrateful brute to desert him after he had lost his
chance for help at the tavern by giving his hand in my
behalf.

We had halted on our way, and in the darkness we
came to the agreement each to stand by the other so
long as a chance to help remained. 'Twas a compact
hurriedly thought of and hurriedly made, but there,
under the stars dimly showing overhead, was completed
a bond that failed not. 'Twas made through necessity
and became strengthened by love. Not conceived in an
excess of happiness nor backed by the exuberance or
fictitious generosity of strong drink, not even expected
to extend beyond the present period of danger, it held
through life like an invisible chain.

There was no delay in getting into the house.
Though every window I could see was closed by solid
wooden shutters, the back door stood wide for entry,
and I soon found myself in what was probably the
kitchen. It was pitch black within, but Ames knew
his whereabouts, and I, with my hand on his shoulder,
followed him through this room into a hall and up a
flight of stairs. At the top a man's voice broke out
with—

"Who's there?"

"Seven!" spoke Ames in return.

"Five!" was the answer.

"Well enough! And I have a friend," said my

companion. And without more parley he went ahead and up more stairs, opening a trap or hatch, and landing in the garret at last, where he struck a light.

The room was undivided, and took in the entire ground plan of the house. So large was it that the single candle failed to clear the gloom from the corners, and made the great rafters spanning the space overhead, deeply mysterious. Two immense chimneys pierced the floor and went out at the roof, but beyond these the sweep of level was unbroken save by a large bed with curtains, a table, and several chairs. A half-moon window at either gable end was let high into the wall. A long ladder leading to one of them showed it had been used as a post of observation, but now both were carefully covered to prevent any interior light reaching abroad.

Here, then, were comfortable quarters at last. It was none too cool, but there was plenty of air, and could I but get a bite and a few hours' sleep I felt something might come of it, especially as there was a safe hiding place near at hand which could be used at a pinch, and such a possible refuge would prove a mighty factor in preventing demoralization.

I was looking at the trapped hole in the floor through which we had come when I heard a footstep on the stairs and a man appeared from below. He rose into sight as though there was no end to him, so tall and gaunt was he, and as he came to the light I saw that he possessed but one eye, and that set in a face which had the length and expression of that of a horse. With barely a glance at me, he took my companion aside, where they held a whispered conference. Suddenly turning, he held out to me an arm like a flail and grasped my hand. Then with a smile which disclosed a magnificent set of teeth, and like magic transfigured the expression of his face, he said in the purest English and with a voice of wonderful modulation:

"Donald Thorndyke, you are heartily welcome to the poor house of Peter Burt. I trust it will hold you in safety until a way of escape is made clear. Your deed is known to me. I honor you for your generosity, bravery, and patriotism. Pardon me," he interrupted as I was about to speak, "I know your present needs, and will supply them at once; then we will talk." And with this he abruptly turned and went below.

He had barely disappeared when a strange thing happened. I was facing the bed when I heard an exclamation come from behind the curtains which were drawn close, and at the same time they parted, discovering a youth clad in a long Quaker cloak which descended halfway down his shapely calves. For the moment I was startled, but at once surmised that he was the dumb brother of my companion. Ames sprang forward to meet him, the boy greeting him with a smile and a hand clasp, but, pushing past my guide, he advanced to where I stood by the table, and with a rippling laugh where there was no mistaking astonished me by saying:

"Donald Thorndyke here! Has he, too, escaped? Heaven is indeed good! I have no need of counterfeiting dumbness with him.—Beverly, by what fortune——"

The flow of words were cut short here, for Ames let out a cry just as I cleared my muddled brain and recognized the girl, Gertrude King, disguised as a Quaker. With the cloak gathered about her as though to conceal her altered apparel, and slightly bent as in shrinking modesty, she stood with eyes and lips apart, while my late guide grasped my hand and said:

"By the Lord! but I struck better than I knew. Why, man, 'twas you who gave me the first hand in help, and that at the fire, but I have never seen your face closely till now. I knew you as the savior of my sister, but had no guess I was in your debt for myself."

"We're quits, as you said, but 'tis a small debt. She *is* your sister, then!" I exclaimed, in my bewilderment referring to the matter which had been bothering me. "How is it I am thus hoodwinked? Have we not just sworn——"

"Nay, friend," he broke in entreatingly. "I but guessed at you at first. This dumbness has been a mask from the start. 'Twas that and your pass which got Gertrude through the lower lines. I but continued it with you, fearing you would shirk the risk of having a girl share what adventure we might have in store. You gave me to understand that much. Be not offended."

"Nay, Beverly, I could have told you better!" said the girl.—"Captain Thorndyke, you must pardon my appearance, nor think I am unsexed inwardly as outwardly when I say that I know you will not refuse your help to me; for, as you once risked your life for mine, you will not leave us and put it beyond my power to do my share in making good the debt. The same feeling which bade you defy Clinton will surely not allow you to leave me while I am still unfortunate! And I can help. I will not faint nor lose my head and cry out if danger comes. I can shoot; ay, and will, if need be!"

She was a striking object as she stood there in the light of the single candle. As she spoke she stepped forward, the cloak slipping from her hands and falling about her in graceful folds. Not a whit less of a beauty was she for all that her hair was shorn for more than half its length and stained almost black, for in her male attire there was no mistaking the grace of her sex, which in her was accentuated. In her present rig she seemed less tall than in her proper costume, but it

gave freedom to her movements, and there were ease
and suppleness in even the small gesture of extending
her arms toward me as if to add weight to her words.
From top to toe there was witchery about her, and I
little wondered at Scammell's infatuation. How on
earth she had passed the lines without having been suspected was a puzzle, unless, indeed, she too, like her
brother, was skilled in acting a part.

"Mistress Gertrude," I replied, bending my head,
whereat she attempted a courtesy, which, to say the
least, was graceful despite the lack of sweeping drapery, "you need not think me generous when I tell you
that the oath which binds me to help your brother
binds me to help you also, and to the last extremity.
These may be but empty words; danger lies in every
quarter, nor can I probe a way through. Madam, do
not count on the success of my best efforts, but for the
sake of all know them to be my best. And now for
your story; but, first, how is it that brother and sister
bear different names?"

"We are but half brother and sister," said Ames.
"Ne'er mind genealogy; let's get below and eat, then
for sleep, then for what God wills. It can bode no evil
to us that we three are thus met, but what a find for
Clinton could he but clutch us!"

CHAPTER XIV.

WHETHER our meeting would prove for good or evil fortune the future alone would tell, but certain it was there was nothing remarkable in the fact of our coming together. 'Twas but natural that the girl had flown straight from Clinton to where she might expect to find her brother, and, as the report of his escape had been true, she there found him. Her freedom from arrest had been due to the same cause or causes that had allowed me to retain my own liberty on that memorable Sabbath; namely, the lack of military precaution at headquarters on that day and the suddenness and unlooked-for nature of the episode. Once under the roof of a Quaker relative, she and her brother had been quickly disguised and passed through the lines as father and son, finding refuge in the house on the shores of Turtle Bay, and they had thus far eluded capture by retreating by day to the concealed quarters before described.

From there Ames had proceeded to Stryker (another link in the chain of secret patriots), hoping through him to find the means of getting to the Jersey shore or above the lines at Kingsbridge; but partly through the fact that all points of possible escape were doubly guarded, and partly through the adventure caused by my going to the Dove, he could obtain no help from the innkeeper. However, as he had further protected his sister by starting Lowney's companion, the trooper, on

133

a false scent to the northward, and had ended the days
of the Tory blackleg himself, his errand could hardly
be considered fruitless.

The only remarkable point in the sequence of events
that had brought us all together was that I should have
met " Rex " in the nick of time and had him made
known to me.

There was nothing in his present appearance by
which I could have connected him with the scorched
youth I had encountered at the fire. He was now clean
shaved, and, with the grime of smoke washed from
his face, his singed hair replaced by a white wig, and
his entire change of costume, he was an aged Quaker if
one peered not too closely at the lines which had been
laid upon his features.

The details of their escape and a recital of my own
adventures were given as we regaled ourselves with a
hasty meal in a room beneath the attic. Though solid
shutters were over the windows, they were further protected from any gleam of light straying outward by a
hanging of sheets nailed to the casing. This closeness
made the heat stifling, but physical discomfort was a
small matter, and was almost forgotten as I listened
in turn to the news from the city as it was given by
our host.

Like a band of plotting freebooters in masquerade
we must have appeared as we sat at the small table with
its single candle, talking in whispers, the girl and her
brother in their incongruous characters making the
strong points of the picture, while the tall, long-fea-
tured man, whose melancholy cast was instantly cor-
rected by a smile, sat opposite me, a more than sufficient
foil to my proportions.

My host never laughed, but his smile was a passport
to favor, making his natural expression sour by contrast or as though he was acting a part when his face

was in repose. Of the little band of those who remained in New York, and were underhanded though active in their devotion to the cause, I saw not one but who was an adept in his ability to mimic or portray a character totally at variance with the one God had given him. Peter Burt was not the least of these, for, though he looked like a graveyard, he was the reverse by nature. This worthy was a typesetter in the office of the notorious Rivington, the official printer to the King, and was the right-hand man to that blatant Tory. His position and his undoubted education made his real sentiments unsuspected, and, while by day he damned the rebels and seemed to lack common compassion for those who by chance fell prisoners or were even suspected of treason, by night he was doing all in his power to get information to Washington or giving a helping hand to refugees or those in distress. Late in life I heard that Rivington himself was in full accord with Burt, and used his post to the confusion of the King's interest, but I know naught of the truth of it.

The matter that roused my greatest interest was the news (or lack of it) of Scammell. As a garner of information Burt was in the thick of it, and I was mightily mystified when told that Scammell had recovered sufficiently to move from his quarters at the King's Arms and had disappeared, leaving no trace behind, though the search made for him was but a trifle less keen than that made for us.

"Has he started his lure for me?" I asked myself, but dropped the subject as I listened to the explanation of his move.

"It comes about through a remark made by Mistress Gertrude," said Burt, indicating the young lady, who laughed lightly at the story she had undoubtedly already heard. "It is possible you may recollect her twitting Clinton with a reference to some officer who

had informed her about her brother. Well, Clinton
took this to mean Scammell, and Scammell hearing of
it, possibly in a garbled recital, and fearing arrest, has
given color to the matter by putting himself beyond
the reach of investigation. He is a sharp fellow, sir,
and knows his broken head will excuse him when the
trouble blows over. Sir Henry is not fond of making
enemies among the line and file of his army, though he
cares little for the staff. As for you, Captain Thorndyke, it were well if you quickly devised some means of
putting yourself into a position of greater security than
I can offer you. There is a large reward for you, and
if you were taken, your trial would be a mockery. Our
friend Ames has but little better chance should he be
caught, and as for his sister, though her life might not
be sacrificed, she would be undone—Mrs. Badely would
see to that. Failure to find you thus far means re-
doubled efforts in the future. They know you must be
still on Manhattan. What can be done?"

"Nothing to-night," I replied, the blackness of our
prospects opening like an abyss before me. "Let me
sleep; in my present condition I am useless."

"Right!" he exclaimed. "You are safe for to-
night. I will not leave here till past daylight, and will
return at dusk.—Now, Miss King, up to your quarters.
—Gentlemen, you will rest here. If I give the alarm,
get to the barn. Look to yourselves by day, and be
wary, for were you discovered here I say, as did Stryker,
my days of usefulness to the cause would be over."

So saying, he blew out the light and opened the
windows, while I threw myself, dressed as I was, onto
the bed, and, drawing in great breaths of the damp
night air, soon slept as only sleep the tired and healthy.

CHAPTER XV.

THE FOG.

I LAY like one dead until well into the morning, waking as blithesomely as a child, only to be shocked as I came to a realizing sense of the toils that beset me. Physically I was a new man, and the feeling of antagonism and defiance with which I met the outlook proved that my spirit was yet unbroken.

But not a hole could I discover through the network of circumstances that had made me a victim. Testing the matter from all sides, the result was the same. It was fight and die, though I was careful not to betray this conclusion to either Ames or his sister. I knew that the youth was equally at sea, but the girl was cheerful and acted as though her troubles would be of short duration, feeling doubtless, as her sex is prone to do, that with two protectors things would go not far wrong.

And, indeed, we needed the fillip of good spirits from some source, and hers aided my philosophy to the extent of causing me to think it were as well to smile at approaching death as to sit and quake over its certainty.

All that day we fed well, this once maiden of fashion preparing our food, while by the aid of the ladder in the attic Ames and myself kept watch by turns through one of the half-moon windows which commanded the high road a mile or so away. But we were undisturbed, though we saw numerous troops going north, and once

feared a squad was about to turn toward us, but they
went on, only halting a moment where the roads
joined.

At sunset Burns returned, bringing the news that
a double cordon of the enemy had been drawn across
the island near the Dove, which body was to divide and
beat up the country both north and south, scouring
every house, tree, and nook and cranny from one end
of Manhattan to the other. This accounted for the
unusual number of troops we had seen that day, and to
this extent had my act stirred to its center the British
army. It almost enabled one to count the hours of remaining freedom, and I figured that by noon on the
day following the forces would have drawn their line
close to the purlieus of the city and caught us as a fish
is caught in a narrowing net.

The thought fairly drove me wild, and in my very
despair I rose from the table at which we had been
sitting and went to the window for air, that I might
be rid of the oppression which like a weight lay upon
my chest. Was this fear? Hardly; for, had the house
been assaulted at that moment, the load would have
fallen away as fell the burden from the back of Christian. Nay, it was uncertainty and inaction still playing on the harp strings of my nerves, but it was an unbearable feeling.

The moon was up, and it cast a lusty light over the
lowlands and the river, though its setting would not
be late. It was a lovely night; in faith, all Nature was
possessed of a beauty which made the thought of yield-
ing up of life bitter enough. Everything suggested
freedom, from the rolling of the distant woodland on
Long Island to the sparkle and dance of the water which
lay betwixt it and me, barring me from liberty and my
inborn right to breathe the free air. The speck that
shot across the brilliant moon path I knew to be a patrol

boat, and a sudden hatred of the bonds that compassed me, as exampled in that small floating thing, brought my muscles into iron bands, and I clutched the sill with my fingers until the casing cracked.

I turned back to the others, and we ate the balance of our meal in silence, even the girl feeling the growing . nearness of the end and glancing furtively at each man's face in turn.

I think we sat in this state of depression for much more than an hour, or long after we had finished eating, and each face was well-nigh lost in the darkness. The window being open, no light was made, and, as there was not a breath of wind, the stillness was only broken by the sounds of night life without. There was a faint shimmer of moonlight on the floor which barely gave form to those at the table, but the only sign of animation existing within doors was the glowing of our three pipes as we men sat and sucked away, each respecting the thoughts of the others.

At length Burt spoke. " I am bound to confess that darkness looms ahead," he began, " and if I make a suggestion, it is not to hint that you should take a hopeless chance in order that I may be rid of you. Could you do aught with a boat? I have one concealed that might be made ready in an hour."

The spell of silence and inactivity was broken, for the girl left her chair and stepped softly to the window as I replied:

" I have thought of boats, but only for the Hudson side. Could we go far and not be picked up by another such sneaking devil of a patrol as I saw yonder? Whither shall we go? I say *we*, for we it must be. I have cast my lot with the others."

He made no answer, and I rose and joined the girl (whom I could hardly yet think of as a girl) at the window. But now the aspect of Nature had changed, and the fair picture I had seen below but a short time before was blurred as a breath blurs a cold pane. With the quick alteration possible in this region and at this season, within the hour the night had grown damp, and a light, low fog hung over the river and its banks, so shallow, so still, and so silvery in the clear moonlight that it was as though a quiet inundation had ingulfed the land and turned the world into a lake. At the elevation from which I viewed it, I looked down upon it as one looks down upon the sea from a low headland. A billowy fullness lifted here and there, slow moving and majestic, but over its vast extent the line betwixt fog and clear air was sharply drawn. No moon track cut across this fleecy ocean, no sharp ripple broke its surface, and a breeze would have wrecked its strange beauty in a second.

The trees rose through the vapor, clear at their tops but invisible at their bases, and one dead sycamore stood strongly out against the light like the masts and rigging of a sunken ship. Its similarity struck me. As my eye caught it, like a flash of lightning an idea shot into my brain and my pipe snapped off at my teeth as I bit through the stem in the intensity of my feeling. With a cry I sprang for Ames, and gripping him by the shoulders with a force that made him cry out, I said, or rather shouted:

"I have it! I have it! Now is the time! Will you follow me and take a monstrous chance? Look, man! Mark the fog! We will to the boat—drift for the Phantom—cut her cable and trust to the ebb and God above to carry us past the fleet."

"The phantom! For the love of God, what phantom? Are you suddenly daft, Thorndyke, that you see ghosts?" was the vehement return of the youth as with a violent twist he tried to free himself from my grasp.

"Nay, man, no ghost!" I cried betwixt a laugh and a sob, so high was my nervous excitement. "My ship— the schooner Phantom! Have I not told you? She lies but a mile below on a straight drift. See, man, see!" said I, hurrying him to the window. "The fog will be our guard! Once away, we are safe! 'Tis death to bide here when such a mask stands ready for our use! We are yet alive! We are not spent! Will you risk the outcome? Let us not stand here and see those scarlet devils hem us in like a ring of fire! Better strangle in the sweet brine beneath the vessel's keel than be jerked into the next world by means of a rope! Never shall they dance me! How now? Shall we sink or swim together in the venture?"

I was beside myself with excitement. As the meaning of my words, which had been poured out in disjointed sentences, caught the youth, he instantly took fire. We were now all standing, and I had released him from my hold. With a bound he gained the side of his sister, who had stood like a statue as my plan was unfolding, and taking her hand, he said:

"Gertrude! Gertrude! do you follow him? 'Tis a grand opening; 'tis like a call to life! I am for it! We have no home, and can lose no more than is already lost if we remain here. Will you cast your lot with him —with us—and risk the danger which can be no greater beyond than in this place?—Come, Thorndyke, make it clear; show her 'tis the last resort, desperate though it be."

There was no need of argument, however, for with one hand in that of her brother and the other stretched toward me, she simply answered, "I dare all you dare! Have I yet failed?" and stood with lifted head and untrembling form as she spoke the words.

Out of sheer respect and admiration for the heroism of this girl, I felt like bending my knee even as a knight

bends before his sovereign, but the practical mind of
Burt put a period to any possibility of mock heroics,
for that individual asked in the calmest of tones:

"Is your ship still where she has been? Is she deserted, or, at least, is she not guarded?"

"Three days ago not a gasket had been touched
since the broad arrow was painted on her bow," I answered. "By night she is guarded by a single man, but
that troubles me less than would a fly on a hot day.
He has seen his last sun if he thwarts me. I care not
for one man nor three if I can but guide my approach.
From aught I have seen—and I have watched her well—
nothing has been done to her, naught carried away. She
was thought fit to go on an errand to Pigot, only wanting in men, arms, and provisions; even the fresh water
stowed forward may be good!"

"Arms and provisions you can have. They are
even now in the barn room," he answered slowly and
in strong contrast to my excited speech. "But," he
continued, as he closed the shutters, blocked the windows, and lighted the candle, "might you not overshoot
your vessel in the fog, or run into some of the anchored
fleet when once adrift?"

"Ay, all is chance!" broke in Ames; "and 'twere
better to take the chance than to be run to earth like
a tired fox, as is like to happen in biding here. What,
then, would come to you, Peter? Like enough you
would help weight a third string, and we all hang together!"

"When does the tide ebb to-night?" I asked.

"Near eleven, or at about the setting of the moon,"
Burt answered. Then after a moment he continued:
"Well, God be with you, gentlemen! I will do my part.
Like the refuge in the barn, I made the boat and hid
it while yet Washington held the city. I clearly foresaw
the outcome of his collision with Clinton, and little

doubted the ultimate use of both barn and boat. Either is at your service."

With the opening of possible escape before me, and one demanding immediate action, my spirits went aloft in the measure of their former depression. Nor did I fear their reaction, as enough uncertainty lay before to keep a man's eyes and wits awake, and that, too, without the aid of liquor. Even after the decision to trust to the boat was made, my mind misgave me. Was it better to drag this girl into the danger of an attempt to fly through a plan which might be nipped in the bud and end by our running at once into the hands of the enemy, or lie in a suffocating box with the doubtful chance of being overlooked? Even if safer, the latter would become more than awkward if necessity demanded protracted concealment, and if discovery ensued it would but serve to damn our generous benefactor. Besides, to tell the truth, I had no wish to be found like a scared rabbit in a hole. A man's pride hangs on nigh as long as his breath, if he be properly balanced, and I had made a reputation of which, to say the least, I was not ashamed. Nay, I would make a bold and novel move, and, if it must so come, end my life like a man with his liver of the proper color.

This much settled, and in less time than it had taken to write it, I thought and spoke no more of the barn room, but turned with the rest to making ready. Beyond the boat, the bundle of provisions, an extra brace of pistols, and a rapier, we mulcted our host of nothing. In an hour the boat, which was no more than a flat-bottomed scow squared at the ends, was brought from its hiding place. It was fitted with the roughest of oars and but one thwart, and was a damp affair altogether, its concealment having been made through covering it with boards on which had been piled a mass of wet salt weed. It proved tight, though terribly heavy,

but as I worked I completed the details of the start, and
had determined that the use of oars would but menace
our safety, so that speed, or lack of it, would be a quality cutting no figure. We would but drift and steer.

After cleaning it, there was little else to do but load
the boat, getting the arms snugly bestowed, and then
wait for the slacking of the flood tide. It was tedious
and impatient waiting, for I feared me that the wind
might rise and wreck the fog. If this should happen
before dawn our prospects would be wrecked with it,
and then—and then——

But I am not prone to borrow trouble, though it
was with half relief and half regret that toward midnight I finally heard the swashing of the ebb as it eddied
along the rocks, and knew the time to start had come.
The full realization of the risk came upon me as I stood
with painter in hand giving my last farewell to Burt.
" God keep you safe! " he said. " If I find the schooner
gone to-morrow, and hear not of your capture by Thurs-
day, I will thank Him as never before." The next minute the three of us were out on the Sound River, and
the black land was hidden by the fog that closed
around us.

I at once sculled out into the stream until I struck
the free current, and then sat myself on the boat's bottom, using an oar as a rudder to keep the scow's head
down the river, letting her drift with the tide which
was here running at a great rate. All night sounds from
the land were lost in the thick cloud, and an almost
dead silence ensued as we whirled southward, the only
break being an occasional sucking noise in the water,
due to the hurrying whirlpools.

It was nervous work. Ames was forward as a lookout, his figure even at that short distance being almost
lost in the combined darkness and blur. The girl,
seated upon the center thwart, held herself as straight

as an arrow, though her head was slightly bent as in intense listening. Fears of her becoming an incubus had long since vanished, and if her heart beat thickly at our dubious adventure, it did not show in the quiet and confident smile with which she had adopted every suggestion and obeyed every order with as little hesitation as though she had been a disciplined soldier. In her hand she held a pistol which was huddled closely in her cloak to keep the damp from its priming, and in an emergency I fully believed she would use it without a qualm.

I had given orders that no shot should be fired save in extremity, determining that interference should be met by cold steel only. At the onset I feared nothing beyond blundering into a patrol, and in that case the use of firearms might alarm the enemy ashore.

In the above fashion, then, we drifted along for perhaps twenty minutes, the wet dripping from my brows and lashes like tears. I had no means of getting at our definite whereabouts save by guessing by our speed, that making me think we should be abreast of the highlands below Turtle Bay. Turning the boat's head inshore, I ran close to the rocks, and then slid along (more slowly for being hard by the bank) just beyond what I thought to be the loom of the land. By this I had gotten into the swing of the situation and had less fear of interruption than of missing the Phantom. 'Twould be an easy matter to slip by her, and even could I once mark the height of Corlears Hook, with its alarm beacon always ready for the touch of a torch, I would then be an unusual sailor if I could make a straight course for the schooner, though she still lay at her old anchorage. In the darkness both beacon and heights would be beyond vision, and I was approaching what was very like real worry when my fears were relieved and our present situation indicated by the sound of eight bells struck in true

man-o'-war's-man's style that came floating over the
river about off our larboard beam. I gave a fair guess
that the measured beats came from the Bellerophon
striking the hour of midnight, that ship being the only
vessel of size which had been anchored above the Jersey
prison hulk to dispute a possible passage of the Sound
River from above. I was sure of this when, after intently listening, I heard no other striking, for had the
fleet been near there would have been a harmony of
bells in quick succession.

My mind being thus relieved, I turned the tub's
head into the stream again, and for awhile we floated
rapidly and silently along, a boat with three figures
that might have been carved from stone so rigid were
our attitudes of watchfulness and expectancy.

I fear I am none too strong a believer in the doc-
trine of special providences, though I have seemed to
see its workings in my own behalf, as instanced in the
breeze that saved me from the knife of the negro; but
if ever the Almighty carried three human beings in the
hollow of His hand, and pointed out the way of deliverance from pressing danger, He did it this night, and that
without the working of a miracle. Suddenly, and without the intervention of a breeze, we were floating in clear
water. Before us rose a white, impenetrable cloud of a
dull luminosity, while behind us lay the moist veil from
which we had just drifted. Its height was clearly
marked, and showed the mist extended not more than
twenty feet above the river's surface. We had struck
a chasm in the fog, and once when on the high seas I
had marked the like, then, as now, there being no wind
to mix or drive the vapor.

The rift was but a few hundred feet across, though
it apparently extended from shore to shore, like the
waters rolled back for the passage of the children of
Israel. Not a boat was in sight. On either hand the

water lay black and flat, only shimmered here and there by the light of the stars that shone clearly overhead.*

It was a wonderful, an awe-inspiring sight, but the quick exclamation I involuntarily made—the first sound from the boat since it left Turtle Bay—was followed by almost a shout as I marked a height of headland from the top of which, faintly outlined against the pale sky, stood up the beacon. It was Corlears Hook past doubt, known not alone by its rounded outline, but by the unused alarm signal which Clinton had caused to be placed there to warn the fleet in case of a sudden attack by the Americans. A watch was always kept from this point, but I doubt that the eye of an eagle could have caught the tiny speck of our boat with its load of three as it floated over the space of open water.

In less than five minutes we were plunged into the opposite bank of fog, and then I passed the girl to my place in the stern, quietly shipped the oars in the muffled tholes, seated myself on the thwart, and held me ready to alter our course and feel for the schooner as soon as we had gained a trifle more way down the river.

---

* This incident must not be considered forced. The writer saw these exact conditions while on a ferry boat from New York to Brooklyn during a foggy night in the summer of 1895. The phenomenon is probably due to a warm and comparatively dry streak of slowly moving air, and lasts but a few moments.

CHAPTER XVI.

THE CABIN OF THE PHANTOM.

WITH my mind lost to all else save the calculation of the speed and distance we were making, and my body braced forward awaiting the proper moment to swerve the boat's course, I was suddenly startled by a quick exclamation from Ames, which was at once followed by a rasping bump and the heeling of the scow until the water poured in over the gunwale. At the same moment the starboard oar received a blow that almost tore it from my hand, and what seemed a huge black object arose alongside and quickly vanished in the mist and darkness astern. The suddenness and smartness of the shock were startling; but, quick as were the appearance and disappearance of the obstruction we had fouled, I recognized it to be the spar buoy which marked the outer edge of the reef extending from the Hook into the river.

One might have cruised a week under the conditions besetting us and failed to have picked it up. It was like groping through the proverbial haystack and finding the proverbial needle without having looked for it, and, though its greeting had well-nigh been disastrous, it gave me the one point I wished with absolute accuracy. I now knew that we were nearly dead on the Phantom, and not two cable lengths away; indeed, had we missed the rude warning of the spar, it was but fair to reckon we would have fouled the schooner herself unless in my miscalculations I had altered our course, in which case we would have missed her altogether.

Quickly turning the boat's head about, I let it drift stern first, and even before I expected, heard the rush of the tide against a vessel's stem, while almost instantly, magnified through the fog, loomed up like a blank wall the bow of the schooner.

So suddenly were we upon it that the jib boom was well over us before I sighted the black hull, and with all my might I checked the boat's way, grasping the bobstay in time to save a collision, while Ames whipped the painter about the taut cable, and we came to a rest. The suck of the rushing waters against the broad, flat end of the scow made me fearful that the noise would call the guard's attention forward, and, whispering into the ear of Ames to hold all fast until I returned, I gently rid me of my boots, took my sword betwixt my teeth, swarmed up the stay to the bowsprit, and stood again on the deck of my own schooner.

At last 'twas done. The exultation I felt would be but natural to any man who sees the successful ending of a difficult undertaking. Fog and darkness were as nothing to me here; my way aft would have been clear had I been blind, but hardly had I gotten abreast the foremast when I heard the burly tones of one man addressing another, and the noise of oars as they fell into rowlocks came plainly to my strained ear. Stepping softly over the bulwark, I lowered myself to the channel and listened.

" An' ye get astray in the fog an' come not back by dawn, I'll have ye in the guardhouse for bein' off post," said the voice from the deck.

" Nay," came the answer from a boat; " ye do me a good turn by giving me this leave; fear me not. I'll ne'er betray you or fail to be back in time for you to get

ashore.   'Tis a summer's fog, an' will melt by sunrise!
Tell him I will fetch the rum."

"Fetch it, then, but not in yer skin," was the return.   "If they speak o' me, say ye heard I was going
on a quest to Kingsbridge, to be back on the morrow.
Ye had better belay yer lip, for ye are off post, an' I
hold ye in my hand."

"Ay, ay! Never fear! Good-night!" was the answer, and the boat moved off with steady strokes of the
oars, while the first speaker evidently entered the cabin,
as I heard the companion door open and close.   Then
all was again silent.

Here was an unexpected situation made more mysterious from the fact that there was something familiar
in the voice of the man who had just gone below.   I
could not place it, only noticing that both men spoke
with the savor of sea brine in their words, and though
one was totally strange to me, the voice of the other
hung in my ear as a misty dream hangs in the mind
after waking, naught but its effect remaining.

Getting to the deck again, I moved slowly aft, stopping as I noticed a slight luminosity at the side of the
cabin, but on further cautious approach found the cause.
The cabin was lighted.   To prevent the light from going
beyond the vessel a tarpaulin had been stretched over
the cabin house from rail to rail, thus leaving an open
space betwixt the rails and the deadlights, whereby was
served the double end of obtaining air and guarding
the outward show of light.

Here was deviltry for sure.   Dropping on to my
stomach, I snaked myself beneath the tarpaulin, brought
my eye to the swung back port, and nearly betrayed
myself by the start I made.

A lighted lantern hung from a carline, the remains
of a meal were spread on the table, and there, half reclining in a bunk and with his head in a bandage, was

Captain Scammell, haggard from fever and somewhat the worse from liquor, while on the transom and by his side sat my whilom mate, John Lounsbury, of Rye, late risen from the dead.

Here, then, were my two arch-enemies; probably the only living souls whose animosity toward me was both of a personal and political nature, saving perhaps that of Clinton himself. Possibly my gorge would have risen sooner against Scammell than at the man by his side, though the latter was none the less a villain, and it seemed as though Fate, having given me friends when in need, had guided me hither to test my mettle to extremity.

Giving no thoughts to those in the boat, I settled myself to hear the opening dialogue of the two, for it immediately transpired that Lounsbury had but just arrived.

" My God! I thought you would never come! " were the first words by Scammell. " What news do you bring? "

" None to warrant a grin," was the answer. " I can give ye no end o' advice though, an' 'tis to get from this an' have it out wi' Clinton while there's yet a chance."

" Damn your advice! What's your news? "

" Well, Belden goes scot free, an' is back in favor an' on the Sprite. He lays the fault o' palming off that devil Thorndyke to ye. He says ye called Thorndyke by my name in the tavern yard, and that he is innocent of all fraud."

" Curse the stunted coward! And is not Thorndyke caught? or—or—the girl or her brother? "

" Nay, but a peg worse. Thorndyke has brained Lowney, whom ye must know, and then escaped, God knows how, being mixed up with a Quaker at Stryker's tavern on the road. Stryker was arrested, but after-

ward let go, for he was not thought to have had a finger
in the pie. As for the boy an' girl, naught has been
seen o' them—not a smell—and there ye have all I
know. They say the girl is in the woods to the north,
but she may ha' gone to heaven by this!"

"What? what?" said Scammell, stärting up, but
sinking back with a curse as he placed his hand on his
bandaged head. "In the woods! Known to be there
and not taken! Are ye all cursed babies on the trail?
'Fore God, you are right! I was a fool to fly at a shadow!
I'll back to Clinton and plead fever to explain my absence. I'll back with you this night. The first tale told
is the best! Is it not known whose name she mentioned
to Clinton?"

"Nay, man, she gave no name that I can find.
Clinton but suspicioned ye. Go to him, an' yer not a
fool, while I bide here the while. What made ye pick
this spot to hide in?" he continued, carelessly passing his hand over the smooth woodwork of the bulkhead.

"Because 'twas right beneath their noses, and the
guard was in my pay. In faith, Lounsbury," he went
on, with something like relief in the easing away of his
body and the long breath he took while he laid his hand
on the brace of pistols sticking in his belt, "there was
another reason, one with money——"

"Ah! what?" interrupted the other, suddenly withdrawing his wandering hand and bending eagerly forward.

"Ay, the reward, you know; I'm nigh done up for
cash. That and revenge, for, mind you, I thought that
Thorndyke might take it into his head to come aboard
his own ship, thinking, like me, it was the least likely
place to be searched. His paper gave me the idea. I
hoped to lie by here until the trouble blew over, or roll
in the glory of taking the hound if he came. He is

equal to attempting a surprise, but I was ready for him. The guard is none too bright; had you not better step up and take a look about?" And with this he patted the gleaming pistol stocks and looked toward the companion way.

"There will be no guard to meet him this night," answered Lounsbury with a laugh which also betokened relief. "I let him go till sunrise, and his musket lies fog-soaked on the deck, the ass! Ye have the vapors. We be safe enough. The fog lies like a fleece, but—but——"

"But what, you fool?" was the irritable rejoinder.

"I meant 'twas a new thought, that o' the chance o' his coming. Ne'er mind. Go ye ashore with the guard when he gets back, and I'll bide here against Thorndyke's boarding the schooner."

For a moment or two there was silence, and during it I fancied I could trace the working of the minds of both: Scammell's bent on the probable result of delivering himself to Clinton, and Lounsbury's on the dawning chance to get his finger on my gold still safe in the bulkhead. Presently the cavalryman smote his knee with his fist and broke out:

"My God! why—why did I not spit the fellow while I had the chance two days since, or shoot him? Why d'd I not know him for a spy? 'Twould have saved all this! Is there no trace of him?"

"None since he passed the lines an' put Lowney to sleep. They tell me he killed the green sentinel with his fist. Faith, my head aches at the thought o' him, an' ye may thank God the ewer was cracked, else 'twas your skull that broke an' not the pitcher. By the powers above, I begin to fear him, an' ye——"

"Shut up!" was the ungracious answer. "Hand out the bottle and help me get on deck for air. I hate this hole! I have been buried three days!" And with

11

this Scammell struggled into a sitting position, reaching out his hand for the dram Lounsbury was already pouring.

Now that I had these two at twice a sabre's length, it went against me to think of their coming on deck and possibly spoiling the plans I had already hatched in their behalf. Slipping from my cover, I crawled over the cabin house and got to the door. There was a lock on it, but the key had long since gone and I had been used to make a shift of fastening the companion by padlock, hasp, and staple. As I felt over it I missed the padlock, though hasp and staple were still intact. While fumbling for my knife to use as a bolt, in the light from the cabin window I caught the glint of a musket lying along the deck under the tarpaulin, and, quickly unshipping its bayonet, thrust the steel through the iron loop, and the two below were prisoners. There was another door in the cabin, but it opened into a small space, or " 'tween decks," and I knew a mass of lead had been piled aft and against it to give the vessel a proper trim, so that mode of egress was blocked.

My scheme was simple enough. I would now go the whole pace and take with me a couple of prisoners, and if I failed I would be no worse off than before. In any event there would be a sudden ending to my difficulties if I was to be taken, and the kidnaping would not hasten my final swing.

Still unshod and silent, I made my way forward, and with some difficulty, owing to the darkness and need of stealth, the scow was emptied of her load, and at last we three stood on the deck. So far all had gone well. My next move was to cut away the ground tackle, leaving the boat's painter still belayed to the cable. As the last strand parted and the schooner shot away leaving the scow still fast, I fancied the astonishment of the guard on finding the Phantom had dwindled to a rusty, mud-spattered contrivance but a peg removed from a raft.

As the schooner gathered force and fled, now broadside to the ebb, I told in whispers what I had found and what done. I was well aware that not many minutes would elapse before those below would discover something out of gear. Between the covered dead-lights and the fog they could have no notion that the schooner was free, for the water was as flat as ice, there being no more apparent motion now than before. Unless we fouled something, they could make no guess at what had happened, but the door would bother them, and in all likelihood they would end in an attempt at breaking it down.

To balk this I led the way aft, bidding Ames be spokesman if it came to words, and to act as he saw fit if it came to blows. Placing Mistress Gertrude on the top of the house, and so out of harm's way, Ames and I bent our ears to the door, though I kept my eye open for what might at any minute confront us from out the depths of the fog.

We had not long to wait ere hearing from those within, for soon a hand was placed on the fastening, and the door rattled in the forcible shaking it received. Its failure to open was followed by a round oath, and we plainly heard the voice of Scammell suggesting that it be broken down. After a parley betwixt them as to what was the probable cause of the trouble, another attempt was made to force the door by shaking, and then there was worked through the joint of the companion way the blade of a sword. This I could not see, but felt the steel with my hand, and, thinking the situation had better be known at once, I picked up the musket and with a blow of its stock broke the protruding weapon close to the panel.

To the two below this was the first intimation that

aught was going wrong, and their consternation must have made a fine show. Possibly ten seconds elapsed before they recovered from their surprise, and then the voice of Lounsbury demanded, "Who's on the deck?" but on receiving no answer, the panels were assaulted with a force that well-nigh sprung them from their frames. Now I bade Ames speak, and, placing his head conveniently near a dead-light, he called out:

"Below there, Scammell and Lounsbury, you two be prisoners in the name of the United Colonies, and I demand the surrender of your arms! If you force the companion, it will mean death to both; you are outnumbered."

"Who are you?" came from within, this time from Scammell.

"Call me the ghost of Donald Thorndyke, if you will, but pass out your arms." At which I laughed outright, despite the situation.

The laugh must have been heard by them and my locality fairly well marked, for there came a volley of curses, and then through the door two pistol shots in quick succession.

It was fortunate that I was well at the side of the companion, else the assault would have finished me. It showed the temper of my captives, as well as the necessity for protection against another similar attack, for should it come to our getting off and using the sails the helmsman would be in sore danger of being shot as he stood at the wheel. There were no window openings in the cabin fore or aft, and, save the door, no possible weakness in the structure; but this door exactly faced the helm and was in danger of being forced or so riddled with bullets that it would become an outlook for the two royalists who could thus command the wheel and adjacent deck.

It would have been an easy matter to shoot either

or both of the prisoners and so put an end to our internal danger, but at this juncture I did not like the report of firearms, nor had I yet arrived at a blood-thirsty mood. Moreover, I felt that the bringing into the patriot lines of a brace of live Tories would redound more to my credit than a tale of a couple of carcasses, which must needs have been thrown overboard at once.

With this menace from within, and without a danger even greater, my nerves were keyed to a pitch that equaled if not exceeded their state at the time Scammell held me at his pistol's point. At least an hour of uncontrolled and uninterrupted drifting must elapse before I might draw a long breath and begin to count on the final success of our attempt to escape; and in that hour there was no knowing what the desperadoes below might not venture upon. At all odds, the door must be secured. There was no time to fumble about for tools, so bidding Ames shoot down both Tories should they force the way, I went forward, and by sheer strength of arms and back lifted the main hatch cover clear from its combings and, carrying the unwieldy mass of timber aft, set it upon edge against the companion.

Here, then, was a shield of solid oak which would resist any pistol shot, and I had no further concern as to the danger of being winged from the cabin while steering the vessel, should fortune get us to sea.

CHAPTER XVII.

THE PASSAGE OF THE BAY.

Now for some time after this no sound came from within, and I stood by the helm anxiously keeping one eye on the fog and the other on the cabin. As there was now no knowing whether we were drifting by the bow, stern, or broadside, I sent Ames forward to hold a lookout at that end of the vessel, standing guard on the quarter-deck myself, that I might control any possible outbreak from below.

Still on the cabin house sat the young lady, apparently unmoved by what had occurred, and certainly unmoving, as her form, which was just to be made out from my post, was as quiet as the schooner's figurehead. Once I had gone close to her to mark her state (somewhat marveling at her self-control), and found her pillowed against the great main boom with its furled sail. She had greeted me with a touch of her hand, the first she had ever vouchsafed me, while the quick turn of her eyes and the gleam of her small teeth (which was all I could see of her face) showed me that she was alert and still self-contained. But not a whisper of a question did she bother me with, though for that matter she had spoken not a word since leaving Turtle Bay. I had a mighty respect for her if only for her knowledge of how and when to keep from obtruding her helplessness, and would have lifted to my lips her smooth finger tips, only I dared not. Even had she not resented the act, it might be but for the reason that through gratitude she would save my feelings, and the thought was not comforting.

Dropping her hand, therefore, with the word that all was going well, I returned to my post. In my expectancy and dread of I knew not what, the minutes seemed to lengthen to quarter hours. The white muffle of mist appeared thicker than ever, and once or twice I fancied I caught on my wet check a cooling breath, as though the dead air was giving a first faint heave of coming activity. I felt that the wind was not far off, and feared it, but come what might I must now hold my course and drift into freedom or eternity.

And still no sound from the cabin save now and then a cough, showing that the lungs of the two were harried by their own powder smoke. I dared not explore the interior for fear of being greeted by a shot, and could only await some overt act to show me what was afoot. Suddenly from below there came a dull, jarring thud, and the fog about the quarter-deck was lighted by a brilliant flash, apparently from beneath the tarpaulin, while at once following came the voice of Lounsbury calling for water and " Air, air, for the love of God! " Almost on the instant, and before I realized that something untoward had happened below, seemingly from the muck directly overhead a hoarse voice shouted:

" The deck, ahoy! There's a schooner adrift and almost on us! Did ye see that light? "

" Ay! Where away is she? " came an answer close at hand.

" On our starboard bow, sir; coming stern first and no sail set. She's like to foul us! "

" Can you make her out? "

" Naught but the foreyard and topmasts show above the fog, sir."

" What the devil can be the meaning of it? " came

the return, and then I heard the scuffle of feet on the stranger's deck, followed by a quick call:

"Schooner ahoy! What schooner's that?"

Hitherto my policy had been silence, but now it instantly struck me that to pay no attention to the hail would be but to precipitate ruin while yet there was a forlorn hope. If we came in collision, unless I answered they would board us in the twinkling of an eye, while if we missed they would be suspicious and start a search, which, blind as it would be, might end by their running across us. Therefore I at once sent my voice back with all my power and without the least hesitation:

"Ay, ay; we've parted a shackle and are losing ground. Will bring up in a couple of cable's lengths if we clear you. Stand by to take a blow. What ship's that?"

"His Majesty's sloop-of-war Ajax! What schooner's that?"

"The Sprite," I returned at a venture, that vessel being the only schooner I could then call to mind. The answer hurled back at me was startling.

"Ye lie! The Sprite went outside this morning on patrol. Come to, or I'll sink ye!—Stand by for quarters! On deck, the watch below!" Then, evidently to guard aloft: "Where away is she? Damn the fog!"

In the quick bustle, the shrill rattle of the boatswain's whistle on the deck of the enemy (which sound seemed to fill the harbor), and all that followed, I heard no answer to the call aloft. There was enough close at hand, for from our own cabin there came a bedlam of shouts that drowned the details of the notes of preparation made on the Ajax.

"Treason!—treason! Help!—help! 'Tis the Phantom cut out by the rebels! 'Tis the villain Thorndyke! We are prisoners in the cabin!—Board us, for God's sake!" and matter of this tenor which crossed the water, and was as plain to the ear of the officer on the adjacent vessel as it was to mine.

And now for us the game appeared to be played to the end. With faces evidently pressed close to the open dead-lights of the cabin the two below had sent forth the alarm and made the muss past mending. From the Ajax came loud orders, and just as I caught the glimmer of that vessel's anchor light as it swept by in a thick yellow halo, there came the rattle of a drum beating to quarters, and it was at once followed by a similar but faint alarm from some ship anchored east and toward the Brookland shore. Then we slipped into the darkness again, and went whirling on our way.

We had missed a collision, but by a close shave only, as I think there lay not two rods betwixt me and the light I had seen. Our move had been exposed, and the only thing gained by us was a knowledge of our speed and whereabouts. The Ajax I knew had been anchored for upward of a month about a mile below the " grand battery," and the way her riding light had slid by us betokened the fact that just then we were moving at the rate of four or five miles an hour.

Therefore we were now off Nutten's Island, but the bulk of the British fleet still lay below. They were fairly close to the Staten Island shore, however, and there would be small danger of fouling them, the tide always setting the fairway well into the center of the Narrows. But of danger from the forces below I was not now thinking. More fear had I of the boats that would put after us from the vessel we had almost fouled, for as we passed her and the noises on her deck faded in the distance, I heard the dull clashing of tumbling oars and the sharp splash of a boat as it dropped from the davits into the water.

As though to guide the enemy, ever and anon there came a cry from our cabin—a cry that shot into the

quiet air like an alarm gun and drove me to madness.
I was now as one who, having broken through a quick-
set, was carrying the thorns in his flesh. Danger hung
over me like a descending bludgeon, though instead
of cowering beneath the coming blow it set my blood
on fire. With a curse which must have caused the girl
to shudder, I seized the musket, and, driving its butt
through the nearest dead-light, felt the iron stock shoe
crunch against flesh and bone. There came from within
a yell of agony, and after silence, and then I spoke:

"Another shout, ye villains, and I'll fill the cabin
with flying balls. Mind this, if yonder boats board us,
before being taken I'll kill ye both! Ye are dealing
with Donald Thorndyke, and now lie and stifle, and may
God have more mercy on ye than have I, ye spawn of
the devil!"

And with this I cut away the seizing that held the
tarpaulin and rolled the heavy covering close to the
windows, thus blocking all ventilation below. So long
as this remained undisturbed it would muffle any noise
they might make, and, I fancied, soon bring them to
terms from lack of air. Hailing Ames (who had thus
far stuck to his post) in a voice which I took care should
be heard by the prisoners, I ordered him to fire into the
compartment at the first attempt they made to move the
smothering cover, and then I hurried forward to prepare for being overhauled by the boats.

Being on my own ship, everything was familiar, and
I easily got a lantern from the galley and dropped into
the hold, carrying with me a line. Here I selected four
or five of the largest lumps of lead which in my hurry
I could light upon, and, drawing them to the deck,
placed them at different points near the rail, that they
might come handy to drop into and stave any boat that
came close alongside. This done, I reprimed all firearms, even to the guard's musket, which was loaded,

and from the after davit quietly lowered the dingy, that, if worse came to worse, it might be possible to escape by our getting into her and disappearing. Then I waited.

I had worked with feverish haste, knowing that the outcome of this episode with the Ajax would terminate for good or evil in a mighty short time. Once they ran off our track we would be comparatively safe, though, to lessen this possibility, I surmised that they would themselves be guided by the drift, only using their oars that they might make their speed greater than that of the schooner. By so following they might hope to overtake us, and doubtless would have done so only we were now at the point where the rush of the Hudson meets that of the Sound River, and the rips and whirlpools formed by the mingling of these waters off and below Nutten's Island were constantly creating counter streams and cross currents that shifted and spun with the minutes, ever changing and never at rest save at the brief intervals of slack water on the turning of the tides.

Beyond the gurgling and rushing of the stream not a sound could I now hear, though once or twice I was sure I caught the thumping of oars in their tholes and heard voices of men. But if I did, they went wide of us, for the minutes swung into half an hour at least, and the half hour into a whole one, yet nothing of the boats from the Ajax did I see.

And now I took a deep breath and moved, for during this time of terrible suspense we on deck had barely stirred. Not a sound had come from below, nor had an attempt to uncover the windows been made, and yet I knew one man had a broken nose from a musket butt, and both must be pressed for want of air. Mistress Gertrude still sat on the cabin top, and crouched low near the companion door, with pistol in hand, was her brother.

As patient as was this girl, she was human flesh, and
a delicate bit of femininity at that. The cabin top
could not be made permanent quarters for her, and,
though I believe she would have collapsed from sheer
exhaustion ere offering a word of complaint, it was an
uncalled-for sacrifice for her to remain longer unshel-
tered and seated on bare, hard planking. Up to the
present comfort had not been considered, but now that
immediate danger was past, I turned my thoughts to
the young lady, and cast about for a retreat to which
she might retire. Save the hold or the forecastle, no
spot was available, and either would be repugnant to
one of her fastidious tastes. Still, shelter she must
have; I would see to it presently, but now I became
more than curious to know what devilment was meant
by the continued silence of the two desperate men caged
in the cabin.

It struck me that the quiet, coupled with what had
gone before, might bear a mighty significance, and going
softly to a corner of the tarpaulin, I quickly threw it
up and looked in. The light was out. Drawing back
out of range I called Scammell by name, and then
Lounsbury, but received no reply. Putting the threat
of death in my demand for an answer, I still received
nothing in return; so, clambering to the cabin top, I
laid my ear above a dead-light to catch a sound of movement within, but had hardly taken my position when
both nose and lungs were assailed by such a mixed
stench of burned powder, lamp soot, rum and foulness in
general as to almost turn my stomach, though it at once
cleared up the mystery.

Here, now, was my threat to stifle them carried out
better than I knew. Dragging off the tarpaulin, I
pushed away the hatch cover, drew the bayonet from
the staple, forced back the companion slide and entered. The first thing I did was to stumble over a man's

body on the floor, and then I turned and got to the deck, for the air in the cabin was more than I could at once endure. Letting the place clear for a little, I fetched the galley lantern and went down once more. The cabin was yet filled with a heavy blue mist, and the sulphurous fumes were choking. Lounsbury lay on the floor with his face covered with blood, apparently dead, both eyes being swollen and his countenance blackened beyond recognition. His companion sat on the cushioned transom, jammed into a corner betwixt a berth and the bulkhead. He was unconscious, and, with his tongue hanging out, was breathing feebly. Physically he was alive, but, through liquor and foul air, was so dead drunk that nothing could have roused him. Three empty brandy bottles lay about, together with Scammell's sabre, a broken sword, pistols, and tobacco pipes, while on the table, the cotton cover of which was burned to ashes, were the remains of a leathern powder pouch rent by explosion.

No wonder they had succumbed. In their tipsiness, or through the carelessness of desperation, they had fired their ammunition, the amount not having been sufficient to cause more than the muffled blow and flash I had heard and seen on the instant of our being hailed by the Ajax. This, with the smoke of their previous firing, together with the heat and closeness of the quarters, had created a smudge and foulness in which none but a drunkard could have lived a minute. They had evidently been deep in some scheme to blow open the forward door (which showed signs of attack) when a spark from a pipe caused the plot to harass the plotters. Lounsbury had been the chief sufferer, and thus was accounted for his blackened face and his cry for air and water.

However, it could not have hit my turn better had I laid the train of events myself, nor was it long before

I had the two lying on the deck and knew the cabin was sweetening and would soon be a fit retreat for Miss King. Neither was it long before I discovered that Lounsbury was not as dead as he was drunk, though hardly as far gone in liquor as Scammell, who could have been pitched over the rail and passed to the next world without the slightest inconvenience to himself. And more's the pity 'twas not done.

Like bags of dunnage I took them by their collars, hauling them amidships, and then clapped the wrists and legs of both into irons, articles which in those days stood somewhat ahead of the medicine chest in importance, and frequently in use. With a mingled feeling of pity, hatred, and disgust, I soused the sots with a bucket of salt water, and then left them for Nature to bring to life. As I moved aft I caught the freshness of a small, early morning breeze, and felt that ere long the protecting blanket of fog would be rolled away. Much would I have given for a knowledge of our exact whereabouts, but as this was impossible, nothing remained but to prepare the schooner for sailing as soon as we could get our bearings. 'Twas a small job to cast off the gaskets and get loose the headsails ready for hoisting, but another matter for Ames and myself alone to run the heavy canvas of the main and foresails to their mast heads. I was fearful that the rattling blocks and rustling of the great cloths might herald our situation, but nothing came of it, and after a deal of hauling we got something like a slack set to the sails which for months had been mildewing against their booms.

Gradually a lividness came over the fog, and, as the light of the coming day strengthened, it showed the mist driving across us like wads of smoke. As the light broadened I went to the binnacle to see how we were heading, but found the compass gone from it, and, on examination, discovered that all my instruments had been confiscated saving the telltale screwed into the cabin ceiling. This, like the hanging lantern, was begrimed by a white deposit from the explosion, but, on clearing it with my palm, I found we were heading north by east, or still going stern on toward the south.

So matters went till sunrise, the wind growing fresher as the time sped, and at last, while Ames and myself were putting the cabin into some shape and the girl had gone to overhaul the pack of provisions, I heard her give a great cry, and rushed to the deck to find its meaning.

It was no alarm. She was standing by the fore shrouds looking at the sudden transformation which had come over the face of Nature. Often have I seen the sun rise, but never did it appear in such a grandeur of pearl and grays. The glory of its coming was none the less for the lack of vivid coloring. The fog had rolled off as rolls a curtain, and to the east and north lay piled in towering masses ranging from thunderous blackness to the opalescent clearness of a seashell. Through its misty caverns shot dazzling shafts of sunshine, which wavered and played over the face of the bank like the tremulous shifting of the northern lights. Astern, clear as far as one could see, lay the ocean blank of all sail, the small summer waves glinting back the strong light from the east. To the west and over our larboard beam stood out the green heights of Staten Island, and under their shelter I marked two heavy ships of the line, while toward Sandy Hook lay two others with sails furled and at anchor. Gravesend Bay also held one, a mammoth, which I took to be the Cerberus, but not a ship was alert. No more were in sight, and I marveled that we had run the gantlet of the fleet, thinking, naturally, that most of them had gone up the bay and must have lain close to our track. Little I knew that the bulk of Lord Howe's flotilla had sailed

east the day before, and thus opened the path that otherwise would in all likelihood have been blocked. But
so it was, and later I knew we had the French to thank
for having drawn them away.

Doubtless we were marked by a hundred eyes on
board those about, but the leviathans were powerless to
harm us, their very size and ponderosity shackling them
against quick action. Close aboard and on our starboard
beam lay the white sand spit of the lower island which
goes far to make New York harbor the haven it is, and
once past this wilderness of beach, now known as Nor-
ton's Point, we would be on the sea.

With a shout of relief almost delirious I sprang
forward and mastheaded both jib and staysails, while
Ames jumped for the main sheet and drew it in. It was
the first inkling I had that he was anything of a sailor,
and the knowledge was mighty welcome. Slowly we
came about until the schooner nosed into the west wind,
and then he ran to the helm while I caught the draught
with the headsail to help her getting past the point of
" irons "; then I belayed both jib and staysail sheets.

But of what use are these details? Enough to tell
that presently we were slipping eastward and past the
Dry Romer, the sails swung wing-on-wing, and an air,
which turned to a calm as we fled, pushing us from over
the taffrail and toward the rising sun.

CHAPTER XVIII

PURSUED.

ALL that morning we sailed almost as blithely as ever pleasure seekers sailed a summer sea. True it was that a measure of anxiety still hampered my spirits, but, as compared with what we had undergone, we were at heart as light as the filmy mares' tails floating athwart the blue above. And even now, while tragedy might be lurking near, there was an element of the ridiculous in our appearances, too marked not to be noticed by each of us. The girl, with a natural care of herself, was the most presentable of the three and looked to be but a proper youth; but 'twas Ames who gave color to the ship's present company. He had retained his wig—to make his hat fit, he said—and what with his fresh face, white hair, and clothes still mud-stained from his fall into the ditch the night before, he was a sight to behold. As for myself, I appeared to be in the last stage of dilapidation. A four days' growth of dark beard, my clothing burned, rain-soaked and ragged, my linen a shock to the eye, my queue ribbonless, and my hair streaming about my shoulders, I made a picture fit to repel the girl. Two days before, her likes or dislikes would not have caused me a second's thought, but now somehow my very size seemed to me obtrusive, and, coupled with my outward state, shamed me into an avoidance of her close observance.

But no change could I mark in her manner when

12   169

necessity brought us together. Her smile was as bright
—ay, brighter—than the dazzling sea about us, her
voice as free from nervous tremulousness, and her manner as self-contained as though she was treading a ball-
room floor instead of the grimy, slowly heaving deck of
a fugitive schooner. Once she had laid her hand on
mine as I stood at the wheel, and seemed to be about
to speak to me, giving a quick upward glance of her
dark eye, though lowering her gaze as quickly; but as
her brother hove aft just then, she turned away and
went below to the cabin, which by this had been given
over to her exclusive use.

I minded me that it was I to whom she first brought
an allowance of salt beef and ship's bread, and let her
brother wait. Somehow the fact warmed me, and then
I apostrophized myself for a fool for having thought
of it. How she regarded her *ci-devant* lover I had
easily seen in the way she turned her head and made a
wide detour when necessity compelled her to pass him
where he sprawled on the deck, his repulsiveness as
much, if not more marked than his companion's, owing
to the tarnished richness of his once glittering uniform.
The prisoners had so far recovered as to be maudlin,
and in their restlessness had rolled into the scuppers.
The sight of them was an evil easily remedied, and, as
air and light were no longer imperative to their well-
being, I had taken them into the forecastle and laid
them each in a bunk, that they might finish off the
fumes of liquor without offense to decent eyes.

Once onto blue water we held a council to determine our destination. It was safer, I thought, to land
my passengers on the Jersey coast and by myself try to
work under short sail to New London, where was consigned the schooner's cargo. But neither brother nor
sister would hear of such a move. Washington having
withdrawn to the north, there could be no telling the

state of southern Jersey, especially as it had been over-
run with bands of marauders known as "Sandhillers,"
and, there being no safe objective for the fugitives,
to land would be but beginning anew a search for refuge.
Without money (though I would make a shift to remedy
the lack of that), without friends and with a price on
their heads, a change to the pine wilderness of the western coast would be scarce an improvement over the deck
of the Phantom, outlawed though she was. Such was
their argument.

As for myself, nothing would have now tempted me
to desert the vessel. By holding a course well south,
clinging only to the loom of the Long Island coast as
a guide (for I had no sure compass), I might run across
a Yankee privateer or find protection in a possible
French cruiser. At this moment I had recovered all
I had lost and more. The schooner with its cargo was
intact; the gold was still in the cabin; I had been en-
riched by several rolls of money from Clinton (though
I had not yet counted the coin, only guessing at its
value by its drag on my pocket), while below were
Lounsbury and a prisoner of rank. More than these, I
had the knowledge of a move to be made toward the
relief of Newport by the British, and—here I was honest
with myself as I thus compiled my gains—I had two
friends, one of whom, oath or no oath, should come to
no harm from mankind while I had an arm to interpose.

I had suggested the Jersey shore as a matter of duty.
I had heard their determination to abide with me and
share my fortune, be it high or low, with something
of a feeling that put a new power into me, and, I fancy,
a new light in my eye (had they been looking closely),
not caused by the dazzle of the sun. Our destination
lay, then, first for the Vineyard. There I would place
this now homeless girl in care of my mother and sister,
who were probably mourning for me as lost, then to

New London to deliver prisoners and cargo to the proper authorities, and after that—well, I would wait and see.

Ay, I would wait and see. One need not plan one's life for months ahead. Somehow there was a brilliant spot in the future which I cared neither to define or get behind—a Will-o'-the-wisp both tangible and elusive which I would not analyze, being content with the glow it spread over my mental picture. The radiance lay on the ancient island farm. It fell on the ancient house and livened its homely interior. It went abroad over familiar fields, dusky woodlands and swamps, and gave a color to the stretches of lonely Leach. It made life more than living, and changed the dross of existence into something very like gold.

I knew I was dreaming dreams and building air castles as I stood my trick at the wheel and hove it over to meet the low-running swell and forestall the vessel's yaw. But what picture equals that of the brain? In progressive stages I mentally doubled Montauk, raised Block-house Island, sunk it, and saw the mist of Norman's Land, and then swept around the great western clay cliffs of the Vineyard, and was at home. Every detail was real, yet fairer than reality. By some queer change in me I looked less for glory now than I had the month before. War was well enough if it must be; glory was a prize easily gotten, but there was nothing to equal peace. I had tamed wonderfully; nothing to equal the delights of home and domesticity. I had acquitted myself before my fellows, and for a time would rest on my honors. In short, I had by then gotten into a weak-kneed mood, the like of which every man knows at some moment of his life; harmless enough, possibly, and for the enjoyment of which he can thank God for withholding the knowledge of what the next hour has in store.

By this it was about four in the afternoon as I figured from the height of the sun, which, though clear, shone from a sky that had become flaked as though a fine-drawn smoke had settled over it. Though the wind hung still from the west, it was lighter, and the schooner dragged through the water as if it was traveling uphill. Its sluggishness I knew was due somewhat to the character of its cargo, which was the deadest of dead weights, but more to the marine growth which had collected on her bottom during her long anchorage, and which could easily be seen streaming below like a long and ragged green beard. Beyond the dull gurgle of the cutwater and an occasional sob in our wake, not a sound broke the intense stillness of the afternoon. Ames was forward, guarding the forecastle hatch, and his sister had gone below. From the prisoners (who had come at last to a realizing sense of their position) nothing had been heard beyond a demand for water, which had been given to them, and air, ocean, and schooner, with all on board, had quieted into what bade fair to become a dead calm.

We had seen a number of sail during the day, but nothing had as yet come hull above the horizon, even these showing south and west mere specks of light against the pearl of the sky line. I thanked God for the scare given the British by the advent of the French fleet, and knew that each cable's length we made to the east brought us so much nearer safety. The day was waning; night would soon be on us, and if the wind held, under cover of darkness we would be secure in our flight, and possibly the morrow's sun might rise and show me the gorgeous reds and yellows of Gay Head bluff with its cap of green turf, a sign that we were in home waters.

Even as my heart warmed at the thought, I cast my eye landward over the larboard quarter and saw coming out of the haze which had all but blotted out the

Long Island coast, a topsail schooner bearing southeast, or directly toward the Phantom. She was some five or six miles away, but even at that distance I could see by her slope that she had found a fresh slant of wind, and that from her forward cloths to the tip of her main boom every rag was drawing, her progress being mightily helped by the square sail set on her foretopmast.

There was no knowing what she was, but the fact that any craft had gotten so close without having been marked, gave me a start, and I put the helm down that the jib and staysails might draw, which would at the same time bring the stranger over our taffrail. A land-lubber could have seen she was no Frenchman, for the Gaul had a style of cut, rake, and carry, all his own, besides which they were not given to sailing small craft in these waters. She might be a privateer, in which case all would be well, but if not, and I feared my own intuition, then my air castles were doomed to ruin, my borrowed happiness was but the swan song of hope, my dream that of a condemned man.

The jibing of the foresail and my hail to Ames brought Miss King to the deck. Her brother joined us, and we three stood looking at the oncoming vessel which had appeared like a cloud to mar the brightness of a perfect day. There was no need to explain the men-ace lying beneath that bunch of swollen canvas. By the faces of the two I saw they realized it was a plain case of chase, the only doubt being whether it would prove for good or evil. I would have given the gold in my pocket for a good glass with which to make her out, but, as that was impossible, it took me but a few seconds to come to the conclusion that our only hope (and that a slim one) was to make the chase a stern one and give the poor Phantom with her foul bottom, all the speed possible. Putting the wheel in charge of Ames, with no loss of words I went forward, clambered up the fore shrouds and managed alone to unfurl the square sail, settling the bracing and the sheet and tack on my return to the deck. In the present light air the pull of the canvas was small, but it was something, and I knew the stranger would mark the increase of sail and read as plainly as print that we wanted nothing of her.

As time went, we saying little or nothing betwixt us, I marked our follower's growth as she drew on. Little by little out came the details of her canvas, and, as I picked point after point, there dawned on me the almost certainty that our pursuer was none other than the Sprite, the last vessel of his Majesty's flotilla I cared to meet.

From the deck of the Ajax I had been informed of the Sprite's absence on patrol, and through the whole morning had held in my mind the dread of meeting her, only feeling safe from that particular craft since noon. Probably she had been sneaking under easy sail along the Long Island coast, and had only fairly sighted us after the westering sun had thrown a broad light on our canvas. Then with a keen nose for anything less than a three-decker, she had piled on her clothes the sooner to come by about what business a trader had to sail the King's sea without being under convoy. I dared not unfold my suspicions, but the girl, with the eye of a hawk and the instinct of a woman, saved the necessity. Turning to me after a long and searching look at our pursuer, she said:

"Captain Thorndyke, that vessel looks like the one that took me from Philadelphia to New York. I hardly know why I think so, but I fear me 'tis the same."

"Ay," I answered hoarsely, "I have that fear, and God help us if they overhaul us, as they are like to do, barring a miracle!—Have you aught to offer, Ames?" said I, addressing her brother whose face had taken

on a look of hardness the like of which I had marked
at the Dove when he was posing as an old man.

"Nay, friend," he returned, suddenly falling into
the Quaker style of speech, and without taking his eyes
from the vessel astern—"nay, friend, I have but a light
knowledge of sea possibilities. To run as thee be running means but to be beaten in the race. Thee has a
head for tricks. Are thee lost? If so, there is but one
thing for thee and me." And turning his eyes to mine,
he made a quick gesture toward the water, which motion
I thought was unobserved by the girl. But I was wrong
in my surmise.

"Has it come to this, then?" she ejaculated with
sudden terror in face and voice. "Am I to be left alone
and at the mercy of those yonder?—Beverly! brother!
you will not commit suicide and leave me without a
protector!—Donald Thorndyke," she continued, her terror giving place to an imperiousness royal in its effect,
"you have sworn not to desert me! Are you nerveless
at last? Nay, I know you too well. I ask your pardon,"
she faltered with a bend of her head and a rapid change
to humility; "I am wrong. Better give back to the
Almighty direct the life he gave you rather than have
those yonder, if enemies they be, take the giving into
their merciless hands. I was wrong. I let the woman
in me speak first. Your burden is greater than mine!"
And with this she placed both hands to her face and
sobbed aloud.

I listened in silence to this outburst with its shifting emotions. There was no answer to make. The
blackness of the last few days seemed to gather and settle
itself over me like a pall. We had been on the brink
of safety, the threshold of content, honor, and success,
and to see the prizes snatched away at this late hour was
beyond human endurance. The softness of the air, the
mellowing light, the silky veiling on the sky above us,

and the lively sparkle of the ocean, suddenly changed from gay congratulation to a hideous grin of irony and malice. Without a word in return I grasped the spokes of the wheel with my whole heart seemingly bent on meeting each surge in a manner to save our speed. To comfort the girl was beyond my power even had it lain in my province, and in real life no man, I fancy, ever juggles with the truth (be it never so bitter) while looking squarely into the face of death.

Neither did Ames go to his sister's rescue. As though to let her gather the full import of the future, he stood apart, only saying, as the poor girl's sobbing decreased, "There is a God in heaven, and what must be, must be."

If, however, I had remained silent it was not because I was stunned, for, though my tongue was dumb, my brain was active enough. There was one chance in a million that our pursuer was not the Sprite, or even one of the British fleet. If so, well. If not, I would sell myself at such a price that there would be but little triumph for them over my carcass. Turning at last to Ames, I said:

"Until it be made certain that we be lost to one another, I shall hold my life as dearly as ever. The mere capture of the schooner—unless that fellow astern be the Sprite—need not bring despair. We will run as long as run we can, and then fight; after that the action of each lies with his own conscience. As for me, I shall not be hanged from a British prison, but I swear again that while you or your sister live and I can lift an arm for either I will still cling to the breath God has given me. If, becoming powerless, I choose to cheat the rope, I will but be like many a captain who goes down with his ship. I take it 'twould be no common suicide, for my honor would not have suffered."

"Ay, I said naught to mean the cowardly taking of

one's own life," answered the youth stoutly. " Fight we will so long as powder and shot hold out, Quaker or no Quaker. We be scant of the first, though. I would to Heaven a sudden darkness like that which fell on Calvary would settle on us now! We might then take to the dingy astern and sneak for the Long Island shore."

He had hardly spoken when the mainsail flapped, and the wind, which had been rapidly growing lighter, almost went out. I cast my eye on the following schooner, and saw with some satisfaction that she, too, had lost the breeze she had been carrying with her, for no longer did she heel to its pressure, and, I thought, no longer were her sails bellying, but, like ours, hung in folds, only occasionally rounded by the dying puffs. By this she had drawn to within a couple of miles of us and was still coming on. Under our stern there was barely a wake (so slowly we moved), the froth from our bends and rudder having given place to an oily flatness filled with tiny eddies, through which the boat we still towed slowly dragged its way. Now there was a yellow haze on all the horizon, that told of the waning day, but the sun's broad light still lay over the ocean, and it would be hours ere darkness could furnish us shelter. By then our fate would be known.

CHAPTER XIX.

THE CAPTURE OF THE SCHOONER.

I WONDERED mightily that they had not fired at us, but the solution of the riddle came to me when I remembered that the Sprite had but one powerful gun forward, and hitherto she had not been in a position to use it on us without blowing away her own forward rigging. Her silence thus confirmed my fears as to the identity of the vessel, nor were we long in doubt as to the malevolence of her purpose. Still she glided toward us, wafted as is a feather over a smooth pond, while we rolled to the long reach of the surges without more way than would take us a fathom in a minute.

For all the deadness of the Phantom, I still stuck to the wheel, that she might not round into the wind. Ames and his sister had gone below to reload the firearms and lay out ammunition, when, just as the last gasp of wind went out and the shivering sails set the reefing points beating the canvas with a musical ripple, the enemy slewed a couple of points to the south, and a ball of white smoke broke from her bow. Plainly as day I marked the shot as it struck the water and in great leaps came skipping toward us. It passed us well astern, for, with the fall of the wind, we had swung into the trough of the sea, and the Phantom was now parallel to her pursuer, the latter lying off our starboard quarter.

There she might remain, and, using us as a target, sink us at her leisure, though I had little fear of this action on her part, as the British policy was ever to capture anything that could be of use, only destroying that which they could not carry away.

I watched the flight of the ball until the spouts sent aloft as it struck the sea became smaller and the missile sunk in the distance. It was a command to come into the wind and show our colors, and hoping (though without reason) to defer to the last the fall of the bolt, I descended into the cabin and fumbled through the flag locker for the Union Jack. I had the ensign in my hand when the girl looked up from her work and quickly asked:

"Are you to make a last stand under that? Nay, then, Donald," she said, with an appeal in her voice, and for the first time giving me my first name alone, "unless you hope to blind them for good and all by the sight of that bunting, 'twere a weak thing to do. You say you will fight; then fight under your own colors. It will make no difference in the end." And with this she bent to the locker, picked up the ensign of the colonies, and, holding it out, dragged from my hand the red flag of the enemy. It was a noble act, and worthy of the spirit which had been equal to bearding Clinton in his own quarters. It put into me the stimulus I needed. Without a word I turned and bounded up the companion, and in a moment the Stars and Stripes were hanging at the main peak, barely unfolded by the zephyr that was still playing aloft.

It was a plain defiance, and met with a ready answer. The bunting had been aloft no longer than was necessary for those on the distant vessel to have made it out with a glass, when again came a spurt of smoke and another ball leaped toward us. It was a well-aimed shot, and, had the gun been trained a trifle more to the right, it would have ended matters on the instant. As it was, the ball dipped close to our stern and beneath the trailing dingy. There was a swirl of spouting foam, a tearing crash, and the little boat leaped into the air amid a shower of splinters, spun over and over like a top, and then settled, keel upward, with a clean-cut hole yawning in her bottom.

I could almost hear the shout of triumph that undoubtedly took place on the enemy's deck as the result of this piece of marksmanship, but in the end, had they but known it, they were whetting the tiger's teeth instead of pulling them. Hardly had the smoke thinned from the shot, when from under the cloud I marked a boat putting away. There was little need of a glass to tell me it was filled with a boarding party, and that the drama was rapidly nearing its close. With the few minutes left for preparation we made haste to get what arms we had on deck, and, while yet the yellow flash of the oars was distant, our arrangements were completed. For defense we had two rifles, four pistols, three cutlasses and my rapier, though the latter and one of the cutlasses, being of no use, were left in the cabin. The lady was to take charge of the ammunition and reload the firearms as used, for, though her brother and myself both begged and commanded her to remain below, she had for the first time drawn for herself her own line of action by simply shaking her head and following us to the deck. She was white as chalk as she stood and watched the near approach of the boat, but I will swear that her fear (if fear it was) was not for herself.

Just before the enemy drew into rifle shot I went forward and opened the forecastle slide, calling both prisoners to come up, for I had a mind that I might use them to make a show of numbers on our deck. But in return I received a volley of curses only, and, as I had no time to try discipline, I shut and again fastened the hatch, rejoining the others aft.

Even at this stage I was possessed with the forlorn

hope that we might drive off the approaching boat, and, if they were short-handed aboard (a condition not unlikely), and failed to cripple us with their long gun, something might happen in the way of wind from another quarter or the coming darkness to enable us to escape. The hope, however, was not enough to give life to my spirits or make it worth the telling to my companions. I had put my past behind me, never hoping to reap what I had sowed, and with set teeth awaited with little fear and less doubt for the result of the coming hour.

Ames lay along the deck with his rifle over the counter; the girl sat in the companion door ready to reload the arms as they were passed to her; and I, looking for the proper moment to open fire, stood in plain sight above the taffrail.

Slowly they came on until I could count ten men and an officer, and as I marked the easy range I told Ames to let them have it. The crack of his rifle was yet in my ears as I saw the bowman pitch forward, his oar slipping from his hand into the sea. There was a slight commotion aboard, and the boat's progress ceased; but it was only to recover the lost oar, and then on they came again. Resting my gun over the rail, I calculated the roll of the schooner and in my turn fired. This shot told as well as the first. A man in the waist sprang to his feet, beat the air with his hands for an instant, and then toppled over the side, hanging half in and half out of water, as limp as a bag of wet salt. At this there was more delay, and by the time they were again well under way both rifles had been reloaded, and as yet there had been no call for the services of Miss King.

"Let them come nearer," said I, "and then give them both barrels at once, and after that the pistols." There was a grim determination in the way their oars flashed now, and as they came to within two hundred feet we both, by this time under the shelter of the rail, fired on the count of three.

Through the smoke that drifted on us I saw the officer sink back in his seat and the rowing cease, then there came a yell from the boat, and two muskets were discharged at us, but without effect. What fools they were to delay, for I had reloaded before the first motion had been made to continue the course! But to my amazement it was for only a moment they held on their way. As I fired again, apparently without hitting, I saw the boat's head slew about, and then they quickly hauled off and started to return to the distant schooner.

It was so far a triumph. Out of ten men we had disabled and perhaps killed three at least, one being an officer. Why they had fled still numbering enough to have vanquished us could only be accounted for by the supposition that they knew naught of our weakness, and feared the plain showing of our colors was but a sign of strength and fearlessness, if not a lure beckoning them to ruin. I had not dreamed of such an easy conquest, and for the while it was all I could do to restrain the extravagance of my feelings. I turned to Miss King. Her pallor had given way and left two bright spots of excitement which glowed on her cheeks and matched well the brilliant sparkle of her eye. She was trembling with suppressed emotion, and as I held out my hand to her in unspoken congratulation, she took it, and, lifting to her lips my grimy fingers, rose without a word and hurried forward.

The impulsive spirit of her brother showed itself in the cry he gave as, with half a sob and half a laugh, he danced about the deck and then threw himself into my arms, breaking therefrom, shaking his fist at the retreating boat, and in mighty un-Quaker mood, though in Quaker style, damned the British high and low, afloat and ashore.

" A curse on thee, thee white-livered, scarlet-backed cowards! " he shouted at the end. " To let two men and a girl drive thee! Oh, by the Lord God above me, the battle is not with the strong! Donald! Donald! mark thee well! I tell thee we will yet best them though they send the whole ship's company! We will rise from the depths! Thy hand and head have so far shown the way! Thee will yet prevail! "

I was well aware that this exuberance was but the reaction following strain. I felt the relief myself, but knew, despite the fact that we were so far safe, the repulse would prove but a respite. The lump that had risen to my throat when I saw that the enemy was beaten off, still held me speechless, but it passed presently, as did also the wildness of the youth, and ere long we were speculating as to the next probable move of the discomfited redcoats. It was true that I had realized the first part of my secret hope of overcoming the boat, but, on scanning the horizon, there was no sign of a rescuing wind, though I thought the south held some promise of a later breeze. There was naught to do but stand at bay and await the issue.

Nor did we await it for long. The sun was sliding rapidly to the edge of the sea, being but an hour high, its path lying in a line with the now thoroughly becalmed schooner off our quarter; its glare throwing a dazzling pathway betwixt the two vessels. It is more than likely they scented the advantage given them by their present position, for not long after the return of the first expedition against us I saw three boats leave their side and proceed along the track of blind'ng glitter.

To aim into this eye-watering brilliancy with any but a mere chance of hitting a mark was an impossibility, but, with the old determination to face the worst, Ames and I repaired to our posts, though the girl still lingered forward.

As I saw the uselessness of protracted defense, I let her bide away, knowing that at the bow she would be clear of flying bullets when the boats should come near enough to return our fire. How the attack was planned was at once apparent, for to cover the onset of the boarders the schooner again opened on us with its forward piece. In evident fear of striking their own men, they abandoned their former manner of rico-chetting the ball across the water, and instead drove point blank at us. Although we lay a plain target, and their schooner, like the Phantom, was at rest, the first shot flew wide of us; the second passed somewhere aloft, yet so near that I heard the horrible humming of the ball, and the third—— To this day they know not all they did, nor, for the matter of that, did I at the time.

We had let the boats come near, that we might shoot with effect, and I had fired and was about to pass the rifle to Gertrude, who in my excitement I fancied had by this time returned to the companion, when to my astonishment I saw she was not behind me. There was no time for protracted search, for, as I sprang from the cabin, where I had gone to look for her, I heard her brother discharge two pistols in quick succession and saw a boat sweep under our counter. In an instant it had hooked on to our starboard channels. With a round oath Ames seized the two remaining pistols and poured their contents into it with scarce a chance of missing, while I rushed to his side, and, lifting the heavy hatch cover from the cabin, against which it had been leaning, hurled it on to the heads of the packed mass below.

Beyond the fact that no man boarded the schooner at this point, what execution was made by the broad and bulky timber I never knew, for at that moment the third shot from the schooner struck the foretopmast just above the hounds. In a thundering crash down

13

came the spar with the squaresail, the outer canvas, top-mast, fore and back stays, blocks, and upper running gear in general, the broken mast smiting the deck with the sound of an explosion.

The din of the shot and the tumbling wreck slewed me around as though I had been on a pivot, but it was only to see that all was lost. From beneath the foresail boom I saw that the other boats had boarded us on the larboard bow, and already half a score of men were swarming over the side. Even then my thoughts went to the girl, but she was nowhere in sight. Body and brain work quickly in times of excitement, and thinking that possibly she had fallen through the gaping hatch and into the hold, though time was scant, I sprang for the opening and looked down, calling her by name. There came no answer, neither was her body in sight, the dull gray of the lead alone meeting my eye. Springing again to my feet, I drew my cutlass and retreated to the quarter-deck where stood Ames with drawn steel, his back braced against the wheel and his breath coming and going as though from violent exertion.

" 'Tis the final stand, my lad!" I exclaimed, as I ranged myself by his side and turned to face (for the last time, I thought) the enemy, who were now pouring aft. " Gertrude is gone! I could find her nowhere!"

"I know it!" he panted. " The game's up; I marked her when she——"

I lost the rest, for at that instant an officer whom I at once recognized came running up, followed by half a dozen marines. As he caught sight of me he halted, and, eying me with profound astonishment, suddenly broke out:

" Good God! 'tis Thorndyke! Touch not that man, on your lives!" he shouted. " Here's game worth a whole watch!—Surrender, ye rebel! Throw down your arms and surrender! Can't you see you are beaten?

You doubly damned spy, the rope will have its own!—
By Saint George, but this is luck!"

"Surrender to ye, Lieutenant Belden?" I vociferated in turn. "By the Lord, no! Come and take me
if ye can, but 'twill not be alive. Your rope is not for
me, nor will the colors aloft be struck while I stand on
this deck! I have given over this world, and fear neither
ye nor the pink shrimps at your back! Come, now, and
clutch your luck!"

If I was strong as two men before, I felt the strength
of ten within me as I spoke. The swath I would have
mowed through that press would have brought the bullet
I invited, but there was no advance. True, the crowd
showed a tendency to rush in as I thus defied them, and
several muskets were leveled at us, but Belden nipped
the act by waving his sword and threatening punishment to the first man who fired a gun or advanced
without orders.

It was plain that to him the prize was a tremendous
one, nor would he have the glory of defeating me
dimmed by my death, and to this ambition to take me
alive and see me hanged was doubtless due my final
safety.

Saving the two shots from the first boat, not a
small arm had been fired by them up to this time, their
determination to carry the vessel by cold steel alone
being apparent all through the attack. As my eye
ranged over the circle of men that spread about us and
hemmed us to the taffrail (yet for all their numbers were
held off by the command of their officer), I saw many
a face well known to me ashore, but not one expressing
an atom of mercy. With a watchful look I anticipated
any possible onset, and yet through all the pent vigor
of tightened nerves and stiffened muscles my gaze played
beyond their lines and marked the details of the surroundings.

The broad ocean lay almost like glass save for the
regular heave that passed over it like a wave over the
surface of molten metal. Off our starboard beam was
an upturned boat floating lazily away, it probably having been stove or capsized by the hatch I had cast into
it, and near it drifted the hatch itself: On deck the
fallen canvas covered the vessel amidships, and aloft
the ragged stump of the topmast, standing clear against
the dappled sky, looked like a pine shivered by lightning. A profound silence had fallen where a moment
before had been a din of shouts and crashing timber—
profound save for a dull thumping forward, which I
knew came from the prisoners, who were thus signaling
for release. The moment was near at hand when I
should pass my soul to its Maker, and yet, though the
resolve was as strong as ever, I wavered, not in fear of
the next world, but dreading the terrible struggle that
would come when a healthy body like mine wrestles in
the grip of suffocation. If our captors could not be
goaded into shooting me, nothing was left but to cast
myself into the sea, and this I would not do so long as
the young Quaker stood at my side.

A sudden cry from the bow, soon followed by the
sound of metal striking metal, told me that the prisoners were out and being freed from their irons. Belden,
without vouchsafing to answer my defiance, hung hesitating, evidently awaiting the arrival of his superior to
direct future movements. Disarmed save for the bare
steel in our hands, we were an easy prey to him had
our deaths now been his object; but as there had been
no show of force after boarding us, the peppery royalist,
still smarting from the disgrace under which I had been
the means of placing him, felt sure of his ultimate triumph over me, and, giving the order to hold us where
we stood, turned toward the point of the disturbance
forward and hurried off. I was a step in advance of

Ames, who still leaned against the wheel, when I heard his voice in my ear.

"There's a fair chance for a leap, Donald," he whispered. "The last tie is gone. Be thee ready?"

"Nay, lad," I answered softly. "We are not yet parted. I still hang to my oath. I have seen nothing of Gertrude. Where can she be?"

"She is past the sight of this, thank God!" he returned. "She is dead, man; dead and gone, and we will soon follow her. I saw her——"

Again he was interrupted, this time by a wild yell from the bow, and the man who uttered it started aft chased by half a dozen marines. It was Scammell. With little upon him save a shirt and his small clothes, he broke through the half circle that compassed us, halting just within its limits. He was a horrible object. His hair hung tangled over his shoulders; his eyes were fierce and bloodshot; his face was distorted by rage, and its pallor was startling. Without a word of warning he called me a vile name, and with an oath raised a pistol he had probably snatched from some one and, leveling it at me, fired. The ball passed betwixt my body and elbow without touching the skin, but it struck Ames, who was just behind me. I heard a deep groan as the youth fell to the deck, his head striking the planking with a heavy blow, and a number of hands sprang upon the infuriated officer and dragged him backward.

It was done in an instant. The shock and suddenness of the attack came like a thunderbolt, and yet I retained my presence of mind. With my eye still fixed on my enemies, I stooped to one knee and felt for the hand of my friend, calling on him to speak; but no sound came to my repeated appeal, and the hand I found, gave no answering pressure. He was dead past doubt, and had quickly joined his sister, who, in some manner unknown to me, had gone before him.

It was the culminating wave of disaster, and for the moment I felt like sinking beneath it. Within a quarter hour by violence I had been bereft of my two companions, and thus was I suddenly freed from my obligation to live. With none left for whom to combat, surrounded by triumphant enemies, and before me ruin in the shape of the noose, it was now my right, as well as considered duty, to preserve myself from the disgrace of being hanged as a spy. 'Twould be but a short struggle, a moment's wild agony, perhaps, and then the end. I braced myself for the ordeal. Rising to my feet, I gave a last glance around, my eye taking in the vast sweep of the sea, on deck the marines still wrestling with the murderous royalist, and, hurrying aft, Belden, followed by Lounsbury. Then turning my thoughts aloft, I made a silent prayer ere taking the final step, when, like a revelation, without the slightest mental effort, without the slightest bending of the mind toward any refuge this side of the great unknown, a possible—ay, probable—way of escape opened before me. As the angel of the Lord at the last moment called on Abraham to desist from the sacrifice of his son, so burst this light out of thick darkness and showed me my work was not yet finished. More than willing was I to grasp this more than chance. As though a stone had been rolled from my chest, I took a deep breath, and quickly unloosing my belt, threw both cutlass and scabbard to the deck, then turning, with a stride I reached the rail and cast myself headlong into the sea.

CHAPTER XX.

THE SHELL OF THE DINGY.

NEVER was my love of life or the certainty of my saving it greater than when I shot beneath the surface of the ocean. Like a plummet I went down, the air bubbles I carried with me roaring in my ears like a cataract. As I lost the impetus of the dive I turned and looked up. Having gone over at the starboard quarter, I was almost under the stern, and the clear green of the water magnified the great shadowy hull of the schooner as she stretched forward into seeming infinity. Like a blot on the silvery surface above me lay the overturned dingy, still held to the vessel by its painter, and in her lay my salvation.

With a few vigorous strokes I swam under it, and, regulating my rise as best I could, came to the surface within the shell of the wrecked boat. The move had been successful. If the trick was unsuspected, I was safe. Letting go my pent breath in a blast, I thanked God for His sudden intervention, and prayed that His hand be not removed from me.

Settled low as was the overturned dingy, my head barely cleared her bottom, but that was sufficient. Sustaining my position by a light hold on the thwart, that my weight should not prevent the regular and natural roll of the wreck, with nerves now tuned to their highest pitch, I hung and awaited developments. The hole

191

in the boat's bottom furnished me with air, and, to my astonishment, this vent in the hollow which now sheltered me gave to my retreat the character of a trumpet, and every sound was magnified, though its quality was changed to the deep sonorous roar such as one hears come from the heart of a conch held to the ear. It was an indistinct babble of cries and oaths that first greeted me, and from the few words I could disentangle I guessed that the whole host had rushed to the schooner's side in the hope that I would rise. Had I still courted death, I might easily have met with it by means of a bullet through my head, for through the confused humming of voices I distinctly heard the sharp clicking of gunlocks, and knew that had I appeared I would have been made a target for a score of muskets.

The sound of voices decreased as the moments flew, and when at last it seemed certain that I had gone to the bottom, there came a general awakening, and a sharp order was given to search the hull, strike the flag, and hoist the British ensign. The clicking of boot heels and the rattling of arms were more distinct than words, but the marines had barely scattered to obey the last commands when, above all else, I heard an unknown voice:

"Overhaul that carrion, and then pitch it overboard!"

This I knew must refer to the body of my poor friend, but before I could realize the necessity of the order thus brutishly given, as clear as the order itself rose the voice of Scammell.

"Look, look, Belden! Damn me, but I thought I had brought down a buzzard in missing the hawk, when, after all, I have struck but a peg lower than Thorndyke himself! By the crime of Judas, I wish it had been the other way! If this young, old broad-brim be not Beverly Ames, I'll lose fifty pounds to any one of you!

Quick, man! See, he is not dead! 'Fore God, but mayhap he can yet give us some news of his sister! Overboard he goes not! Dead or alive, he must be taken to
Clinton, else your commission is in danger! Know you
not that he is connected with Mrs. Badely? Send off
for help! Is not that long-legged Irishman yet aboard
you?"

Here a number of voices joined in and turned to a
confused roar all words at once following. In the space
of a few minutes I heard a boat putting away from the
side, the thud of oars in the water making a jar on my
ear drums, almost painful. For a time there reigned
comparative silence, and then came what was doubtless
a marine's report.

"The hold is clear of all life, sir. Nawthin' but lead
below, an' cabin an' forec'sle all cleaned out barrin'
some arms an' the captain's old clothes."

"How's this, Scammell?" said Belden, evidently
turning to that officer. "We saw three men aboard,
and but two are accounted for. Thorndyke has gone
to hell over the side, and this lad of yours is like to
join him by another route! Where's the third?"

"There was no third," came the sharp response.
"Two it was that smothered us below. I know of none
other; no more does Lounsbury."

"Nay," said that worthy, speaking for the first time,
and with a thick burr to his speech, "there was never
more than four legs to the lot. Mayhap that giant split
hisself in two for the sake o' looks—there was enough
o' him. Thank God for his loss! I would ne'er sleep
easy again knowin' him alive."

Here words fell to a murmur until Lounsbury again
spoke, evidently addressing himself to the one who was
in authority on board:

"Now I take it, leftenant, that by rights this craft
is mine."

"Yours, ye toasted mug!" demanded the unknown voice. "What mean ye?"

"Ay, only by right o' prize, I mean," was the answer. "'Twas I who first laid hand on her, an' got a split skull for my pains, an' not a damn sovereign to help heal it, neither so much glory as shines from the buttons o' yer coat. Prize be cussed! Now, if yer capting wills to let me take her into port—as I came nigh doing awhile agone—'twill go far to put me right with the admiralty an' get me a job, mayhap, like that lost through Thorndyke takin' my name, damn his soul! D'ye see?"

"Ay, I see, ye sweep! And is that all? No prize money?"

"Ay, all, all. Only to sail her home; no more."

"No more, eh? Ye are a cursed deep villain, but I'll touch the captain on it. Go get the grime from your face and look less like a toad. Had he seen you, 'twas no wonder Thorndyke launched himself over the rail. —What now, Scammell? Does the lad still live?"

"He lives, indeed," was the answer, "but whether or no he will bide long I can not say. He was better on deck than he is below. The cabin still stinks. I hope 'twill not be forever before the doctor gets here. Was he drunk at mess? It is possible he can hold the lad's life long enough to allow him to speak; he does little now but moan."

At this the two walked forward, and I heard nothing but the coarse voices of the marines as they sang out to one another or laughed uncouthly.

The knowledge that Ames still lived gave me a quick sense of relief—a relief which fled on the instant as I thought of the probable future in store for him. My own position was infinitely better than his, even were he not suffering from a wound, and, as for his sister, after all was done, was she not better off than either?

But was she dead? If not, what could have become of
her? I had heard that the vessel had been searched
without finding a trace of the third party to whom
Belden had referred. On seeing all was lost, was it possible that she had thrown herself overboard that she
might not witness her brother's tragic end? It was like
her. It would have been an act showing her strength
of character, as well as the weakness of her sex; a natural recoil from physical and mental suffering without
a purpose; a heroic self-sacrifice. It were as well she
had not suffered captivity and long-drawn misery. With
her brother at death's door, or perhaps saved to die by
military law; her property confiscated, without a home
or relatives and at the mercy of Clinton's heartless mistress, life would have held no more for her than the
doubtful benefit of mere existence in confinement for an
indefinite period.

And yet was my reason against the idea of her self-
destruction. There was mystery in her disappearance,
but its solution lay not in that. The attacking party
had boarded us from either side, yet not an eye had seen
her cast herself into the sea. There was more than this
to make me doubtful. For her brother's sake she had
sacrificed herself before Clinton, yet on my hand was
placed her last kiss. Had she left the world thus, without a word to him, without a warning to me? It was
unnatural, unholy; it was monstrous to think of, and
yet—— The possible solution of the riddle as it drove
into my brain had scarce time to find lodgment before
it was put to flight by the voice of Belden, which seemed
to come from directly overhead, his words showing that
the continuance of my present safety was not assured.

" Think you that dingy could be hauled aboard and
repaired? 'Twas a neat shot, and the ball seems to have
cleft her like a knife."

" So it looks," came an answer, " but I'll warrant

you'll find her full of fissures. The work will barely
repay the trouble. Better cut her adrift. If wind
comes, the wreck will drag like a sea anchor. You
might give attention to the quarter boat yonder, and
get the hatch aboard."

"The hatch, yes," Belden returned; "but the boat
is stove badly. Curses on the rebel; he has cost us ten
men in all, and only to give us the slip! 'Tis small
wonder Lounsbury has the shakes at thought of him!
Think of the nerve——"

"Damn him!" was the retort. "What about the
schooner? Lounsbury wants to take her in. There's
nothing gone but the foretopmast, and with three men
he could work her if the captain consents. In the face
of our being short-handed, the idea is not bad if the
villain can be trusted."

"He'll scarce run off with the schooner," answered
Belden, "and lead is no temptation, though I'd be shy
of trusting him with anything more valuable. I know
him of old. He was scavenger to Clinton, and to Howe
before him.—Here, lad, cut away that painter."

The last words was an order probably given to a
sailor, for presently I heard the splash of the severed
line. At the same moment a boat swept by, and from
the few words I could gather I guessed the Irish surgeon had arrived and gone aboard.

After that more boats passed and repassed as time
dragged on, and finally the bulk of the vessel's captors
returned to their own schooner, for, saving now and
then the sound of a single man tramping the deck, the
stillness was unbroken.

It was with mighty satisfaction that I had heard
the final order to cut the tie binding my refuge to the
schooner. I gave no thought to what might come of my
being adrift on the broad ocean. Beyond each moment
as it came and went I seemed to have no interest. The

future was blank, nor need I consider it so long as the wind held off, for in the calm the dingy and schooner would not part company, and until darkness fell I would be compelled to remain in my present pinched quarters.

Hooded as I was, up to the present my hearing had been my only sense brought into play, but with the departure of the last boat load of men I used my eyes for the first time. The interior of the shelter under which I hung was lighted almost entirely from below, and a delicate greenish-blue tint played over the planks and ribs of the wreck. Shielded from direct light overhead, the shell gave all the effects of a water telescope, for, on turning my eyes downward, my sight pierced the ocean for fathom after fathom, the color of the depths growing from the most tender blue to a clear and then dark green, showing me that the bottom lay beyond vision and far below. It was only by turning to the hole in the keel that I could guess the hour, nor was it long before the sun had set and darkness came on apace. By the natural attraction of floating bodies, the boat had drawn near the schooner, and, as they struck and crunched together, I heard the voice of the surgeon as he left the cabin and came on deck.

" Well, by the powers, I suppose I must obey orders. If the boy is moved, he dies—that's flat—an' by me soul, he may go, spite o' me skill! I must bide here the night, must I? Ay, well; send aboard a couple o' bottles, Belden, or, by the piper, I'll mutiny. Why should a dirty rebel be worth more than our own men? Is Scammell to bide with me? "

" No," answered Belden; " he's sent for by the captain. I'll fix the liquor, McCary.—Now, Mr. Lounsbury, you have heard your instructions. Follow us as soon as the wind rises; you will have it ere long—the glass has fallen. We will stand near you.—Are you ready, Scammell? "

There was suppressed conversation after this, and then another boat put away. In perhaps an hour it returned and was hoisted to the davits, and then again there was silence—a deep, brooding silence, such as is only known in a night calm on the sea.

CHAPTER XXI

DE PROFUNDIS.

As I have said, I had given no thought to the future
or what consequence my present situation might entail
should the schooner follow her captor. But as the darkness deepened and a chill due to my protracted sub-
mersion struck to my bones, I realized that, except for
having put myself beyond the sight of my enemies, I
had accomplished nothing. True it was that I might
have laid a course ere this, for I had hung unmolested
for a number of hours; but, instead of turning to my
own interests, I had let my brain play over the mystery
of the disappearance of Miss King. What this portended I had failed to dwell upon. Knowing that for
myself there remained nothing to do but stay where
I was until chance should open a way for me to gain
the shore or mischance deliver me a prisoner or send me
to the bottom, I had racked my fancy for a solution of
the one question regarding the lady. As a reward for
this constant effort, I had hit upon what I thought to
be the correct answer to the puzzle, but to verify it had
been thus far beyond possibility. Now the darkness,
the warning chill, and my general uncertainty brought
me up with a round turn, and I gave attention solely
to my own affairs.

Further than that I must leave my shelter and gain
the schooner, I could not proceed in laying my line of
action. To use the wreck as a support and push the

unmanageable thing for an uncertain number of miles to the Long Island coast would result, in my present condition, in collapse and death. It did not take me long to determine that my only hope lay in the near-by schooner; a forlorn hope at best, for the attempt to board her would immediately place my life in jeopardy. Nor would I have turned a thought to her had I not overheard that she would be manned by Lounsbury and three hands only. This handful of men (the doctor counting as nothing in my eyes), the calm, and the probable total lack of discipline which would follow the transfer of the sailors from a vessel of war to a half-dismantled prize under unofficial command, might allow me to gain foothold on deck. Ay, I thought, by some possibility I may reclaim my loss and become master of the situation, only let me fairly see the chance.

It was now so dark that the sky showed but faintly through the hole in the boat's bottom. As time advanced and there became great danger that the wind might rise, thereby rendering my attempt abortive, I sank myself into the water and came to the surface clear of my late shelter. The tide or some unknown force had drawn the wreck from the schooner's side, and I found I had been slowly drifting south, being now some ten or a dozen rods off the vessel's starboard bow. By the most intense listening I could hear a subdued sound of voices, but from what part of the deck it proceeded I was too far away to determine. All around me was black water, with nothing in sight saving the shadowy hull of the Phantom and a guiding light, evidently swinging over the stern of the Sprite, though that craft was swallowed by the distance and general gloom. Not a star was in sight, not a breath broke the glassiness of the silent swell as it rolled northward. The ocean never seemed so vast nor its depths so repulsive as now, when in the darkness it clung to me with its chilly fingers.

The fathoms below gaped like an open pit, and it was
with a convulsive horror that I let go my hold on the
dingy and struck out for the schooner, resolute, come
what might, to rid myself of the frightful loneliness
which all at once was magnified before me. Indeed, I
felt that my time had come. For good or evil there
would be a sharp turn in my affairs, but if evil, I would
die by shot or sword; not to the black element about
me would I give myself.

Like a frightened child fleeing from the dark, I at
first swam boldly, but, as my vigor sent before me a
small surf that roared through the silence, I abated my
speed, and with slow and noiseless stroke headed myself
toward the schooner's bow, that I might approach her
as I did when drifting through the fog. The gold in
my pockets dragged on me, but not once did I think
of ridding myself of the burden, for the swim was short,
and I had won the money hardly. However, it seemed
an age ere I saw the Phantom's bowsprit outlined against
the sky over my head, and by the time I felt the firmness of her bobstay in my hand something like confidence had come back to me, and my momentary horror
of the deep was past. The touch of the rigging put
strength in me, and I slowly drew myself out of water,
that the torrent from my clothes might not attract attention from the deck. I could now hear the sound of
voices plainly, and knew it came from forward, but it
was too muffled for me to make head or tail of the conversation. It would guide my actions in a measure, for,
so long as it continued, my presence would be unsuspected.

Carefully I dragged myself up until I came within
reaching distance of the bowsprit, and then I brought
my head to the level of the deck. The jib and staysail
hung motionless from their riggings, but from beneath
the latter I marked the figure of a man leaning against

14

the larboard fore shrouds and smoking a pipe as he looked over the water. He was partly turned toward me, and as long as he held his present position I could not advance. As far aft as I could see the deck was otherwise deserted, though a light, hitherto concealed by the rail, gleamed from the cabin window. A slight yellow haze spread from the open hatch of the forecastle, and from there came the voices I heard.

Putting myself astride the bowsprit, I sat concealed from the larboard side by the schooner's head cloths, though by bending my body I could peer beneath the sails and see the figure that blocked my further progress. The talking from the open hatch drowned the drip of the small streams still flowing from my clothing, though it seemed to accentuate the mournful creak that from the top hamper occasionally answered the heavier rolls of the sea. I was now momentarily at my wits' end, for neither forward nor backward could I go. Had I wished to return to the wreck, I could not have found that speck in the darkness, and my plans had not extended beyond getting on to the vessel, and this had been accomplished. But I had not remained passively seated astride the bowsprit for many minutes before a scheme opened before me. It was born of necessity, and, unless he should soon move, demanded the life of the fellow standing by the shrouds. I had barely come to this conclusion when, as though he read my thoughts and felt the sinister threat they contained, he knocked the ashes from his pipe and turned himself toward his companions below.

As he came into the radius of light that shot from the hatch, I saw he was an ordinary seaman—a regulation man-of-war's-man—from his light pumps to his oiled and eelskin-cased pigtail curling clear of the collar of his shirt. With a light remark to his fellows, he seated himself on the top step of the ladder leading down, and, resting his elbows on his knees and his chin on his clinched hands, started to palaver with those below, probably enjoying to the fullest extent the contrast in the discipline of the two vessels.

His action was a glaring piece of marine carelessness, but it both saved his life and opened to me a way to act. Now, with the dazzle of light full in his face, he might lift his head yet fail to see me, and, as the time was ripe, I felt for the foot ropes and silently slid to the heel of the bowsprit. Once there, I crept to the cathead, and from there with a spring I reached the forecastle opening behind the unsuspecting sailor. With a sudden push I sent him headlong on to his fellows, and then I quickly closed the doors, slid the hatch cover, fastened it, and for the third time I had made the Phantom's forward quarters a prison.

There was now little time to spare, for I knew the rumpus that would come would attract the cabin, and it behooved me to get command of that ere Lounsbury could act on the offensive. Snatching a belaying pin from its ring on the mast, I ran to the galley, but found it dark and deserted. From there I hurried aft, and, without the precaution of peeping through a window, presented myself at the open door of the companion way. I knew not what I would find, but was far from expecting the sight that met my eyes. The lantern swinging from its beam had been trimmed and washed, and cast a strong light over the interior. Though no one was at the table, it showed that a makeshift meal had been sent from the Sprite, for on the Phantom there were now no means of cooking, as pots, kettles, and table gear had gone the way of my instruments. In a bunk, the curtains of which were flung wide, and at the side of which stood a bucket of water, lay Ames, his face like chalk and his eyes closed, but whether in death or sleep I could not tell. On a transom locker at the other side of the cabin sprawled the doctor, somewhat more than tipsy, his head rolling to and fro with the plunge of the vessel, while in his hand was a bloody rag or bandage. He was vainly trying to reach a bottle and glass that stood near him on the floor, the heave of the schooner throwing him off his balance at each attempt to raise himself. At the extreme end of the compartment was Lounsbury on his knees, working at the bulkhead with a carpenter's chisel and calking mallet. Ignoring the presence of the drunken surgeon, he had torn away half the casing to the partition, and had finally struck upon my hidden gold, which now lay as plain to my eye as to his. For this, and probably for this alone, he had once attempted to betray me, threatened my life, and well-nigh lost his own. He had guarded the secret as well as I, and now, after months of waiting, hard fare, and harder blows, he doubtless felt a full measure of sordid pleasure as my little hoard lay uncovered before him. And not so little, either. Five hundred pounds would make him passing rich among his fellows.

Though his face was from me, its exultation seemed to strike through him and shine from his back. I could almost see the dry, greedy grin and close set of his ragged teeth as he laid his hand on the bag to judge its worth by lifting. With the inborn suspicion of the everfearful thief or miser, he threw a cautious look over his shoulder, and as he did so his eyes met mine.

I once saw a laughing man shot clean through the heart, and the sudden change of his expression as death seized him, was appalling; but it was nothing to the swift alteration that came over the face of Lounsbury as that villain recognized me. Crouched low at the top of the companion way, with one foot on the steps and the other on deck, I remained immovable as I witnessed the effect of my sudden appearance. Without shifting his position, the wretch held his head craned over his left shoulder, his jaw dropped, and his small, piglike eyes opened to their farthest extent, glaring at me as though their owner was in a trance. His face was too blackened and weather-beaten to allow of a change of color, but pallor and fright were plain in his very attitude. Not a sound or movement was made by either of us as we thus faced each other, and the surgeon, marking nothing amiss, still made desperate though ludicrous bobs toward the liquor on the floor.

Perhaps for a minute Lounsbury held his position, and then with a slow, snakelike motion, his eyes still fixed on mine, he twisted till his back was to the bulkhead, where, extending his arms against the woodwork, he flattened himself as though trying to shrink through the partition, horror and dread written over his swollen and repulsive features.

It had never been in my mind to play a part, but it was plain that to this ignorant and superstitious man I was nothing less than a veritable spirit of the dead. Indeed, the glistening of my dripping clothes, the plastered hair on my head, unshaven, and with the paleness of long immersion on my face, these, with the probable glitter of excitement in my eyes, all tended to make me uncanny in appearance, especially as my figure was backed by the absolute blackness of the night. Lounsbury had seen me in apparent desperation plunge overboard, and doubtless thought I had been drifting fathoms deep below the Phantom's keel, yet in the hour of his success I had come to torment him. Like Banquo's ghost—and ghost I was to him—I would not down.

The agony working in his mind would soon find an outlet in some fashion, but it stirred him in a way I hardly expected. Still piercing me with his glance, his broad chest heaved spasmodically and his right hand gradually moved to the hilt of the cutlass hanging on his left hip. Slowly, like a man asleep, he drew the blade, and with slaver now running from the corners of his mouth, he left the bulkhead and crept toward me. Fascination ruled him. The pent-up energy of the man showed in his crouching, catlike step as he glided along the edge of the table and into the space between it and the foot of the ladder. Madness, murder, and every evil flamed from his eyes, and I knew that now he or I must die, though I would have mighty small qualms in killing him, and had still smaller doubts as to which was to be killed.

Though I was armed with naught but a belaying pin, while he possessed a sword, the chances were more in my favor than in his. In the narrow passage of the companion, to which he must come to attack me, his weapon would be of no avail save in the thrust, while the short and fairly heavy club I gripped would be untrammeled by want of space, and my position above him gave me an advantage I had seen from the beginning.

As the fellow reached the foot of the steps, his manner suddenly changed. Pulling himself upright, he let out a yell that was blood-curdling, and clapping his left hand over his eyes as though to shut out the sight of me, he thrust his sword at arm's length before him and rushed blindly up the ladder as though to impale the uncanny spirit he had seen at its top.

As the steel came near me I beat it down with a blow of the belaying pin, and, reaching forward, struck him fairly on the head. He threw up both hands, balanced for an instant, and then pitched backward, striking the floor head first, the weight of his body doubling and breaking his neck as though it had been an icicle.

Before I followed him by a leap that carried me the length of the companion, I knew my enemy had come to anchor forever. It was not to him I turned my notice as I struck the floor, but to the now half-sobered surgeon who was fumbling beneath his pillow, from under which he drew a pistol just as I reached him. Grasping him by the throat, I threw him on to his back on the locker, and, with my knee on his thin chest, twisted the yet uncocked firearm from his hand and sent it spinning across the cabin.

It was done. Once again I was master of the Phantom.

Hurriedly searching the prostrate man and his immediate surroundings for more weapons, and finding none, without further attempt to conceal my voice or purpose, I commanded him to lie where he was on pain of instant death, and, as I saw the cowardly noncombatant shrink away from me and knew I had nothing to fear from him, I left his side and crossed the cabin to where lay my wounded friend. To my astonishment his eyes were open and he was regarding me curiously enough, though the greeting he gave me was but a movement of the lips, for from them there came no sound. I grasped his hand. There was but the faintest trace of fever in it, and a slight answering pressure was returned. Again his lips moved, and, by bending to them, I made out the word " Ghost? "

" Nay, my lad," I answered heartily. " We are once more to the good. I had small hopes of ever again seeing you alive, but God has willed differently. Are you badly hurt? "

The only answer was a tremor of the lids, and I might have known that weakness would hold him dumb. " Where was the boy hit? " I demanded, turning to the lank redcoat who had not shifted his position but lay looking at me with intense interest. The royalist raised himself on his elbow, and, instead of answering, asked:

" Who are ye, man, and where from? "

" Know ye not Donald Thorndyke returned from hell for a substitute? " I thundered, striding up to him.

"Answer my question, ye sot! Where was the boy hit?"

"In the right lung; the ball passed clear through him," he answered as he shrank back, and then, as his curiosity struggled for mastery, he continued, "They told me that overboard ye had gone."

"They told ye the truth," I returned, stooping for the pistol I had wrenched from him, and cocking it. "Put me aside and tell me, will the lad live?"

"Ay, like as not if he has the pluck," he snapped back, eyeing and dodging the muzzle of the firearm. "Faith, I'll do my best if ye will honor my calling and play that damn thing to some other point. Have ye murdered all but meself?"

"Nay, ye skewer," I answered, almost amused by his fear and amazed at the way it had overcome the fumes of the liquor in him. "I but gave the crew a rest from duty; it is their watch below, and if ye dare call me murderer for taking and defending my own, I'll act the part in truth."

"By me sowl, ye are the devil himself!" he ejaculated, but I cut him short.

"Whate'er I am, ye are my prisoner. Now take your choice betwixt irons and parole; the hold or this cabin. Speak fast! I have business on hand."

"A prisoner only, is it?" he exclaimed quickly, sitting bolt upright and raising his hand aloft. "Then, on the honor of an Irish gentleman, I take oath not to sneak from ye or bear arms," he answered, as though relieved by the terms I offered.

"And bide in the cabin until allowed the deck?" I added.

"That same," he answered.

"And care for the wounded lad?"

"Oh, ay! oh, ay! an' now——"

"Then 'tis ten to one that before long ye will be

back among your fellows by exchange," I interrupted,
being in a hurry. " Bring the boy to his feet, and 'twill
be money in your pocket; but no more liquor."

So saying, I picked up the bottle and took a long
draught of what proved to be good whisky. 'Twas a
well-earned and sorely needed dram, but a mighty
uncivil way of taking it, inasmuch as I had just cut him
off his own grog. The act may have been the means of
fanning the spark of malice held in his nature—a spark
that glowed, smoldered, and burst into flame when I
least expected. The cunning in his brain made up for
the lack of sinews in his body, for when I turned from
locking up the bottle and sliding the key into my pocket,
I noticed a malevolence in his face; but he shifted his
eye from me, and, getting to his feet with an effort,
walked unsteadily across the cabin and bent over Ames.

CHAPTER XXII.

FROM UNDER THE SQUARE-SAIL YARD.

By the rules of civilized warfare I had rendered the surgeon incapable of offensive action, but, apart from his word of honor, my best defense seemed to lie in his cowardice and ready acquiescence to my demands. Even in my intense interest in the welfare of my friend I did not follow the doctor to his side. I had matters on my heart and hands requiring immediate attention, but my first business was to rid the cabin of the repulsive carcass that cumbered the foot of the companion way.

With as little feeling as though I was handling a bale of goods, I turned Lounsbury over that I might be sure of his death, and by the limp and hideous way his head fell to his shoulder I knew he was past all surgery. Grasping him by the collar, I hauled him to the deck, and from thence to the rail, launching him over the side with the feeling that with him went the last of my ill luck. With the dead man's cutlass about my waist and McCary's pistol in my belt (a poor place for a dry priming, as I was still reeking with wet), I went again into the cabin, and with an apology to the doctor for leaving him in the dark, took the lantern from its hook on the beam and hurried to where the wreck of the top hamper still covered the deck about the foremast. Though the light was seen from the Sprite, it would create no suspicion; so, seizing the lantern to a hoop in the mast, I attacked the mass of broken

spar, gear, and canvas, that I might verify or prove
groundless the more than half hope which had come
to me while I hung beneath the wreck of the dingy.
Then the hope was but a flimsy tissue; now it was tinged
with fear. If the girl had not been struck down by a
falling spar and hidden by the folds of the square sail,
then she must have been translated, for of her deliberate
self-destruction I would not now believe.

There was a desperate thumping on the forecastle
hatch by the imprisoned trio, but I paid no attention to
it, and indeed I was so engrossed in my present business that nothing short of the splintering of the cover
or the arrival on a belated errand of a boat from the
Sprite, would have caused me to desist.

The first I uncovered was what I thought to be a
pair of booted legs, but they proved to be no more than
my own foot gear which I had stowed near the mast
the night before, for since boarding the Phantom in
the fog I had gone unshod. The wreck had been thrown
into a fairly compact mass by the side of the hatch,
and it was perhaps five minutes before I had gotten
to the bottom of it. But I was well rewarded. Ere I
had cast aside the last of the fallen hamper I heard a
slight groan, and, on pulling away a mixture of torn
sail and tangled line, I saw the object of my search.

My conjecture had been right. The girl was lying
betwixt the combings of the galley and the butt of the
splintered topmast, a position allowing her enough air
to prevent suffocation, at the same time partly protecting her from the weight of the stuff piled over her.
She lay on her face, and across her thighs, pinning her
fast, was a small end of the broken topsail yard. Her
cheek and neck, with the hand that lay along the spar,
were covered with blood, and blood stained the planking of the deck about her.

I lost no time in feeling for life, as the groan had

told me life still existed. Cutting the lantern from the hoop, I slung it on my arm and, lifting the girl, strode toward the cabin, now in the strangest state of mind that had ever possessed me. If I moved quickly with my body, my brain outpaced it. As I look back at it, the passage from the foremast to the companion way was a long one, though it was compassed in twice ten steps. In the time it took me to traverse it I lived over the five days I had known this lass, and felt them to have been as many years. I suddenly knew the source of my daring, which had grown with the time until at that moment I was ready to face the devil himself, and knew, too, for whom it was meant. I now knew that my head had not been playing over the mystery of her disappearance because it was mystery, but because this girl had usurped all other interests. I was now aware that my resolve to board the schooner was not so much to recapture the prize (though that motive, hopeless as it had seemed, had been strong) as to overhaul the wreck of the foretopmast in quest of Gertrude King, and see her again dead or alive. I gave no name to all this; I raised no fine points anent the strength or weakness of my feeling, nor did the word "love" cross my mind. I only knew that alive I had found her, and that one day she might know I had saved her from both death and her enemies. In a purblind fashion it was all the reward I looked for, and it seemed reward enough.

If I was not fairly subdued by the beauty and heroism of this girl, my pity for her carried me far on the way, and though burly, sea-roughened, and a man to boot, in this case of need I felt that for tenderness I could pit myself against the gentlest woman who ever made a sick-bed a dream of pleasure.

Beyond getting at the extent of her injuries, I determined not to let the now sobered surgeon lift a finger. When I brought my burden down the companion way he was placing a wet compress on the boy's wound, his management of this in the darkness speaking loudly of his skill. My prisoner was evidently past being surprised, for he did little but give a grunt as he saw me bear her in; but when I told him the new patient was a girl, and the sister of Ames, he cast on me a quick, hard look. It was only after I mentioned her name and he remembered the former passenger of the Sprite that he showed real interest, and as he examined her for injuries I heard him grumble the name of Scammell beneath his breath.

Pending the outcome of his search I went on deck. Although a nearly full moon was behind the clouds, the night was unusually dark. The roll of the schooner was growing heavier. It caused a rattling of blocks overhead, and a jerking of the foresail boom on its traveler until it sounded as though the deck must be ripped up. There was a sullenness to the sea that boded mischief, but the cause of it was still at a distance. Betwixt the clashing of blocks aloft, the kicking of the rudder, the mad clank of the boom travelers and the excited tattoo of the reefing points, there was sufficient fuss to at once tell a seaman that the present condition of calm would not be protracted. The look of the sky was enough for me (for beyond the immediate vicinity of the moon a pot of tar could not have been blacker), and in the momentary intervals of partial silence that ensued as the schooner balanced on the tops of the surges I thought I could hear a faint moan far above the truck, as though an unseen and troubled spirit was winging through the depths of space aloft. The horizon had drawn close to the vessel, and the repelling blackness of the water sent a chill through me as I considered what might have been my plight had the schooner sailed, leaving me on the broad ocean with no support but the frail shell of the dingy. A sudden coldness had settled from above, though not a breath of wind had come with it, and, though there was nothing to be distinctly marked through the heavy gloom enveloping the schooner, there existed in the surrounding elements a menacing something which, like an invisible monitor, sent to me an inarticulate warning.

The change had been rapid. Plainly enough I scented the vague threat of the weather and set about to meet the outbreak. Minding me that I was both captain and crew, with the extra weight of having on my hands three prisoners in the forecastle and a shaky one in the cabin, I saw that if it came on to blow I had more than sufficient work cut out for one pair of fists. Determined then to take time by the forelock and be safe in all weathers, I let go the foresail halyards and quietly lowered that canvas, putting it in stops only that it might not blow out, but, as for the furl, 'twould have made a landlubber laugh to see the bulge of the bunt. The shot from the Sprite had reduced the head cloths to jib and staysail, and yet so impressed was I that we were face to face with impending disaster that I lowered and, after a fashion, stowed the jib.

The more I worked the more I felt the necessity, and, though I was on fire to return to the cabin, I held away and turned my attention to the great mainsail which was hurtling to and fro, the subdued thunder of its thrashing bunt and quick patter of its reefing points playing out of the mysterious darkness overhead like the sounds of a distant storm. Alone I double reefed that canvas, though I remember very little of it, the only thing coming to my mind being the horrible smooth inkiness of the water beneath me when I crawled out on the boom to pass the ear-ring and haul taut. Though my hands worked on deck, my heart was below, and it was with a deep breath of satisfaction that I saw the last of more than an hour's hard labor. Casting off the main sheet, that I might not be taken unaware, I gave a glance at the light on the Sprite still lying on our quarter, and then went below, filled with a mixture of hope and dread.

McCary was sitting by the side of the girl as I entered. He looked up before I was fairly off the steps, and said in a surly voice:

" Ye had best be no niggard with the whisky; pass it out! "

" What do you find? " I asked.

" Shock," he answered shortly.

" And naught else? "

" Be not so d—n quick," he replied. " There may be enough else inside, I know not. Outside there's a nasty bit of a blow on the nob and a fractured clavicle. There's the shock to nurse, but if all's well within she'll mend in a few days. It was a narrow escape she has had! How came she here? "

" 'Tis a long story, and one with mighty little to flatter your side of the fight, my friend," I answered. " Let that pass. If you can save both these children, and will settle down ashore and swear by Congress, I'll see that your fortune's made as a doctor. You will be a rare hand! "

" I'll see ye and yer Congress d——d first! " he returned with an ugly scowl. " What I lay hand on, be it rebel or loyal, I do me best with. I'll do it here. I have little against the like of Gertrude King. She is a true lass."

" That's well," I answered as I went to the locker for the whisky. " But Gertrude is flying like myself from Clinton; her loyalty is to her country, and not, as you think, to George III. The title of ' rebel ' is one to be proud of." And with this I handed him the bottle which he took with a dogged air, pouring therefrom a dram which would have been more than respectable for a man. I watched him closely as he put it to the girl's lips. He held it there until a small quantity had disappeared, then, as though no longer able to restrain himself, he lifted the remainder to his own and drank it in a single gulp.

I was about to jump on him, when down the open companion way there came a faint wailing followed by a roar that grew into a shriek appalling in its intensity. It was the first howl of the great tempest of '78, and, turning, I made for the companion. Ere I was halfway to the deck we were laid over to larboard in a manner that for a moment prevented my further progress. A mighty gush of damp wind struck my face as I hung on to the rail, and before I could grip my way hand over hand up the ladder the schooner righted and hung on an even keel, trembling like a suddenly affrighted animal.

In an instant I was at the wheel. As quickly as the squall came it passed, but I knew the weight that must be behind it. Well it was that I had reduced sail and let go the sheet, for in such a sudden blast we would have been thrown so low that the cargo would have shifted and the end come in the twinkling of an eye.

As near as I could guess the first rush of air had been from out the southeast, but the whole gale that followed struck us fairly on the bow, and, in spite of my jamming the helm hard over, I think for a space the schooner made direct sternway. Without a sail drawing, the din of the thrashing canvas drowned all other noises, and in this fashion we hung in irons until it appeared that the mainmast would be shaken out of the vessel. I could not man the wheel and staysail sheet together, and the former I dared not leave; but the wind settled my dilemma, for after a time, and when I was getting desperate, it whipped a point to larboard, and in the half glimmer that now came from the sea, which looked like a dish of froth, I saw the foot of the stay-sail streaming over the starboard bow.

How I lashed the wheel with the helm up and got forward, I hardly know. I remember it was like dragging against a stone wall to get the sheet halfway in, but I did it, and ran back again before we were fairly paid off. Now I lashed the helm down and put my weight on the main sheet, but 'twas past my power to move it a foot. As I had no wish to lose time by running toward South America, I bawled to the doctor to come up. He did so in a hurry, but demurred when I told him to lay hold of the line and haul. The sudden tongue lashing I gave him and a sight of my face in the light which poured from the cabin made him think better of his manner, for he gripped the sheet and fell back with it like a born sailor. It was an almighty tug at best, but grew easier as we hauled into the wind, and when the line was belayed I commanded him to take the wheel while I sheeted home the staysail.

The veriest duffer can not follow the sea for year in and out without learning something of the handling of ships, and, though McCary had probably never laid hand on a spoke from necessity, he may have done so for pleasure, as he seemed to know how to hold the Phantom somewhere near the wind's eye. There was no difficulty, then, in getting a proper trim to the head cloth, and by the time the sheet was belayed and we stood off on the starboard tack the schooner was well under way, her bows smiting the seas, which had risen like magic, in a way that threw a curtain of solid water into the air, which, catching the wind, blew in and came aboard a deluge. I was wet to the skin before, but it was a dry wet as compared to the way the water shot through my clothing, the drops stinging my face like a discharge of small shot. Even under scant canvas and pointing as close as the schooner would go, she lay down to the blast until at times the brine gurgled in the lee scuppers. The channels sheared through the black

15

seas and turned up a smother of froth as they tore along,
while the noise of the roaring wind and water was
enough to deafen one.

Knowing that all now unsafe must be left unsafe, I
turned to get aft, when I bethought me of the men in
the forecastle. During the past hour they had not entered my mind, for I had felt that I had them secure.
With the light they possessed, together with the rations
I knew had been supplied them, they were better off regarding comfort than though they had been free seamen
on duty. Other matters had taken my attention, but
now that I was forward I would give a look to the hatch
fastening. It was right enough, and I laid my ear over
the crack below the slide that I might hear if aught was
amiss. Ay, there was. A clear sound of rasping and
splintering wood greeted me as I stopped the other ear
with my hand to keep out the surrounding racket, and
I had hit the spot on which a knife was at work.

Drawing my cutlass, with its hilt I smote the woodwork. The sound instantly ceased. Unfastening the
slide, I drew it back an inch or more and sang out
through the opening:

" Keep at it, my lads, and when ye have the hole the
size of a pistol's barrel, I'll put one there and give ye a
quick trip to Davy Jones. Mayhap ye have heard of
Donald Thorndyke. Well, I am he. Now mind yourselves! "

'Twould have been a fine chance for them to have
put a ball in me had they foreseen my coming, but they
seemed in no mood to act offensively, only standing
under the flare of the swinging lamp and gazing through
a mist of soot toward the spot whence came my voice.
One had a knife in his hand, and all three were stripped
to the skin, for the heat in the forecastle was no joke,
especially with the hatch closed and an oil lamp, which
they dared not put out, filling the close quarters about

the schooner's eyes with a rank and greasy smother. I changed my ideas regarding their comfort, but in my present situation all the pity in my nature was either hibernating, had gone to the girl in the cabin, or was waiting a fairer chance to blossom. I certainly felt none for them.

With another dire threat I again closed the hatch, fastened it, and betook myself to where the doctor hung on to the wheel, which had almost mastered him in his endeavor to keep the vessel off the wind. Grasping the spokes, I motioned him below. He hesitated a moment, glancing forward and astern as though in quest of some sign of the Sprite, then crawled back to the cabin, closing the doors behind him, a thing I was glad enough for his doing, as the light below dazzled my sight.

And now I settled myself for a night of it, putting aside all matters save the ship's safety. I was lucky to have a doctor in the cabin to care for my sick; as for myself I needed none. So long as I was holding east, I cared little for the blow if nothing carried away. I had hopes that the suddenness of the storm bespoke its shortness, but never did I dream it was affecting my destiny. Beyond the elements I had now little to fear, and, as I knew my own boat as a mother knows her child, felt there was but small danger of her inability to weather the gale.

But the tempest was not of usual temper. Its approach, its violence, and duration were beyond common rules, and had it held aloof but a day longer it would have doubtless altered the history of the colonies, and perhaps have put a period to my own career. One has but to turn to history for the truth of this. The great storm which suddenly sprang on the coast the night of August 11, 1778, and which lasted for more than three days, was of such a nature that it has been set apart by historians as worthy of especial mention, both from its results and its more than fiendish force.

As I have said, the absence of the bulk of Lord Howe's fleet had enabled the Phantom to drift through the fog and from the bay in comparative safety, and this absence was due to an attack planned against the French who were besieging Newport by water, as the patriots under Sullivan were doing by land. The British general Pigot was in desperate straits when Howe appeared off Point Judith, and, had the English admiral been possessed of the sluggish and procrastinating nature of his brother (lately commander of the British land forces in America), he would probably have been a day or two later, and Pigot would have followed the example of Burgoyne at Saratoga and laid down his arms. As it was, Howe arrived in the nick of time, and the French sailed out of the harbor to fight him. The English took to the ocean for sea room in which to maneuver, but from all I could ever gather, each was mortally afraid of the other. The French followed. For two days they played about, either seeking to get the weather gauge of his opponent before opening hostilities. Here at last there must have been fought a battle which might (and probably would) have altered the complexion of the war; but the storm stepped in, and, after damaging and partly wrecking both fleets, drove them asunder. Howe returned to New York to refit, and D'Estaing gathered his scattered ships and sailed back to Newport. What my fate would have been had the tempest held off leaves little to guess, as, had my hoped-for programme been carried forward, I would have run into a network from which there could have been no escape.

By the same storm which had prevented a conflict on the sea the patriot force on land had suffered well-nigh as severely as the fleets. What with ruined ammunition, destroyed stores and demolished shelter, the ferocity of the hurricane even causing several deaths, Sullivan's army was in a forlorn and desperate state, and, though in no condition to make an assault, the gallant commander furthered preparations to that end. Knowing, however, the ticklish temper of our allies, the attack was postponed until the French should return, an event which occurred on the 19th of August. Mighty was the joy of the patriots as D'Estaing sailed up the bay, but the joy was short-lived, for, giving his damaged ships as an excuse, he refused to remain at Newport, and, turning away, sailed for Boston for repairs, leaving Sullivan with a discouraged and rapidly dissolving army close to the strengthened lines of the British.

CHAPTER XXIII.

IN THE HEART OF THE STORM.

But, barring the storm, of these matters I knew nothing then nor for some time after their occurrence. Now I stood and strained at the wheel, squeezing the vessel into the wind as close as she would go, having an unreasonable objection to making the least southing in the course. And yet I was uncertain as to the exact point to which I was steering, possessing no compass save the telltale which was set into the cabin ceiling and out of reach of my eye. If I escaped the pitiless and treacherous sands of the coast of Long Island I would be well content, and by holding to the present tack I had little fear of disaster from that quarter.

I figured that we had made half the length of Long Island up to the time we had been overhauled and the calm set in, and that in a wind for the most part light. If this was so, at the rate which we were now going I hoped to enter Vineyard Sound by noon on the morrow, barring disaster, and twenty-four hours from the present would see me at my own hearthstone. The thought of it warmed me, and great was my need of warmth of some kind, for I was as empty as a drum, fagged by excitement and lack of sleep, and had not known comfort for so long that my memory of it was misty.

But by midnight even the fleeting comfort of thinking was gone, and soon after in feeling I was little better than a block of stone. That which I had gone through might not be reckoned by time alone; it seemed the experience of years. In my half-dazed state I felt that I had been an outlaw for years; for years I had been fleeing and each day fenced with death; for years known and protected the girl and her brother; and for years, it appeared, must I stand and face this howling wind which bore against me like a living thing.

Thank God it was not bitter weather, else I would have frozen stiff as I stood at the helm. As it was, so tortured had I become that I grew rigid under the mental and physical strain—rigid in either quality, and guided the schooner by instinct alone. Hours ago the light on the Sprite had vanished, and now to me the sky, the ocean, the crash of the boarding seas and the shriek of the gale was but a monotone of color and sound, giving me no lightness of hope, no qualm of fear. With the strength of an ox my muscles did their duty and saved me, but there was little brain back of the power. What the end would have been had the conditions remained unchanged there can be no telling.

The tempest, which had come in the teeth of a smiling day, was marked as well by capriciousness as by violence. As the ghastliness of early dawn broke in the east, and I gradually awoke to the fact that morning was at hand, the wind fell as though chopped off or as if we had suddenly shot into the lee of a vast wall. In a half-senseless fashion, like a man under a drug, I tried with fruitless efforts to shake off the feeling of utter carelessness which had fastened to my senses. With the calmness of absolute indifference I marked the sudden dropping of the wind, though I knew full well that it portended an increase of the gale, but when, for how long, from what quarter or with what force, the Almighty alone knew; as for me, I cared not if it blew the vessel out of water. With the same dull indifference I marked our new danger and every detail attending it. With the sudden calm we were at the mercy of the long, green, foam-capped billows which charged toward us like moving hills. They came not, like rollers, with the regular swing of the ground swell, but every surge was the head waters of a mighty dam broken loose, its crest made up of a mad, throbbing mass of liquid torn into shreds and cross seas by its own weight and violent motion. The face of the world was a vast tumult of yeasty, ash-colored madness cut by the darkness of its hollows; a terror (if I could have felt it), not a horror; more sublime than grand, more awful than sublime.

In five minutes we were in the trough of it. Without a zephyr to steady her, the schooner wallowed like a crazy thing. The roll, the sidelong heave and lurch, the jerking pitch and recovery were terrible tests to the stanchness of the vessel. Alternately the bow and stern rose to a dizzy altitude, then sank with a rapidity that even to my trained nature, was sickening. Each joint and block found a voice which complained in notes ranging from a bang to a squeak, of its unnatural treatment. Alow and aloft the poor Phantom protested, and, as I looked calmly on, I knew that if the conditions continued she would end in rolling her masts out, leaving us to finally founder, a sheer hulk. The maintopmast swayed like a whip, cutting through the arc of its motion with amazing swiftness. The diminished sail beneath it, with its spars slashing hither and thither, shook out a report like a cannon, and threatened to burst as its slack bunt drove from side to side. Everything loose or insecure fetched away and wandered at random about the decks. The lumps of lead I had brought up the night before rolled betwixt the hatch combing and bulwark, banging the latter with blows that threatened to drive out the planking, and would have done so had I not gripped my way to them and thrown them overboard. The scuttle-butt sprang from its skids and came aft with a bound, halting and spinning like a top when in the waist, then dashed to larboard only to be stopped by a sidelong lift of the stern which shot it into the bows where it hung fast, bung up, jammed betwixt the flukes of the spare anchor and the bulwark stanchcon.

I noted these things with an eye more interested in the antics of the barrel than in aught else. Its speed and agility were wondrous, and I thought more of its fearful force and erratic movements than of the general straits in which the schooner was now held. Through it all I felt my impotent numbness, and it was with the mere animal instinct of getting food for a craving stomach that I wearily moved to go below.

Stiff, sore, and dispirited enough I was as I staggered toward the companion way and entered the cabin. The first sight of its interior was enough to break one's heart, and that fact probably did much to pull me together. The surgeon, the cowardly, besotted wretch, lay drunk on the floor, and also on the floor was Gertrude King, dead, I thought for an instant, but soon found she was not only alive but conscious. Having been thrown from her bunk, she had crawled over to her brother to prevent a like disaster to him, and now lay or leaned against his transom, powerless alike to help him or herself. She was almost dead from sea-sickness and pain, yet when she saw me, the fright that came into her eyes reminded me of Lounsbury's last look. It was plain that McCary had but given her a dram to revive her, and when this had been accomplished, without going further or vouchsafing an explanation of the day's later events, started in to finish the drunk I had so suddenly interrupted. The fever for rum was upon him, his manhood and morals having been consumed along with the liquor.

Notwithstanding the suffering his actions had en-

tailed, I could almost have thanked him for being the
cause of putting into me a sense of real existence, for
there was a slight awakening from the heavy lethargy
that held me as I stooped to the poor girl and lifted
her in my arms as though she was a child to be comforted. The instinctive shrinking she had shown when
I reached for her gave way to a moan and the limpness
of total abandonment as she felt the strength of my arm
about her. As I laid her on the transom by the side
of her brother, whose eyes were shut and whose height-
ened color now betokened fever, she placed her un-
wounded hand against my check as if to make sure of
my being mortal, and faltered out:

"I thought you dead! O Donald! Donald! I thought
you dead!"

In the mere sound of a human voice there was something that stirred me to a livelier sense of myself and
surroundings. But her words did more than this. Of
themselves, as I set them here in cold black and white,
they hold no significance, but as I heard them there
was something which caused the waning spark within
me to burst into flame and shoot through the dullness
of my exhausted body and overtaxed brain. The touch
of the smooth hand, the look, and the simple tones of
this ill-used, wounded, and bedraggled girl were beyond
misinterpretation to me, when to others it might have
been but a trifle more than commonplace. Like a shock
the attending danger of our situation rushed upon me,
and again I realized my responsibility; a feeling that
had been dead for hours, and which was now resur-
rected by the light that burst upon me at the girl's
words.

She was a pitiful object as she lay prone at her
brother's side. Her left arm was powerless, and the
blood from her wounded head still stained her face,
neck, and hand. The flow had ceased, but through her

bright hair I could see the location of the gash. I was no surgeon to dress either the cut or fracture, and, as for the sake of all, my own necessities were paramount, I would lose no time in experiment without more warrant.

My own necessities, forsooth, and for the sake of all! I lost no honesty through dreaming of heroism. If my finer sensibilities had awakened, so had my coarser, and I knew I was now working for a purpose, the roots of which lay in selfishness, but of a stripe easily forgiven.

As I put the maiden down she closed her eyes, and either fainted or slept from exhaustion, and I, like a famished wolf, groped about the floor for the food which had been tipped from the table, holding her onto the transom the while with one hand, and with the other drawing together the fragments of the but half-eaten meal.

'Twould have been a moving sight to an onlooker could one have peeped into the cabin at this time. The wounded brother and sister, abject in their misery, even the ocean allowing itself no rest in its efforts to throw them from where they lay; the lengthy bulk of the drunkard sprawling half under the table, his body swaying with the leap of the vessel, and about the floor a mixture of broken food, the bag of gold and empty bottles which ran hither and thither with the acute and ever-changing angle of the deck, all seemingly chased by the overturned bucket which had stood by the side of Ames.

The light of the low-burning lantern swinging madly from its hook in the beam gave a melancholy effect in contrast to the pale dawn now gleaming white and cold through the windows, and in this muss, to the accompaniment of the groaning woodwork, was I half on my knees cramming my mouth with bits of hard bread and such matter as came rolling within reach.

I ate like a man in despair, and yet with a hunger which gave a sweet taste to each morsel, unsavory as I commonly would have thought it. As I snatched and swallowed, now possessed by the fear that the gale might rise again while I was below, I marked the unholy aspect of the surgeon. He did not present the disgusting appearance of Scammell, but beggarly enough he looked—a rum-sodden brute, outshining his surroundings in the glory of his scarlet uniform. I held a firm hatred for him as he lay there, feeling that half my present trouble was due to his infernal weakness or deliberate carelessness. Had matters gone well below, I might have made a shift to keep to the deck and yet have food and drink supplied me, but now the whole business was on me, and my wounded were without proper care. I wondered how it could have come about that such an accomplished swiller of liquor had found it possible to have gotten dead drunk on the short allowance of whisky left in the bottle I had given him, but I soon gave over thinking of it. The question to be settled was how I could leave Ames and his sister, but it was soon solved. Letting them take their chances for a moment, I seized the snoring redcoat by the collar and hauled him up the companion way, he making the third drunkard I had pitched from the cabin in this fashion. As I dropped him with small ceremony there came a sound as though he had struck the deck with a muffled club. This made me suspicious of still concealed arms, but, on turning him over, I found the cause and supply for his latest debauch. In the skirts of his coat were two bottles like that I had taken from him, one full, the other two thirds empty. It was a Godsend, and then and there I took such a dram that ere long the contents of my veins were less akin to the ice water they had seemed to be holding.

Going back to the cabin, I hauled the larboard bunk

mattress to the floor and laid the girl upon it. Close
to her I laid Ames, lifting bed and all, and thus both
were beyond danger of a bad fall, however the vessel
might ramp. The lad opened his eyes as I placed him
by his yet unconscious sister, but I bade him not speak,
and tried to hearten him by telling him I was yet master, that Gertrude was by his side, hurt, but not badly,
and that we would, by the help of God, be safe ashore
ere sunset. He smiled faintly, and made as if to nod,
by which I guessed he was already aware of his sister's
presence. I knew that whisky was no medicine for his
complaint, but I managed to get a dram down the throat
of the girl, whereat she soon opened her eyes and came
to life with another moan.

Though I wished to linger by her, I dared not; there
was much to do—too much for one mortal. It was the
work of a moment to clear the floor of the bounding
missiles and heave them above (all but the gold, which
I threw into an empty bunk), and I followed after for
a brief look about.

Since I had taken the whisky my energy had come
back full fledged and in fighting mood, as though the
numbness of the past few hours had been a waking
slumber from which I had just recovered. The broad-
ening day put hope in me, though clearly and with a
quick sensitiveness I marked the anger of the sea, the
sinister scowl on the face of Nature, and the wild disorder reigning aboard the Phantom from her bowsprit's
end to her remaining truck. Bestowing a glance on the
drunkard, who lay on the wet planking not a whit less
comfortably than on the carpet of the cabin floor, I
gave my attention to the shrouds, finding as yet nothing
had let go or sprung. I then carried aft the main throat
and peak halyards, that they might act the part of a
back-stay and give some relief to the standing rigging.
I was engaged in making fast the lines when there

passed beneath us a wave of extraordinary height and sharpness. It was a cross sea, and it well-nigh tripped the schooner, which term betokens a capsize from lack of supporting surface beneath a vessel's bilge. With a twisting lift it bore the stern so high in the air that the deck slanted like the sides of a steeple, forcing me to drop the halyards and cling to the rail to prevent falling into the bow. For an instant I thought of a surety we would plunge sidelong below the following sea, pierce it, and be swamped inside the tenth stroke of my pulse; but the send of the water flung us partly out of the trough, and as it passed lifted the bow to a terrible incline, and, giving us an extra vicious lurch, left us almost stern on to the run of the billows. Had it broken as it reached us, the tons upon tons of water which would have fallen on our deck must have driven the schooner beneath the surface as though she was no more buoyant than the lead in her hold. It was a wonderful view I had of the ocean from the height of the mighty comber. The sharpness of its ridge foretold the coming cascade, and, though it drove us down on our beam's ends and made the schooner groan like a suffering mortal as she recovered, it was not evil in its effects on me or mine.

Two things on deck there were which seemed to catch the infection of motion, one being the surgeon, who was shot into the scuppers with a violence which did something to sober him, for, like a man waking from a deep sleep, he threw out an arm and began rubbing his eyes, muttering words that might have been a protest at his rough usage. The other was the runaway scuttle-butt which had been captured by the flukes of the spare anchor. As the stern of the Phantom sank to the hollow and the bow pointed higher than it had ever been my lot to see it, the barrel, like a wild thing waiting its chance, dropped from the position in which it had been held and with a rush tore aft like a spent cannon ball. At the break of the poop it was met by the lifting stern, and, retracing its course, drove against the door of the forecastle hatch with a force that split the panel from top to bottom. As a ball it sprang from the impact, spinning on its chines for an instant, the water flying in a circular shower from its now open bung, then hurrying to larboard amidships, it reached well aft in time to be caught by the mounting stern. With a wonderful agility and seemingly with the instinct of one mad to escape environment, even if it ended in self-destruction, it jerked itself on end as though to look about, tottering and falling again on its side with the lift of the bow. For a brief space it hung seesawing and gurgling thickly as though choking, then it shot forward with the fury of a bolt. Nothing intervened to check its course, and, as though it had wings, it ran up the mass of rope and wreck which had now become jammed near the heel of the bowsprit, leaped into the air, cleared the low bulwark, and plunged, shrouded in its own spray, into the frothing sea below.

I would sooner have fought the three prisoners than been forward in the path of that insensate thing, and, though I was aware that our available stock of fresh water went with it, I was glad to see it spring off the deck.

CHAPTER XXIV.

A SMALL TRAGEDY.

THE scuttle-butt had barely disappeared, and I was about to get back to the cabin to see how had fared its inmates, when my ears were assailed by a violent hammering forward, and I at once perceived that my prisoners had assaulted the weakened panel of the forecastle door. With my blood well up, I got myself hand over hand along the bulwark, and by a leap from the cathead came to the hatch and boldly threw back the slide. The three were jammed on the ladder at work together, but the suddenness of my move caused them such a surprise that they tumbled from the perch as though struck. The lamp was out, and from the black hole came a hot and reeking smell that was suffocating.

"What's amiss there?" I roared, hanging on to the hatch with one hand and with the other showing the barrel of my pistol.

They scrambled to their feet and looked up, little but their white flesh showing in the wan light entering the half-open hatch. The sailor with the pigtail whom I had pitched below was a trifle in advance of the others, and, stepping a pace forward, he shouted back:

"Wot's amiss? Everything's amiss! Wot kind o' treatment is this to give a man? Split me! but I'd rather go overboard and stifle in a jiffy than smother by inches. Wot's amiss above, man? Who be you? Where's the cap'n?"

"Never mind me!" I answered. "'Tis enough that I am master here, Lounsbury being some two leagues back. Pass up your arms! You are prisoners to the colonies, and the first finger that lifts in fight belongs to a dead man! Pass up what you have below there!"

"Prisoners, is it?" said he of the pigtail, turning to his fellows. "Heard ye a sign o' the gang that boarded us? Cuss me, mates, but they must ha' come on wings then, for the sea was as smooth as a pan o' warm grease two minutes afore I was hurled on to ye, an' not a speck in sight, barrin' the Sprite! Prisoners, is it? Cuss me, list to that!"

"Ay, prisoners it is, and to the colonies; so no more palaver. What have you below?"

"I care not a damn for colonies or King!" was the reply. "There be no arms here. D'ye think three men were sent hither to beat off a boarding party, an' the schooner in consort? D'ye take us for sea-loafing marines? We be sailors, we be—that's all. Here's wot I have, an' I'll trade it for air!" Saying this, he pulled his knife from its sheath, and, taking the steel by its point, held it toward me.

"Will you swear to no other arms, each of you?" I cried.

"Ay, that's God's truth!" spoke up one of the others. "Ye say ye are of the colonies—well, so be I. I'm a New Bedford lad, sir, an' I'll thank ye to hold a grip on me that I may not be taken from ye."

"An' that's God's truth, too, yer Honor!" broke in the first speaker. "There was naught vicious in the rumpus we was raisin'. A man has a right to air, an' 'twas all we was cravin'. So be I'm a prisoner, I'm content if it means grub an' water an' a chance to breathe!"

Now I know little of the nature of the black sailor save that his anger is apt to show in treachery, but with

16

the regular white salt I am better acquainted, and have
found that the English seaman, be he Yankee or Briton,
argues his point with a square fist and a flashing eye.
Though there may be wars and wars with the mother
country, it will be open and without back-stabbing by
those of the Saxon race, and, believing this, I thought
I saw a way of scoring a point, and that with little danger to myself. The truth of the statement that they
were unarmed appealed to my reason. For defense three
men armed or not would have cut no figure, and, as the
Sprite had intended to act as consort, the necessity of
force on the Phantom had not been considered. Being
satisfied that my prisoners possessed no weapons other
than the sailor's universal knife, and holding that a bold
face will carry a man further than a too open show of
caution, I flung back the door and, grasping the slide,
hung over the hatch opening and dropped into the forecastle.

"Now," said I, as I gathered myself and clung to
the woodwork, "if you mean fair by me we'll soon come
to terms; if foul, take the last chance you'll have to
settle! Who comes first, or come you all?"

"Look a' here, mister," said the spokesman, who
scarce shifted his position as I dropped near him, "I
spoke ye fair, an' had I boarded ye alongside I would
be fast enough in the fight, mind ye, an' 'twould be
along o' the leftenant's eye on me. But as it be, I care
not for blood. If I fight, 'tis from bein' forced to it.
I was shanghied into this business, an' that's the truth;
an' if I can get out without stakin' my neck as a de-
sarter, I'm willin' enough. Ye say we be prisoners?
Say no more. Do ye drive us to work for rations? Why
so be. We knew naught about bein' tooken captive, an'
only wanted to speak ye fair an' get a breath. That's
why we carved the hatch.—Ain't that so, mates?"

"Ay, that's gospel!" came from the one who had

spoken of himself as a Yankee, while the third held
his peace, leaning with folded arms and a skillful bal-
ancing of his person against one of the bunk uprights.

"You say you are a New Bedford lad?" said I,
speaking to the man who had made the statement.

"Yes, sir; New Bedford, sir," came his ready answer. "I was pressed in Portsmouth three years agone,
sir, while on shore leave from the Sallie Mull, trader,
sir. I've been sailin' in these here home waters for nigh
on two year, sir, with never a chance to run. I say it
boldly, sir. Put me in three miles o' the coast an' give
me leave, sir, an' I'll go over the bow, damn me, an' swim
ashore. But I won't join the Yankee navy, sir. No, sir.
I don't want to hang; but, for God's sake, sir, don't get
taken, else back to the Sprite I'll have to go, an' I'd as
soon go to hell for a spell o' sufferin'!"

I looked sharply at the third man, expecting some
word from him, but he shifted his eye from mine, giving me something like a sneer and shrugging his bony
shoulders, but vouchsafing nothing in the way of words.
He was a dogged-looking rascal, with a broad, red scar
across nose and cheek, a sabre slash without doubt.
Rawboned and light of weight, he looked like a sleeping
cat as he lolled against the upright, his lack of brute
strength probably balanced by great activity.

"Come, lads!" said I, ignoring the attitude of the
silent man, "I'll be frank with you. I'm Donald Thorndyke, of the American forces. The schooner was taken
by me single-handed, and the Sprite is beyond all bearings. Lounsbury is overboard, there are two sick in the
cabin, and the surgeon is at my mercy. So are you if
you abide not by the terms I offer. The schooner is
in danger, and unless you turn out 'tis like you'll find
the forecastle a coffin. If I make no mistake, we're in
for a waft that will come nigh to blowing us out of water
if we don't roll our spars out before. Get on deck and

work the schooner under my command until we make
Holmes Hole in the Vineyard, an' when you set foot
ashore you are free men. I have no rations and no
water. The scuttle-butt has launched itself overboard,
and I am afraid of the supply in the forehold. There's
not a shilling in it for any of you, but 'tis a fair way of
escaping the King's navy without deserting, for I'll put
you on parole. I tell you, lads, I'm a bad one to foul,
but you'll find I have an easy helm and never miss stays
if handled honestly. Now choose betwixt this hole and
the deck, and choose in a hurry! If you are to save neck
and freedom, throw down your knives as a sign; I've
no more time to waste."

The two who had spoken looked askant each at the
other, and the knife of the original spokesman fell to
the deck. As the hand of the Yankee sought the sheath
the third man spoke, unfolding his arms and scowling
like thunder as he gave vent to his words.

" Ye two be domned fools to be trustin' a rebel an'
runnin' yez head into th' noose. Be yez a couple o'
babbys not to mark his firearm is useless wi' th' wet?
'Ee's in our 'ands! Wot's to 'inder our takin' the craft
an' gettin' th' price that lies on the 'ead of this 'ere——"

He got no further. I strode up to him and snapped
my fingers in his face, then, thrusting my eyes close to
his, I thundered:

" On deck with ye, ye blatherskite! I'll see that ye
sing a tune with old iron in it ere sunrise to-morrow!
On deck, I tell ye! "

Notwithstanding the din already existing in the
forecastle, my voice rose far above it, its violence and
the suddenness of my move making the man shrink back
as though frightened. But he was not cowed. Gathering himself, he uttered a curse and sprang past me, placing himself 'twixt me and the ladder; then whipping out
his knife, he called aloud to his companions:

"Take th' chance, lads, while yet we 'ave 'im! 'Twill be th' makin' o' us, an' 'tis fifty puns to each! Stand by, bullies! we'll make meat o' th' cussed spy!—Up, Larry, an' close the 'atch on 'im! I'll 'old the gangway."

His action and outspoken hostility was so sudden as to take me by surprise, and, had the others responded to his call, it would surely have gone hard with me. But instead of springing to the succor of their mate, they remained standing as though the quick shifting of the situation had for the moment dazed them. The earnestness of the fellow's purpose showed in the rapid change that came over his face. From a sulky expression it had altered to one of wide-awake ferocity, and the listless droop of arms and shoulders given place to tense muscles and rounded chest, through the hairiness of which the perspiration stood out in beads.

Even with this menace before me I could but think what a simple fool the man was. Instead of quietly following my lead and getting me at a disadvantage, he had chosen to beard me against the odds of my cutlass and the lukewarmness of his mates. At the same time, it was no case for argument, nor would it do to temporize an instant. Ere the promise of reward for my capture or the easy chance to regain control of the schooner could act upon the slowly moving minds of the well-disposed seamen, I had nipped the mutiny (if it could be so called), and had the ringleader begging for mercy.

Without drawing my cutlass, I advanced upon the fellow as though to close with him. I mind me now that he was left-handed, and, as the fist holding the knife swayed aloft and came down, I seized its wrist and with a violent turn whipped his elbow out of joint as one twists the leg from a well-cooked fowl. As my hand stayed his he clutched my throat with his right, but as his joint parted he gave a howl of agony, dropped the knife and my collar at once, and sank to his knees roaring like a bull.

Physically the man had been no match for me, and I might have hammered the life from him and met with little opposition or resistance. Holding him for a brief space, that my power might impress his companions as well as himself, I dropped him, and he sank to the deck with a moan that made me almost regret my act.

But the demands of war, self-preservation, pride, and the safety of others leave little latitude for the sentiment of pity in time of action. Had I in anger alone disjointed the groaning man my conscience (which, thank God, has never been seared into inactivity) might have upbraided me, but now I felt no great pang of remorse as I sprang up the ladder, calling the two to follow.

If the plucky resistance of the disabled seaman had impressed the others, such impression seemed to have disappeared as they came with me into the air above. Like owls suddenly brought into sunshine, they blinked in the now broadened light, and, hanging on to the halyards of the foremast, gazed with plain interest at the tumult about them. Sailors though they were, I would have wagered that never had they faced such a sight from so small a craft, and this was made certain when the man named Larry bawled at me, while for a moment I gripped the same rope with him:

"Barrin' an case o' breath, ye might as well ha' left us below. The craft can't live long this here way. 'Tis a matter o' wind or Davy Jones, an' ye had better whistle for the first, let it come high or low.—Belay all, an' stand by!"

His exclamation was caused by a sudden jerk of the schooner, followed by a sidelong dip, and a whole green sea came aboard over the starboard bow. The full force of it was broken by the house of the forecastle hatch, but the bulk swept over all obstacles like a cascade, and, rising to our hips, drove us clear of the deck in a twinkling. In a bunch we hung on to the halyards until the rush subsided and let our feet come to the planking once more. I saw the flood sweep aft and foam over the break of the poop, while torrents poured down the galley and into the forecastle. It was the worst drenching the craft had yet experienced, and a few more such visitors would send enough water into the hold to make her logy, and that would have been the last straw, as I guessed the pumps to be useless for want of care. Had I had a full crew, nothing could have been done to ease our state or render our condition less perilous. The fact that the seas were now more boisterous though the calm had lasted above an hour, told me that a vicious force was still at work over the breast of the ocean. Though the sun might have been fairly up by this, there was no certainty of the fact, for the light was a greenish gray, and the clouds hung low and in furrows, fold on fold, to where the horizon was blotted out in a thick foglike haze. No land was in sight, and all about, nothing showed save the hellish turmoil of the sea and the lowering menace of the sky above.

How long the schooner might have lived thus there can be no surety, and even to me, knowing as I did the soundness of each beam, rib, and treenail, it was a wonder she had thus far held her spars and timbers so bravely.

But she was no longer to test a broadside battering. Having at present nothing to fear from the men (for even had they been given to plotting it were against human nature for them to strike at me while death threatened all), I was about descending into the cabin after ordering the two to take the limp surgeon forward and stow him in a bunk. For a moment I stood and watched them careening along the deck with their burden, wondering if it were wise to allow them to come in

contact with their disabled mate. I saw the passage
made in safety and turned to go my way when, on casting my eye over the taffrail, I beheld a wall of spray
tearing along the sea off the starboard quarter. The
line of its advance was as clear as that of a thunder gust,
and I had barely time to cast loose the main sheet and
raise my voice when the squall struck us. Terrible as
was its appearance, it had not the weight of the blast
that had opened the ball the night before, but it heeled
us far on to our beam's ends, while sea after sea planted
themselves against the bilge and rolled on deck until
I feared we would founder under the sheer pounding
of the brine. Like lightning the boom had flashed to
larboard, and that spar with most of its canvas lay on
the waves. I had grasped the wheel and hung on for
my life. It seemed that we would never right again, and
I was watching the flood pouring over us when, with a
clap like the discharge of a cannon, the staysail burst,
a cloud of rags blowing away to leeward like wads from
a gun. The very angle of the vessel saved her from
carrying the tons of water that had beaten in, and, as the
headsail let go, as an animal goaded to desperation, the
Phantom rose and, gathering way, fled before the gale.

We fled before the gale, and like the spinning spoon-
drift picked up by the wind and scattered broadcast
without form or consistence so also fled my notice of
details. Of the three terrible days during which this
storm lasted I mind me only of a few poignant facts
standing out against a background of remembered misery. The second stage of the tempest was fiercer by
far than was the first, and the wind came from a quarter
almost exactly opposite the point from which it broke
on the night of August 11th—namely, southeast. And
with it came rain—a pent-up deluge that laced the sea
and sky with parallel lines like strings of polished steel
wire. While we held the wind astern it was endurable,

but later, when we bore into the gale, one's face could not suffer long exposure to the blast that drove the liquid pellets before it like volleys of buckshot.

We had not held our way for long when it became plain that to escape by running was impossible, as the following seas reached a height and speed that threatened to poop the schooner at any moment. It had finally come to laying to or being wrecked out of hand, and every opening in the vessel was closed as tightly as possible in preparation for the move.

It was an anxious moment when the maneuver to come about was made. Each one was lashed to his post, and, when I gave the order to jam down the helm, I knew that salvation or destruction might lie in the coming brief minute.

The wind with which we had been fleeing fell as we struck the trough of the seas, the mountainous billows making a fair lee to the deck. I had closed my eyes as the wheel flew over, and when from an instant of comparative calm the gallant vessel rose and I felt the solid blast in my face instead of on my back, I shouted a thanksgiving, and in the ecstasy of my relief from long nervous tension shook hands with the sailor by my side as though he had been my lifelong friend instead of an enemy on whose death I had determined the night before.

Even though we were safely hove into the wind the gale so increased in force as to make it impossible to longer carry even a double-reefed mainsail, and there were no means at hand for further reduction of canvas saving to take all in. I met the difficulty by making a sea anchor of the wreck of the top hamper, binding the mass together and heaving it overboard with a line attached, then, by stripping the vessel of its last rag, to this drag we rode across the fearful billows with less straining, now pointing squarely into the wind's eye.

But though the Phantom's antics were reduced in violence and we existed in comparative comfort, the schooner was far from being secure, since the whole seas that rose and combed over the bows threatened again and again to swamp the craft, for, ere her scuppers could relieve her of the terrible weight of water from one wave, another would follow and tear aft, at times driving her bow fairly under. There was nothing to do but knock away great sections of the bulwarks to give free drainage to the flood, and, this done, we could but stand and wait for what Fate had in store.

It was when we were thus driven to inaction that one life was lost. I was standing by the wheel, drenched, exhausted, and fast falling into my former state of dull apathy. The galley doors had been fastened to keep out the water, and the forecastle hatch was closed, though not secured. Larry and the New Bedford man were close to me, crouched in the lee of the cabin house. To go forward was to court death, and, though the quarter was no place for a seaman off duty, all attempts at discipline and sea etiquette had given way before the common danger, and both men kept aft to be clear of the rush of the sea.

In a half-dreamy way I was conning the horizon dead ahead when I saw the forecastle door open and the man who had defied me stepped to the deck at an interval when for a moment the deluge had subsided. He was suffering agony from his wrenched arm, for his face was working, and he held the wounded limb in his right hand. The pain of it had probably driven him to desperation, or reduced his spirit into getting aft and seeking possible relief to his torment. Behind him appeared the head and part of the body of the now sobered surgeon, at whose advice he had doubtless taken the reckless step of leaving the forecastle. The man in advance seemed dazed, for he hesitated and almost fell as the head of the schooner rose to a billow, but with an effort he turned toward me and staggered a step forward. At that instant I saw a huge sea lifting ahead, its ridge tottering to a fall, its fine crest rent by the wind, blowing to leeward like smoke, and as I marked it I threw up one hand and shouted for the man to get back. Whether he understood or not I shall never know, for ere he had gotten abreast the foremast the vicious roller boarded the schooner with a roar and at once the fellow disappeared. I saw him a second later borne swiftly along the deck toward the bulkhead passage, and before one could shout "Man overboard!" he was swept into the sea as a bucket of water would have swept away a chip. Again I marked him drifting sternward on the crest of a wave, with one hand in the air as in appeal, his set, white face looking like paper as he gave a last terror-stricken glance at me and a shout unheard save by his Maker.

To lift a finger for his rescue was beyond all but divine power, and, though he was no more than the boom's length from me, he was as fairly seized by death as though clutched by a fatal malady.

CHAPTER XXV.

A RESPITE.

IT was a tragic episode, but I had seen so much tragedy crowded into my life for the past few days that this quick and probably painless passing of a human soul made in my state but little impression. I looked for the doctor, but saw the doors of the forecastle fast closed, and afterward found that the force of the water had slammed them on him, knocking him from the ladder to the deck below. A pity it was that there and then it had not been he instead of my plucky enemy who had first planted foot to come aft. Better for my subsequent happiness would it have been if, instead of the sailor, that red-laced drunkard had choked in the element he so despised.

The heaving into the wind and the drowning of the seaman were the only events which roused my blood to a heat that make the details stand out in memory. I might tell of the sufferings of Ames and Gertrude King, and of their utter indifference and total abandonment to what appeared certain destruction, but it would be useless. The greatest agony of either sprang from sea-sickness and its attending miseries. There was not one of us who thought of food, which was probably fortunate, as our stock brought on board was brine-soaked and ruined. Even my toughened self and the tougher sailors lost heart and stomach in the deadening nausea that gradually seized us and kept its hold. The doctor, imprisoned forward by the seas, and too cowardly to show his head after his one attempt to come aft, might have been in another world for all we heard or saw of him. The last drop of stimulant had gone, and with it had gone the last of even fictitious spirits. An unshakable apathy clutched our little company, and, save that one lurch of the vessel was of greater violence than another, nothing marked the events of hours. Fear had passed; anxiety was dead; day and night were meaningless terms. We were only waiting the final stroke; a wrench, an open seam, and then the blessed end.

Mechanically I placed rain-soaked cloths on the wounded ribs of my friend and on the gashed head of his sister, and offered to them rain water squeezed from a square of clean canvas. It was not because my interest in either ran high; friendship for one and love for the other had fallen with my nerve force into a latent state, and I barely responded to their needs—to my own I responded not at all. Mechanically I went to the deck, only to meet the same lead overhead and the same towering majesty of water, neither of which impressed me (for I was far past being impressed) more than I have since been by a flat calm. The pitiless rain in my face and eyes would rouse in me a dull sense of discomfort, just as a sleeping child unconsciously resents disturbance, but that was all. I would go below, meeting the lack-luster eyes of the sailors, who had also sought shelter in the cabin, and the deathlike forms of the two on the floor, and feel that we were all sinking into the languor of starvation and prolonged strain.

By the end of the third day the Phantom was practically a floating wreck, though for all I could see not a line had parted, nor a spar, other than the topmast, been displaced. But there was no longer a buoyant lift to her bows, and the seas ran dangerously near the level of the deck—a fact that plainly spoke of water in the hold, it having drained from above or leaked between her strained planks. There had been no attempt at pumping, for no man could have stood at the brakes in the deluge that came aboard, and now we were settling, helped mightily by the nature of our cargo. But the knowledge of it gave me no trouble, nor was there a comment made on the fact, though to three of us at least the conditions were clearly apparent.

On the night of August 14th I went below, fully expecting that but a few hours would elapse ere we went to the bottom. Once in a while my vitality would assert itself, and a quick apprehension, a living sensibility, would shoot through me like the running flash of driving sparks in burned-out tinder, but without enough heat or force to rouse me to action. I slept heavily, as one sleeps in the fumes of burning charcoal, dead to harm or happiness, and was waked from a dream of feasting by the sound of a report like that made by a bursting sail. Half conscious I crawled to the deck to see what had happened. The dawn was well forward, a strip of bright sky of pearly clearness heralding the sun which was already scattering the clouds aloft. Patches of the deepest blue flecked with fine vapor like clotted cream sailing far above the rapidly dissolving storm wrack, foretold fine weather. The wind had sunk to almost a calm, and was blowing a soft warm breath from the west. The sea was a vast series of hills and valleys, their crests no longer like teeth, and so rhythmical was their run that the half-submerged vessel swung with the regularity of a pendulum, only at times a swollen surge brimming over the bows, sending a cascade to the deck. Just visible to the north was a clear, dark, indigo-colored lift of land, which I instantly knew to be Montauk Point, and even my dull senses responded to the knowledge of the wonderful drift we had made.

I noted these details with a slow, dreamy satisfaction, but, on turning my gaze southward, I became fully alive to the fact that the awakening day had put a period to our misery. There on our larboard quarter, two cable lengths away, lay a schooner twice the size of the ·Phantom, her sides pierced for guns, and forward of her foremast the brine-tarnished brass of her pivoted rifle stood out against the horizon. She had luffed into the gentle breeze, and all her sails were shivering and swinging as she bowed to the swells. From her main peak blew out the flag of the United Colonies, and over her taffrail was drifting the tawny smoke of the shot that had aroused me.

For a space I stood like a man of stone, my look fixed on the ensign so long a stranger to me. As I gazed at the gorgeous bunting my heart rose in my throat, the tears welled from my eyes, the frost which had long bound me suddenly thawed, and, putting all my remaining power in my voice, I gave vent to a wild shout, threw both arms above my head, and staggered below.

That night, under her own remaining canvas, the Phantom sailed into the harbor of Holmes Hole and dropped her spare anchor. We had been rescued by the American privateer Jenny, of New London, out of that port bound home with prisoners and booty after a four months' cruise.

With my story told, there had been enough help offered to have equipped me for a voyage to the Indies, but I asked for only provisions, water, fuel, and a couple of hands, determined to gather to myself the glory which had well-nigh slipped my grasp. We were freed from the load of water taken in during the storm, the Jenny standing by and lending men to the work until the pumps "sucked," and then, promising not to lose sight of us until we entered Vineyard Sound, stood for her home port.

Not a word did I say about the two sailors whom I had captured, and who had served me well. The doctor I had found half dead from fright, the effects of his debauch, starvation, and seasickness, and I determined to hold him myself still as a prisoner on parole. I had no idea of transferring Ames or his sister, for I doubted if the Jenny crowded as she was, would prove more comfortable than the Phantom. The remainder of the trip would be short; at my own home there would be the best of nursing, and my surgeon prisoner would make a fair attendant if he could be kept sober, a matter I would take in my own hands.

There were other reasons why I would not consent to be separated from my friends even had they been willing (which they were not), the weightiest of which not being the danger of transshipment, but one I deemed unnecessary to mention, and which as yet I would not fully acknowledge to myself.

Knowing nothing of the march of events, I confided to the captain my fears of General Sullivan's safety, and told him what I had learned of Clinton's intended movement to the relief of Pigot, hoping he would be able to transmit a warning to the American general in time to prevent surprise. I did this that, should my own future attempt prove abortive, the message might arrive at the patriot camp from another quarter.

Thus suddenly relieved of care, we sailed away under mainsail, foresail, and jib, and had made the remainder of the voyage without incident. It was with emotions almost boyish and uncontrollable that I marked the mingled reds, yellows, and blues of the great clay foreland of Gay head, doubly brilliant in the light of the westering sun. By then our consort was well to the northwest, but I now feared neither the British nor the devil, for, if closely pursued by the former, I should have run the Phantom ashore and taken to the woods, even though it broke my heart to do it.

But no further necessity for heroic action presented itself, and we slipped into the haven of Holmes Hole and dropped the only anchor we had left, creating a flutter among the inhabitants of the hamlet, who were mightily alarmed at seeing a schooner bearing no flag sail up within gunshot of the shore and round to as though for a broadside. Heretofore they had not been molested, but perhaps it was an inward sense of trouble impending which made them quake at the mysterious action of the Phantom, for barely a fortnight was to elapse ere Grey, the "Hand of Iron," sailed up as I had done, and under the guns of the fleet demanded the usual tribute of blood and an unusual one of forage.

But now, saving a few fishermen drawn up on the beach, there was not a craft in the harbor. The peace of the evening, the quiet beauty of the green land, and the feeling of safety fell on my spirits like a benediction after an impressive sermon, and I breathed as one breathes on waking from the horrors of nightmare. War and danger had vanished as had vanished the storm clouds of the day before, and, indeed, so far as the events of the past few days had affected me, they had been but as a nightmare or as had been the storm to the land, leaving but few marks to tell of its fearful reality.

In a week I had recovered from the terrible strain to which I had been subjected, noticing only that my head had taken on a few white threads I had never seen before, but my nerves, which have been my mainstay through life, were neither loosened nor frayed by the desperate tune circumstance had thrummed upon them.

I had suddenly shot from an era of conflict to one of peace, I thought, nor did I dream I should be aroused again unless I voluntarily took the field. I became a hero, too, nor was my notoriety a cheap one. From

17

Edgartown to the heights of Gay's Head the fame of my achievement spread, even the half-breed Indians, whose ground lay about the latter point, being unstinted in their sober congratulations to the " big Thorn," as I was called by them.

Seafarers and those drawing their subsistence from the sea are stolid to apparent indifference as to the fortune, be it good or bad, Fate deals out to them. They become inured to the fickleness of the great element which is at once a threat and a mainstay, and the rack of uncertainty on which they are stretched for most of their lives makes wild demonstration impossible, be their joys mighty or their griefs deep.

And so when I appeared before my mother, who, as I had feared, had given me over as dead, there was no violence of emotion; only a stunned, ghost-seeing look on her white face as I entered her presence and opened my arms to her, and the single articulate cry of " My son! my son! " as she fell into them. It was but little more from my sister, who had been brought up in the same stoical school, and by the time my long story had been told, much as I am telling it here, the quiet round of daily life had been regained, the sick and wounded transferred to the small house overlooking the Sound, and the doctor, full of protestations as to his good intentions, and yet surly withal, installed medical attendant.

After my arrival my earliest business was to clear my mind of two responsibilities weighing thereon: the first to get word to General Sullivan of the intended move of Sir Henry Clinton, as I feared that by some slip my first message through the Jenny's captain might have miscarried; the second, to have the Phantom's cargo delivered at New London.

The news of the arrival of Howe and the departure from Newport of the French to fight him had already reached the Vineyard, but I was not deceived by this into thinking that Clinton had worked ahead of his expressed intention of relieving Pigot in the course of two weeks. It would be too unlike the man to act with such promptness, and there had been no force landed to succor the beleaguered royalists. Lord Howe's maneuver had been a move to open the gates for re-enforcement, and it had been successful. The doughty British general to whom I had offered personal violence would hardly have altered his plans because they had been breathed into the ear of one who, according to report, had never escaped to transmit a warning, and who now presumably lay dead at the bottom of the ocean. With his mistress he doubtless felt a villainous satisfaction on hearing that the Phantom, with Beverly Ames on board, had not followed the Sprite into New York, but had foundered in the great storm. I to this day wonder as to their thoughts regarding Gertrude King (who to them had entirely disappeared). To the man she must have been the sword of Damocles, which dropped at a time when he had gotten to live in the fancied security of believing it would never fall.

If my conjectures regarding Clinton's movements were right, I had something like a week in which to act, and, as luck would have it, there staggered into the harbor a privateer sloop-of-war, storm scared, under a jury mast, and in a sinking condition, with half her men lost in the tempest. And hardly had her anchor reached bottom when she suddenly tilted and followed it, taking with her most of her remaining crew, and to-day her oaken ribs lie petrifying in the salt sands just east of West Chop, from whose bluff the red eye of the lighthouse now winks its warning.

Her captain, whom I well knew, was a Providence man, though his ship hailed from New London (as did most of the privateers cruising to the east), so to him

I committed the Phantom and my message to Sullivan, and within three days, from the pine heights abreast of the house I saw my schooner disappear west of Naushon, and felt that my duty had been done.

I never saw the Phantom again. She discharged her cargo and lay neglected at New London, too strained for further service without repairs, while I, becoming active in other quarters, waited for more auspicious times before again cruising in a defenseless trading schooner. And there she continued to lie, a partly dismantled hulk, like an old sailor sinking to sleep with the scars of old actions and the peace of old memories to comfort him, until two years later, when Arnold made his famous or infamous raid up the Thames. Then, while the town of New London was burning and the battle of Fort Griswold was at its height, the schooner caught fire, and in a shroud of flame reeled to the bottom, where her bones still rest.

But that was later. Now the waning summer's days were as a dream of perfect tranquillity. There was nothing to mar the lassitude that came over me as the quiet I had so long unknown stole into my very vitals, until I wondered how I had ever been active. There was not even anxiety for those who had suffered so severely during the flight from New York, for, though the life of Ames was for awhile overshadowed by uncertainty, his youth plucked him from death, and he began to mend, soon being beyond danger.

His sister showed little of the effects of her ordeal. It was determined that shock, her fractured collar bone and lacerated scalp were the extent of her injuries, and after a season of rest, nourishment, and a sense of perfect safety, she appeared as radiant as an arm in a sling and a bandaged head would allow. In something like a week her head was well, and clad in proper feminine garb, the contributions of neighbors (though we had no near ones), she shone with a light unknown to the plain-visaged damsels of the island.

We of the Vineyard are a hardy race, but make no boast of our beauty. Health runs riot among us, but the strong salt air, the stronger winds, and the glittering sun, though they make broad chests and deep lungs, fail to fine the skin or give the delicacy of color and grace of figure possessed by the woman I had rescued, and who in my eyes stood for a model of both courage and feminine perfection.

I can not give McCary much credit for the recovery of his patients. Not but that he gave them sufficient attention (he gave the girl too much, to my mind), but neither case was one demanding either instruments or medicine; the air, the nursing (done by my mother and sister), and the sweet, strong elixir of youth and vitality leaving little necessity for other assistance.

But the doctor troubled me somewhat. He never came from seeing Gertrude without a wildness about him for which I could not account (poor fool that I was!), and at those times he regarded me as though I was something to be barely endured. Gertrude plainly disliked him, though she always treated him very respectfully. He was light-hearted at times, but never when I was about, and his marked sullenness to me became greater as the days wore on. Clad only in his gaudy uniform, he had created as much curiosity and animosity when he was taken on shore as though he had been an extra brilliant red rag flourished before a herd of bulls of doubtful temper. And from the day of his landing until I saw the last of him he never entered the village again or ventured east of the low woodland bounding our farm in that direction.

After his patients were beyond the necessity of his attention, he turned to leading a half-nomadic life, passing much of his time with a borrowed gun in the

stunted forest (which was then well-nigh as wild as
when Columbus discovered America), or wandering into
the Chappaquiddeck territory and hobnobbing in a
patronizing way with the lords of that soil, who in their
degeneracy paid profound respect to his scarlet uniform
and called him (knowing him to be a prisoner) " Cold
Blaze," or " The Fire that's Out." I hardly wondered
at his withdrawal from the immediate vicinity of the
farm, as it was only by so doing that he could enjoy the
open air and escape the curiosity of the visitors who
flocked to catch a glimpse of a genuine red-coated in-
vader of America. He was a *rara avis* to the quiet
islanders, and caused as much comment as though he
had been a freak of Nature or had dropped to earth
from a distant planet.

CHAPTER XXVI.

But his fire was not out, though there was nothing cheery in its sparkle. The lurid heat within him lay hidden among the cold ashes of his calm exterior, only flaring up at me at times. I thought this was due to his sullen disposition and his natural resentment at feeling himself a prisoner, and perhaps it was, but when I told him I was ready to deliver him to the Massachusetts authorities to be placed in the regular lines of exchange, he begged me, after the fashion of a man given his choice between being hanged or shot, to let him bide where he was, though liberty might be longer in finding him. I knew very well that he hated me, but his hate was so tinged by cowardice that he cringed like a dog when I was by, and, though I never doubted his will to bite, I little dreamed he had either the courage or would ever have the opportunity.

So I let him roam in, out, and about, thinking that mayhap he might be needed for his skill, yet hoping that my official notification of his being on parole would ere long end in his being taken off my hands. I might have suspected (but did not) that something was amiss when one day Ames bade me look in his pocket for certain important papers he told me had been taken from Mrs. Badely's desk by his sister. It was the first I knew of his possessing documents of any kind, and, though I searched high and low for them, they were

255

gone. This led me to suppose that they had been taken from him at the time he fell and was overhauled, but he assured me it was impossible, Gertrude having had them sewed in her vest until two days before, and he declared they had been stolen, though by whom he could give no guess, they being of no value to any one save himself, his sister, Mrs. Badely, and Sir Henry Clinton. I told him I would probe the matter, but, as nothing further was said, I forgot the thing, especially as Gertrude thought little of the loss, saying she had the contents of the documents at her tongue's end, though, of course, the originals were preferable to any copy she could make. I remembered then that when Mrs. Badely burst into Clinton's presence and fainted, she had prefaced her collapse by crying, "He has been back and taken all those——" going to the door ere completing the sentence. Gertrude now informed me that these papers were meant, and from that remark of her guardian's she had known it was her brother whose escape was referred to.

"It was not Beverly, but I who took them," she explained laughingly, "and if they are lost, it will do Sir Henry no good, as I have them here." And she tapped her white forehead with her white finger.

A few days after, Ames again spoke of the writings, and asked me to give McCary an overhauling, a thing I promised to do the next day.

I mind me well it was the last of August when he made this request and I the promise. I had become anxious at the nonappearance of the Phantom, and had taken the habit of going to Gay Head, looking over the immense expanse of the ocean, and hoping, as one will, to hasten the coming of a longed-for object by constant watching. Each day I returned home disappointed yet buoyed by a doubtful encouragement in believing she must heave in sight the next.

The great bald headland was now no longer the bleak uplift of a once submerged clay bank. The wide sweep of meadow, the rank grass and tufts of low, bushy growths, the patches of heatherlike blossoms, which accentuated the melancholy loneliness of the immense field topping the cliff, had now a meaning, a poetry I had never marked before. The quick notes of the birds rising by twos and threes from the seed beds and fluttering away to the blue line of woods to the east, caught the ear sharply. The chirp of the kitydid seemed a perpetual protest against the tremendous desolation of the place, and its constant cry broke the otherwise universal hush. The wind bent the tall grasses and whispered as though the upheaved land was close to heaven, and became sacred ground therefore.

And to me it was sacred, or at least removed from common earth. More often than not I was accompanied hither by Gertrude (who had gradually gained strength for the somewhat long trip), and her presence it was that threw enchantment over all things—an enchantment which only a secret lover knows or can know.

· . From this height even on the cliff's edge no sound of the surf reached us unless the sea was heavy, though far below the thin, white line of its froth lay like a writhing bar of snow. And here had I often wandered apart from the girl, that I might watch her as she stood looking out over the sea, her skirts swept backward or perhaps only trembling in the breeze, which in varying force was here always blowing. Long would she stand there, and as long would I gaze (with my soul in my face doubtless), her tall, graceful figure cleanly cut against the blue of the background, and a half-melancholy and wholly abstracted expression in her eyes; and then by and by she would turn and come toward me with a bright smile that was like an apology for her momentary forgetfulness of my presence.

Gods! may the memory of the sweetness of those days never dim! The rush of the free salt air is still in my nostrils, the sweep of the sea comes to me like a vision, the purring of the wind is yet in my ears, and by these I know that, though my body is now withered, the ancient ichor of youth lies somewhere in the depths of my nature; and even now my old heart throbs quicker as I call up the picture of those hours when to myself alone I admitted I was worshiping Gertrude King.

I knew then why the landscape was no longer barren; why there was music in the homely sounds of bird and insect life; why there was beauty in the plainest growing thing, and magic in this seeming forsaken bit of God's footstool.

But on the day I gave Ames the promise to touch the doctor on the matter of the missing papers I was alone. The sky was threatening, and it was getting late before I started for Gay Head, and Gertrude had remained with her brother. I had grown to think my walk but an irksome duty when she was not with me, but perhaps her absence on that day fell out for the best—perhaps otherwise.

As I walked up the gently sloping cap of the cliff which suddenly breaks away to the sea in an almost sheer precipice, by the bit of scarlet on its edge I knew I was not to remain alone. Seated on a tongue of projecting earth, with his gun betwixt his knees, sat McCary, apparently looking seaward with such intentness that he heeded not my approach. I had seen him thus many a time, often sprawling out on the turf as in an excess of laziness or half dozing, and sometimes as rapt as a poet nursing a fancy. But whatever his mood, he had hitherto sighted me before I was well upon him, and prevented closer companionship by scrambling to his feet and making off until out of my sight. A surly dog, I thought, and mightily obliged was I for the room he gave me.

However, to-day he was far gone at wool-gathering, or I thought so until I gained the edge of the steep, when I saw that he was intently watching a man halfway down the cliff, who was making his way to the beach below by a dangerous path known only to those who have haunted the headland and dared the perils of its face. By creeping along the narrow clay terraces, dropping in some spots, and in others sliding through the ragged, rain-washed gullies with which the front of the height is seamed, one might from the point on which the surgeon was sitting reach the level of the beach in safety. But woe to him who by mishap or misstep loses control of himself, as the chances are that he rolls to the bottom and is dashed to death against the huge bowlders which at the inner edge of the beach make to this gigantic clay bed an effective sea wall against the encroachments of the ocean!

Gay Head cliff, like most of Nature's stupendous efforts, is to be admired from a distance, and nothing can be more awe-inspiring than from its top to view the perpendicular strata of reds, yellows, blues, and whites which by some power and at some time of inconceivable remoteness have been heaved from the bed of the ocean and cast upon end.

I had never hazarded the cliff from here, but a quarter of a mile northward there was a safe descent along a broad and easy sloping buttress, and I wondered why a man should take the dangerous route to the level below.

But I ceased to wonder when, on looking closely, I discovered the fellow was a half-breed. There are no better sailors in the world or men more daring on sea or shore than those who have a strain of Chappaquiddeck blood. To this day the few of the tribe spared by rum and disease are wreckers and life-savers, although the negro blood predominates. They vary their water life with the less dangerous one of making pottery from the party-colored clay of the headland, and, though now they are less venturesome than their fathers, their light boats go skipping about like water spiders on a smooth pond, going far asea, but I never heard of a drowning.

That the fellow below was at home on the cliff I could plainly see, for he made his way so easily and skillfully, always with face downward, that he reached the white level of the beach and disappeared among the bowlders ere I could identify him. One of the companions of the surgeon mayhap, I thought, for I had often marked him wandering with them, though mostly he was alone, and then it came to me that his growing intimacy with these people might bode no good, for, like many of their betters, they had curious notions of right and wrong, and might be bought body and soul for a sovereign—and McCary had plenty of money.

This flashed through me as the half-breed disappeared, and then it was that the surgeon looked up and saw me near him. With unusual alacrity he got himself to his feet and turned away without a word; but minding me of my promise to Ames, I had no notion of letting him beyond my reach, and, as there could be no better time or place for unfolding the matter of the documents, I hailed him, making my way toward him.

He halted and wheeled about at the sound of my voice, and now stood with the gun in the hollow of his elbow as he waited my coming. I think I had never disliked the man as I did the moment I neared him. There was something about him so dogged, so cold and calculating, yet so sullenly defiant, and withal so crafty and cowardly, that I felt like striking him in the face. The sight of him changed my softer mood completely. The little charity (or perhaps it was pity) I felt for him, blew away in the brisk wind, and what policy I had intended using in my manner went with it. His dim gray eyes were bloodshot and betokened a free use of liquor, though where he could have gotten it was past my wits to fathom. He held himself as though awaiting a simple question to which he would fling his answer as one flings a dog a bone, and then go his way; but if this was in his mind, I must have given him a shock, for with no attempt at gracefully coming to the point, I shot the question at him.

"Dr. McCary, where are the papers you stole from Beverly Ames?"

His red eyes blinked as though crossed by a flash of lightning, and the butt of the fowling-piece dropped to the ground in the start he gave. If I had held doubts before, I knew now that he was the thief, and following up my instinct that he had not dared to secrete the papers about the house, I took a stride toward him and ventured:

"They are upon your person, and here and now you will hand them to me!"

Some kind of a sound came from the man's throat as he recoiled from me as though fearing an assault, and the gun slipped to the ground. The thud of its fall drew his attention to it, and it was doubtless to cover his confusion and gain time to frame an answer that he stooped to raise it. But partly to bring the matter to a head and partly in fear that the weapon might be loaded, and in his desperation he would use it on me, I advanced quickly and, placing my foot on the barrel, looked him squarely in the eye without speaking.

If he had intended an attempt at hoodwinking me by a smooth answer, my action brought his villainous temper to a pitch past restraint, and, drawing himself upright, he gave me a return look so full of venom that

if looks could kill I would have fallen dead at his feet.
Then he spoke, or rather exploded:

"An' ye are a black-hearted rebel to beset a man
in your power with such a charge! Am I the likes
of a thief? What would I want with his papers? Am
I not under your thumb, and have I done aught but me
best by the boy an' girl? 'Tis a thankless job to have
wasted me skill on such a lot! By the powers, ye infernal weed, 'twill not be long ere ye will be beggin'
mercy at the hands of Dr. McCary, for once beyond ye
I'll do me endeavors to haunt ye down to hell! Lave
me alone, man, an' thank God for the free time ye have
left to ruin the silly girl yonder! 'Tis short enough!
Never will I forget the way I was trated aboard the
schooner by ye, or the slight of her overbold looks to ye
to pay for all I did for her. Go your way, and damn
me no more with your talk of stolen papers. They be
gone for good an' all. Scammell took them; he showed
them to me. Go to him, an' ye dare, an' call him
thief."

The fury with which he threw these words at me is
past all telling. His face, usually of an unhealthy pallor, flushed until its color matched his bloodshot eyes.
His lean fingers clutched into his palms, and he shook
as though palsied. His anger was so real, his indignation at having his honor impugned so apparently genuine, that I believe I should have offered an apology and
let the matter drop had it not been for two things:
First, the insult he had offered Gertrude King; and, second, his last words. The former roused me as though
I had been struck, while the latter exposed the studied
falsity of the man (a falsity justifiable, perhaps, in one
in his position), for Ames had assured me there was
nothing in his pockets at the time he was shot.

But my anger was nearly as high as his as he finished
speaking. As he completed his speech, he gave a wave

of his fist and turned to leave me with an air of contempt, but like a shot I leaped for and laid hold of him.
Catching him by the collar, I twisted him about with
one hand and with the other smote him across the
mouth; then diving into his breast pocket, I pulled
forth a mass of papers before he could check my movement, and with a finishing push thrust him from me.
He staggered backward for several paces in fruitless
effort to save himself, then pitched to the ground, while
I, having uttered no word in return to his tirade, hastily
ran off the small sheaf of papers I held in my hand.

By the time he had gotten to his feet and pulled
himself together I had found what I wanted—four ob-
long sheets folded and tied with a string, all addressed
to Henry Clinton, Esq., or General Henry Clinton, showing that the correspondence antedated his knighthood.
They were signed George Germain. I presumed these
were the papers I sought, as they were indorsed " F. B."
(which I took to mean Florence Badely) in fine writing,
and the word " private " was under the initials of each
document. The rest of the papers, together with Mc-
Cary's wallet, were his own private matters as I saw at
a glance, and throwing them to him, I placed the abstracted writings in my pocket and picked up the gun
at my feet.

Though barely three minutes had elapsed since I
thrust my hand in the surgeon's coat, I had regained
command of myself by the time I completed the survey.
My finding the missing papers probably had much to do
in saving the scoundrel from chastisement for the insult
he had offered the lady. In my hands he was so puny
an individual that I should have regretted further violence toward him, and when I considered that I myself
had both lied to and robbed Clinton, and that the papers
in question bore witness to thieving from another quarter, it would be hardly consistent for me to put too

fine a point on the conduct of the man standing before
me.

But my temper at that moment was none of the
sweetest, nor was my charity for him made broader
because our sins (if sins they were) had been similar.
As he held away from me, his face now turned from red
to white, and his eyes full of impotent rage, I held something more than mere dislike for him, but I said quite
calmly:

"Dr. McCary, you have evidently forgotten that you
are a prisoner on parole, sworn not to act against the
United Colonies until regularly exchanged. Though
you have forfeited consideration, I shall not press you
too hard, but, sir, if you dare again to darken my door,
I will see to it that you regret the intrusion. From
now on find your own food and shelter. Go your way—
to your fellows, if you wish—but let me not be cursed
by the sight of you again!"

And with this I turned my back upon him, threw the
gun over my shoulder, and walked off without even looking around to see what might be his next move.

CHAPTER XXVII.

WHAT HAPPENED ON GAY HEAD.

THAT night, as I tossed the papers to Ames and noted with what satisfaction he received them, I told him the story of their recovery, and laughed as I drew a word picture of the discomfited redcoat as he stood despoiled and disheveled on the brow of the cliff. But the lad took a mighty serious view of the matter, and, though he did not question my right to lay hands on McCary, and considered my having forbade his return to the house a stroke of wisdom, he was far from treating lightly the threat the doctor had made, and told me he feared I had not seen the end of the business. It set me thinking, too, when he asked me what possible motive the fellow could have had in preferring to remain in this out-of-the-way spot when, by taking my offer to send him to the mainland, he might have by this obtained his exchange, or at least found a society more to his liking. The question was beyond my ability to answer, and I asked him in turn what his ideas might be; but the lad gave me no satisfaction, only casting at me a queer look and turning in his bed, as though my stupidity tired him.

The next day, after a fruitless and lonely trip to the headland, I started beating up the woods for a couple of stray cattle. Gertrude and my sister stood in the low porch of the doorway waving me a farewell, and, just as I was looking back at them from the edge of the

18   265

home lot, the horse I was riding suddenly shied violently, the cause being my late antagonist and an Indian
companion, who rose from behind a clump of bushes
and walked away in the most innocent manner possible. I had it in my mind to hail the doctor and ask
him why he was venturing so close to forbidden ground,
but then I thought the fellow miserable enough if he
had taken to living with the Indians (who were, indeed,
the only ones likely to welcome him), so held my tongue
and rode on.

I saw him again the next afternoon, and, God wot,
it came nigh being the last time either saw aught again.
It was the 28th of August, and as glorious a fall day
as ever presaged a season. The air was suggestive of
the coming glory. The crisp, cool shadows of the trees
swung over the grass, and the heat, so long oppressive,
gave way to a life-giving temperature. A sprightliness
was in and on all about, and, had I not been beset with
peculiar conditions of heart and mind, I should have
responded to the spirit of the weather with a boyish lack
of dignity. There was a freshness of life and motion
everywhere, and the beauty of it all was made perfect
by the deep blue of the sky, the piled-up masses of snowy
cumuli banked against the western horizon, and the
lusty sparkle of the sound in the distance. The strong,
livening breeze blew fair from the west, and if ever the
belated Phantom was to appear, it should be on this
day of days.

This was in the morning, and by that night it had
been the day of days—to me, at least.

I went to the great headland that afternoon accompanied by Gertrude. The day was as fine as ever, though
its character had changed as the sun passed the merid-
ian, and out on the wide, moorlike meadows of Gay
Head the march of the season was more marked. Now
the distant woodland and the hollows were veiled in a

smoky haze, and the faded herbage of the field showed
a rustiness that spoke of the coming change. The few
poor stalks of golden-rod were already hanging their
withered heads, the katydid's note was sharper in its
complaint, and the trailing vines of the thorny dew-
berry threw out a blood-red leaf here and there, as
though to attract attention to its shrunken and seedy
fruit. The bold blue of the morning sky had gone and
given place to a brooding tenderness, while over all the
land hung the nameless pathos of the coming autumn.
The waning day held the beauty of Indian summer
without its dreamy stillness, for the wind on the height
piped merrily in my ears, though below at the sea's level
it was but a zephyr.

I wandered along—far from hurrying now—filled
with the spirit of the surroundings, and filled yet more
with a passion which I knew ere long must burst its
bounds and hurry me on its flood to happiness or disappointment. We could be talkative enough in our
walks in other directions (though I had hard work to
guard my words at times), but on the long and lonely
trips to this point there was little said by either the
girl or myself, though to me my dumbness held more
meaning than any flow of words. I dared not speak,
and yet I was afraid of my silence—ay, afraid my eyes
would shout what my tongue shrank from whispering—
afraid that the rest, the blissful content I was now enjoying, the spirit of her presence, which had become a
part of me, might be blown away by a single word. And
I would rather dream on like a coward than suddenly
be waked and find I was no mate for this girl, who,
though treating me familiarly as a friend and equal
(from gratitude, perhaps), would scorn an alliance with
one so far removed from her in birth, if not in breeding.
I feared the passing days, for I knew this state could
not endure forever. I feared—God knows what—only

they were the fears of every lover whose love is too deep to babble lightly like a shallow brook, and whose passion lifts, a mighty stream, finally bursting all bounds.

And mine was near the bursting point that day. For the most part I walked at Gertrude's side, and, when we reached the foot of the long incline which raises until it meets the brow of the cliff, I tried to talk, but said less than though I had not spoken. The folly of it struck me, and I left her, going a few paces in advance to kick away the brambles, that they might not catch her trailing garments. Thus we pushed up the slope, Gertrude sauntering behind, looking into the bushes as she passed or picking some belated flower, and I with my eyes now on the level just beyond, hoping to catch a view of the ocean as it opened over the edge of the headland. I looked back and asked if she was tired and wished help, but she said "No," and that she would follow slowly, bidding me hasten if I was impatient. So I turned away. A few more steps brought the blue of the sea before me, and I gave a shout as I sprang forward, for there in the distance lay the Phantom or her ghost.

The few hundred feet that intervened betwixt me and the edge of the cliff I passed on a run, but when I reached a point where the sea presented a clear field, my joy was turned to consternation. If the distant schooner was indeed the Phantom, she was a prize in the hands of the enemy, for as I reached the brow of the promontory and looked away I saw lying before me, wafted by the light west wind, the British fleet strung out, vessel after vessel, for miles. The heavy ships of the line and the transports lay off against the haze of Cuttyhunk and Naushowena, but the lighter fore-and-aft rigged craft hung on their flanks like skirmishers, and one was so far inshore to the Vineyard that I had my doubts of its clearing the Devil's Bridge, a reef that pushes its way for half a mile or more northward from the foot of Gay Head.

As a spectacle the sight of those ponderous moving forts was magnificent. More than a score of the enemy's ships with every sail set and drawing were creeping eastward, and the significance of their presence here threw me into a state bordering on panic. It was so unlooked for, so foreign to the peace of the island, its full meaning so uncertain, that I stood and looked without realizing that such an expedition bound along the Vineyard Sound could have no such small game for its object as our poverty-stricken island. The fleet was already east of every port of importance on the southern coast, and then it came to me that its destination could be no less a point than Boston; its object, the French flotilla which had there taken refuge.

There was no possibility of mistaking the cumbrous English build, rig, and rake, and had there been, there was no mistaking the small crimson speck hanging from the main or mizzen peak of each vessel.

As I looked keenly at the craft I took to be my own schooner, I saw it was not she, but I had scarce come to that conclusion and settled in my mind that this scowl of war was not directed toward Martha's Vineyard, when from behind me I heard a piercing shriek, and, turning, saw Gertrude throw herself into a clump of low bushes about a hundred feet from where I was standing. Even before she fell the spot was blotted out by a puff of white smoke, and at the same time I heard the horrible humming of a bullet mixed with the report of a rifle, and my hat was lifted from my head and sent over the precipice.

For the briefest instant I was dumfounded, but for the briefest instant only. That I had been marked for assassination and had been missed was the idea quickly leaping to my brain, but all thoughts of self and all uncertainty as to the identity of my assailant were immediately dispelled as I saw the scarlet-coated figure of a man rise from his concealment and try to shake off the girl who was clinging to him as a woman clings to an opponent.

Even in the whirl of the struggle I recognized McCary, and before I could get halfway to him he had torn himself loose and thrown Gertrude to the ground, where she lay without moving. For a breath or two he stood over her as though at loss how to act, but seeing me approaching unhurt and at full speed, he shook his fist at me and with a yell bounded over the body of the prostrate maiden, and, taking a course diagonal to mine, ran northward and toward the cliff.

For a few more steps I followed the dictates of my heart and continued toward the girl, but knowing that further harm could not come to her, I altered my direction and put after the flying royalist, casting aside coat and waistcoat as I ran.

He had the start of me, and his long legs carried him swiftly over the ground; but if he was spurred by fear, I was goaded onward by vengeance, and the latter is the sharpest prick known to the heart of man, remorse excepted. He threw a backward look at me with nearly every leap, and with every leap I gained upon him. My blood was on fire; pity had gone from me as though that virtue was yet unborn; to kill was a spirit as strong in me as it was in him.

I soon saw how he had mapped his flight. He was pointing himself toward the tongue of earth which marked the top of the perilous path to the beach, and if he took it I would follow, though we both went to the bottom together.

As he flew on it evidently became plain to him that if he continued his course in that direction he would be headed. I had clung to a line parallel to the precipiece, and was cutting him from his goal, when he suddenly veered and made for the safer descent farther on. It was a foolish move, for now I felt that I would soon have him. Hard living and harder drinking had sapped his strength, and by the way his legs dragged I knew the end of the race was at hand. Suddenly he veered again and ran straight for the edge of the cliff, stopping short as the sea with its host of vessels met his vision. As he halted I could hear the blast of his breath as it came and went. Bending, he looked over the brink as though to fathom the depths below, then glanced up at me.

I was within three rods of him, but he still hung like one driven distraught betwixt the choice of death below and death above. As I neared him he made his decision, and with desperation flaming from his eyes he flew to meet me. Without a word he sprang on me, gripping me by the throat ere I could prevent him, and twining his supple leg about mine as though his were jointed in a dozen places. Like a devil leech he hung, striving with all his power to push me over the abyss behind, his teeth set in his nether lip, and the veins on his forehead standing out like marline.

But it was fruitless. He little knew my power or the spirit that had turned me to iron. With a violent wrench I tore him from me, and, staggering to a fall, I shifted about, bore him backward and hurled him over the cliff, the exertion bringing me to my knees on the brink of the height from which I had flung him.

The spot where McCary went over was on neither the steepest nor loftiest part of the headland, but it was a fearful fall. Here in a vertical line the height was perhaps a hundred and fifty feet, though on account of the pitch of the face of the wall a body would pass over fully two hundred before reaching the level of the beach. As I sunk to all-fours, I watched his flight to the bottom. He struck the first terrace, which was but ten or fifteen feet below, and with a desperate effort tried to cling to the narrow clay shelf, his hooked fingers, like talons, digging into the friable earth, while his body hung over the greater drop beneath. But the season had been dry, and the substance of the cliff turned to powder under his hands. Slowly though surely his fingers slid, his upturned face was horrible in its despair, and, as his eyes met mine peering over the edge of the brink above him, he cursed me as only a hopeless soul can curse. As the last words left his lips his failing support crumbled away, and he shot downward to the next step or terrace, off which he bounded, glancing into a washed-out gully, the passage of his body and his exertions to check his flight starting an avalanche of loose stuff in his wake. He made a magnificent fight, but it was seemingly to little purpose. Greater and greater grew his speed as he bounded from one step to another, until when more than halfway down he was rolling helplessly along, a confused mixture of clay dust and flying legs and arms merged into the effect of a scarlet ball shooting toward the beach. In the end his body came to a rest betwixt two huge bowlders, and there it lay motionless, though the track of his fall was yet marked by a stream of bounding lumps of clay which followed him. If he had not broken his neck in the wild progress of the latter portion of his descent, he was still alive, for he had, fortunately for him, missed striking the natural sea wall on the beach.

Though possibly alive, he would soon have choked in the smother of powdery stuff piled upon him had it not been that other eyes than mine had marked his terrible tumble. As I rose to my feet, awed though not subdued by what I had seen, I noticed a man running along the white sands below, and then marked for the first time an Indian's boat drawn just beyond the snowy line of the surf. I had no dream of collusion in the attempt on my life at this time, but I was soon led to suspect and then know of something approaching it. The running man I recognized as a Chappaquiddeck, and as he arrived at and bent over the body of McCary, scraping away the clay under which he was half buried, I turned and hurried to where lay the motionless form of Gertrude King.

CHAPTER XXVIII.

BEYOND her disordered garments, there was nothing to denote the violence with which she had been handled, for she lay on her back, her white face, clear and un-bruised, turned upward as peacefully as though marked with death, and, indeed, my first thought was that death had claimed her.

The horror that smote me as I saw her lying there so still was all the punishment I needed for any wrong I might have done the surgeon, but as I bent over her with a groan, and then felt the clear yet feeble beating of her heart, the reaction coming upon me was the final force which broke the barrier of my feelings. I forgot everything, my own late peril, the murderous redcoat, the struggle, and his meteorlike fall over the cliff; the off-sailing fleet, which might have run ashore and sent a host swarming up the height for all it would have troubled me then; the sky, the earth, the past and future —all these were lost to mind as I lifted my beloved and poured into her deaf ears the passion I had so long held dammed within me. Ay, more: I dared profane her lips with mine, and never dreamed of the unfairness of the thing I did.

I confess to having been irrational, but not more so than any man of strong feelings placed in a like posi-tion. I was deeply in love (for which I have no excuse,

and need none), and if for a time my heart got the better
of my head, in extenuation I have only to plead the
depth of my passion, its repression, and the sudden reaction on discovering that the girl was yet alive. I can
not recall what I said, but as I chafed her cold hands
and spoke as a man will speak but once in his life, her
eyes opened, and with a smile, half weary and half con-
tented, she closed them again and relapsed into her
faint.

As though caught in a flagrant act, my tongue ceased
its clamor and I felt the blood creep to my face in the
fear that she had been sensible of at least part of my
outburst. But I recovered both my natural color and
my confidence when a few minutes later she reopened
her eyes, and, lifting herself quickly from my arms, sat
up and gazed wonderingly about in the bewildered way
of one suddenly awakening from a deep sleep. She
looked at me steadily for a moment, as if to gather her
wits, I silently returning her gaze, and then her lip
trembled and her soft dark eyes filled with tears.

"Ah, my friend!" she said tenderly though very
calmly after a space of silence—"ah, my friend, I was
in time then! You are unhurt? Where is—is——"

And here she looked about as if expecting to see the
body of the man who had laid in ambush. With a rush
the past came back, and my heart set hard for an instant as I answered:

"He lies on the beach below. I threw him from the
cliff."

She shuddered visibly and put both hands to her
face, and then for the first time I saw that it was probably through her action that my life had been saved.
I was on the verge of prostrating myself before her and
again opening my heart, but, great idiot that I was, I
let the moments speed until in very shame at my own
weakness I dared not loose my tongue. I had more

courage in the face of death than in the face of the woman I loved, and so let the opportune minute pass until my confession was then made impossible, for, dashing away her tears with a defiant movement, she held out her hand for me to assist her to rise. The time had gone.

No schoolboy ever felt more awkward than did I as we stood together, neither speaking, she shaking out the folds of her garments, and I, like a clown, looking on with my soul in my eyes, my heart a lump and my tongue a useless block. A sudden change had come over her. The frank friendship of the hour before had given place to a distant preoccupation, and I was smitten with the consciousness that my fears of her having heard my wild outburst were well founded, and that she was mildly resenting my daring. But I soon comforted myself with the knowledge that no fainting woman can hear, and then I warmly enough asked her if she had been injured in the scuffle with McCary.

To this she answered quickly though quietly, as if glad to break a silence which was rapidly becoming strained: "No, Donald, not greatly. I think he may have wrenched the lame shoulder, but, as in my former accident, it is nothing worse—nothing unless perchance there be an internal hurt. Come, shall we not return home?" Then hesitating a moment as she cast a side glance at me, "Did you—— Is—is he dead?"

"Dead, Gertrude," I returned, "I know not. I had not thought of him! Your need was the greatest, or at least I—you—I will go and——"

"Nay, not yet. Tell me what happened. Tell me all that happened."

She stood half facing me, her eyes downcast, her short, bright hair now freed from its stain, loosened and falling a mass of tangled ripples, one hand grasping her skirts and the other pressed to her heart as to subdue its beating, though there was no apparent agitation.

Then I told her of my sight of the British off the coast, of hearing her shriek and seeing her throw herself onto the would-be assassin, of the shot, the chase, the short struggle, and the fall of McCary, and so on up to my return to her side. She listened with a wondering look, which was turned away from me, and when I had finished she flashed one glance into my eyes and said:

"Donald, is that all—*all?*"

I felt my cheeks turn to fire and my pulses jump, but, without seeming to mark it, she continued, her countenance growing tender even as the clouds grow tender under the light of the rising sun:

"Have you no more to tell? O Donald! I thought you brave! Have you only courage while in the grip of a murderous monster and—and over the body of a lifeless woman? My poor boy—my hero—oh, my love, why will you make me help you?"

Think her not unmaidenly. If she was, then it is unmaidenly for a maid to love—then it is unwomanly for a woman to stoop for the happiness she sees lying at her feet. I thought not of this then. For all my strength, I had been but a weak and tongue-tied child as I stood before her, but her last words turned me into a giant. The hand she held out to me lifted me off the earth. Sparks flashed before my eyes, and I choked with the violence of the emotion that rose and overwhelmed even the recollection of what I said and did. In the end I only know I held her where she belonged and she was answering a question:

"Shamming? No—or not at first. Was it shamming, I wonder? In the beginning I fancied I was dreaming, and then I gradually thought it was true, though I lay still; but at last I was sure, and—— O

Donald! I am a woman, and I loved you. When, after opening my eyes, you became dumb, I felt my heart would break—then I think I grew a little resentful—and then—when I saw your face as we stood together—I—I—my dear love, I know not which of us is the greater coward."

And so it came about that on that glorious day on the glorious heights of Gay Head I found a content beside which my past content was turmoil. The dangers we had endured together sank away; the future lay ahead unknown, unfeared. In the happiness of success I shrank from nothing; storm and sunshine would be all one to me; the horn of plenty had been emptied for my sake, and Fate could hold nothing from which I would quail, save death; not mine, but my love's. And yet, for all my inward boasting, it was well I knew naught of the terrible tempest I was so soon to face, or that the spark which started a fire that well-nigh consumed me was fanned to activity when I threw the murderous surgeon from the cliff.

How long we remained exchanging our mutual confidences is a matter of conjecture only, but finally I became sane enough to be interested in knowing the details of Gertrude's finding the hidden royalist. And he had been well concealed. At the spot in which he had lain in ambush awaiting my usual visit (and he had timed me surely) there was a ring of low bushes which made an excellent cover for one lying on the ground. When I had run to the cliff Gertrude was some distance out of my track and to the rear of me, and possibly my enemy knew nothing of her proximity to him. As she wandered aimlessly along, she came full upon this patch of shrubbery, and saw a man lying on his stomach taking deliberate aim at my figure, which was clearly outlined against the sky beyond. I made a fair mark and one not easily missed, and had her arrival on the spot been delayed but a few seconds, I should doubtless have fallen a victim to the doctor's venomous hatred.

The sight of the redcoat and the poised rifle, with the knowledge of the story of the missing papers reclaimed two days before (together with other matters unknown to me at that time), opened her eyes to the sinister purpose of the prostrate scoundrel, and, as her only resource, she had given vent to the scream I had heard. At the same moment, in the desperation of knowing the man she loved was in danger, she had thrown herself upon the villain before her just as he fired. He had probably been too intent on his intended victim to notice Gertrude's approach, but her shriek, given at the instant he applied pressure to the trigger, slightly disturbed his aim, and he had missed me by a hair.

Her recital (somewhat interrupted by unnecessary punctuation and the violence of my thanks for her timely intervention) brought to mind the fact that even a fallen enemy demands attention at the hands of his conqueror, and that I was both hatless and coatless. Nothing could induce Gertrude to accompany me to the edge of the height to see what disposition the Indian had made of the body of McCary. With all her nerve, there was nothing morbid in her curiosity, and, though she was willing and even eager to have me know the fate of the surgeon, she recoiled at the idea of seeing his carcass.

I left her, therefore, and took my way to the cliff. The fleet was still holding along the Sound, but its distance was so great and the wind so light as to make it appear to have made little progress. When I advanced to an elevation commanding a view of the sea inshore, though I could not yet see the beach below me, I was nonplused at the action of the schooner I had before marked as sailing dangerously near the land. She had hauled fairly southward, and with only her mainsail trimmed for her altered course was creeping slowly along parallel to the face of the cliff, and at about a quarter of a mile from the sands. I could have planted a rifle bullet on her deck with ease, and was wondering what motive she could have for thus abandoning the fleet, when I reached a point allowing me a view below. Then her motive was plain enough. The body of McCary was gone from where I had seen it settle, and, instead of being laid out on the beach or elsewhere, that individual was in the Indian's boat, and, under the lusty strokes of its owner, was being carried out to the hover-- ing vessel.

I marked him plainly as he sat low in the stern, anon lifting aloft his red coat as a signal to those aboard the schooner, though from the feeble way he raised the garment and the suddenness with which his arm dropped I took it that he was fairly well shaken by his fall. Neither his neck nor any other bone was broken, I imagined, for, though I could not at that distance mark the details of his actions, they were far from those of a seriously injured man, as it took him scarce thirty seconds to transfer himself from the lesser craft to the greater, and that without any assistance. The boat hung to the side of the schooner for a space, and then it shot away toward the Indian village on the northern shore. I hastily called Gertrude, and by the time she joined me the schooner had swung into the wind and gone about, laying a course for the distant fleet. It may have been imagination, but I thought McCary was on the quarter-deck, surrounded by a group of red-coated officers, pointing to the figures of Gertrude and myself as we stood boldly prominent on the height above. If he was so looking, and held a modicum of feeling, he must have been awed by the aspect of the declivity down which he had rolled, for below its full extent shows to a greater advantage than from above.

It was with a mixed feeling of disappointment and relief that I noted the escape of the fellow—disappointment that he had slipped from me without adequate punishment, and relief that I had none of his blood on my hands. His coming off as he had was a miracle at first thought, but it ceased to be as I considered how his struggles to restrain his fall had broken its severity. Though the latter part of his descent had been uncontrolled, it was a declivity down which he had shot, and not a sheer drop, and, as the face of the height, stupendous as it is, is made up of soft clay in which there is not a stone larger than a pebble, and he failed to strike the sea wall at the bottom, I could easily understand how he had, with the help of the Indian, escaped with his life. Doubtless he had been stunned by his bounds from terrace to terrace, and was well bruised and twisted, but with assistance he had recovered his senses and prevailed on his dusky friend to take him to the vessel, which by some chance was sailing near the land.

This was the way I accounted for the matter, and, saving the detail anent the Indian, I was right.

The next day I knew that the Chappaquiddeck below had waited by appointment for the appearance of McCary, having been hired to take him to Newport, where he was to join Pigot, the perilous voyage to be made in an open boat. There was no tale of murder to be done, but the surgeon had borrowed the fellow's gun and promised to meet him on the beach at the very hour he did, though great was the astonishment of the innocent red man to see his patron keeping his appointment and approaching down the face of the cliff like a falling star. He had not marked the struggle aloft, and he had been in collusion with McCary only as I have explained. The advent of the British fleet was evidently as great a

19

surprise to the surgeon as to me, and the schooner, " a flight o' luck " (as Lounsbury had once expressed it), the villain little deserved.

The clew leading to all this was gained through the abandoned rifle I picked up on our way home. It was a common grade of firearm, but its stock opened the way to the truth, for on it was carved a rude semblance to a fish's head, and still more rudely cut was the name of " Tummasee," a full-blood Chappaquiddeck I had known since a lad. Realizing the power of money wherever applied, I little wondered that the Indian could have been hired to aid the prisoner in an escape, but I hardly think he could have been brought to act as an accomplice to the murder of an old and well-known inhabitant of the island. His innocence of any consciousness of wrongdoing was clear in the open way in which he claimed the rifle when I showed it to him, he even going so far as to exhibit the gold piece McCary had given him.

CHAPTER XXIX.

A BIT OF HISTORY.

FOR one week I lived in a trance, a state of delirious beatitude which a man of character would not wish forever to endure, and which in later days I have tried to recapture as one tries in vain to hold on awakening, the spirit of an entrancing dream. Even when enjoying a more tangible happiness have I turned and sought for the mood possessing me during the first days of my betrothal to Gertrude King. But it was as futile as is my present attempt to hale back the lost spirit of my youth. Like a flash of lightning or the unreal shadow cast by the Will-o'-the-wisp, it comes for the briefest space, and flits away before I can grasp it. An old sight, an old odor, an old tune throws me for a moment under the old spell, but quickly the fire of the past dies out and I see its ashes in the present.

For seven days I lived apart from all common things, a dreamer, a visionist, but on the eighth day I became a man.

In the meantime had come the news of the relief of Newport by General Clinton. He had arrived just in time to see Sullivan retreat in safety, and his rage was boundless. I know not which of my messages reached the American camp, but I do know that I received no credit for the warning given. Sullivan admitted that he was forewarned, but by whom or through whom was a subject on which he forever remained silent.

The British general, baffled by the turn of affairs on Rhode Island, started for Boston to try his strength on the French, who had deserted Sullivan in his hour of need. It was his fleet I had seen, and my surmise as to its destination had been correct. It turned out, however, that our allies also had word of the coming of Clinton, and on his arrival he found the hereditary enemy of England drawn up to receive him in such an advantageous position that he hurried away from the vicinity of Boston and returned to Long Island Sound, his temper not having been improved by this second setback.

That the expedition might not be fruitless, he next planned an attack on the town of New London, but here the Almighty interposed. For three days a strong north wind blew down the river Thames, preventing the entry of the fleet, and by the time an attack was possible the town was prepared to make a brave defense. The administration of Clinton showed that he was never quite ready for a pitched battle on even terms, and, as it was no longer possible to surprise the old harbor town, he withdrew his forces. But he had by this been long from New York and Mrs. Badely, and, as neither his health nor his temper could brook opposition or failure, he turned the expedition over to General Grey, and placing most of his fleet at the disposal of this able though cruel lieutenant, ordered him to ravage Buzzard's Bay and Martha's Vineyard, while with a few vessels as an escort he fled to the ease and comfort of New York.

The wanton destruction of defenseless points now took the place of dignified warfare. What Grey did is well known. After the almost complete destruction of New Bedford and the adjacent coast (which was accomplished on the Sabbath and in the space of twelve hours), he turned his attention to Martha's Vineyard.

Historians all agree as to the extent of the robbery (contributions under pain of death) which took place on that quiet island, but they do not agree as to the shedding of blood. I myself doubt any official sanction of violence (the suddenness of the descent and the character of the inhabitants making resistance impossible), but the annals of the house of Thorndyke prove that violence *was* done, that blood *was* shed, and that immediate vengeance was taken therefor. Ay, and more that was not immediate—a blood vengeance which ran through the rank and file of the British army during the following two years, and finally a bloodless vengeance which struck the head and front of the host—Sir Henry Clinton himself. It smote him in a way that bowed him low, and, though the hand dealing the blow was hidden from the public, he of all others knew who had cut loose the sword so long suspended above him.

Four days from the time I saw the British fleet sailing eastward I saw it return and sail westward. No news had then arrived as to its mission, but whatever that mission had been I knew no general action had taken place, for every spar was entire, and not a hole showed in the white cloths that bellied in the wind. Ship after ship they trailed away like a flock of birds, finally melting into the haze toward Long Island Sound, and I thought that was to be the last of them.

On the morning of the 5th of September my mother was too ill to rise from her bed. This was alarming, for I could hardly remember the day she had ailed, and with a strange, depressed feeling, which, however, soon wore away, I tore myself from Gertrude, and, putting the ancient horse to the more ancient chaise, set off to Edgartown for the doctor.

John, or Bow-peg Phillipse, as the doctor was generally called (the nickname referring to his extremely bandied legs), was a man for whom as a practitioner I had mighty little respect, nor is it saying much for him in admitting that he was the best physician on the island. We had little use for doctors in those days, and have not a great deal even now. The rust of years had obliterated most of this man's learning, and, beyond the knife and a bolus, he had but few remedies on which to rely in case of need. As a man, however, he stood well, and for his opinion on two subjects, if nothing more, I held him in high regard—those of admiration for the character and person of my lamented father, and the British, whom he hated. The doctor, a sturdy, hard-fisted, soft-hearted, rather excitable man, with a figure as gnarled and twisted as a root, had served in the English fleet during the French War, and had been a witness at the depopulation of Acadia, the inhumanity of which act being at the bottom of his detestation for all things emanating from England. Moreover, he was no coward (though he overflowed with policy), and had not a bullet in his leg and seventy years prevented, he would have been far from the last to serve his country in its present trouble.

But as a physician he was my only resort, and I went for him more for his opinion as to the ailment of my mother than in belief that he could cure her if her malady should prove to be of a serious nature. I started for him on the Sabbath, and the quiet of the day was in the air and over all the land. Not but that it is always quiet here, but even to me, used as I was to the stillness of the place, there was an unusual hush, a breathless calm, and one portentous had I but known it. It was a good eighteen miles' drive to Edgartown, and, after giving the horse a rest, I returned with Phillipse in the chaise by my side, not arriving at home until somewhat late in the evening.

That night he lay in our house, and that night New Bedford was burning and the fleet was creeping toward us through the darkness, and not a soul on the island knew what was in store.

The next morning the doctor made his examination of the patient, and then took me aside.

"Nothing ails your mother, Donald," he said, " saving the disease we are all bound to take if we be not cut off too soon. I mean old age. She has been beset with worry, but we'll give her a draught to mend the feebleness, and then all she needs is quiet and the will o' God. You may have her with you for yet awhile, but she's tender, lad."

I had lived years enough to be prepared for this, and it scarcely came as a blow, only it pressed me hard to have thus clearly brought to me that my dear mother, who all her life had been the embodiment of tenderness, was at last nearing the threshold of her long home. Peacefully she lay in her bed, looking through her great horn spectacles at the early sunlight streaming across her chamber floor, and alas, poor soul! (should it be poor soul?) none of us dreamed how nearly it was sunset for her, and I stooped and kissed her, comforted in thinking that the end might still be in the future—the indefinite future—words always soothing to a fearful heart.

Setting at rest the anxiety of the household, I put a bottle of rum before the doctor, and, bidding an adieu to Gertrude, started off on horseback to the village to obtain a supply of simples the physician had prescribed.

But I did not go to the village that day nor for many days thereafter. I had gone no more than three miles on my way (and the store was off six at least) when, as I cleared some woods on the top of a hill, and was nearing the farm of neighbor Ashcroft, over the stretch of open country I beheld his barn burning merrily. With a shout I pressed forward, but not for a great way, for as I drew nearer I saw his cattle running madly about a field, chased by a number of men wearing scarlet coats, and then as plainly as though it had been told me I fathomed the whole business. The British had landed on Martha's Vineyard.

For only one minute did I halt, and then turned about and regained the cover I had but just left.

The certainty of invasion came like a bolt from the clear blue above, and knowing of this mode of warfare used by our enemies, and the extent to which it had been pushed in Norwalk, Danbury, and at other points, my heart sank within me. I fancied their place of landing must have been at Holmes Hole, the most central and by far the most convenient point from which to start a raid, and, though my own home was well removed from the anchorage of the fleet, I little doubted it would receive attention from the raiders, who were evidently bent on replenishing the commissary by robbing the island of its cattle and flocks even if they went to no greater length.

As I stood under the shelter of the woods, I was sorely troubled how to act. To gather a force and repel the enemy was impossible, for the Vineyard was as helpless as a stray chick under the swoop of a hawk. Even successfully to defend one's own house from the hands of the spoilers was out of the question, as to defeat one squad would be but to bring on another more determined. I knew not the strength of the landed force, but I did know that from Tryon up and down they took few chances through being weak in numbers. Ravishing an undefended and prostrate coast line would figure well in a general's report if he spoke not of the weakness of the section, but dwelt heavily on the immense number of troops (which presumed an immense opposition) required to subdue it.

I was therefore in a quandary as I strained my eyes on the distant farmhouse and its blazing barn, but my mind was somewhat hurried as I marked a wagon with two horses turn from the home-lot lane into the road and slowly climb the hill toward me. Mightily hurried, indeed, when I saw that the vehicle contained a number of redcoats, and caught from a musket barrel a quick flash of sunlight, as though the weapon had been exploded.

Then I turned and started toward home. The old horse must have been astonished and outraged at the way he was urged onward, but I gave him little chance to draw an easy breath until I reined up at the kitchen door.

The unusual sound of a galloping steed brought out black Sam and the servant Cathy in a panic, and their panic was increased as I shouted to the man: "Drive the cattle deep into the woods! The British are coming! Waste not a second!" at the same time dismounting and hurrying him into the saddle. His not too brilliant intellect was quickened at the dread word "British," and he was off ere I gave him a chance to ask a question.

Running through the house, I tore up to my mother's room, expecting to find Gertrude, but she was not there. My sister sat by the invalid, and, quietly beckoning her from the room, I told her the news. She nearly fainted as she listened, and it was all I could do to get from her that my love was with her brother. Bidding her be careful to hide her agitation, I hurried to Ames's room, only to find him alone. He was greatly stirred as he heard the short story I blurted out, cursing his own inability to act, but of his sister he could only say she had left the house for a walk to beguile the time against my return, but in what direction she had gone he knew not.

The fear I had was not one I dared to express to him, but deep in my heart it was that she, himself, or myself might be recognized by some of the group which was undoubtedly making our farm the objective point of their drive. If Gertrude was in the forest and would remain away, I should have little to fear for her, and, as there were many preparations to make, I could not desert my plain duty and go in search of her, especially as I knew not in which direction to first turn.

My next move was to find the doctor. That worthy was drowsing beneath the north porch in blissful content with the world, but the way the old gentleman fired up when I retailed what I had witnessed was a comfort, albeit his plans to meet the difficulty were hardly practicable. He would barricade the house and defend it as if a fort. He swore no redcoat should invade the roof covering him, be it his roof or no, and live a minute. In short, he acted in a way to drive me wild, inasmuch as he was unreasonable in his rage; not a feasible plan had been laid or even suggested, and there was not a moment to lose. In the end a council of war was held in Ames's room between him, the doctor, my sister Rachel, and myself, in which it was clearly shown that force, save as a last resort, would be foolhardy; flight out of the question, as neither my mother nor Ames could be moved to the woods on such short notice; while a tame surrender of person and property would be cowardly, and was not to be more than mentioned. It was true that the doctor might withdraw, and so might I, leaving none but noncombatants about the house, but to me this looked to be little less than desertion on my part, a cowardly contrivance; and the doctor swore in strange oaths, for which he apologized to the lady, and at once repeated, that he was not to be driven off by a pack of lobster-colored, sheep-stealing rogues while the son of his old friend was in straits. I think the stubborn-headed practitioner little dreamed of danger to himself, but he won my eternal gratitude for his stanch determination to stand by me and by the way he bore himself when put to the test.

The result of our conference was that policy (otherwise deceit) should be used, and it was agreed that the doctor should pose as the head of the house, with Ames as his son, my sister and Gertrude (should the latter appear) as his daughters, while my mother would unknowingly take the part of the dying wife of the old gentleman, who under his own name and in the company of Rachel and the servant would receive the visitors in the kitchen.

As there was more than a chance that I would be recognized if I presented myself, it was arranged that I should lie concealed in the woodhouse off the kitchen, that I might be at hand if violence or an open rupture ensued.

With the recapture of the schooner, my rifle, sword, and pistols had been rescued, and, loading the firearms, I gave one pistol to the doctor for use in an emergency, and one to Ames, who was removed to my mother's room, the privacy of which, out of respect for her supposed condition, might not be violated. I had my doubts about any part of the house being safe from search, but I could see no other disposition to make of either my mother or my friend, and trusted the doctor to disarm any suspicion that the house was aught else than the abiding place of a peaceable and harmless family with Tory proclivities.

Then I turned attention to my own hiding place. The woodhouse, a flimsy, pent-roofed structure, was built against the gable end of the house itself, that fuel might be obtained therefrom without exposure to the terrible storms of winter. It opened into the kitchen on one side, and near this door was a small, square window, sashed, glazed, and curtained with thin muslin. On the opposite side of the room, if room it could be

called, was another door leading into the yard, and close
by it an immovable window, matching in size those of
the house, this being likewise glazed, and protected on
the inside with solid wooden shutters.

The first thing I did was to nail up the outer door
and bar the shutters. By so doing I was protected at the
rear, and, as the only light now entering came through
the small window on the kitchen side, the place was so
darkened that a man standing in the corner, though
uncovered, might not easily be seen by any one entering
the apartment, though he could command a view of all
going on in the kitchen itself.

CHAPTER XXX.

THE ATTACK.

WHILE I was thus busied in fortifying my retreat, Rachel had been posted in the garret watching for both the coming of the enemy and any signs of Gertrude. Since I had met her this was the first time I wished my love would remain away from me, and, as my trip to the village, had I made it, would have consumed at least three hours, I hoped she had taken the notion to stay from the house until my expected return. My fear now was that she had gone to meet me and would fall into the hands of those in the wagon.

They were evidently taking their time or had lost their way, for I had finished my preparations, had pointed out the liquor closet to the doctor, and was trying to get through the thick wits of Cathy that whatever happened or was said she must pretend to be dumb, when Rachel came flying downstairs with more color in her face than I had seen for years, and announced that the team with its burden of royalists had just cleared the edge of the woods, where the redcoats had left the vehicle and were advancing toward the house on foot. There were five men, one apparently an officer, she said, as he carried a sword in lieu of a musket, and walked ahead of the others. Gertrude she had not seen.

With a ready wit that commanded my respect, the doctor at this whisked the spinning-wheel into the center of the room and bade Rachel seat herself and work; then, pointing to the half-dying fire, told Cathy to clean the hearth, after which he sat himself in my mother's rocker, stretched out his legs, and, throwing a kerchief over his face, to all appearances was fast asleep. He was the very man for the part selected if he would but keep cool.

Stripping myself of coat and waistcoat, I buckled my sword to my side, and, taking both rifle and fowling-piece, stepped into my quarters, closed the door, and fastened its latch by jamming a slip of wood into the loop of the fall. Then I stood with my face at the window, through the thin drapery of which I could see quite plainly.

The silence as I waited seemed intense, though there was the ticking of the clock and the low humming of the wheel. A fly which had blundered betwixt the pane and the curtain set up a thunderous buzzing over the window, as if drawing attention to my place of conceal-ment, and the time dragged (or appeared to) to such an extent that I was about to call through the partition when I heard footsteps on the path without, and then a voice in a tone of command bidding two men to repair to the rear of the house and allow no one to leave it.

I heard the guard pass the window at my back, and presently there was a shuffling of feet, followed quickly by the entrance of the officer.

As his shadow fell athwart the door-sill the door itself was blocked by two marines, who, however, did not at once follow their superior across the threshold, and, as he boldly advanced into the room without a rap to herald his coming, I nearly fell backward, for before me stood Captain Scammell! He was as sleek as on the day I first saw him, though his face now bore the desperate look a man puts on when he is about to do a desperate deed. His drawn sword was in his hand,

and a single pistol stuck in his belt. Driving the point of the former into the planking of the floor, he said in a loud tone:

"For giving shelter to the enemies of the King, in the name of his Majesty the inmates of this house are prisoners. I demand the bodies of one Gertrude King, one Beverly Ames, and one Donald Thorndyke, outlawed by proclamation, and known to be concealed, succored, and comforted under this roof."

This well-rehearsed bit of formality had not been half delivered when the doctor pulled his kerchief from his head and opened his eyes as though waked from a deep sleep, his face indicating profound astonishment. Rachel half rose to her feet, and the servant stood in open-mouth wonder.

For one instant after the completion of the speech the scene was a tableau—not a soul stirring; but Phillipse recovered from his feigned surprise, and before Scammell could move or speak again he bounded from his chair with the exclamation:

"What! A King's officer! Thank God for a sight of his Majesty's colors! You are welcome, sir, thrice welcome!" at the same time advancing and holding out his hand as he continued: "I can at last speak out with no danger! God knows how I have prayed that his Majesty would establish his authority on the island! Come, sir——"

"Who are you, sir?" was the stern demand of the officer as he ignored the hand extended to him and eyed the doctor suspiciously. "Who are you? I wot not of one of your description. Is this not the house of Thorndyke?"

"Ho! ho!" returned the wily physician, "and are you seeking that arch-rebel? Curse me not with the suspicion that my roof ever harbored one of his breed. I am Dr. John Phillipse, an honorable practitioner, a man loyal to his Majesty. You have mistaken your road. The house of Thorndyke lies two miles to the south. If you came by Holmes Hole, you passed the proper turn as many miles back. Is that villain to be brought to book at last?"

At these words Scammell's face lost its desperate cast and took on a look of perplexity, and it was plain that he was both disappointed and uncertain how to act. It showed in the way he pulled his sword from the floor, sheathed it, and removed his hat out of deference to the lady, who had reseated herself at the wheel. Then he said with some hesitation:

"Is it possible that two farms can be so alike? This house answers in every detail."

"You may find many on this plan," quickly interposed the doctor, "the difference being in a chimney, window, or door only. We of this section are prone to build alike. It is a peculiarity holding good throughout the colonies."

"True enough," returned Scammell. "Who have you in your family?"

"This is my daughter Ruth, my eldest," returned the physician, lying with the greatest of ease and smoothness as he indicated Rachel by a wave of his hand. "My youngest is away. I have also a son—a boy whose wit is lacking—the Lord smites his children, sir. My wife is nearing her end, and the youth is with her upstairs. I hope you will respect her condition, but if you insist, you may search the house."

"I have no intention of intruding on the privacy of a loyal man," returned the Tory, "but I was plainly directed to this house, and noticed no turn in the way as I came along. You, sir, must know of this Thorndyke. He was on the island a week agone; is he still at home? Are those he brought still with him?"

"Indeed, I know not," was the ready reply. "I

hold no intercourse with his family, but I have heard of a lady and her brother having returned with him barely three weeks since. He also has one of his Majesty's naval surgeons, taken somehow and put on his parole.— My dear, bring out a bottle and some glasses.—Will you not drink the King's health before you move on? I would be your guide, sir, but a bullet in my leg gotten in the King's service in front of Louisburg, prevents."

The plausibility of Phillipse's speech, backed by his open manner, could not do otherwise than deceive the Tory, who was upon strange ground, and, bowing to my sister, who had risen and placed upon the table a bottle of liquor and the glasses, he seated himself with his back toward me and so close to the window through which I was looking that but for the partition I could have driven my sword through him without moving a step.

"It seems, sir," he began as he tipped the bottle, "that I owe you an apology for this intrusion and thanks for your good will. I fancy I can now find the house I wish. Two miles back, you say, and to the south. I must hurry, else he will get wind of us. The King's health, and yours, madam, and yours, doctor." And lifting his glass to his lips he drained it, then rising, prepared to depart.

"After all, you will have more than your own force, captain, or major; I know not your rank, sir," volunteered the doctor. "There is the surgeon, who will——"

" No, indeed, sir," was the laughing reply. " McCary took himself off a week ago, and it is through him that I am posted. Regarding Thorndyke," he continued, walking to the door, " I confess to personal enmity, but McCary's extends through the whole household. It is perhaps fortunate for you that the capture of this fellow is my sole mission. I may be followed by others less considerate than myself, but, as you lay out of the track

20

of the regular highway, you may escape. I wish you good day, sir—the same to you, madam."

Now this looked to be a fair ending to the matter, for a time at least, and I was congratulating myself that we would gain several hours and be prepared for their return, when the hall door opened and Gertrude entered the room. Her face was flushed, as though she had just been awakened from a nap—as, indeed, she had—her hat was in her hand, and she was about to raise it to her head when she caught sight of the group upon the threshold. With pretty embarrassment she glanced from the party to my sister, and exclaimed: " Why, Rachel, what is the matter? What is——" but suddenly stood like one paralyzed as she recognized her *ci-devant* lover.

My heart gave a terrific bound and stood still. For a moment Scammell returned her stare, then the light broke on him, for his sword flashed out as he thundered:

" Aha! I have it! Nearly tricked, by God!—Forward there! " and he sprang toward the girl, who, seeing his approach, uttered a scream, and turning fled through the door by which she had entered the room, slamming the portal behind her.

The action now became as quick as it had hitherto been slow.

As Scammell turned to follow the fleeing maiden, he wheeled on the doctor, who was now across the room, and, drawing his pistol, fired. The shot brought the old man to his knees, though he was on his feet again before his assailant had gotten from the room. At the same moment Rachel sprang to the closed door, placing her back against it, and, as the officer threw down his pistol and shouted, " Let none escape! " one of the marines ran to my sister and, seizing her with one arm, dragged her roughly from her position, while his companion bounded through the now opened door, followed by Scammell.

The noise of the scuffle brought one of the outside guard into the kitchen, only to be grappled by the doctor as he entered, and the two were at once sprawling on the floor in close embrace. As my sister strove in vain to release herself from the grasp of the marine, she shrieked my name, and in my hurry and excitement I broke the light slip of wood in the fall of the latch, and could neither unfasten or force the door.

But rescue for Rachel came from an unlooked-for quarter. Still tugging desperately at the jammed latch, with my eye yet at the window as I worked, I saw Cathy run to the hearth, snatch a brand from the fire, and dash it into the face of the soldier. With a yell of pain he released the girl with whom he had been struggling, throwing her violently to the floor, and, turning upon the old servant, he shortened his musket in his grasp and with an oath drove the bayonet into the heart of the faithful woman. Without a word she fell backward, while I, goaded to madness at having unwittingly made myself a prisoner, dashed down the sash in front of me, and from my fowlingpiece poured a charge of buckshot into the head of the villain who looked up, his attention attracted by the noise of the splintering glass. Like lead he fell across his victim.

It was a terrible moment for me. The room without was already a shamble, and every soul in it was on the floor. The opening through which I had fired was far too small to pass me, one door was jammed, and the other nailed. But there was the second window. Hastily throwing back the shutters, with a log I shattered the sash in half a dozen blows, and, snatching my rifle, jumped out.

The crashing of glass evidently brought on the fourth marine, or else he was running for help, for as I doubled the corner of the house we collided with terrific force, the blow sending me staggering against the side of the building, while he bounded off and fell to the ground motionless, probably stunned by the shock.

As I recovered and ran through the kitchen door I saw the doctor's opponent had gotten the mastery and was astride the physician's prostrate form, striving to hold him, and at the same time endeavoring to reach the old man's pistol which lay just beyond his grasp. Without a word I brought the edge of my rifle's stock down on the bared head of the redcoat. I marked the wood sink into his skull, but saw nothing more, for, stopping only to deliver the blow, I ran through the room into the hall and up the stairs, whither I knew Gertrude must have fled and been followed.

CHAPTER XXXI.

As I tore along, short as was the distance, there was ample time for my head to be filled with a tangle of horrid thoughts as to what had happened above that served to make the way seem endless. As I reached the top the sound of loud voices directed me to my mother's room, and in a moment I was at the door. My mother, who until the violent invasion of her apartment had probably not dreamed of danger, having partly lifted herself from her pillow, was calling for me in a weak and tremulous voice. Ames leaned against the wall at the foot of the bed, and in front of the bed itself, as though to defend those behind her, stood my brave girl with a cocked pistol in her hand. Confronting her brother was the marine who had followed Scammell, and opposite Gertrude, held away by her pistol, stood Scammell himself, with his back toward the open door. Above the feeble noise of my mother's calling I caught the words that Gertrude had given in answer to some question or demand of the officer: " Never alive, sir! Settle with him! I am the promised wife of Donald Thorndyke!" and then I was upon them.

Unnoticed by either of the royalists, I deliberately aimed my rifle at the marine and pulled the trigger, but the priming had been dislodged by the blow I had given the man below or it had become wet with his blood, for only sparks flew from the descended flint. Casting the now useless gun aside, I drew my sword, and with the cry of "Turn, you villain, turn!" I smote Scammell across the shoulders with the flat of the blade.

Such an insult he had never received, and, wheeling about, he confronted me on even terms for the first time. I never saw such rage on a human countenance as on his when his look met mine. A flame appeared to shoot from his eyes, and as our swords crossed with a crash he shouted: "Shoot him down! Kill the damn villain as he fights!"

He had swung himself around to bring his back to the light, thus throwing me face to face with the sea soldier. Though I was well engaged with my opponent, I saw the man raise his musket, and at that instant Gertrude fired, presumably at him, as he staggered against the wall, his musket falling to his side. With apparent effort he struggled to retain his position, and, again lifting his gun, he now pointed it toward the heroic girl and fired, falling to the floor at the same instant.

In the close room the crash of the explosion was deafening, but through it I heard the shriek given by my love, followed by a deep groan. I heard Ames spring around the bed and utter an exclamation, but I dared not shift my eye from the man before me. For me the blow had fallen. My heart turned to stone, my nerves to bands of steel, my muscles to iron. Even then I felt the glory of perfect and invincible strength, and knew for what purpose it had been given me. Now that my darling had fallen, I should kill this man who had been the cause of her murder had it been ordained that I should suffer in hell for the act.

But he was not so easily made way with. Through the smoke that spread in the room I could see his devilish face with its bared teeth, as though he was smiling at my agony. I pressed him close, giving him no opening, and as we shifted, now with his back toward the door and mine to the bed, he suddenly made a furious lunge which I parried, but ere I could counter he turned and fled from the room and down the stairs.

Without a look toward those I loved best on this earth, I followed him. His move was so sudden that he was at the foot of the stairs as I reached the top, and he was at the outer door of the kitchen when I arrived at the one leading from the hall. Whether he meant to elude me and escape, being frightened at the look on my face (as well he might have been if it exhibited my feelings), or whether he hoped to gain the assistance of one of his men below, I know not. Mayhap he only wished for a more open space in which to play his sword.

However, if flight had been his hope it was nipped by a sudden frost, for as he cast a backward glance at me he ran fairly into the embrace of black Sam, who threw his arms about the Tory, pinning his elbows at his sides, and causing the officer to drop his sword. Struggle as he might, he could not loosen the powerful grip of the farm hand, and when I reached them they were tottering over the smooth turf, the negro calling on me to "kill the Britisher!" even as Scammell had called on the soldier to kill me.

Standing a pace or so away, I ordered the black to release his prisoner, which he at once did, stepping aside and eying me as though I had suddenly gone mad.

So far as possessing any Christian quality, I had gone mad; and, likewise, so far as possessing more than a modicum of any feeling (save hate for the man before me), I was dead. I may have held a faint glimmer of honor in my mind, else I would have stabbed the miserable royalist while he was held by the negro, though this scrap of consciousness was, after all, but pride. I am glad I gave him a chance.

"Hand him his sword!" I shouted fiercely. The black did as ordered, and then I spoke to Scammell for the last time:

"Now, you hound, defend yourself! Strip off your coat and be a man. *À l'outrance* you once said, and now *à l'outrance* it shall be! If you run again, I will stab you in the back, and I care not for foul blood! If you slip, it means no quarter. Here ends it! I will not waste time in giving you that once promised beating, but, as for my contempt, let this show."

So saying, I advanced toward him with my sword down, and with the palm of my left hand struck him across the cheek and quickly sprang on guard.

The blood flew to his face and out again. Driving the point of the weapon into the ground, he tore off his scarlet coat, tossed aside his hat, and, grasping his sword, without a sound came toward me with a rush.

I had a taste of his style of fence by this, but I dared not try my own trick while his anger was at such a height that he would not mark the fine opening I meant to show him. At first he fought wildly but too well for me to try to force his guard, and, in order to cool him, I gave ground, that he might gain encouragement. Not for a fraction of a second did I shift my eye from his, though somehow I was conscious that we were being watched from the door, though no one interfered. Not for a fraction of a second did I fear this man, who, far from smiling now, was working earnestly to wipe out the last insult and my life together. It gave me a fierce joy to mark his rage (and the depth of it was plain enough), though not a word was spoken. He played my wrist as if to test its strength, and found it steel; he feinted, he tried both inside and outside of my guard, our blades biting and snapping together as though alive.

The glory of that fiery moment comes back to me

as I set this down, but it is dulled by years agone. I hear the smooth sibilance of the sliding steel and the sharp ring of the parry. I see the clear sky above me, and feel again the hot air of that early autumn noon, and know my age is that of the flesh and not the spirit. Oh, for my lost strength! O God! for eternal youth!

I drew the fellow foot by foot, still holding away until his fruitless efforts to undo me had made him desperate, and then I threw my wrist out of line and my point fell off. Like lightning he took the bait, and like lightning I stepped back. The next second his sword was spinning through the air. Before the whirling steel reached the ground I had passed my blade through Scammell's throat and saw the awful spasm on his face. And then I turned away before I heard his body strike the sod.

When I looked again he was lying on his back with arms and legs spread wide, his half-closed eyes turned to the sun, as dead as a man with a severed jugular could be.

I came back to the world then, and looked broadly about me for the first time since my enemy had entered the house. The doctor, with his kerchief about his head, came running from the door, followed by Sam, but with no greeting to either I turned my thoughts to those upstairs and started in. As I neared the door I marked the man I had run into still lying prone upon the ground, but I gave him only a passing glance.

When I re-entered the kitchen the room was filled with a smoke and the smell of burned cotton, which I had not noticed as I came through. Rachel was no longer there, but on the floor was the soldier I had killed first, lying athwart the body of his victim, while the one I had brained with the rifle stock lay where he had fallen.

The doctor hurriedly explained that the ball from

Scammell's pistol had but grazed his temple, and, after having been relieved from his assailant, he had discovered that the brand picked from the hearth by Cathy had fired the rag carpet and the flooring beneath, and his efforts to extinguish the flames and save the house had prevented him from joining me above. Rachel, he said, had recovered and gone upstairs.

I listened to him dully and went on, fascinated and repelled by the horror of what I had seen and expected yet to see.

The scene that met my eyes as I cast my first fearful look into my mother's room occasioned such a revulsion of feeling that I stood still.

On her knees in the center of the apartment was my sister, weeping as though her heart would break, and by her side, bending over to comfort her, stood Gertrude. On the floor lay the marine she had shot, and by the bedside was Ames, looking down at my mother. The room was blue with smoke.

Quickly leaving the weeping girl, Gertrude flew to me, throwing her arms about my neck, her face and freedom of motion showing she was unhurt. There was no hysterical outburst from this noble woman, who had now twice saved my life. She simply looked wonderingly at me and drew me across the room, whispering:

"She is dead! O Donald! and the shot was meant for me!"

There on the bed lay the body of my mother, the ball intended for my love having struck her fairly in the temple, killing her instantly.

Was I shocked? Ay, but only for the moment. The peace of her face was the peace which passeth all understanding, and, beyond the dark stain on the pillow, there was naught about her to indicate that she was not hearing the music of which she had often dreamed.

I bent over and kissed the transfigured countenance,

and then my rage grew boundless as I realized that she had gone without a word to those she loved. Lifting up my voice, I swore a vengeance which should not cease until my country was rid of the butchers invading it or I had been struck down. And Ames in silence reached out his hand and pressed mine. It was in no unchristian spirit I thus swore, but the spirit abode with me, and now the charity which has come with age is broad enough to cover the curse of England's hatred for her own children because they demanded their rights.

Though my heart was sore as I stood by the corpse of my mother, I felt it was no time for mourning then. I was beset with a fear that others would soon follow after Scammell, and evidences of our successful defense against the first incursion were too plain not to bring a bloody reprisal. Of the five men who had left the wagon, four were dead and one was a prisoner. I say four were dead, but the fellow whom Gertrude had shot and whose wavering aim had caused him to misdirect his bullet lived for more than an hour after.

We gathered the bodies of the slain enemy and hid them in the barn. The remains of my mother and Cathy were placed tenderly in the wagon that had brought our assailants, the evidences of the fray covered as hastily and thoroughly as possible under the circumstances, and we fled to the woods.

The prisoner was the man with whom I had collided. He had been found by Sam, the negro having returned from driving off the cattle just as the man was recovering consciousness. With little ado he had knocked the fellow in the head with his own musket, turning and running to the kitchen door in time to intercept Scammell. The marine was fairly well subdued by the two concussions he had received, and when he again recovered his senses there was little of the fighting mood left in him. He was bound by the hands, put under the eye of Sam, and taken with us.

The tragedy of the day, which had been precipitated by the untimely entrance of Gertrude into the kitchen, might have been entirely avoided had we but known in the beginning that, instead of going into the forest for a walk, the girl had gone to her room and slept, hoping thus to easily be rid of the time which would intervene before my return from the village. It is true that if the course of events had been thrown into another channel we know not what might have happened, but what God wills is not to be questioned. Her entrance into the kitchen was the signal for the ending of the greatest episode of my life, just as her appearance in the companion way of the Sprite was the beginning of it.

For the two days the British remained on Martha's Vineyard we hid, living in a disused shed deep in the heart of the forest. 1 have but a misty recollection of the details of that time, only remembering in a general way the scouting done by Sam and the wholly inadequate preparations made to beat off the enemy, were we discovered. There was no lack of arms now, and we were desperate enough, but there came no occasion for more fighting, though had we been found we might easily have been taken.

On the second evening, under cover of darkness, I returned alone to the house, surprised to find it still standing and showing no evidences of having been entered since we had fled from it. There I constructed two rude coffins, and my mother and the brave old serv-ant were buried side by side in the woods near the edge of the home lot, Dr. Phillipse doing the last offices. The time was midnight, and the land was being drenched by a sudden thunderstorm, the whole party standing through it while we filled in the shallow graves in a darkness only broken by the glare of the lightning. To me the peals of thunder were a salute to the dead, the pouring rain a proper winding sheet, and the aisles of the forest, roaring with the voice of the short tempest, a grand cathedral, and one well fitted for the silent forms there committed to earth.

And there they still rest, marked by a stone I have lived to see begin to crumble under the hand of Time.

CHAPTER XXXII.

CONCLUSION.

My tale is nearly done. I know it has been almost wholly in the line of my own adventures (thus laying me open to the charge of egotism), but I have told it in a fashion that best suits myself, be the reader's conclusion what it may. It was not written for self-glorification, but for the purpose of showing how my love was sanctified in a baptism of blood, and how a man's self-interest and his patriotism may be so solidly welded as to be a single thought.

The day when I was first threatened by Lounsbury had been a day of promise (though I had known it not), and the run of my life for the following three months, which I have here set down, but a trial of my worthiness. That I was weighed my story has truly shown; that I was not found wanting is proved when I swear that I won the sweetest, bravest wife God ever gave a man.

Of those who threw themselves between me and my fate but little need be said. On the 8th of September the British left Martha's Vineyard, after extorting a heavy price for the peace its inhabitants had enjoyed. They went, laden low with the spoils of their invasion, leaving many aching hearts behind. That day we returned to the house. That day, in the sands of the beach, we buried the repulsive bodies which had been hidden in the barn. Even while we worked to hide them forever, I marked the ships as they streamed away to New York, and in fair view of them filled in the ditch holding Scammell and the three marines.

I know not if that officer ever made his peace with Clinton, but the fact that he accompanied the fleet when it descended on the coast leads me to think he had, though I know not to this day how the dragoon came to be doing sea duty. Nor do I know of any search having been made for either him or his fellows. His was an irregular expedition, born of spite and requiring no report.

Of McCary I never heard again. Two months after the death of my mother Gertrude and I were married, and then my wife told me a secret I never would have guessed, and which cleared up the animus of the surgeon's hate for me.

One week after our rescue by the Jenny, and while the girl was convalescing, he had asked her to be his wife, promising to throw aside his commission and guaranteeing a free pardon to herself and her brother from the King. His possessions in the old country were considerable, and these he laid at her feet. He wooed her well, excusing himself for his impetuosity on the plea of the depth of his passion and the surrounding circumstances. At her flat refusal his love had turned to indignation, and he had openly damned me as his rival, restraining himself at last, and begging in abject terms that she would keep the matter from me. And she had promised.

As for the blow that humbled Clinton, it worked slowly, though none the less surely. Immediately after her marriage Gertrude began a correspondence with a distant relative in England, one close to the British ministry, inclosing the papers (or copies of them) which she had taken from Mrs. Badely.

It finally resulted in the recall of the British general,

who was placed at the bar of Parliament charged openly with cowardice only, since to question his right to his knighthood would be striking too near the King himself. I know from more than hearsay that his bitterest enemy, and the man who in all England he most feared, shook the hateful papers in his face and swore his ruin. Did not Clinton then know who had made good her promise and dealt the blow? From that day, after a lame excuse which any man may now read, the ex-general in chief was a broken political reed, and with him, from the public eye, sank his paramour.

And this is all. With the ending of the war and our dependence to the British crown, the properties of both Gertrude and her brother were restored to them. They were fair days. Within six months after my marriage Ames and I again entered the fight, still as irregulars. What we went through side by side is not a part of this tale, but Gertrude herself buckled on our swords with streaming eyes, and with streaming eyes she took them off when we returned after the great day at Yorktown, but not till then.

And the pledge made by her brother and myself under the stars that night at Turtle Bay, still abides, for he still lives. The oath spoken over the body of my mother, and indorsed in the hand clasp of my more than brother, was made in no unholy spirit. And it was carried through coolly, as though we were but instruments of that mighty prophecy which is written in that book of books: " Vengeance is mine, saith the Lord. I will repay."

THE END.

www.ingramcontent.com/pod-product-compliance
Lightning Source LLC
Chambersburg PA
CBHW060534030726
47498CB00004B/1192